It was their dream.
It was their nightmare.
It was their *home* . . .

GREELY'S COVE

They knew that something evil had come there to live.
But could they destroy it? Or could they even survive
it?

CARL TROSPER—a successful Washington,
D.C., political consultant, he came back to claim
his son, Jeremy . . . after his wife mysteri-
ously killed herself.

JEREMY—an autistic child, he was suddenly
able to see and hear and speak . . . but was his
soul truly his own?

DR. HADRIAN CRASLOWE—the brilliant psychologist responsible for Jeremy's cure. What
terrible methods of treatment had he mastered?

LINDSAY MORELAND—Jeremy's aunt, she
wanted custody of the child . . . but could she
control his strange behavior?

HANNIE HAZELFORD—an eccentric old
woman, she dared to fight the evil with a frightening power of her own.

ROBINSON SPARHAWK—a forensic psychic,
he came to Greely's Cove to help solve the
townspeople's disappearances.

STU BROMTON—the town police chief, he was
tied to a community he had grown to hate.

Would anyone survive the agonizing terror of . . .

GREELY'S COVE

GREELY'S COVE

JOHN GIDEON

JOVE BOOKS, NEW YORK

GREELY'S COVE

A Jove Book / published by arrangement with
the author

PRINTING HISTORY
Jove edition / March 1991

ISBN: 0-515-10508-2

Jove Books are published by The Berkley Publishing Group,
200 Madison Avenue, New York, New York 10016.
The name "JOVE" and the "J" logo
are trademarks belonging to Jove Publications, Inc.

PRINTED IN THE UNITED STATES OF AMERICA

10 9 8 7 6 5 4 3 2 1

GREELY'S
COVE

INTRODUCTION

Lorna Trosper needed darkness.

She stumbled through the small house, scrabbling at switches, shutting off lights. The filth and squalor of her world—the injured furniture and broken walls, the tattered monstrosities that she had called her paintings—all were more than she could bear. Darkness was a refuge from an ugliness that her artist's eyes could no longer endure.

More terrifying than the tangled disorder and the carnage of her house was the sight of her son, Jeremy, whose own hazel eyes radiated an insane sense of satisfaction that things had come to this. He followed her from room to squalid room, giggling his silken giggle, turning the lights on again.

Darkness, then light.

Darkness, then light.

Lorna knew that she could not defeat him, because even though he was only thirteen, he was so very strong, and this was a "game" he could play for hours, if not days. He seemed to thrive on the ordeal, to suck strength from it, even as Lorna felt herself growing weaker by the moment. How much *longer?* she wondered, fearing that her hours, perhaps even her minutes, were numbered.

A new terror seized her when she caught sight of her own image in the full-length hall mirror, which through some miracle had survived the debacle of the previous week: Her once-pretty face belonged not to a vibrant young artist—which is how she had dared to think of herself—but to an emaciated harridan with horrid, overly bright eyes, blond hair ragged and wild, mouth contorted in a rictus of unthinkable pain.

How long had the transmogrification taken? Weeks, maybe, or months.

Or millennia.

Time had become meaningless, just as she herself had

1

become meaningless. Her body had become a vessel of fear, a demon's plaything. Staring into that alien face in the mirror, she knew that she could endure no more.

She gathered her final store of physical strength and staggered crazily into the kitchen, where a stark ceiling lamp cast a pall over the garbage that had collected since she last cared about cleanliness and order. Piled on countertops and chairs, heaped on the table and linoleum floor, dumped mindlessly into the sink, were mountains of broken and encrusted dishes, mounds of reeking refuse and food wrappers.

Her eyes fell on a butcher knife that lay on the floor amid the clutter, and for a fleeting, maniacal moment she saw herself seizing it and whirling to confront Jeremy—falling on him, screaming from the depths of her tortured soul, stabbing, slashing, escaping. But deep within her a remnant of the original Lorna Trosper fluttered to life, a surviving artifact of love and motherliness that had somehow withstood the ordeal of her son's "awakening." That remnant throbbed feebly, yet with force enough to intervene, to prevent her from murdering her own child. Letting the knife lay, she steered herself to a drawer that had been her catchall place—her repository of trading stamps, coupons, pens, and pencils.

Clawed through the clutter until she found a pen and pad.

Scribbled something, tore the slip from the pad, crammed it into the pocket of her paint-spattered smock.

From behind her, and fearfully close, came a sound that knotted her stomach: Jeremy's soft giggling. Keeping her eyes low and away from his face, she lurched through the rear door into the tiny garage and slammed it behind her.

Mercifully, the garage was as black as dreamless sleep. Lorna Trosper leaned against the door and listened to her racing heart, to the winter rain on the roof, to her son's breathing on the other side. Finally she found the strength to move and, needing no light, made her way to the jointed door that ran on tracks overhead. She made sure that its lower edge lay flush against the cement floor, then felt her way to the old Subaru station wagon that she had gotten in accordance with her divorce settlement. (How many centuries ago?) She slipped in behind the wheel and pressed down the lock buttons. The key was in the ignition lock, where she routinely left it, cold to her quivering fingertips. She turned it and the starter wound, and the trusty four-cylinder engine grumbled to life and filled her mind with its comforting sound. Her head fell against the seat back.

Lorna Trosper needed darkness. Soon she would have all the darkness a person could ever need: one richly black and luxuriantly vacant; one devoid of the terror that had driven her to this; a darkness from which there would be no tormented awakening.

One final obscenity, however, lay in store: As the Subaru filled with acrid fumes, Jeremy pushed open the door between the garage and the kitchen. A crack of dreaded light fell across the windshield and assaulted Lorna's eyes. The boy stood a moment with his small hand on the doorknob, framed in the hellish yellowness, grinning a lunatic's grin.

Lorna tried to force her eyes shut, but she couldn't. The image of her son's face, with its dazzling white teeth and wild, glowing eyes, imprinted itself on her mind, and she knew that to live would be to carry the horror of it always. Her stomach heaved, but only acid came up, for she had not eaten in days. The pain was like a fire in her chest and throat. Still she gazed at him through a blur of hopeless tears, yearning to see something in his face besides unspeakable pleasure, something a mother could love in her final moments.

What she saw, however, made her pray that the dead don't dream.

PART
I

There are things far worse than death, my son.
Far worse, indeed.

—C. L. Calliossa

1

Carl Trosper had not cried real tears since the age of fifteen, not since the moment his father's casket started its slow descent into the grave, riding some sort of mechanized sling that spared the backs of the pallbearers. Young Carl had borne up well before that moment, just as his mother had. Together they had endured the heartrending eulogy delivered by his dad's best friend and law partner, the tearful *I'm so sorrys* from scores of family acquaintances, and bleak thoughts about a future with a gaping hole in it. Carl had suffered all this without working up much more than a mist in his eyes. *I'm a man now,* he'd told himself throughout the ordeal. More than that, he was Jeremy Trosper's only child, a combination not suited to blubbering.

But blubber he did when Matt Kronmiller, the town's only mortician (and one of its richest citizens) hit the switch that started the casket's downward plunge into that god-awful, muddy hole in the ground. Carl watched the contraption sink slowly out of sight, feeling his chest tighten and his throat grow hot, hurting under a dreadful weight of finality. Later he tried to forgive himself for the unmanly flood of weeping but failed.

Now, more than twenty-three years later, his eyes were again smart with real tears.

Lorna, his former wife was gone.

The coroner had called from Greely's Cove, Washington, his old hometown on the west shore of the Puget Sound, to tell him that Lorna had killed herself. Carbon-monoxide poisoning. She had locked herself in the Subaru, which itself was locked in the garage, and had started the engine. She probably had not suffered, opined the coroner, struggling to say something helpful.

Fortunately Carl had been alone when the call came, which was unusual on a Saturday morning. Melanie Kraft, his latest regular squeeze, was in Chicago on business—something about a midwinter meeting of the National Association of Manufacturers' executive board, for whom she served as assistant counsel. On any other Saturday morning, he and Melanie would be recovering from a Friday night out, having dined at The Palm, or Le Pavillon, or Joe and Mo's, or any of a hundred top-drawer Washington, D.C., restaurants. They would have taken in a movie or a play and downed three-too-many nightcaps at The Hawk 'n' Dove, their favorite Capitol Hill watering hole. On any other Saturday morning they would have been lounging around his fashionable Wisconsin Avenue condo, wearing plush terrycloth bathrobes, sipping Bloody Marys and listening to old Steely Dan records, decadently satisfied after an energetic session of the "root dance."

But Melanie was in Chicago, and Carl was alone. And, being alone, he could cry without degrading himself in anyone's eyes but his own. So cry he did, even as he had stopped himself from doing just that a year earlier, when his mother had passed away after a long illness, leaving him without the living roots of family.

It was nearly eleven o'clock by the time he finally pulled himself together. He ducked into the shower and tried unsuccessfully to wash away the hurt, then dragged himself out again to pull on a pair of faded Levi's and a boatneck sweater. Standing before his bathroom mirror, he contemplated trimming his short, reddish-blond beard with its silvery tinge of the approaching forties, wondering whether the distraction of a small, everyday chore might be therapeutic. He decided instead to have a Bloody Mary and call Melanie at her hotel in Chicago.

She answered after the sixth ring, sounding sleepy and red-eyed.

"Mel?" Carl didn't like the sound of his own voice.

"Carl, is that you? What a pleasant surprise to wake up to. How's my favorite big-time political consultant?"

"Melanie, I've had some—bad news. I—"

"Carl, what is it? You don't sound good, lover."

"Mel, it's about Lorna."

"Lorna? Your ex? Carl, what's wrong?"

"She's—she's dead. Killed herself. I got a call this morning from the coroner in Greely's Cove."

"Oh, God." A long silence ensued, during which each groped for something more to say—Melanie for something to comfort, Carl for anything at all. Melanie recovered first. "Honey, I'm coming home. Stay right where you are. I'll grab a cab out to O'Hare and be on the next plane."

"Melanie, don't do that. You've got your meetings—"

"To hell with the meetings. You need me."

"Look, I'm holding up okay. I appreciate your good thoughts, but I only called to tell you that I'm going out to Greely's Cove and that we might not see each other for a while. I assume that I'll have to make the arrangements for the funeral and—"

"Plus you'll have to do something about Jeremy."

"Yeah—Jeremy." His voice caught. Jeremy Carl Trosper was his only child, named for Carl's own dead father, the sole product of his union with Lorna. *Doing something* about Jeremy would not be easy.

"Sweetie, I'll give you a call as soon as I get a chance," he said. "Don't worry about me, okay? I'll be home as soon as I've taken care of things out there."

"Okay, I understand, kiddo. But I'll miss you. I already do. And remember, I love you."

Carl winced slightly, as he always did whenever Melanie told him that she loved him, for he always felt as though good manners demanded that he say it back. After Lorna, he wondered whether he would ever be able to say those words to another woman.

"Thanks, I needed that," he answered, lying just a little.

2

The smashup had not been fatal, thank God. A foggy, rain-streaked window had denied the driver of the Le Baron a clear view of the approaching Bronco on Highway 305, and he had turned left off Frontage Street directly into the truck's path. Blammo. Easily a grand worth of damage to the Le Baron, the police chief figured, and the Bronco was probably totaled. But both drivers, fortunately, had used their seat belts, and neither had gotten more than minor bruises.

Stu Bromton, chief of the Greely's Cove Police Department, supervised the men who came in wreckers to drag the junk away and then wrote out a summons to the Le Baron's driver, who complained hotly. The guy in the Bronco had been going too damn fast, and the intersection should have had a traffic light rather than a fucking stop sign.

Stu, who was not in a mood to field complaints on this particular afternoon, handed him the summons and said, "Listen, Mr. Taylor, you're a very lucky man. In the first place, you're lucky you got hit in the front quarter panel and not in the driver's door, or I'd be sending you off in an oversized garbage bag instead of giving you a ticket. In the second place, I'm too busy to bother with the paperwork of charging you with reckless driving instead of failure to yield, which saves you about five hundred dollars in this jurisdiction. And in the third place, you're lucky I haven't imprinted my knuckles on your nose for being a general asshole. Now stop your cussing and be nice, okay?"

Stu Bromton turned on his heel and steered his tree trunk of a body toward his cruiser, leaving Mr. Taylor to be thankful for his flood of good luck. Before the police chief could squeeze behind the wheel, one of his patrol officers, Dean Hauck, hurried over to him. "Had lunch yet, Stu? I'm buyin'." Hauck had been the first cop to arrive at the scene of the accident.

10

Stu groped for a reason to decline the offer. Hauck was an inveterate brownnoser who never ceased trying to impress the boss with his determination to be a first-rate cop. He never stopped talking shop, which drove Stu crazy, and he wore those aviator-style sunglasses with the mirrored lenses, which Stu hated.

Trouble was, Hauck *was* a first-rate cop, which Stu was not and never would be. And someday soon Hauck would see an opportunity to leave this one-horse department with its three shifts of two men each, and he would seize the opportunity, forcing Stu to undertake again the distasteful task of luring in another rookie who was desperate enough to work for chicken feed until a better job turned up. Getting another Hauck wouldn't be easy.

The chief was opening his mouth to accept the invitation when the radio in his car crackled. He answered it, and the dispatcher informed him that representatives of the medical examiner's office and the prosecutor's office had returned to the police station after a trip to Matt Kronmiller's mortuary. They wanted to see the chief.

Stu was off the hook with Hauck. "Guess I'll have to grab a bite later, Dean. Sorry." The young cop gave a regretful smile and nodded.

The rain eased a bit as Stu drove toward the station, and the streets of Greely's Cove began to show signs of life. Saturday shoppers had ducked into coffee shops and storefronts to escape the downpour, giving the streets the atmosphere of a ghost town, but as the rain diminished they ventured out again to finish their errands.

Stu fell into his newly acquired habit of scrutinizing everyone he happened to see, even slowing the car to get a good look if necessary, a habit he had taken up eight months earlier when the disappearances had begun. Eight citizens of Greely's Cove had vanished from the face of the earth at the rate of one per month, for no apparent reason, leaving no trace. Police Chief Stuart Bromton had solved not one of the mysteries—had collected not even a gossamer lead—and the townspeople, not to mention the city council, had become impatient. He occasionally heard reports of someone having seen one of the missing people, always under strange circumstances and never in the broad light of day. He hoped that through heightened vigilance he might see a face that had appeared on the state ID bulletin of wanted felons, a face whose owner could explain why the population of Greely's Cove was dipping at the rate of one per month.

Greely's Cove, a salty town of 2,000 year-round citizens, lay on the west shore of the Puget Sound, a short drive southeast of the slightly better known tourist trap of Poulsbo. Twenty-odd miles across the Sound lay Seattle and its satellites—a metropolitan area of two million scurrying souls, the vast majority of whom wouldn't recognize the name Greely's Cove, even though many had driven through its outskirts en route up the Sound to the fjordlike Hood Canal, or to Port Townsend on the Strait of Juan de Fuca, or to the majestic Pacific shore.

Nestled in a dense wood of pine and cedar, Greely's Cove was still small and quiet, still unconquered by the venal legions who see beauty in strings of service stations and colonies of condos and files of fast-food franchises. At the center of town, astride Frontage Street, was a cluster of old but smartly restored structures, mostly of ancient brick with bright Victorian filigree. Attending the older buildings was a coterie of newer ones that housed year-round businesses: the West Shore Insurance Group, a chiropractor's office, a law office, and a cramped ladies' boutique called Hannie's. Sprinkled throughout the commercial quarter were the tourist establishments, some of which closed during the winter while others struggled on: the West Cove Motor Inn (bar and restaurant), the Old Schooner Motel ("Modern/Kitchenettes/Under 12 Free"), and Bailey's Seafood Emporium. Toward the edge of town, near the intersection of Highway 305 and Frontage Street, where the Bronco and Le Baron had met violently in the afternoon of Saturday, February 8, 1986, lay a scatter of "all-American" establishments, including a McDonald's, a liquor store, and a spanking new Safeway.

Stu Bromton began his life thirty-eight years earlier in the hospital at Bremerton, Washington, the nearest real city to Greely's Cove, less than half an hour's drive south. A strapping ten-pound baby whose entrance into the world had almost convinced his mother to have her tubes tied, Stu was big and freckle-faced like his father, Morgan P. Bromton, whom everyone called "Tiny."

Big did not mean *fat*, though, his father had always said. *Big* meant *heavily muscled*, or *beefy*, or *strong as an ox*, like defensive linemen are supposed to be. Following his dad's example, Stu had guarded against becoming fat, which meant jogging four miles daily, lifting weights in his basement, and limiting himself to 3,000 calories a day—except for beer, that is, which didn't count against the total. Beer was his only bad habit, which really was not so bad, because it never seemed to make him drunk. As Tiny had always done in his younger years, Stu Bromton went out once a week with the boys, usually on a Friday night, and pounded down between ten and twenty beers.

Like Tiny in his prime, Stu stood six-three and weighed two hundred and forty-five pounds. Like Tiny, he had played on the defensive line in high school, had gone to college at the University of Washington and then on to law school. But *un*like Tiny, Stu had not become a lawyer and thus could not join his father's lucrative, small-town practice, as had been the family dream ever since Stu could remember. Unable to cut the mustard academically, he had quit law school and returned to Greely's Cove to become a policeman and ultimately the police chief—possibly because he had married the mayor's daughter. Since failing in law school, he had never been able to look his dad squarely in the eye. Or himself, either, for that matter.

He parked in the muddy lot of City Hall, which dominated the corner of Frontage Street and Sockeye Drive. At the rear of the ancient building was the firehouse, with its huge, jointed door. Inside it was a single late-model pumper truck, painted not the traditional red but a regrettable yellowish green, which had become a standard color of the fire service. On the first floor were the city offices, such as they were, and upstairs was a council chamber that sometimes doubled as a courtroom. In the basement—or "garden level," as the police laughingly called it—was the headquarters of the Greely's Cove Police Department.

A visitor who came down the concrete steps of the main entrance would find himself looking through a steel-mesh screen into a cramped cubicle, where sat the dispatcher, who doubled as a receptionist. If the visitor's business were legitimate, the dispatcher would press a button that unlocked a door in the reception area, and the visitor could enter the "inner

sanctum," which included a squad room that smelled of
cigarette butts and Lysol; a detainee cell with steel bars and a
heavy door; and the chief's office, which Stu shared with his
secretary.

Big-time operation, Stu Bromton often said with a wry
chuckle.

Two men waited in the chief's office. One was Dave Putney,
assistant county prosecutor, a wisp of a man with prematurely
thinning hair. Because this was a Saturday, he wore a yellow
sou'wester rain jacket, unzipped and open at the front, over
khaki trousers and running shoes, rather than his customary
Brooks Brothers three-piece and brogues.

The other was Dr. Alvin Lonsdale, a forensic pathologist
summoned from the state medical examiner's office to assist in
"processing" a suicide. Lonsdale was near retirement, paunchy
and jowly faced, possessed of a wrinkled grin and a belly laugh
that reminded Stu of Ed McMahon.

"The team of Putney and Lonsdale," said Stu in his
radio-announcer voice, pushing through his office door, "is on
the case, so don't worry, Virginia, we're in good hands." Both
men smiled, even though they hated being called out on
weekends, especially to out-of-the-way little burgs like Greely's Cove. "You guys get any coffee?" asked Stu after trading
handshakes.

They hadn't gotten any, but a bellow from the chief brought
the dispatcher scurrying in with two Styrofoam cups full of
something very much like coffee—steamy, black, and more or
less liquid.

"Careful with that stuff," Stu warned his visitors, "it'll grow
hair on Formica."

Dr. Lonsdale grimaced after taking a sip, then opened the
manila folder he had brought with him. *"Trosper, Lorna Ann
Moreland,"* he read. "Age thirty-six, artist, divorced, mother
of a thirteen-year-old boy. God, what a waste." He glanced up
at the police chief. "I've seen her medical records, Stu, and
I've seen the coroner's preliminary report. We've been over to
the mortuary to look at the body, and everything we've got so
far shouts suicide. But before I say so without an autopsy, I
want to know everything you do."

"Fair enough," said Stu, taking the chair behind his paper-
strewn metal desk. "I go way back with her, ever since she

married my best buddy back in law school. They were good people, both of them. Had some bad breaks, though."

"Like a kid who turned out to be a drooling basket case?" interjected Putney, the assistant prosecutor.

The chief managed a small smile that masked his annoyance over the remark. "They never got a definitive diagnosis on Jeremy, as far as I know," he explained. "Some doctors said he was autistic, others said he was severely retarded. Whatever it was that he had wrong with him, he was a real burden—not only financially, but emotionally. Carl and Lorna's marriage couldn't take the strain of it, which isn't so surprising, if you ask me. Marriages go belly-up over a lot smaller things than that."

"Amen," said Putney, whose tone suggested that he spoke from bitter experience. "But I hear that Lorna finally found a doctor who could help the kid. That would seem like a reason to go on living, wouldn't it? I mean, you find someone who can help the son you thought was beyond help, and life takes on new meaning, wouldn't you think? You'd have every reason to live, right?"

"Maybe not," said Stu. "I talked to the doctor this morning—name of Craslowe, practices right here in town."

"What kind of doctor?" asked Lonsdale.

"Clinical psychologist, specializes in kids. I've seen his sheepskins, and they're impressive as hell. He's English— went to Oxford, Cambridge, some big school in Austria, or some-damn-where. Anyhow, he moved to town last winter and hung out a shingle on the old house at Whiteleather Place. Lorna heard about him and took Jeremy to see him. Now, I don't have any idea what Craslowe did, but whatever it was, it worked—almost overnight. Suddenly Jeremy's talking, playing with other kids, learning things, even reading—"

"Oh, come on, Stu," said Lonsdale, with a chuckle. "These children don't attain reading skills that quickly, and many never do."

"I swear to God, Doc: The kid learned to read. Before Lorna took him to see Craslowe, he couldn't even dress himself. Within months—weeks, really—he could read and carry on conversations just like an adult. Sounds kind of eerie, I know. Like everybody else in this town, I was blown away by it, I really was."

"You were going to tell me," said Putney, "why this miracle caused the mother to kill herself. Why wasn't she wild with joy?"

"According to Craslowe," said Stu, "her son's rapid progress threatened her definition of herself."

"Come again?"

"She always saw herself as Jeremy's provider and defender, know what I mean? Fed him, washed him, cleaned up his messes, protected him from the cruel world. We're talking about a creature that only a mother could love, and she loved him with everything she had. Then all of a sudden—almost without warning—he turns out to be a real person who can look out for himself. He can even *read!*" This he aimed at Lonsdale specifically. "Lorna finds out that he's probably been learning things all his life, that his condition has misled everyone to think he's hopelessly retarded. It dawns on her that she's been deceived all these years—"

"And it also dawns on her," interrupted Lonsdale, anticipating, "that someday Jeremy may no longer need her as a provider and protector."

"Exactly. Her definition of herself unravels. She's no longer the person she had forced herself to be during all those years when Jeremy was sick. Being an artist, she's the sensitive type anyway, and she can't cope. She falls into a deep, dark depression, her personality disintegrates, and she ends up in the Subaru with the engine running." Here Stu Bromton's voice became dangerously thin, and an uncomfortable silence ensued while he collected himself, while the medical examiner and the prosecutor studied the black-and-white tiles of the floor, the mint-green paint on the walls.

"I'm still having trouble with this miracle recovery," said Lonsdale finally. "As a doctor myself—"

"Yeah, some *doctor*," jabbed Putney, grateful for an end to the silence. "You're a forensic pathologist, for crying out loud. You do *autopsies*. You wouldn't know what to do with a patient who's still breathing and giving off heat."

Lonsdale gave out one of his trademark belly laughs. "Okay, so I'm not an expert on the inner workings of the human mind, but I took the mandatory psych courses in college and med school, and I know enough about the subject to be skeptical of miracles, that's all. I'd say an autopsy is in order, under the circumstances."

"And I'd say he's right," chimed in Putney. "A rule of thumb with any suspicious death is to order an autopsy."

"Oh, come off it, guys," protested Stu. "This is hardly a *suspicious* death. You've got a suicide note in Lorna's own writing. You've got statements from her friends about her depression over the last six months and a plausible description of her mental state from a respected shrink. Plus, you've got my personal voucher that she didn't have an enemy in the world. Why do you need to cut her up and put pieces of her in bottles, for Christ's sake?"

"We getting a little squeamish in our middle age, Chief Bromton?" asked Putney snidely. "I thought you were a seasoned cop, big guy. You *know* why we do autopsies. As for the suicide note, I'd like to run it by the questioned-documents examiner in the Seattle crime lab. It's scrawly enough to raise a question about whether it's really Lorna Trosper's handwriting, and on top of that, I'm a little confused about the content. A professional opinion wouldn't hurt."

Stu was on the verge of pleading, something he detested and almost never did. "Dave, Al, I *knew* Lorna Trosper. My wife was one of her closest friends. I—we loved her. If there was the slightest chance that she died because of foul play, I'd be screaming for an autopsy, and I'd be pounding on somebody's desk in Olympia to get the State Patrol in here with a homicide team."

"The Patrol's probably thinking about opening a branch office here"—Putney chuckled derogatorily—"since you've been keeping them so busy looking for your missing citizens. Death investigation might become the major industry of Greely's Cove! Disappearances, suicides—all you need now is a bona-fide homicide, Stu, and you'll have it all!"

The chief ignored the crack. "Look, guys, I *know* Lorna killed herself, and I'm satisfied about the reason. My oldest buddy—her former husband, who still loved her a lot, by the way—is on his way here from back East to take care of the arrangements. Spare me the ugliness of telling him that Lorna's body is in Seattle, being sliced open and chopped to pieces in a medico-legal autopsy. Can you do this for me? For old time's sake? *Please?*"

Against their better judgment, after trading long and leery stares, Putney and Lonsdale acceded to the chief's request. They affixed their signatures to official forms, certifying their findings that Lorna Trosper died by her own hand.

And they ordered no autopsy.

Mitch Nistler's mind swam upward toward full consciousness, upward toward light and sound, guided by Dr. Hadrian Craslowe's strong and reassuring voice.

". . . three, four, five—you are nearly awake now, Mitch—six, seven, eight . . ."

He was ready to break through, and he was glad. The sleep of hypnosis was never a refuge for him, never a place of warmth and rest.

". . . nine, ten. There, now. You're fully awake. That wasn't so bad, was it?"

Mitch blinked several times, but he doubted that he was fully awake, for Dr. Craslowe's face was still hazy and indistinct. Ripples of distortion floated through his field of vision.

"Why don't you have a sip of water?" offered the doctor, and what Mitch saw next assured him that he was not yet fully awake but still tied with dream threads to the hallucinatory world below. *(Below?)* An antique crystal pitcher ascended from its spot at the far end of the ebony table and glided through the air to the good doctor's strangely deformed hand. The old man poured water into a long-stemmed glass and handed it across the table to Mitch.

The cold water jolted him to full alertness, and he became aware of the horrid taste in his mouth. *What in the hell have I been eating?* he wanted to croak. Even before guzzling the water he had felt full, as though having just devoured a huge mound of rotting meat. The hellish taste coated his tongue and throat, extended up into his nasal passages. He tried unsuccessfully to flush it away with water.

"You're experiencing the taste again, I see," said Dr. Craslowe, smiling his craggy smile. "Nothing to worry about, I assure you."

Mitch Nistler gulped a little more water, then set the glass aside. "It's more than a taste this time," he gasped, nearly gagging. "There's a *smell* with it."

"Hardly abnormal, dear boy," said the doctor in his broad,

British accent. "Taste and smell are closely affiliated senses. You are merely experiencing a psychosomatic artifact of the hypnotic experience. It's rather common, actually. The sensations won't last long."

Mitch wanted to believe him, but the taste, the smell, and the lump in his gut gave no signs of leaving. Once he had gotten food poisoning—years before, while doing hard time in Walla Walla. A friend of his, who worked in the prison cafeteria, had smuggled three pounds of roast beef into the cell block and stored it unrefrigerated under his bunk. Mitch had shared in the "feast" late one night and had awakened hours later with cramps, chills, and an ugly taste in his mouth. He'd known that only one thing could cure his agony: throwing up, which he did in the uncovered toilet that occupied a corner of his tiny cell. He had clung to the toilet bowl like a drowning man to a rock, flinching and trembling throughout most of the night, wishing he were dead.

He wanted to throw up now, but he fought the urge with deep breaths.

"Well, I suppose that will be all for today," said Dr. Craslowe, rising from his huge, wing-back chair. "I'll see you next week, then?"

Mitch fought down another wave of nausea and steadied himself against the edge of the massive ebony table. These sessions were taking their toll. Each one seemed to produce a stronger "psychosomatic artifact," or whatever the hell the doctor called the demon in Mitch's mouth. He felt sick and weak, and he wanted the sessions to end, even though Dr. Craslowe was treating him without charge.

To make matters worse, the treatments were not working: Mitch noticed no softening of his hunger for alcohol, which the therapy was supposed to cure. As a matter of fact, he fully intended to duck into Liquid Larry's on his way back to the mortuary for a triple threat (three shots of gin in a beer mug, over ice, topped off with tonic), after which he would crunch down a roll of Breath Savers in order to hide his boozy breath from old Matt Kronmiller's nose. Kronmiller was the mortician, Mitch's boss. Today especially, Mitch would need the jolt of a triple threat—to deaden the horrific taste in his mouth and purge himself of the dark unease he was feeling.

"Shall we say Saturday, as usual?" pressed Dr. Craslowe,

donning his thick, steel-framed glasses, enlarging his watery gray eyes. "The weekends are best for me, I daresay." He rendered his craggy smile again, and Mitch caught a glimpse of ancient dentures. "My regular patients demand the lion's share of my time during the week, I'm afraid"—meaning that he reserved weekdays for those who could pay, Mitch figured— "and Mrs. Pauling has asked for Sundays off."

As though on cue, the doctor's assistant glided into the room, carrying Mitch's anorak. She was a lithe, olive-skinned woman with almond eyes. Nearly as tall as the doctor himself and young enough to be his granddaughter, she carried herself rigidly erect. Unlike the doctor, she seemed never to smile.

Mitch Nistler struggled with himself. If he could just find the strength to utter the word *no,* he would be free. He desperately wanted to see the last of this sunless mansion called White-leather Place, where the doctor lived and practiced. He wanted to be free of Craslowe, whose unsettling eyes and long face suggested impossible *oldness,* though the actual wrinkles and folds marked a man in his midsixties or not much older. A simple *"No!"* would deliver him of hypnotic jaunts into the chilly well of the subconscious, from which he always emerged with vague fears and, lately, a putrid taste in his mouth.

But the *"No!"* would not come. Mitch's tongue confronted it, tripped over the *n* sound, and got no farther.

"Are you all right, Mr. Nistler?" asked Mrs. Pauling in her middle-class English clip. Her strong hand clamped around his elbow, shoring him up. "You seem a bit off balance." Her voice seemed full of genuine concern, perhaps even pity.

"Nonsense," said Craslowe. "He'll be right as rain in a moment. He's had a particularly lively hypnotic confrontation, that's all. Isn't that so, Mitch?"

Mitch gazed into the doctor's avuncular face as the latter helped him into his anorak. The smile never wavered. It beamed kindness and concern and confidence; but more than anything else, it conveyed authority, ancient and incontestable, not to be denied.

"Yeah," said Mitch hoarsely. "I'll be right as rain." He dropped his shivering gaze to the Persian carpet beneath his feet and wished with every cell in his scrawny body to be out of this house, away from its dusky antiques and smothering tapestries. He craved sunlight, the smell of rain, a clean breeze. He craved distance between himself and Whiteleather Place.

"So, it will be Saturday next, I presume," said Craslowe, helping the little man with the zipper of the coat, squaring him away.

"Saturday next," agreed Mitch Nistler.

Seconds later he was out the door and down the walk of the looming Victorian mansion, climbing behind the wheel of his rusting '73 El Camino. The engine burbled to life, and the rear wheels of the half-car/half–pickup truck sprayed rock chips into the clumps of yellowing shrubbery as he roared away.

Behind the front door of Whiteleather Place stood the doctor and his helper, staring into each other's eyes, searching and reading, scarcely needing spoken words.

"Will he be all right?" asked the raven-haired Mrs. Pauling at length, breaking the silence.

A smile—this one was anything but avuncular, from impossibly old lips. "Oh, yes, Ianthe, he will be all right. In fact, he will do nicely. Nicely indeed."

"Then you have chosen well?" she asked, her almond eyes brimming with sadness.

The doctor's smile grew broader, darker. "Chosen well, yes. And very soon I'll have the proof of it, I daresay."

3

A few minutes after noon on February 8, 1986, the day after Lorna Trosper died, a Boeing 737 ascended from National Airport near Washington, D.C., and set out for the city of its birth—Seattle. After a journey of more than seven hours, with intermediate stops in Minneapolis and Billings, it touched down in a perfect instrument landing at Seattle-Tacoma International Airport, a short drive south of the massive Boeing manufacturing complex. Carl Trosper got off the plane and, since he had checked no luggage, went directly to the Avis counter, muscling along his expensive leather carry-on bag. He used his American Express Platinum Card to rent a metallic-brown Olds, which he picked up in the subterranean rental car terminal. Minutes later he was on Interstate 5, northbound for the Washington State Ferry Terminal in the heart of Seattle.

By now the winter dusk had deepened to night, and the Saturday rush hour was in full swing. The ferry terminal was clogged. Weekenders who lived on the west shore of the Puget Sound were homeward bound after a day of shopping and frolicking in the city. Carl Trosper fell into the long, slow-moving queue for the ferry to Bremerton, feeling alone amid the throng, listening to the thrumming rain and swishing windshield wipers, thinking sadly of the countless times he and Lorna had waited together in this very spot for the ferry.

He followed the taillights of the car ahead of him into the cavernous maw of the huge vessel, and a crew member directed him to a spot near the bow, meaning that he would be among the first to get off on the Bremerton side. He cut the engine, locked the Olds, and climbed the stairs from the parking deck to the passengers' lounge. A glance at the nearly deserted observation deck told him that *that* was where he wanted to be, despite the chill and steady beat of winter rain, a place where he could think and reflect—alone. So he turned

22

up the hood of his blue Henri Lloyd parka and leaned against
the cold rail, face into the wind, eyes slitted against the rain.
Through the soles of his boat shoes he felt the churning of huge
engines as they imparted their energy to propellers, and the
ferry began to move. The *whoot* of a powerful whistle sliced
through the sharp air, announcing departure, and the rush of
excited waters came to his ears.

So it's come down to this, has it, Old Carl? said the voice in
his head—his father's voice, from the depths of a long-dead
boyhood. His father had always called him "Old Carl," even
when "Old Carl" was an infant with fat, unflawed cheeks and
bright red hair. *So it's come down to this, has it? You bugged
out on your pretty young wife, leaving her to handle Jeremy
alone, and she couldn't make a go of it without you.*

No, it wasn't like that at all. We broke up because that's
what we both wanted. Jeremy had nothing to—

The *lie*. Once again, the *lie*. The same one he had told his
mother when his divorce became final, the one he had told
himself so often. The same smelly, implausible falsehood he
thanked God his father had not lived to hear.

Jeremy had nothing to do with it.

The ferry, engorged with motor vehicles and human beings,
lumbered away from the docks, away from the sting of auto
exhaust and the clamor of the city, into the blackness of the
Puget Sound. The rain slackened, and strings of jewel-like
lights popped through the mist from the opposite shore. Carl
glanced at his watch: just thirty-five minutes to Bremerton.

*So it's come down to this, has it, Old Carl? The big-shot
political consultant—or whatever you call yourself these
days—is coming home, wearing his fifty-dollar haircut and his
oh-so-casual yachting clothes, to bury his pretty little wife,
who killed herself because he deserted her.*

For the love of God, Dad, cut it out!

For a horrible moment Carl worried that he had blurted the
words aloud. A young couple had come through the doors of
the passengers' lounge onto the observation deck, carrying
Styrofoam cups of hot chocolate, braving the weather for a
little privacy. He stole a quick look at them: They were leaning
over the rail, faces close together, cooing to each other, paying
him not the slightest heed. The ferry slowed, honked its
arrival, and insinuated itself into the pier, nudging the dock and

halting. The ramp clanked into place; car engines gunned in anticipation of freedom; and the wave of a crewman's hand caused the ferry to disgorge upon the floodlit shore. Greely's Cove lay less than twenty-five minutes away, a leisurely drive northward on Highway 16.

The night was velvety black, for the sky was without its moon. *A new moon,* Carl had read in the *Minneapolis Tribune* during the long flight from Washington, D.C., so the night would have been dark even without its thick blanket of rain clouds. The town of Greely's Cove began to materialize from the darkness on both sides of the highway. Amberish streetlights peered through the dank branches of pines and cedars. Traffic signals flashed yellow in all directions, since traffic was nearly nonexistent despite the early hour. Neon signs announced Safeway, McDonald's, and Gunderson's Chevrolet-Subaru. Carl knew every streetlight, every sign, every crack in the cement sidewalks of Greely's Cove, for here he had launched his life. Here he would make his new beginning.

His plan began to form as he steered into the drive of the Old Schooner Motel, where a "Vacancy" sign shimmered in pink neon, and he felt better than he had all day.

"I'm going to make a suggestion, Sonny Butch, so listen up."

Liquid Larry, who called nearly every man and boy he met "Sonny Butch," leaned across the bar until his beefy face was mere inches from Mitch Nistler's. "You go ahead and finish up that triple threat, you hear? Then you ease off that stool and get your ass down the road while you can still drive. What d'ya say?"

Mitch raised his glassy eyes and tried to return the barkeep's diplomatic smile, but his facial muscles weren't cooperating. "You cuttin' me off, Liquid? 'S that what I'm hearing?"

"Like I said, Sonny Butch, just a suggestion. I don't want to lose any of my best customers." The diplomatic grin widened. "Besides, I expect your boss is probably waiting for you over at the chapel. I hear you boys got yourselves a suicide last night."

Mitch cringed at the mention of his boss, Matt Kronmiller.

It was indeed likely that the old batfucker was waiting at the Chapel of the Cove, no doubt cussing his assistant embalmer with every passing minute and working up a good case of mad to hurl at Mitch when he finally showed up. " 'S that what you hear?"

"That's what I hear," said Liquid, "suicide. Artist lady who lived with her weird kid over on Second—ran that little art store next to the Mariners' Bank. Used to be married to the Trosper boy, Carl."

"Matt doesn't like his employees to talk about the decedents," said Mitch, downing the last of his drink. "It's not professional. Just like saying 'body' in front of the bereaved isn't professional. You're s'posed to say 'Mr. Smith,' or 'Mrs. Hansen,' but never 'The Body.' " He thumped the mug down on the bar. "Do me one more time, Liquid. Then I'm out of here, I promise."

The barkeep's smile fell away, and his beefy face hardened. He drew himself up to his full height, which was six-three, and sucked in his gut. Though well over fifty, Liquid Larry was an awesome sight behind his bar, surrounded by sparkling glasses and mugs hung upside down in long racks. Few rowdy patrons ever argued with him if he requested their absence.

"I'm tryin' to be reasonable with you, young fella," he said to Mitch in a low voice. "I'm not throwin' you out, you understand, but I don't want you to embarrass yourself, either. Four triple threats is enough booze for anybody."

Mitch Nistler chuckled hoarsely and plugged a Pall Mall into his lips. "You of all people should know that I'm not just *anybody*," he said, coughing out smoke. "I'm a pro. I could suck down eight or ten of these things and shave your wife's snatch with a straight razor, and she'd do nothin' but smile, smile, smile!"

"*Now* I'm throwin' you out, Sonny Butch."

Liquid Larry didn't mind rough talk, and God knows he'd heard enough of it through twenty years in the Marine Corps and another fifteen running a blue-collar roadhouse. In fact, he could go toe-to-toe with the raunchiest bos'n and cuss the son of a goatfucker blue. Only one subject was off limits: his family. If you talked about his wife, kids, or mother, you didn't cuss, a lesson that Mitch Nistler learned the hard way.

• • •

The Old Schooner Motel was rich in middle-class tackiness, but it was also comfortable and quiet. In fact, *quiet* was not the right word, thought Carl; *tomblike* was more accurate, which was not surprising in the dead of the off-season. His room had vinyl-covered furniture, ham-handed seascapes on the walls, and fake wood paneling in the kitchenette. But the TV worked well, and everything was spotless, if not slightly antiseptic.

After a long and languorous shower, he argued with himself about whether he was too hungry to sleep or too tired to eat. He had started the day on Eastern Standard Time and was ending it on Pacific, having gained three hours during the flight from Washington, D.C. In Greely's Cove it was a few minutes after 7:00 P.M., but Carl's bioclock insisted it was past ten. He was tired as hell since he had slept only fitfully on the plane, but he was also ravenous: the airline's food had proved inedible except for a pathetic little bag of cashews that a flight attendant had dropped in his lap between Minneapolis and Billings.

His gnarling stomach won the argument, so he decided to trot down the street to Bailey's Seafood Emporium, a rustic establishment founded long before his birth and renowned for its steamed mussels. He threw on a fresh shirt, a gray corduroy sport coat, and his parka, because a glance out the window told him that the rain had resumed with a vengeance.

"Carl!"

The voice stopped him as he was about to push through the glass door from the motel lobby into the downpour.

"Carl Trosper!"

He turned around and saw a plump, fiery redheaded woman behind the registration desk, not the young, gangly girl who had waited on him when he checked in. This woman had snapping green eyes made enormous with eyeliner and a blue denim jumpsuit that flowed over an amply curvaceous body.

Carl took a halting step toward the desk, openmouthed. The woman smiled hugely, and Carl was transported back to his school days at Suquamish High, when the owner of this dazzling smile wore the school's colors. She had been a cheerleader with flaming pigtails, a spanking high-kicker in her bulky green sweater, tiny silver skirt, and satiny green panties.

"*Sandy?*" he breathed, scarcely above a whisper. "Sandy Cunningham, is that you?"

She laughed sweetly. "It used to be, but it's Sandy Zolten now. My husband, Ken, and I own this place. We live in the big old house across the alley. Carl, you've hardly changed at all—except for the beard, of course!"

Carl felt his face beginning to flush. In high school he and a close buddy, Renzy Dawkins, had worked on the school newspaper as photographers. During games and pep assemblies, they had taken pains to position themselves in front of Sandy, as close to floor level as possible, supposedly to get action pix of the cheerleaders for the paper. What they really wanted, however, were "beaver shots" whenever Sandy kicked especially high—outtakes, of course, that never made the paper. Only the photographers' wallets. Carl's skill had earned him a nickname that he hoped no one still remembered.

"It's nice to see you, Sandy. You—uh—you look terrific. I mean it."

"Oh, come on! I'm three sizes bigger than I was in high school. I guess that's what motherhood does for you."

"I don't care what size you wear; the years have been good."

"Still the charmer, I see."

"Me? A charmer? Since when?"

"Since *always!* Every girl in the school would've killed to go out with you, and you know it!"

"God, I must've been deaf, dumb, and blind. I wish someone would've had the human decency to tell me what a hunk I was." They laughed loudly. To Carl, laughing seemed like something he'd not done in a century.

Further chitchat revealed that Sandy had married her college boyfriend, an accounting major from Spokane. They had lived and worked in Portland, Oregon, for six years—Ken as an associate in an accounting firm and Sandy as a real estate agent—before deciding to go into business for themselves. Sandy's mother had written to say that the Old Schooner was up for sale and within the Zoltens' reach, a nice little business that was manageable by a hardworking couple.

The rest of the story hardly needed telling. Two daughters, Teri and Amber, sixteen and thirteen. An English setter, neutered. Kiwanis, PTA, summer vacations in Colorado. Middle-class story, predictable as hell, but easy on the ears.

"I envy you," said Carl during a pause, meaning it. "You've

got the life most of us dream about. I'm glad for you, I really am."

"I'd ask how *you've* been, but I already know," she said, fixing her gaze on the countertop rather than on Carl's face. "I can't tell you how sorry I am. Everybody in town loved Lorna, and even though you guys were divorced . . ." She stammered, not knowing what to say next. Finally: "If there's anything we can do, all you have to do is ask."

"Thanks. I appreciate that."

Sandy wondered aloud whether he needed help at the house that had once been his and Lorna's. Cleaning, maybe, or cooking. Someone to look after Jeremy.

"I'll know more tomorrow," he answered. "I talked to Lorna's sister on the phone this morning, before I left D.C. She and her mother have come over from Seattle, and we're getting together first thing in the morning. Jeremy's staying with them."

"I know—down the street at the West Cove."

Carl smiled: no secrets in a town this size. He had picked the Old Schooner because Lorna's sister and mother, two people he had disliked thoroughly from the very moment he met them, were staying at the West Cove Motor Inn. Though he was anxious to see his son, he wanted no part of his former in-laws, at least not tonight. Tomorrow would be soon enough.

Suddenly the front door whooshed open, admitting a bounding teenaged girl who wore a slouchy camouflaged jacket over a man's dress shirt, the shirttails of which flapped below the jacket with her every stride toward the reception desk. A second look told Carl that this was the same gangling kid who had been working the registration desk when he arrived, but now she was costumed in New Wave grub, replete with Cuisinart hairdo and heavily made-up eyes, ready for a night out with a pair of chums who waited outside in a car. Despite the studied dishevelment and the layer of cosmetic goo, she was a remarkably pretty girl, blessed with her mother's huge green eyes and rusty hair.

"Mom, I need twenty dollars. Can I—"

"*Teri!*" Sandy's tone carried a mother's rebuke. "I'm having a conversation with a guest."

"Oh, I'm sorry," said the girl, her cheeks growing suddenly red. She cast a lightning-quick glance at Carl, who smiled.

"Teri, this is Mr. Carl Trosper."

"I know. I was behind the desk when he checked in."

"Mr. Trosper and I were friends in high school, back before the Civil War."

"Hi, Teri," said Carl, offering his hand. The youngster shook it ever so briefly, as though it were a rubber glove full of worms. For a split second she seemed on the verge of offering condolences for the dead Lorna, like a grown-up would have, but adolescent bashfulness intervened and choked off her words.

"Now, you said something about money?" asked Sandy.

"Yeah, Gina and Leah and I are driving up to Kingston to see *The Karate Kid,* and we're going to stop at the Pizza Hut on the way back, and I only have six dollars and seventy-five cents, and I'll pay you back out of next week's check, and—"

"Honey, twenty dollars seems a little steep for a movie and a pizza. Besides, you've already seen *The Karate Kid.*"

"Mom, we've seen it twice, but we want to see it again before *Karate Kid II* comes out. Can I *please* have twenty dollars? I owe Gina and Leah, because they bought the food last time we went out."

The muscles in Sandy Zolten's face tightened with apprehension, and she asked who was driving.

"Leah," answered Teri. Leah Solheim was seventeen, went the prepared statement, and a very good driver. She had gotten an A in driver's ed, or her mother would never have trusted her with the family's brand-new Toyota.

"Okay," said Sandy with stiff reluctance, digging into the till for a twenty. "But I want you to come right home after the Pizza Hut. And remember: no beer, no dope, and no chasing around in boys' cars—"

"Mother!"

"—and stay away from strangers, you hear? We've had more than our share of weirdness in this town lately."

"Mother, *please.*" Teri cast a darting glance at Carl, who pretended disinterest in this mother-daughter tête-à-tête. "It's not like we're going to Miami or something. Kingston's not even ten minutes from here and we're only going to see a movie and eat some pizza. There's absolutely nothing to worry about."

She snatched up the twenty and crammed it into her

camouflaged jacket. "Thanks, Mom. Nice to see you again, Mr. Trosper." She bounded to the front door, turned and blew a kiss to Sandy, and was gone.

"Seems like a great kid," said Carl, a comment that hung feebly in Teri's aftermath.

"She *is* a great kid," said Sandy. "Gets good grades, puts in a shift every day here on the desk, doesn't drink or do dope that we know of. Oh, we had a minor incident with marijuana about a year ago, but I think she learned her lesson. As teenaged girls go, she's good as gold." But the look of taut apprehension still had not left Sandy's face. "I just hope I can get through her high-school years without ending up in the state home, that's all."

"Oh, you'll make it." Carl smiled. "No matter what you moms think, there isn't much trouble a kid can get into in these parts. Believe me, I know from years of trying."

"Ordinarily I'd agree with you, but things have gotten a little strange around here lately."

"How so?"

Sandy fixed him with a green-eyed stare that conveyed something stronger than the usual mild worry that mothers endure over teenaged daughters who go out for movies and pizzas. This was fear, undiluted and potent. She opened her mouth to speak, then cut herself off. "Carl, you don't need this. You've got enough trouble of your own. Look, you were probably going out for some dinner, and I'm tying you up."

"Bullshit. Just because we haven't seen each other since high school doesn't mean we're not friends anymore. If something's worrying you, I'd like to hear about it." He leaned an elbow on the counter. "For old time's sake, if nothing else. Now what's this about things getting strange in good old Greely's Cove?"

Sandy took a pack of Merits from a drawer under the counter and lit one. "Well," she began, exhaling a cloud of smoke, "about eight months ago, people started disappearing, just like they walked off the face of the earth. The first one was a friend of Teri's, a girl named Jennifer Spenser, only sixteen. That was—let's see—about the first week of June. At first everyone thought she'd run away with some boy, naturally. But her parents, Tom and Linda, said she hadn't taken any luggage or clothes, not even her makeup kit. Besides, she'd seemed perfectly happy at home, like any other normal high-school kid. Stu Bromton, our chief of police—remember Stu?"

"We grew up together," Carl reminded her. "In fact, our fathers practiced law together. Stu and I were planning to do the same one day, only . . . well, that's a long story. Go on."

"Stu decided to call in the State Patrol after she'd been gone a few days, and they organized a search. Carl, it was one of the worst things I've ever gone through. People fanned out along the shore of the Cove and started walking through the woods, calling her name, poking into bushes and holes, looking for some piece of her clothing, anything at all. Needless to say, they didn't find anything. The Patrol put out a nationwide bulletin through the missing-kid network and drew a total blank. The Coast Guard scoured the shore all the way down to the Bainbridge Island bridge. She just—disappeared."

She paused for a drag on the cigarette. "This is a small town, as you well know, and everyone knows everyone else. We all felt like it had happened to one of our own family. We watched Tom and Linda Spenser become walking zombies because they couldn't sleep at night, because they couldn't stop wondering when some policeman would call on the phone and tell them that a hiker in the Olympic Forest had found Jennifer's mutilated body, or that she'd washed up on the shore, or—" Sandy shuddered, causing Carl to do the same.

"It's hard to imagine anything worse," he said, interrupting the pounding of rain against the huge window in the lobby.

"I would've said the same thing eight months ago. But there *is* something worse: when it happens *again*. About a month later Elvira Cashmore disappeared."

Carl's face went slack and whitened a shade. "Old Mrs. Cashmore? Frank Cashmore's widow?" He had known the Cashmores as a boy. In fact, he had cared for their yard, mowing the lawn, trimming the hedge. They had paid him well and treated him like a favorite nephew. "Who could possibly want to hurt Elvira?" The question was rhetorical, and he immediately regretted asking it.

"She was sixty-eight years old and one of the sweetest people I've ever known—left a rhubarb pie in the oven. She didn't take any clothes with her, and she didn't withdraw any money from her account at the bank. Never let on to anybody that she planned to go anywhere—just disappeared. So we went through the whole bloody exercise again: state police officers, the organized search, the Coast Guard, and, well, nothing ever turned up. Nothing *solid,* that is."

The term "nothing *solid*" gave Carl a twinge of discomfort. But before he could ask her to explain what she meant by it, Sandy went on: "That wasn't the end of it. The very next month, someone else disappeared. This time it was—let me think—oh, yes: Monty Pirtz."

"I don't think I've heard of him. He must've moved here after I left."

"He was a little younger than you and I, a Vietnam vet who was confined to a wheelchair. Ran a small repair shop up the street and lived mostly off his disability checks. Anyway, he vanished into thin air just like Jennifer and Elvira, and nobody's seen him since."

The following month, September, it was a ten-year-old girl, Cindy Engstrom, who disappeared.

In October it was Wendell Greenfield, age fifty-one, a service-station owner who was the husband of Sandy's close friend, Debra Greenfield.

In November it was one of Teri Zolten's teachers at Suquamish High: forty-two-year-old Peggy Birch. Shortly afterward her husband, George, had a nervous breakdown and blew his own head off with a shotgun.

December: a fifteen-year-old boy named Josh Jernburg.

And January: a pretty waitress who worked at Bailey's Seafood Emporium, Elizabeth Zaske, not yet twenty.

"The last one was exactly a month ago," said Sandy, "on January 8, and that's the way it's been ever since last June. During the first or second week of the month, someone vanishes." She pounded her cigarette into an ashtray that held a matchbook on which was printed: *For Our Matchless Friends.* "Other than the timing, there doesn't seem to be any pattern. The victims can be young or old, male or female. The State Patrol is baffled, and so is Stu. Worst of all, there doesn't seem to be anything anyone can do." She raised her green-eyed stare to his, and he caught a dose of the apprehension she felt. "Maybe now you can see why I worry about letting Teri go out."

Carl tried to be comforting by pointing out that people *do* walk away from their homes and communities, often without telling anyone and without making the preparations that most folks would consider normal. They leave behind clothes, luggage, and bank accounts. Others fall into rivers and streams, never to be found. And, tragically, some fall victim to child-killers and molesters, but this is comparatively rare, despite sensationalist news coverage. It seemed like a good sign, he offered, that Greely's Cove's "victims" were of all ages, both male and female, because virtually every serial killer that Carl had ever heard of did his evil deeds according to a rigid pattern. Even though people had disappeared with monthly regularity, the likelihood of coincidence seemed strong.

"Mind you, I'm no detective," he concluded, "but I'd bet a year's salary that these things aren't connected. If I were you, I'd stop worrying. You can't shut yourselves away and stop living, after all. Life has to go on."

Sandy Zolten pretended to be comforted. "Oh, you're probably right. Ken and I have told each other the same thing, but it helps to hear it again. Anyway, I'm sorry I burdened you with this, Carl."

"Don't be. My load of trouble is small compared to having a child disappear. I've lost Lorna, but I'm getting my son back. I can't imagine what the Spensers and the Engstroms must be going through, having lost their little girls."

"Or the Jernburgs their son."

"I'm glad you told me about this, Sandy," said Carl. "It's reminded me that I'm a lucky man. I'm getting a second chance with my boy, and this time I'm not going to blow it." He reached over the counter and patted her arm. "You take care. I'll see you later."

Outside, he raised his parka hood and zipped up tight, as the rain was falling in stinging sheets. But he did not hurry toward Bailey's Seafood Emporium. Sandy Cunningham Zolten's disturbing story had killed his appetite.

Having traveled half the distance between the motel and the restaurant, he nearly turned around and went back. He had forgotten to ask her what she'd meant by "nothing *solid*." Elvira Cashmore had disappeared, and nothing *solid* had turned up. Did this mean that something *un*solid—an insubstantial clue or an ambiguous explanation—had?

Just then he stepped smack into the roiling stream of a

gutter, soaking his shoe and sock. He swore wildly as the cold shot up his leg, into his guts. He shivered and forged on toward Bailey's, no longer thinking of steamed mussels. What he needed now was a good stiff Scotch.

On any other Saturday night Stu Bromton would have gone out with his buddies to pound down some beer, maybe to the Moorage out on Marina Street, or, if they felt like slumming, to Liquid Larry's. Stu would have allowed himself a steak sandwich and fries, knowing that he'd need to jog an extra mile the next day to keep the fat off.

On any other Saturday night he would have pounded down his final brew just before midnight and, after announcing to his buddies that all good things must end, gone home to his prefab house with its beige aluminum siding, smelling like a brewery but not even close to being drunk. Being a big man has its advantages, he often said, especially if he happens to be the police chief in a small town and needs to stay respectable. Lots of body weight, lots of capacity.

But this wasn't an ordinary Saturday night. This was one month to the day after the latest disappearance in Greely's Cove, Washington, when a cute young waitress named Elizabeth Zaske stepped into a crack in the earth and shot straight to the molten core. Or climbed up a ladder into an alien ship to be whisked to another galaxy. Or was eaten by a cave bear.

One month to the day.

Stu Bromton, chief of the Greely's Cove Police Department, didn't feel like drinking beer tonight, but neither did he feel like going home. He didn't feel like listening to Judy, his wife, whine about the payments on the satellite dish. He was in no mood for his sixth-grade daughter's complaints about school, her "tacky" clothes, and lack of privacy. And he certainly did not look forward to the din of his four-year-old boy's violent fantasies with Go-Bots.

Unfortunately, Stu Bromton had no other choices. This, more than any other frustration—the lack of choices—made his life a hell.

"I guess I'll head home, Bonnie," he said to the dispatcher, who sat in her steel-mesh enclosure. "Give me a buzz if anything happens."

"Okay, Stu," said Bonnie Willis, glancing up from her log

sheet. She was a big woman, maybe thirty, who looked as though she had applied her police uniform with a spray gun. "I thought you'd be going out for a few cold ones, after putting in such a long day and all. Do you realize it's almost eight?"

Stu realized it. He had purposely made it a long day, finding put-off paperwork to tackle, chores to do, letters to write. But all good things must end. "Have a nice shift," he said, incurring a sympathetic smile from Bonnie. The heavy door swung closed behind him, and the smell of rain filled his lungs.

As was his custom, he took a turn around town before heading home, just to verify that things were quiet, not that doing so would cure the unease that wormed in his guts. The disappearances never gave any warning. Nothing ever seemed out of place during the hours and days before someone called the station to report a missing person. No strangers were seen prowling the alleys, and no strange lights appeared in the woods. The plague that had crept into Greely's Cove operated under the maddening guise of normalcy.

He cruised down Frontage Street, past the West Cove Motor Inn and the Fox Theater. Here and there pedestrians darted, their collars turned up against the rain. Though this was a Saturday night and still early, remarkably few cars were on the streets.

He turned onto Second Avenue, a shady residential street overhung with winter-naked maples and elms, lined with cramped bungalows built in the late 1940s. As he approached midblock, he slowed to get a look at a particular house, the one where Lorna Trosper had lived with her son. Because there were no streetlamps, he saw little more than a dark hump of roof, guarded on either side by towering pines. He knew well what the house looked like. One-sixteen Second Avenue, Greely's Cove, Washington: white clapboard siding and dark green trim. He had wanted merely to be *near* it, if only for a few seconds.

He felt a pang somewhere near his solar plexus. There, in the cluttered garage of that house, Lorna had breathed carbon monoxide until every cell in her body was cold and inert, and in so doing she had shattered another of Stu Bromton's ragged but precious fantasies. Oh, he had long ago given up any notion of actually winning her and making her *his*, even before she had taken up with Renzy Dawkins, who was Stu's oldest buddy next to Carl Trosper. Even if he had still been single, Stu would have been no match for Renzy in a contest for Lorna's affection. Renzy was rich and rakishly handsome, and he had an aura of glamor and adventure.

Still, good fantasies are hard to come by, and Stu Bromton mourned the loss of this one. Feeling empty and more than a little worthless, he headed home.

4

Ralph Macchio, playing the Karate Kid, rose to the challenge and vanquished his dastardly rival in the final minute of the film, doing his kindly mentor, Mr. Miyagi, proud. His reward was the tumultuous adulation of a horde of bloodthirsty spectators, a gratified and almost tearful smile from Mr. Miyagi, and a contract to star in the forthcoming sequel, *Karate Kid II*.

The house lights came on while the credits still rolled, and a crowd whose average age was under sixteen gorged into the aisles and out the doors of Kingston's tiny Rialto Theater. Though the rain had stopped, the street glistened wetly with the reflected glare of neon and headlights.

Teri Zolten breathed in the night, clearing her head of the cloying fumes of popcorn and cigarettes, relishing the salty breeze off the Puget Sound.

"My *gawd*, can you imagine getting nailed by Ralph Macchio!" exclaimed Gina Walsh after the trio had piled into Leah Solheim's mother's new Toyota. She closed her huge brown eyes and pretended to swoon in the rear seat.

Leah, a lissome blonde whose hazel eyes looked much older than seventeen, retorted, "In your case, can you imagine getting nailed by *anybody*?"

Teri Zolten laughed shrilly, and Gina snatched up the gauntlet.

"At least I have some taste," she said. "Not like some other people who happen to be driving this car. You wouldn't catch me peeling my pantyhose for a salmon-face like Rory Pressman."

Teri found this to be unbearably funny and cackled. But Leah did not.

"Fuck off and die," she said, betraying a raw nerve.

The Pizza Hut was less than two blocks from the Rialto, near

37

the intersection of Highway 3 and Bond Road, which led south to Greely's Cove. Teri hoped that her two chums weren't really mad at each other, though their silence was not a good sign.

"Let's be outrageous and get a Deep-Pan Super Supreme," she said as they entered the restaurant's parking lot. "A big one."

"Speaking of *big* ones, Leah, has Rory asked you out again?" Gina apparently was not prepared to let the matter lie.

"At least I know what one looks like, which is more than you'll ever know!"

"But unlike you, I'll never have the desire to know what they *all* look like," counterpunched Gina, and this time Teri almost choked with laughter, though she wanted desperately to avoid taking sides in this spat.

"Oh hey, you guys, look who's here!" Leah was pointing frantically at a deliciously black '67 Chevy that was thundering to a stop a few parking slots away, its monstrous V-8 burping and shaking. One of its smoked windows was down, and visible inside were two shaggy-headed boys whose hair grew down the backs of their necks in fashionable rattails. "God, it's Kirk Tanner and Jason Hagstad! Can you believe it?"

Kirk Tanner, the owner of the Chev, cut the engine and the lights. Both doors swung open, and both boys swung out. They wore nearly identical bulky jackets of dark satin, with sleeves pushed almost to their elbows, and sweatshirts over threadbare jeans. Jason Hagstad wore sunglasses on the top of his head, like Don Johnson, even at night.

"Oh *gawd*, Jason is such a fox!" breathed Gina. "Doesn't he look like Rob Lowe?"

"They're gorgeous," said Leah, scarcely above a whisper.

"You *guys*, they're *seniors*!" cautioned Teri. "Leah, I'm warning you, don't you dare honk!"

"Seniors don't have leprosy," chided Gina. "Leah will be one herself next fall, for Christ's sake."

Leah honked. The boys halted in midswagger to look back at the girls in Mrs. Solheim's shiny white Toyota Celica, and much to Teri's dread, they swaggered over, hands in their hip pockets, faces smug with certainty that they had hooked into serviceable prey.

Their ritualized small talk was smooth and easy, laden with

"y'know" and "excellent" and "man," and before long they had thoroughly charmed Leah and Gina.

"Hey, man," said Jason, getting down to serious business, "we were gonna go in and have a pizza, but what the fuck, do you guys wanna head down the road and—y'know—do a little smoke? We got a case of Mick on ice in the trunk, if the doobage makes you thirsty." He grinned, and Teri saw Gina squirm with delight.

As if the proposition weren't sweet enough already, Kirk Tanner leaned through the window to whisper, "We got half a dozen hits of crack, man. Ever been high on crack?"

Teri felt her stomach churn. She had never been high on crack, and she had only smoked marijuana four times. Her parents had caught her with a joint in her purse about a year ago, and the whole damned world had almost come to an end. She resolved never again to risk going through that God-awful, tear-drenched hassle—not *ever*.

But here were Gina and Leah, considering taking up with two seniors. Not just *any* two seniors, but the most notorious pair of reprobates at Suquamish High—Kirk Tanner and Jason Hagstad. To drink and smoke and fuck and do crack.

Not that Teri considered herself an angel. But doing *crack*—it was the worst stuff anyone could smoke: high-intensity cocaine, horrifically potent and addictive. Teri felt like vomiting.

"Now where did you get some crack?" asked Leah, trying to sound sophisticated enough to disbelieve an implausible story.

"New guy in town," answered Kirk Tanner, meaning Greely's Cove. "Hangs out in Liquid Larry's. His name's *Cannibal,* if you can believe that! He got us the beer, too. So how about it, man? You guys interested?"

Gina and Leah were—y'know—interested.

"It definitely sounds more exciting than what *we* had on tap," said Leah.

"Definitely!" confirmed Gina. "I'm ready to party!"

"You *guys,*" protested Teri, "I was going to buy the pizza tonight. I almost had to wrestle my mom to borrow twenty dollars."

All eyes turned to her—silent ones, but eloquent. The boys' eyes said "Well, what the fuck, go in and have yourself a pizza, little girl!" The girls said "Really, Teri, don't be such a slug!"

The meaning of the deathly silence was clear: A foursome is company, but a fivesome is wet toilet paper.

"I s'pose we could split up," said Gina in a low but hopeful voice. "Don't you have to go home early, Teri?"

Teri Zolten got the message. "Yeah, I guess," she said, fighting an ache in her throat. "But I hate to make you guys take me all the way back to the Cove."

"Oh, hey," said Leah Solheim, "you can take this car, if you have to go, Ter. Just park it up the street a ways from your house and leave the keys under the floor mat. I'll pick it up later." Leah's tone was that of a close friend who was riding to the rescue, as though Teri could always count on Leah for help.

"There you go!" said Kirk Tanner. "Problem solved!" And it was.

So Teri Zolten found herself alone behind the wheel of Mrs. Solheim's new Toyota Celica, headed south on Bond Road, blinking away tears. Fortunately the car had an automatic transmission, because Teri had no idea how to work a stick shift. She strained through blurry tears to see the road and its painted lines, remembering her lessons from driver's ed. *Accelerate smoothly, not like a jackrabbit.* And: *Apply even pressure to the brake pedal—don't stomp on it.*

By now she loathed herself, the whole world and everyone in it.

She loathed the transparent Leah, who was actually more the predator than Kirk Tanner or Jason Hagstad. Tonight's exploit, when retold at school Monday morning, would enhance Leah's already considerable mystique among her rivals and pursuers. That's what Leah wanted: to be thought of as exotic and spicy, and she worked at it. A brush with criminality couldn't hurt the image.

Gina was hardly any better. Though she loved to accuse Leah of nymphomania, Gina would fuck anything with an erection, Teri suspected. Teri was also sure that she herself needed some new pals, regular girls who liked regular things and regular boys. She wanted no part of drugs anymore, and she wanted no part of criminals like Tanner and Hagstad.

The night grew darker as the lights of Kingston fell behind, and the highway led inland through the tiny Port Madison

Indian Reservation, where Teri always assumed Indians lived, maybe in little huts nestled in the dense forest or in long lodges made of animal skins. Though she had lived virtually next door to the reservation for seven of her sixteen years, she had never laid eyes on an Indian—at least none that she knew of. But then she had never actually set foot on the reservation, either, except to ride through it in a car.

As Kingston had, the reservation fell behind, and the aura of the Toyota's headlights became a world unto itself, a gliding island in a cold ocean of dark. Here, a few miles before the lights of Greely's Cove would start to wink through the trees, the vegetation grew to the very edge of the asphalt, a tangled wall of mossy bark, sword fern, and tawny grass. Now and then a bright pair of eyes glowered through an opening in the undergrowth, captured and betrayed for the barest moment by the passing headlights. Animals' eyes, of course: maybe a deer's, a cat's, or a raccoon's—eyes made differently than humans', able to gather light and concentrate it for use in a world of black.

Teri thought about turning on the radio: A few tunes might have made her feel better. But she couldn't let go of the wheel with either sweaty hand. Too tense, she told herself. Too uncertain of her driving skills. For a girl her age, driving was hardly routine.

But this was not really the problem. The *darkness* was. It seemed to make a sound that floated on the edge of the satiny rush of tires on wet asphalt. Teri could almost *hear* the darkness as it devoured the edges of her gliding island.

She thought of her mother's admonition to stay away from strangers: *We've had more than our share of weirdness in this town lately.* How stupid, Teri had thought at the time. The old bag's going crackers because of the disappearances, just like half the other adults in town. But now Teri wondered whether she herself teetered on the edge of crackers, for the sound of the dark was giving her gooseflesh. She longed to see her mother's face, to feel the old bag's protective arms around her, to be safe at home.

A pair of eyes appeared up ahead on the shoulder of the road, on the very edge of the headlights' reach, eyes that seemed too high off the ground to be a cat's or a raccoon's. Teri's own were dry of tears now, and she narrowed them in an effort to focus on the indistinct shape that supported the two pin-pricks of reflected light. Her foot went instinctively to the brake pedal, and the Toyota jounced wildly, for she had stomped in violation of the Doctrine of Even Pressure. As she straightened out the wheel, the figure came into clearer view: a *human* figure, a woman.

Teri slowed the car, but her mind went into high gear. How could a human's eyes glow like an animal's? Why would someone be out walking on this forlorn stretch, braving rain and dark? And what on earth was there to *smile* about, as this lonely pedestrian was doing, while standing in the middle of the road? Teri hit the brakes again to avoid running over her, and the Toyota came to a halt.

The woman in the road was of medium height, dressed in a dark and shapeless coat that covered her from neck to knees. She had a wide forehead and a long, sloping nose that ended in a sharp point above her mouth.

An accident, thought Teri. *There's been an accident somewhere*, for the woman had only one shoe, a white canvas sneaker. Her brown hair stood crazily away from her head in tangled fingers, and her wild, reflective eyes were open so wide as to expose white all around the pinpricks of color. And that *smile* . . .   More a grin, really, wide and toothy.

Yeah, there's definitely been an accident. The poor woman's car is probably in a ditch somewhere, thought Teri, *maybe overturned, and she's crawled out to flag down—*

"*Teri!*"

The voice seemed to come from inside the car, or from inside Teri's head, even though she had seen the woman's lips move. A blanket of icy needles enfolded Teri's shoulders. She cramped the wheel to the left and hit the accelerator, causing the Toyota's wheels to *screeee*. In a fraction of a second, the woman's figure was behind her, a shrinking gob of red in the rearview mirror, bathed in the bloody glow of taillights.

"*Teri! You've got to help me!*"

This time Teri almost gagged with fright, for the voice was clearly audible, and it sounded inexplicably familiar, though the figure was far behind on the road. The image of the woman's face formed again in her head: wide forehead, chalky white flesh that drooped a little around the eyes, and a radically sloping nose that came to a point.

Suddenly Teri *knew* her. She was Peggy Birch, her former social-studies teacher at Suquamish High, who had disappeared three months earlier, as though she'd fallen into a giant grinder that reduced a person's body to mere molecules. Teri had not recognized her at first. Under normal circumstances Mrs. Birch had been an impeccable dresser, even though her taste had been grotesquely middle-age. Her hair and face were always skillfully made up, and when she smiled, it was an intelligent smile that complemented the friendliness in her eyes—not at all like that lunatic grin on the face of the woman in the road.

Teri fought down her fear and brought the car to a complete halt. Poor Mrs. Birch was back there on the road, wearing only one shoe, having been through God-knows-what, desperately needing help. What kind of person would leave her to fend for herself?

And stay away from strangers, hear?

But Mrs. Birch was hardly a stranger, thought Teri in answer to her mother's warning. Something terrible had happened to her, and she needed help. She may not even have known that her husband, crazed with grief and delusions that she had actually visited him in the dead of night, had put the muzzle of a twelve-gauge shotgun into his mouth and pulled the trigger.

Teri lowered the window and stuck out her head to get a look at the roadway behind. A wall of brush loomed on either side, stained red from her taillights. But no sign of Mrs. Birch.

"Thank you for stopping, Teri."

The girl's heart fluttered and tried to crawl up her throat. She pulled her head back through the window and saw Peggy Birch sitting in the passenger seat, her face awash in the twilight of the instrument panel and dash. Teri's mouth worked and yawned and formed a silent *O* before any sound came out. "H-h-how did you—you—"

The smell enveloped her, a horrid mixture of body dirt and rotting meat, a suffusive stench that drew hot tears. Teri covered her mouth with a hand and hacked.

"I really do appreciate your help, Teri," said Peggy Birch, still grinning so tightly that vile little wrinkles appeared at the corners of her mouth. "It was certainly getting lonely out there." She actually laughed, and her throat rattled with phlegm. "You're a sight for sore eyes, I can tell you that."

Teri dared to look at her passenger again and saw that Mrs. Birch was filthy. Her face was splotched and encrusted with grime, her teeth coated with yellow, her clothing positively verminous. She looked very, very sick.

"Mrs. Birch, a-are you all right? W-we've all been really worried—"

Once again, that phlegmy laugh. "Oh, Teri! I've been terrific, I really have. I have so much to tell you that I really don't know where to begin."

"T-to tell me? I don't understand." Teri felt a knot of dread forming in her stomach. "I'd better get you to the emergency room in Poulsbo."

"Teri, Teri, we don't have time for that." She reached out to touch the girl's arm, exposing a hand and wrist that appeared to have been eaten nearly clean of flesh. Teri tried to scream, to shriek, to fill all creation with the sound of her horror, but only a croak came out.

"Tonight's going to be your big night, honey," said Peggy Birch, stroking Teri's arm. "Tonight I'm taking you to the Feast, and you'll find out what dreaming can really be like."

Teri squealed with revulsion and forced away the clawlike hand. She groped for the door handle, meaning to flee the stench-filled car. But Peggy Birch laughed yet again, issuing a sound that brought to mind a vat of bubbling slime, and the door locks engaged with a sharp snap.

5

The first light on Sunday, February 9, filtered through a mist that rolled seaward in the embrace of a tart breeze. For Lindsay Moreland it was a day for taking care of business. In this respect, it would not be much different from any other in her adult life, though the business itself was hardly routine. Today she would arrange her elder sister's funeral. She would plan the future of her nephew, Jeremy. And she would meet and defeat her former brother-in-law, Carl Trosper, on the field of verbal battle.

Carl had apparently decided to become his son's father again, notwithstanding that he had long ago given up that privilege. Carl's audacity never failed to amaze her.

"Jeremy's still asleep," said her mother, Nora Moreland, softly pulling closed the door that joined the two motel rooms. "Sleep is probably the best thing for him."

Lindsay had rented two adjoining rooms at the West Cove Motor Inn, one for Jeremy and another that she shared with her mother. She put an arm around her mother's shoulder.

"Sleep would be the best thing for you, too," she said. "There's absolutely no reason why you should be up so early."

"I can't seem to drop off," said Nora Moreland. "Every time I close my eyes, I see Lorna's face. . . ." Her voice caught, and she swallowed hard, but she kept control. Having wept for most of the preceding twenty-four hours, she was temporarily fresh out of tears—*all cried out*, her husband would have said. "Anyway, there are things to do. What's first on the agenda?"

"Breakfast. After you're dressed, I'll call room service."

"And then?"

"I'm supposed to have coffee with Carl."

"I'd best come along to referee."

"That won't be necessary, Mom. I can handle myself against the likes of him."

"It's *him* I'm concerned about, dear. I doubt that he can handle the likes of *you*."

Lindsay issued a little smile. "Whose side are you on, anyway?"

"Yours, of course. I just think that Carl's entitled to some consideration. He *is* the boy's father, after all. I'm not saying he's my favorite person in the world, but I'm tired of being angry with him. I'm tired of the hostility, Lindsay. It's lasted for more than thirteen years, and I'm tired of it."

"Mom, this isn't a matter of showing good manners; it's a matter of doing what's best for Jeremy."

"And do you really think that coming to live with you is what's best for him?"

"I do. And Lorna would've agreed with me."

"But, Lindsay, you're only thirty-two years old. Your career is just starting to catch fire. And you're not even—you're not—"

"Go ahead, Mother. Say it."

"Okay, I'll say it: You're not *married*. Why would you want to take on the burden of raising a young boy all by yourself? You're a beautiful, single woman who—"

"Mother, I'm a securities-account executive who makes seventy thousand dollars a year. I live in a nice neighborhood, I have nice friends. I can make sure that Jeremy has a good life with good people in it. That's more than a hell of a lot of kids get these days."

"But don't you think Carl could give him those things?"

Lindsay chuckled bitterly. "Oh, Carl could provide the glitzy home in a fashionable Washington, D.C., neighborhood, no doubt about that. He could show Jeremy how to become a sleazy politician. He could teach him the elegant art of sticking his nose up other people's behinds—"

"For God's sake, Lindsay, try not to be vulgar!"

"I'm only being realistic," said Lindsay. "Carl Trosper is a political consultant whose bread and butter depends on how brown his nose is. He thrives on rubbing elbows with senators and cabinet officials and hotshot lobbyists in the halls of power. He flits all over the country on business, and he loves to party. How much time do you think he'll have for Jeremy? And how long do you think it will take him to get tired of being a daddy again, especially to a kid who needs special care? Don't forget, he's already bailed out once."

Nora Moreland knew when she was licked, and she sighed. "I just hope you'll be civil to him."

"I promise," said Lindsay, and she kissed her mother's forehead. "Now, about the rest of the day. After I've talked to Carl, I'm going over to the mortuary to make the cremation arrangements. Since there won't be an autopsy, we can get on with things—meaning we can probably be finished here in a few days. This afternoon I'm going to talk to Jeremy's therapist, Dr. Craslowe."

"That's wise, I think. Maybe he can tell you what you're letting yourself in for."

"I suspect you're right. After that I'm heading over to Lorna's house—"

"*That's* where I can help," said Nora. "Why don't you drop me there after breakfast? I can get started packing Lorna's things and cleaning. From what the police chief said, the place is an ungodly mess."

"Mom, I'm not so sure that's a good idea. I'd planned to call in some movers and housecleaners—"

"Forget about the movers and housecleaners. I may be old, but I'm still good for something. I'll make a start on the cleaning and packing, and Jeremy can help. Having something to do will be good for both of us."

"Whatever you say, Mom."

While her mother dressed, Lindsay looked in once again on Jeremy. He lay on his side, apparently sleeping deeply. Even in the sparse, curtained light of the motel room, Lindsay could see what a beautiful child he was: a perfectly balanced mixture of Carl's ruddy, squared-off features and Lorna's delicate fairness. Of course, he would lose much of his mother's beauty as he grew to manhood, Lindsay thought, and would probably end up a carbon copy of his dad. But for now he was an angel on a pillow, sleeping an angel's gentle sleep.

Lindsay withdrew from the room, troubled just a little that the boy could sleep so peacefully in the aftermath of his mother's hideous death. In fact, Jeremy had shown scarcely any sign of the trauma and grief one would expect in a child who had just lost his mother. Probably a delayed reaction, thought Lindsay. She closed the door gently behind her.

And Jeremy opened his eyes.

• • •

The West Cove Motor Inn had a coffee shop that the owners had named The Coffee Shoppe. It boasted white tablecloths with fresh flowers (even in the winter months), floor-to-ceiling windows that let in the morning light, and a reputation among the locals for the best waffles on the west shore. Its upscale atmosphere was in keeping with the motel itself—quite unlike the Old Schooner down the street, where Carl Trosper was staying.

Lindsay Moreland asked the waitress for a table near a window and, since the place was nearly empty so early on a Sunday morning, got it. Even though she had already nibbled a small room-service breakfast with her mother, the wafting smells of fresh coffee and cooking made her hungry again. She fought down the temptation to order Belgian waffles, needing no lumps on her lithe frame, no hints of "cottage cheese thighs."

At the stroke of nine o'clock, which was the appointed time, Carl walked in and peeled off his raincoat. Lindsay's eyes landed on him, and her breath caught: He was indeed a good-looking man, especially with the addition of a short beard. Six feet tall, reddish-blond hair, longish face with a lantern jaw, slender in a gray corduroy sport coat over khaki trousers and a green V-necked sweater.

The waitress showed him to the table, and he gave Lindsay one of his patented, brown-eyed smiles, the kind that had melted her elder sister's heart back in her college days. But Lindsay's heart did not melt. She had seen plenty of his type in Seattle's business world—guys with proper tans and jaunty clothes and health-club bodies. Guys who traded on charm, not brains or ability.

Lindsay stood up, shook his hand firmly, and managed to return his smile. They exchanged civilities (her mother would have been proud), and Carl ordered coffee and a cinnamon roll with raisins.

After the inevitable *too bad this isn't under better circumstances*, Lindsay said, "Well, how are things at J. Howard Maynard and Associates, Political Consultants Extraordinaire?"

"Busy, this being an election year and all," said Carl,

sipping his coffee. "We're handling four Senate races and ten House races. Plus we're doing some polling and analysis for a couple of presidential candidates."

"Wow, the money must be rolling in," said Lindsay, and the remark hung awkwardly.

"It's a good job," said Carl finally, without disapprobation. "I get to travel around a lot, meet people. Nice benefits; no heavy lifting." He attempted a grin.

"Well, if that's what you're good at . . ." Despite her promise to her mother, Lindsay was making it plain that she didn't hold Carl's line of work in high esteem. Political consulting and lobbying, in her view, were mere steps above parasitism.

"And how's the world of stocks and bonds?" asked Carl. "I trust you're making the best of this bull market."

"I suspect we're in for a slide sometime before the fourth quarter," replied Lindsay, using her professional tone. "But that's all the free advice you're going to get." They both smiled uneasily.

"Then I suppose we'd better get down to cases," said Carl, his face darkening. "Have you heard anything more about the autopsy?"

"Yesterday afternoon I talked to the police chief—what's his name?"

"Stu Bromton; old friend of mine."

"Whatever. He informed me that there won't be an autopsy or inquest. The medical examiner and the prosecutor both agreed that the cause of death was"—here she took a deep breath—"was suicide. We're free to get on with the arrangements. I suppose you know that Lorna had always said she wanted to be cremated."

"Yes, I remember that. We should probably see the mortician today."

"I told him yesterday that we'd want cremation, but you're right—we should finalize things with him this afternoon. It's on my lists of things to do."

"Did Stu say anything else?"

"Like what?"

"About a suicide note—anything like that?"

"There *was* a note. Since there won't be an autopsy or an

inquest, the police don't need it. We can pick it up at the police station, if we want."

Carl's eyes grew heavy with sadness, and for the briefest moment Lindsay felt a surge of sympathy for him.

"Have you seen it?" he asked. "Do you know what it says?"

"No."

"I'd like to have it."

"That's fine with me."

"Is Jeremy awake yet?"

"He was still asleep when I left the room. My mother suggested that I drop her and Jeremy by the house later this morning. She wants to start cleaning the place up and packing Lorna's things. Why don't you come by around lunchtime?"

"Sounds good," said Carl agreeably. "Home is probably the best place for him."

And there it was, thought Lindsay: the first tentative shot before the opening salvo of the battle. *Home is probably the best place for him,* and home is where Daddy is, naturally. Home will become Washington, D.C., is that it? Fat chance.

"I'm glad you brought that up, Carl. We need to talk about Jeremy's future." Lindsay folded her hands on the white tablecloth and fixed Carl with a steady, blue-eyed gaze. She leaned forward slightly, assuming a posture of stiff resolution. "I'm sure you'll agree that he should stay close to Dr. Craslowe, since this man is largely responsible for his recovery. It's unthinkable that Jeremy should start up with some other therapist at this stage of the game. That's why—"

"I couldn't agree more," put in Carl. "Craslowe's been the only doctor who's been able to get through to him. I don't see any reason to switch horses in midstream."

Lindsay wilted a little and blinked incredulously. "But yesterday—on the phone—you said something about becoming a real father again. You talked about how tragic it was that Lorna had to die in order to bring you and your son together. I took all that to mean that you intended to take Jeremy back East with you."

Carl gazed out the rain-streaked window at the rolling mist. The wintery grayness of Greely's Cove seemed a living part of him, like skin or hair, something he'd been born with.

"That's what I meant—then," he answered. "But I've had some time to think, Lindsay. I've thought about what my life has been till now, about the things I've done—to myself and to others—and the things I've missed. I've thought a lot about Lorna and Jeremy, and I don't mind saying that I've had some fairly heavy-duty regrets. It's time to start putting things in order again."

What the hell is this? wondered Lindsay. *A tactic?*

"So what's the upshot?" she demanded, sounding harsher than she wanted.

"The upshot is that I plan to move back here. I'll take care of Jeremy like I should've done a long time ago. I'll probably hang out a shingle and practice a little personal injury law—I've kept up my Washington-state bar dues, thank God. I'll raise my kid and teach him how to sail, play ball, maybe even how to practice law someday. We'll survive, might even prosper."

Lindsay stared at him, slack-jawed, for a full ten seconds.

"Is this really what you want?" she asked.

"It's what I want. It's what I need."

Lindsay's anger took control of her, giving her voice the bright, sharp edge of a straight razor. "Now that your son has recovered to the point that he can behave in a socially acceptable way, you want him back, is that it? Now that he can be trusted not to defecate on the furniture? Or take his pants off in church?"

Carl's face hardened. "You haven't changed at all, have you?"

"I'm too old to change, Carl, and so are you. You couldn't abide the thought of living with Jeremy before he started to get well. You couldn't take his screaming or his messes or the sympathetic looks from your friends. All you wanted was to get away from him, even if it meant leaving Lorna, and that's exactly what you did. You made a life for yourself somewhere else, somewhere far away, the kind of life you've always wanted."

"Know something, Lindsay? You have the diplomatic charm of a tarantula." He pushed his uneaten cinnamon roll away and signaled for the check. The waitress didn't see him at first, for she was talking in urgent whispers with the policeman who had just sat down at the counter.

"What Jeremy needs is stability," Lindsay went on. "He needs someone who'll stay with him and love him; someone he can count on to be there when the sledding gets rough. You don't meet the specifications, Carl. That someone is not you."

"Gosh, it's been nice chatting with you," said Carl, scooting back his chair, anticipating the arrival of the check. The waitress was on her way, scribbling on her pad as she walked. "Let's do it again real soon."

"I'm not going to let you have him, Carl."

"Oh? And what makes you think you'll have any say in the matter?"

"Lorna was my sister. She would've wanted me to take Jeremy. That's what I intend to do."

"Well," answered Carl, dropping all pretense of civility, "I won't presume to offer you any legal advice, because you've undoubtedly got a lawyer of your own. But I will tell you this: I'm Jeremy's natural father, I have a good income, and I live an upstanding life. There isn't a judge in this country who would deny me custody."

The waitress set the check down, and Carl glanced up at her face. She was a pleasant-looking woman of middle age with short black hair. Her face was contorting, her eyes filling with tears, her hands shaking.

"Thank you," the waitress managed to gasp. "P-please join us again."

Carl handed her a credit card and asked, "Are you all right? Is something wrong?"

The policeman who had entered a few minutes earlier came to the table and took the waitress's arm. "Come on, Edna, we'll find someone else to take care of things here for a little while. Until you feel better."

"Excuse me, Officer," said Lindsay. "What's going on here?"

The policeman had a baby face, a pair of mirrored aviator glasses that hung from a buttonhole of his shirt, and a nameplate that identified him as Hauck. "We've just had some bad news," he said. "I hope you'll excuse Edna. If you'll wait a minute, I'll get you another waitress." He put an arm around Edna's shoulders and guided her toward the door that led to the kitchen. "I should never have told you about it, not while you were on the job," Hauck said.

Edna broke down completely then. Heavy sobs racked her body. "I used to babysit for the Zoltens!" she blubbered through a torrent of tears. "Teri was such a wonderful child, so intelligent, so thoughtful!"

Lindsay watched their backs as they moved away, then glanced at Carl, whose face had gone ashen, the color of the smoky mist beyond the window.

Mitch Nistler woke to the crunch of gravel and the slosh of tires through water and knew instantly that a car had pulled into the muddy, unpaved drive at the front of his house. He forced open his aching, crusty eyes and grabbled for his glasses.

Fuck a bald-headed duck, it must be Kronmiller! he hissed. His stomach churned as he remembered that he had not shown up for work at the mortuary last night, but instead had gotten drunk at Liquid Larry's.

Well, not exactly drunk. Just *loose*. Loose enough, in fact, to get thrown out of the place by Liquid himself. Loose enough to decide that his boss, old Matthew Kronmiller, could take his assistant embalmer's job and shove it up his rosy ass, for all Mitch cared.

Now it was morning and the sun had dawned, revealing the world in all its bleak clarity. Mitch's body had burned off most of the alcohol he had poured into it the night before, which included ten beers at home after getting a taste of Liquid Larry's size eleven. Now he had a throbbing head, aching joints, and a different attitude about his job.

He *needed* that job, damn it, despite its less attractive aspects. The money, while not great, was decent—especially for an ex-con who had barely made it through high school. It was the closest thing to a future that he owned.

He ransacked his closet in search of a clean shirt and a presentable pair of jeans, neither of which he found. He settled for stuff he'd worn earlier in the week but had not yet washed. They would have to do, despite the wrinkles, and he hurriedly pulled them on over his skinny body.

He heard a car door slam and then another—more than one person, apparently, meaning that Kronmiller had not come to roust his ass to work after all. Kronmiller always came alone when there was rousting to be done. Mitch breathed a little easier, but not *too* easy. If he knew what was good for him, he would haul his butt over to the mortuary right now, and he would start cleaning up that suicide if the old batfucker hadn't already done so. Mitch hoped that his visitors, whoever they were, would not stay long.

He heard the scuff of shoes on the cement stoop, the ticks and snaps of someone pushing the doorbell button (the doorbell didn't work), and finally, the thump of heavy knuckles on the splintered, rain-bleached door. *Boom-boom boom-boom*.

Mitch stepped into a pair of tattered loafers and dashed out of his cluttered bedroom, stuffing his shirttails into his jeans. He whirled and lunged around the living room, snatching up empty Olympia beer cans and Big Mac wrappers, which he crammed into a black Hefty bag that usually lay next to his Salvation Army armchair.

Boom-boom boom-boom.

He pounded into the kitchen, tore open the back door, and flung the bag onto the rickety rear porch, where it landed atop a pile of half a dozen such bags, all bulging with beer cans and burger wrappers and wadded cigarette packs.

Boom-boom boom-boom.

"All right, I'm coming, I'm coming!" he yelled, and he heard a barking laugh that was somehow familiar. He attacked the scatter of porn mags that lay on the couch, on the carpet, beside his armchair—memorable publications with names like *Cocktail* and *Honey Pit* and *Beaver*, all with gynecologists' views of young women in blazing color on the covers. He chucked the pile behind the couch.

Boom-boom boom-boom.

He fumbled with the safety chain and dead bolt and finally managed to jerk the door open. The face on the other side caused his stomach to flip-flop. It had exaggerated brows that knitted above a fleshy nose, a blockish jaw covered with stubble, and hazy eyes that could not quite hide a wild anger, even when the mouth was smiling, as it was now. The face belonged to Corley Strecker.

Or, more accurately, to Corley the Cannibal Strecker, recent graduate of Washington State Prison in Walla Walla.

"WHOOOOAH, Marvelous Mitch! How in the fuck are ya, boy?" Corley the Cannibal—a mountainous man who chewed bubble gum with loud, pistonlike strokes that caused the muscles in his face to roll and ripple—flung his beefy arms out wide.

Somehow Mitch got his unhinged jaw under control. "Fuck

a bald-headed duck!" he breathed, wanting badly to disbelieve his own bulging eyes, wanting even worse to escape the bear hug, and failing on both counts. Cannibal swung him around as though he were a loose-limbed toddler, laughing the barking laugh. Mitch staggered crazily against the doorjamb when Cannibal finally set him down, feeling dizzy and nauseous from the stench of bubble gum mixed with Cannibal's gamy breath.

"Marvelous Mitch, I want you to meet my lady," said the big man, reaching for the arm of the woman who waited a few steps behind him. "Marvelous Mitch Nistler, meet Stella DeCurtis. Stella, this is my best bud from the old days in Walla Walla, none other than Sir Marvelous Mitch Nistler."

The woman stepped forward. She, like Mitch himself, was painfully thin and as tall. She had white New Wave hair that must have been bleached. Despite her apparently high mileage, she looked not yet thirty. From a knot on the top of her head the hair spewed upward and then down in all directions, like a geyser of brittle ice. Her dark eyes glared from sockets heavily shadowed in electric blue, and though the hollows beneath her jutting cheekbones were powdered in rouge, the rest of her taut face was without color. Her skin-tight pants of black leather and coarsely woven poncho of greens and blues looked expensive.

"So you're the little slave boy I've heard so much about," said Stella DeCurtis, not bothering to offer a pale hand but stepping uninvited through the door. "From what I hear, you're lucky you had a master like Cannibal over in Walla Walla. Otherwise, you might not have lived through it." She flopped down into Mitch's Salvation Army armchair and busied herself in preparing a toot of cocaine.

Cannibal sprawled onto the threadbare sofa and lit a cigarette. "Well, don't just stand there, Mitchie-Witchie, close the door and be sociable. Least you can do is offer us a drink or something." He laughed the angry laugh again.

Mitch did as he was told, fetching his last two Olys from his rusty little fridge in the kitchen and turning them over to his "guests." He felt just like the little slave boy he had once been.

An old feeling wormed up from his guts and threatened to choke him, a feeling he had not endured since Walla Walla, a noxious mixture of self-disgust and mortal fear, of having lost himself in a hell of sound and smell. It all came back: the perpetual din of clanking cell doors, hectoring shouts, out-of-tune guitars and blaring radios; the pukish smells of sweat and urine and antiseptic and mushy prison food heaped on wet metal trays.

"So, did you get off on being Cannibal's slave?" asked Stella in her dry voice, after taking her hits. "What's it like being a slave, anyway?"

Mitch balled his fists to keep his hands from shaking and nearly succeeded. "That was a long time ago," he managed.

"Oh hell, Mitch, it only seems like a long time ago," said Cannibal, chewing his bubble gum violently. "You've only been out—what? Five years?"

"Almost seven."

Strecker launched a short review of Mitch's history for Stella's benefit. "Mitchie Witchie here only had two choices when he got to D Block: be a slave or be a chick. You see, honey, ol' Mitch was only about twenty-two or twenty-three back then, and he looked just like a kid, all scrawny and smooth. He'd gotten himself caught sellin' crank and pot to high-school kids—for about the third time, as I recall—and the judge dropped a tenner on him; made him serve a quarter of that. He'd never been to the joint before, and he'd never heard about the wolves. Ain't that right, Mitch?"

Talk of the *wolves* made Mitch's skin cold and crawly.

"The minute he shows up, the wolves start fightin' over him, right?" continued Cannibal. "Christ, they damn near tore each other to pieces. Young, smooth meat like old Mitch isn't exactly common in the joint, you see, and every fuckin' wolf in the place meant to make ol' Mitch his chick. Well, ol' Mitch got lucky, 'cause D Block was mine. I was the goddamn block boss, the secretary-general of the place, and I was in the market for a slave. I needed somebody to bring me my food, stand lookout when I was in the shower, make up my bunk, little shit like that. To make a long story short, I stepped in and coldcocked the big mean wolf who meant to make Mitch his chick. In other words, I saved ol' Marvelous Mitch from a fate worse than death. Ain't that so, little man?" Cannibal grinned obscenely without missing a beat in the torture of his bubble gum, revealing the teeth that had earned him his moniker.

During his first prison term for burglary (before he moved up to armed robbery and assault with a deadly weapon), he had gotten into a fight with the block boss and bitten two fingers off the older man's hand. The block boss had mistakenly concluded that Corley Strecker's bark was worse than his bite. From then on Strecker used his chompers when he fought, as well as his fists and feet, sometimes tearing whole mouthfuls of flesh from an opponent's arm or leg. Hence the nickname.

Mitch nodded miserably. Cannibal had indeed rescued him from a fate worse than death, and Mitch had paid for his salvation with two years and six months as the indentured servant of a brutal and stentorian master, jumping like a frog on a hot skillet whenever Cannibal bellowed a command. He ran errands for the "secretary-general," delivered his messages and threats, collected his receivables of candy bars, cigarettes, dope, and money. He brought his food, made his bunk, scoured his sink and toilet, folded his clothes. He relayed rumors and gave him the gossip of the yard. Degrading as the servitude was, it was far better than the alternative. As Cannibal's slave, Mitch enjoyed his protection, and no one dared lay a hand on him—not even the meanest of wolves.

"So, when did you get out of Walla Walla, Cannibal?" asked Mitch, trying to keep a nervous quiver out of his voice.

"Nine months and twenty-three days ago—ten hard ones out of forty on that armed-robbery beef." He took a pull from his beer and a drag from his cigarette, always chewing, chewing. "Could've been worse, though: The state could've tagged me with some extra time for some of the shit I pulled inside. Know what I'm talkin' about?" He grinned hugely.

Mitch knew what he was talking about. Cannibal had busted heads and limbs, ordered beatings. He had stolen, extorted, and smuggled. Even killed.

"I must say, I'm glad to be out, too," added Cannibal, shaking his head. "The fuckin' joint has changed, Mitchie. The niggers got their Muslim Nation, the whites got their Aryan Brotherhood, the spicks got somethin' else—I never could say the name. It's gettin' so a secretary-general can't count on anybody anymore. Everybody's got some other loyalty. One guy can't hardly run the block by himself, like I did. If I hadn't've gotten out when I did, I probably would've gotten chopped, I swear to God."

"So, what are you doing these days?" asked Mitch, eyeing

Cannibal's well-tailored leather jacket and expensive boots with suspicious eyes.

"Well, I'm glad you asked me that, little man. See this?" He pulled a small plastic vial from the pocket of the jacket and held it high for Mitch to see. Inside it were four yellowish white cakes of powder, secured by an orange stopper. "You're looking at forty dollars retail. You're also looking at the best goddamn high on the block. Tell you what: Take a hit on me."

Mitch knew what it was without being told. Crack, smokable cocaine, a distillate so powerful you could become an addict after just one hit. He didn't need this. What he needed was a beer, or maybe four, or better yet, a triple threat, but not *this* shit.

"You go ahead. I gotta go to work in a few minutes."

"Oh, I never do crack myself," said Cannibal. "I can afford the good stuff these days—nose candy. The high ain't as intense, but it sure as hell lasts a lot longer. Ain't that right, Stella?"

Stella DeCurtis nodded without betraying the slightest enthusiasm.

Mitch cleared his throat, issuing a frightened sound that he regretted. "It looks like the crack business is agreeing with you," he said to Cannibal. "What I can't figure out, though, is what you need with me."

"Hell, Marvelous Mitch, it's not like I *need* you," said Cannibal, laughing, chewing. "I just wanted to drop in and say hi, now that we're neighbors and everything. We've got a lot of catching up to do, you and me. We've been in the stinker together, right? That makes us asshole buds for life, right? Now, what kind of an asshole bud would I be if I didn't give you a chance to share a little piece of my good fortune?"

Mitch Nistler felt the blood draining from his face.

6

Carl Trosper ran down Frontage Street, leaving behind Lindsay Moreland, who sat alone and mystified at a table in The Coffee Shoppe of the West Cove Motor Inn. He had snatched up his credit card where their hysterical waitress had left it, dug hurriedly into his wallet for cash to toss onto the table, and, before Lindsay could remark about the suddenly ashen color of his face, dashed out the door of the restaurant.

It was less than five blocks to the Old Schooner Motel. Half an hour earlier, Carl had walked from the Old Schooner rather than drive to his meeting with Lindsay, but now he ran. Propelling him was a curious urgency, a need to comfort Sandy, perhaps to help her if he could; *curious*, because the night before he had seen her for the first time in two decades.

Yet, in the lobby of the Old Schooner the previous night, she had shared with him her fears and apprehensions about the dark things that had happened in Greely's Cove over the past eight months—the disappearances of good and decent people who lacked good and decent reasons to disappear—and her worry over Teri. Sandy had opened up to Carl as though he were more than a fondly remembered face from childhood, but rather a real friend who was entitled to hear these deeply personal worries. And he had listened like a friend, had tried to comfort by pooh-poohing the notion that the disappearances were connected in some way.

Maybe that was the source of his urgency, a crawling sense of guilt for having comforted and pooh-poohed instead of grabbing Sandy by the shoulders, shaking her until her teeth rattled, and demanding that she chase down her daughter and drag her back to the safety of hearth and home. Now he damned himself for having discounted the danger. Eight people had vanished from the face of the planet, for the love of

59

everything holy! How could he have failed to be afraid for Teri, having heard the story?

The rain had relented temporarily, and the fog had begun to thin. A sprinkling of pedestrians hurried purposefully up the block or down, some on their way to church, others out for Sunday breakfast.

Carl drew stares as he loped through the mist, his boat shoes flapping on the wet pavement, his raincoat flopping crazily, but he didn't care. The sights of the main drag danced by his eyes in rhythm to his strides—the Mariners' Bank, the Fox Theater, the Masonic Temple, old sights that conjured visions of his youth.

Three boys, ages twelve or thirteen, all wearing baseball caps backward, thundered past him on skateboards, careless of the mist or the rain or the puddles. For a twinkling he saw himself a quarter-century ago, together with a pair of boyhood pals, Renzy Dawkins and Stu Bromton, not on skateboards but on Schwinn Continentals, weaving through the traffic en route to nowhere in particular. Predictably, their acquaintances had called them the Three Musketeers, because they were seldom seen apart. Privately they'd called themselves the Triumvirate, a term Carl had picked up in a Roman history text of his father's. With childish exuberance, the Triumvirate had plotted to rule the town one day, the state and perhaps even the country. To the Triumvirate, nothing had seemed impossible.

Not all the sights were old ones. Sandwiched among the familiar buildings were freshly trimmed storefronts and façades, rebuilt or restored to reflect changing times, changing people, changing wants. A sign lettered in flowery cursive announced *Hannie's, A Carefree Ladies' Boutique.* The old drugstore had become a chiropractor's office, the old grocery an accountant's.

Carl stopped cold, as though slamming into an invisible wall. Directly across the street from Hannie's, between the Mariners' Bank and the Fox Theater, was a storefront with bright green window lattices and a Dutch door to match. Tucked under a well-worn awning was a wooden sign with the name of the establishment carved in stylized relief: *Lorna's Little Gallery.* Barely visible behind the lattices, obscured by mist and the shadow of the awning, were displayed perhaps half a dozen paintings, most resting on short easels.

Carl's feet began to move of their own volition off the sidewalk, over the cracked gutter, across the street. An oncoming motorist slowed and swerved to avoid hitting him, then gave him an angry blast of the horn. He found himself standing with his nose inches from the latticed window, squinting through the smudgy glass at the paintings within.

Watercolors, mostly—some Lorna's, some by other artists. Seascapes, islandscapes, a study in oils of cormorants leaving their webbed footprints on a wet beach.

Lorna's Little Gallery. Lorna's Little Dream. Lorna's Little Means of Eking Out a Living after her husband forsook her and their child for the glitzy world of political consulting and power-brokering.

This was where his ex-wife sold her watercolors, where she displayed the works of her few artist friends, where she dispensed occasional art supplies to local painters and sketchers who ran out of brushes or paper or gum erasers and were too pressed to catch the ferry to Seattle for a visit to a real artists' supply store. Carl had seen the gallery before, but he had never seen it like he was seeing it today.

What troubled him were the cobwebs that festooned the pictures and the easels, the layer of dust on the inside of the glass, the general dinginess. During their marriage Lorna had shown an artist's indifference to housekeeping, but with works of art she had been tyrannically fastidious. A painting had to hang just so. Dust could not be allowed to collect on the frame or mounting. The light had to be perfect. To Lorna *all* art—no matter how amateurish or crude—had been sacred, a gift from God that required keeping up.

She had died less than two days earlier, yet the filth on and around the displays was obviously months old. Carl swallowed hard, feeling empty and cold. Lorna would never have neglected art in this way. Not the Lorna *he* had known. A worry formed and hung in his chest like a stone: Maybe she had started the job of dying long ago, long before her heart actually stopped pumping.

He turned away from the window and headed down Frontage Street again, walking with long, quick strides toward the Old Schooner Motel, hurrying but not running.

• • •

Ianthe Pauling shouldered home the massive vault door and, in accordance with Dr. Craslowe's standing orders, locked it. The comparatively fresh, unbefouled air was a blessing, though a hint of charnel reek had wafted up from the chambers below while the vault had stood open. It hung in the dark passages of the basement like the lingering memory of a nightmare. She hoped intensely that the horrible smell would never creep into the house above. Though she was well accustomed to discomfort, the stench was simply too much to live with, an impossible hardship that she lacked the strength to suffer for more than a few minutes at a time.

Having made her way to her room on the second floor of the mansion, she flung open the velvet curtains and sank into the padded settee that filled the bay window, tired beyond words, too drained even to produce tears in which to bathe her sadness. She tried to be grateful for the morning, gray and damp though it was. The morning had brought an end to the night, which was reason enough to be thankful. But the sadness was a veil that doused even the tiniest joys before they could spark into full-fledged feelings, and blackness once again engulfed her soul.

The taking of children always affected her this way. In the faces of the really young ones, like little Cindy Engstrom— behind their contorting horror-masks and the fearfully glistening eyes—she saw the faces of her own dream-children, whom she and Warren had hoped to bring into the world someday, the sons and daughters who would never be born, thanks to Hadrian Craslowe. Better for Cindy Engstrom if she could have somehow traded places with one of Ianthe's dream-children, the ones who had never known life.

How simple and wonderful everything would have been, had Craslowe never existed, had his predatory magic never found its way to Ianthe Pauling's native Sumatra, where, on the shores of Lake Toba long ago, it had corrupted and enslaved her family. How beautiful life could have been on the fringe of the steaming jungle, where the aromas of rubber trees and wild-growing spices tickled the senses, where the roars of tigers could sometimes be heard in the night, where grown people played joyful children's games and worshiped innocent old gods to the crashing of gongs and cymbals.

Beautiful and simple, indeed. And utterly impossible.

Teri Zolten and Jennifer Spenser were only sixteen, the very age at which Ianthe had become a young Englishman's bride and flown off with him to his home in London. She remembered how much like a little girl she had felt then, how unlike a grown woman or wife. That Jennifer and Teri would never know the fulfillment of real womanhood was an incredible sorrow. But Ianthe Pauling had no tears left—not for them, not for herself.

In the face of the fifteen-year-old boy, Josh Jernburg, she had seen her younger brother, Lionel, who had been just that age when she and Warren had sent for him so he could live with them in England. Despite their different racial backgrounds, both boys were dark and slim. Both were gangly, sweet-faced lads who could have grown up to become strong, handsome men.

And what great dreams Ianthe had dreamed for Lionel. What wonderful things she had dared to hope for him. In England there were good schools and bright prospects, the opportunity to achieve joys beyond the wildest imaginings of the Batak tribesmen from whom Ianthe and Lionel's family had originally sprung. In England there had been the hope of escaping the taint that had afflicted Ianthe's family from the moment its blood commingled with that of an American sea captain named Tristan Whiteleather, her great-grandfather.

This man had burdened his offspring with a curse that could never be shed, one that demanded unimaginably vile sacrifices and deeds. It had enslaved her as it had every Whiteleather child of old Tristan's line; had already taken her husband, Warren. It had made a hostage of her brother, Lionel, who languished in a padded cell of a mental institution in Wales, a seemingly incurable lunatic. Only because of him did Ianthe stay on in service to Craslowe, for Craslowe's magic had made Lionel the howling, jerking, vomiting animal that he was. Only Craslowe's magic could lift the spell.

Someday soon, the doctor had promised, he would restore Lionel to a normal state, to the merry and good-hearted young man he had once been. But only if Ianthe continued to serve awhile longer with selfless, unflinching loyalty. The quality of her service would determine whether Lionel would ever really live again.

How much longer? she asked herself for the trillionth time, and deep within her aching heart lurked the unspoken dread that a cretaure as foul as Hadrian Craslowe could not be trusted to keep a promise.

The Zoltens lived in a two-story, white stucco house that shared an alley with the motel they owned and operated, a convenient arrangement that saved time going to and from work. Their large living room was filled with middle-of-the-line Early American furniture, which in turn was filled with people—neighbors, friends, Sandy's relatives, all on hand to comfort, encourage, and help.

The news of Teri Zolten's disappearance had traveled fast, sped on its way by a sick sense of expectancy that the people of Greely's Cove had acquired during the past eight months. They had *expected* to lose another of their own, and when the expectation became reality, they were ready for it. Despite the early hour on a Sunday morning, they had descended on the Zolten household with hot casseroles, urns of coffee, and ample supplies of reassuring smiles and words. Many would stay with the Zoltens until the vigil was given up, until Police Chief Stu Bromton announced that it was pointless to stay, until hope for little Teri had evaporated like steam from an empty coffee urn.

Stu Bromton sat in a corner of the crowded living room, taxing a spindly-looking love seat with his bulk. Huddled near him were Ken and Sandy Zolten, who sat on folding chairs brought up from the family room downstairs. This was the part of his job Stu hated most—the initial interview with the horrified family of a missing victim: taking down the victim's full name; the color of her eyes and hair; her height and weight; any peculiar identifying marks; the description of the clothing she wore at the time of the disappearance; the names of kids she ran with.

Had she been behaving strangely? Did she have any enemies? Had she been having trouble in school? Any trouble with drugs? And on and on, as though any of this excruciating trivia would help.

Ken Zolten was a tall, lean man in his late thirties, built like the tight end he had been in college, a man who cared about staying in shape. His blond hair had started to recede badly, but he kept it short to avoid drawing attention to it.

"Is that about it?" he asked Stu during a pause in the

questioning. "Shouldn't we be organizing the search party?" His steely eyes radiated agony.

"My people are already taking care of that, Ken," said Stu. "The party's forming up in the parking lot of your motel right now."

"Then let's get on with it. I don't want to waste another damn minute."

"I've got to ask just one more question: Can either of you think of any reason—and I mean *any* reason, no matter how ridiculous it might sound—why Teri might want to run away from home?"

Sandy spoke up, her voice barely under control. "Come on, Stu, we all know she didn't run away. She didn't have anything with her other than the clothes on her back and twenty-odd dollars. Besides, she was happy here. She was just a normal, happy, healthy —" Sandy's voice cracked as she realized that she was referring to her daughter in the past tense. Tears gushed from the corners of her green eyes and flowed down the sides of her nose, leaving muddy trails of yesterday's mascara. "I'm sorry, I'm sorry," she sobbed, while blotting her eyes and cheeks with a pink Kleenex.

Ken reached around her shoulders and enfolded her in his arms. "It's okay to cry, Sweets. It's okay." His own voice was dangerously thin.

"It's *not* okay," said Sandy, after blowing her nose into the Kleenex. "We should be out there looking for her, not sitting in here chatting. I'm done crying. Now I want to go out and find my daughter."

"Then let's do it," said Stu, hoisting himself out of the love seat with a grunt. "Sandy, I suggest that you have a relative or a close friend of the family stay near the phone here, just in case Teri calls from somewhere. If she's in trouble, she doesn't need to hear the voice of a stranger on this end."

If she's in trouble! thought Stu. Cops have to say the goddamnedest things, and oh, how he hated this job.

"My mother will be here with Amber," said Sandy, sniffling. "I'll ask her to mind the phone."

Stu then addressed the hushed gathering in the living room, asking for able-bodied volunteers to help with the search, a drill that most of those present were well accustomed to, having gone through it eight times before. "We're forming up in the parking lot of the Old Schooner, and we'll be kicking it off in about ten minutes. Any help would be much appreciated."

The dozen or so men in the room, and a few of the younger women, headed for the door, following Ken and Sandy Zolten out through the covered porch, down the walk flanked by naked rosebushes, through the alley to the parking lot of the motel, where they melted into a crowd of forty or fifty private citizens who had already gathered to search for little Teri.

Carl Trosper entered the covered drive of the Old Schooner Motel and passed by the front entrance. Lowing crowd noises had reached his ears while he was still a hundred yards down the block, and curiosity now drew him around the corner of the building to the parking lot in the rear.

Scores of people were standing in the hazy rain, knotted in small groups around uniformed police officers. Parked on the periphery of the crowd were a pair of GCPD cruisers and a unit of the county sheriff's department, their blue beacons spinning and pulsing, their radios crackling now and again with scratchy police voices. As Carl watched, a white Washington State Patrol car glided into the lot, with a dour, Smokey-hatted trooper behind the wheel. The trooper parked, got out, and joined the throng that milled around Carl's old friend, Stu Bromton, who had just raised a bullhorn to his lips.

"Ladies and gentlemen, can I have your attention, please?" His amplified voice seared the quiet of the morning and reverberated off the low walls of Frontage Street. *"We're going to divide the search party into four groups."* And he briefly outlined the strategy: two groups on either side of Bond Road, heading both north and south, combing the ditches on both sides before moving deeper into the woods to reverse directions for another sweep, then yet another, and so on. A member of the police department or the sheriff's office would lead each group.

"Just one word of caution," added the chief. *"We've cordoned off the area immediately around the car that we assume Teri Zolten was driving. Please do not intrude into that cordoned area. There may be evidence on the ground, and we don't want it disturbed. Thank you. Now let's move out."*

The crowd then headed for the street, a shambling army of

somber faces under wet-weather gear, and started climbing into cars for the short trip north on Bond Road. Carl stood on the edge of the human stream and watched the faces flow doggedly by. Many were familiar, though no one seemed to recognize *him*. Sandy Zolten was there, of course, arm-in-arm with a man Carl assumed was her husband. There was old Dale Noggle, a town fixture who had been ancient and retired even when Carl was a lad. And Sig Knutson, Carl's former Little League coach. Many more.

Carl felt a chill creep down his back. Familiar as the faces were, they seemed different somehow, marked in a way that mere years could not accomplish. These were faces of a people in bondage, faces contorted and worn by fear. Their eyes had an unnaturally sharp look of great suffering. Carl shuddered as he remembered a photograph he'd once seen in a collection on World War II. An Allied soldier had snapped it outside the barbed wire at Dachau. Clustered inside the wire were half a dozen inmates, their faces hideously ravaged by starvation and disease, their twiglike fingers hooked between the barbs. Their desperate eyes smoldered with the look that Carl was seeing today.

A hand on his shoulder made Carl flinch, and he swung around to come face-to-face with Stu, a human mountain in a damp police jacket. They stood still a moment, eyes locked, mouths frozen in sad smiles, before bear-hugging and clapping each other on the backs. "Hippo, God damn it, it's good to see you!" said Carl when they broke. "How the hell have you been?"

The police chief tried vainly to force a scowl into his smile, and he balled a fist, which he positioned under Carl's chin. "*Hippo!* I oughtta bust your melon, you little maggot! I thought I'd finally lived that nickname down. How old were we when you tagged me with it, anyway?"

"It wasn't me. It was Dawkins, remember?"

Stu put a massive hand on Carl's shoulder and shook him good-naturedly. "Yeah, I guess I do at that. Renzy gave everybody nicknames, but he never had one himself. Yours was the Bushman, as I recall—I can't really remember the significance of it."

"You don't want to know, believe me."

"Anyway, you're probably the only one in the world who

can call me Hippo now and live to see the sun come up. Welcome back to Greely's Cove."

"It's good to be back," said Carl. "I wish it were under better circumstances."

Stu Bromton's smile fell away, and his eyes darkened with that Dachau look. "Carl, I'm sorry I didn't call you personally about Lorna. I just couldn't do it. I couldn't be the one to lay that on you. I hope you don't—"

"Hey, don't sweat it. I understand. The coroner was very nice about it."

Another car from the Greely's Cove Police Department arrived, this one driven by the young cop whom Carl had seen in The Coffee Shoppe, the one who had told the waitress about Teri Zolten. Officer Dean Hauck got out, bearing two Styrofoam cups full of coffee. He walked over, handed one to Stu, and sipped the other.

After prying the plastic lid off the cup and whiffing the steam, Stu asked, "Is this from the station?"

"Negative, Chief," answered Hauck. "I got it at The Coffee Shoppe. Figured you deserved some of the good stuff, with all the pressure you're under and all."

"Did you find out about the dogs, like I asked?" asked Stu, ignoring Hauck's brownnosing.

"Affirmative," said Hauck, adjusting his mirrored glasses. "I called the Seattle PD, and they said they can have a couple of bloodhounds out here within the hour."

"Good. Anything else I should know about?"

"The county says they'll send a forensic investigation unit to go over the car, but not until noon. Their main guy was up in Vancouver for the weekend, and he has to drive all the way down."

"Beggars can't be choosers, I guess," lamented Stu, "and in this town we're definitely beggars. As you can plainly see, the state's arrived." He nodded toward the dour Smokey, who stood with a pair of sheriff's deputies near the middle of the lot. "Why don't you go over and brief those guys, Dean? I'm going to spend a few minutes with my old buddy here, then I'm going out to the scene. When the press shows up, have them wait at the station, and don't say anything to them. I'll be back as soon as I can."

"Will do, Chief." Hauck hurried off to join the trooper and

the deputies, who stood shmoozing with their thumbs hooked into their woven leather gun belts.

"So," said Stu, regarding Carl again, "what brings you out on this damp Sunday morning?"

"I was having coffee with Lorna's sister over at The Coffee Shoppe when I heard your man Hauck tell the waitress about Teri. I hotfooted it over here right away, thinking maybe I could help somehow."

"That's decent of you, old stud, but you've already got all the trouble one guy needs."

"You're probably right." Carl smiled feebly, then glanced around the now nearly deserted parking lot. "What the hell do you think happened to her, Stu?"

The big man removed his visored cap with its plastic rain protector and ran a hand over his bristly scalp, but rain was still falling, so he put it on again.

"A call came into the station a little after one o'clock this morning," he said. "Kid who works nights at the ferry terminal up in Kingston, on his way home to the Cove, found a white Toyota abandoned on Bond Road, lights on, motor running. Our dispatch called the county, and they sent a unit up to check it out. Hell, what are we standing here in the rain for? Let's go into the lobby and get dry."

In the lobby of the Old Schooner they found a pair of vinyl-covered armchairs and a coffee urn. A friend of the Zoltens was minding the counter as the motel's few guests checked out in dribs and drabs.

"Anyway," continued Stu in a low voice, with a cup of fresh coffee warming his hands, "the license number belonged to Mrs. Anita Solheim, a divorcee who lives with her son and daughter here in the Cove. The dispatcher called me, and I called Mrs. Solheim. It seems that her daughter had taken the car up to Kingston last night, where she and a couple of girlfriends were supposed to see a movie and eat a little pizza afterwards. Naturally, Anita was frantic—didn't even know Leah hadn't come home yet. Is it any wonder kids get in trouble, when their parents don't keep any closer tabs than that?" He sipped his coffee. "The other two girls were Gina Walsh and Teri Zolten."

"How about Gina and Leah?" asked Carl. "Are they safe?"

"They're both home with their families, which may be a

minor miracle in itself, considering who they spent most of the night with." Stu went on to explain that the girls had paired up with two of the town's most notorious teenaged subhumans, Jason Hagstad and Kirk Tanner, whom police had pulled over on Bond Road for drunken driving later that morning, shortly before dawn. Teri Zolten had not been with them.

"They'd put down almost a case of beer among them," said Stu, "and we knew from the paraphernalia we found in Tanner's car that they'd been doing grass and crack, too. And judging from the wet stains on the seats, they'd been having an orgy that would've made Xaviera Hollander envious. They were all so loaded that it's a wonder they didn't end up splattered all over the road. We finally got Leah Solheim sober enough to admit that she'd given her mother's car to Teri after the movie, because Teri wasn't in the mood to party, or something like that. Teri was supposed to park the car up the block from the Zoltens' and leave the key in it."

"And that's it? Teri left the Toyota in the middle of Bond Road, engine running and lights on?"

"That's it," confirmed Stu. *"Almost."*

"What do you mean?"

Stu gazed a moment into his coffee cup, inhaling steam, frowning with deep furrows that Carl could not remember him having. Stu Bromton was beginning to look old.

"I checked out the Toyota myself," he said finally. "If you can make anything out of this, be sure and let me know: When I opened the door—it was the passenger's—I was hit with this . . . this incredible *stink*. I don't know how to describe it. It was like something—no, it was worse than a sewer, worse than an open grave. I tell you, it made me want to blow my breakfast. Good thing I hadn't eaten any."

Carl studied the large, freckled face of his friend, then looked away, because it had taken on that haunted look again. "A stink like a sewer or a grave, you say. What could've caused it?"

"You got *me* by the ass. But there was one other thing: the passenger's seat. It was all filthy and grimy, almost moldy. Anita Solheim said the car was cleaner than Mother Hubbard's cupboard when her daughter took it to Kingston, and hell, it's brand new. Except for the passenger's seat, there isn't a spot on it anywhere."

"So you're telling me that whoever got to Teri Zolten, whoever flagged her down and dragged her away—"

"If that's in fact what happened. There were no signs of a struggle."

"Whoever this was, he was one rotten son of a bitch—and I mean that literally: dirty, smelly, so rank that he leaves a stink in the car that last for hours."

"I guess that's what I'm saying." Stu clapped his hands on his knees and hoisted himself up, ready to get on with his duties. "Let's get together real soon, partner. We have a lot of catching up to do."

Carl stood up and shook his outstretched hand. "You said it. In the meantime, could you use another warm body in the search party?"

"Look, Carl, you've got a funeral to take care of, not to mention a con. If you want to know the truth, the search party's already too big. With all those people stomping around, we'll probably mess up any evidence that's out there."

"I guess the whole town figures it's got a stake in this thing, huh?"

Stu blew a long, grim breath between pursed lips. "Then you've heard about what's been happening over the last eight months—the Mystery of Greely's Cove. Sounds like a kids' adventure movie, doesn't it?"

"Parental discretion advised on this one, I'd say. I ran into Sandy Zolten last night here in the lobby, and she told me all about it. I—" Carl bit his lower lip and swallowed. "I even met Teri. Maybe that's why I feel like I have a stake in it, too."

"In that case you're more than welcome to come along. I've got an extra pair of overshoes in my cruiser. Let's go."

Just then a flaming-red Jaguar coupe rolled into the drive outside the lobby. The driver's door flew open, and from behind the wheel bounced a thin, shriveled woman whose perky movements belied her apparent senescence.

Carl did a double take: The sleek Jaguar XJ-S was grossly out of place in the somber, rain-drenched setting of the Old Schooner, but more so was the outlandish woman with her orange slicker, flashy silk scarves wrapped loosely about her neck, and blond Dolly Parton wig. She made straight for the door of the lobby, wasting not a second, and burst through to confront Stu Bromton head-on.

"Oh, *Stuart*, I'm so glad I've found you," she said in a stately British accent. "I've been to your station, and your dispatcher informed me that I might find you here. It's imperative that we talk."

Stu shut his eyes a moment and cringed perceptibly. "Hannie, I really would like to talk, but I'm awfully busy right now."

"I'm afraid this won't wait," she declared, thrusting out her chin. "It concerns the death of my friend, Lorna Trosper."

Carl started at the mention of his dead ex-wife, and the old woman noticed. She turned her turquoise contact lenses upon him and surveyed him, inch by inch, top to bottom. Carl marveled wordlessly at the intricacy of the lines in her face, obscured but not hidden by a thick layer of makeup. Without the elaborate blond wig or the fiery lipstick and cosmetics she would easily have looked a hundred years old, but as it was, she looked eighty. Her voice, while that of an elderly woman, was strong and even.

"I don't believe I've had the pleasure of meeting *this* gentleman," she said, indicating Carl.

Stu sighed, "Miss Hannabeth Hazelford, I'd like you to meet Carl Trosper. Carl, this is Hannabeth Hazelford."

"Trosper," said the old woman. "You must be Lorna's husband."

"Ex-husband," Carl corrected. "I'm happy to meet you, Miss Hazelford."

She offered him a bony, spotted hand adorned with a huge ring, which he shook ever so gently, for fear of breaking something so old. "Please call me Hannie," she said. "All my friends do. Your wife and I were quite close, you know. I was privileged to acquire several of her paintings."

"Hannie owns the ladies' store up the block," said Stu. "She came to town—what? A little over six years ago?"

"It's a boutique, actually," said Hannie, "directly opposite Lorna's gallery."

"Well, I wish we could stand here and chitchat all day," said Stu, "but I've got important business to attend to. What can I do for you, Hannie?"

"As a friend of Lorna and as a member of the taxpaying public, I've taken it upon myself to inquire as to the procedures employed in dealing with her tragic death," said Hannie in her very British way. "I'm given to believe that you plan no autopsy. Tell me, Stuart, can this *really* be true?"

"That's right. The coroner, the prosecutor, and the medical examiner's office agree that the cause of death is apparent. No autopsy is necessary."

"Dear, *dear,* I find this troubling indeed. You see, I've taken the liberty to research the law in this regard. According to Washington State's criminal code, a suicide by a presumably healthy young adult falls into the realm of 'suspicious' death, and the law requires that a medico-legal autopsy be performed in any such instance. But of course you know this, your being the constable and all."

"Hannie, I'm a police chief, not a constable," said Stu, planting his fists on his hips, "and I'm afraid I don't have time to stand here and argue the fine points of the Washington criminal code with you. What do you want from me?"

"Merely this, Stuart: As a taxpayer and a friend of Lorna, I insist that you arrange an autopsy on the unfortunate girl, and that you do so posthaste."

"You *what?* I don't believe this. Hannie, why in the name of God should you care whether there's an autopsy? Usually the friends and relatives of dead people do everything they can to *prevent* autopsies! They don't like to think about their loved ones being sliced up and dissected."

"My concern is the letter of the law," answered Hannie unconvincingly, avoiding the police chief's wide eyes.

"If you've read the law," said Stu, "you also know that the authorities have considerable discretion in these matters, particularly in suicides. In this case there's absolutely no reason to suspect foul play and no reason to inflict the expense of an autopsy on the taxpayers. Now, if you'll excuse me . . ."

"I'm afraid I *can't* excuse you just yet, Stuart," said Hannie with a shade of desperation. "I demand that you carry out your duty under the law! Lorna's tragic passing is indeed a suspicious death and, as such, warrants an autopsy!"

"Look, Hannie," said Stu, becoming angry, "I don't tell you how to run your dress shop, or your *boutique,* or whatever it is. And I'd appreciate it if you wouldn't try to tell me how to do *my* job. You're a very nice lady, and I know you were Lorna's friend, but the way we deal with her death is no concern of yours!"

Carl watched as the desperation in Hannie's eyes turned to blue fire.

"It most certainly *is* a concern of mine!" she shouted, leaning defiantly toward Stu's tree-trunk frame. "You cannot possibly know all that's at stake here. That young woman's body must not be allowed to lie unattended in its present state. I'll say it but one final time, Stuart: Do your duty as an officer of the law, or I shall be forced to do mine as a lawful resident and taxpayer."

"If you're threatening me, Hannie—"

"If I must bring a lawsuit to ensure that the law is carried out, that is indeed what I shall do!"

A bolt of intuition hit Carl, owing to Hannie Hazelford's curious reference to the dead Lorna's *present state*. "Miss Hazelford," he said, "you might be interested in—"

"Hannie. Please call me Hannie."

"Uh—*Hannie*. You might be interested in knowing that Lorna is to be cremated. That's what she always wanted."

"Cremated?" The old woman's turquoise stare bore into Carl's own, and her frown weakened. "And when is this to be done, may I ask?"

"Very soon. We plan to make the arrangements this afternoon, after I see my son. Tomorrow at the latest, I'd guess."

"Cremated," she said again, her eyes narrowing as though visualizing the actual procedure. "And you intend to have this done very soon—tomorrow at the latest?"

"The sooner the better," said Carl, watching relief pour into Hannie's face. "It's what Lorna would've wanted."

"I see. Well, if she's to be cremated, there isn't much point to an autopsy, is there?" She drew her orange slicker around her tiny body and turned slowly toward the door of the lobby. "Forgive my making such a nuisance of myself, Stuart. I do hope you're not angry."

"I'm not angry, Hannie. It's been a bad weekend."

"Yes, quite." She turned back toward Carl when she reached the door and paused before pushing it open. "You *will* see to the cremation, won't you?"

Carl felt a chill but shook it off. "Yes, Hannie," he promised. "I'll see to it."

The old woman smiled feebly, then pushed through the door and headed for her Jaguar.

* * *

Mitch Nistler pressed his tongue against the interior of his broken lip and tasted blood. He watched through the window as Corley the Cannibal Strecker roared away in his new four-wheel-drive Blazer, with its huge tires and blinding chrome roll bars, the ice-haired Stella DeCurtis seated next to him.

"*Fuck* you!" Mitch screamed, now that they were safely out of earshot, spattering the glass with bloody spittle. "Fuck you and that silly cartoon cunt of yours! Fuck you *both!*"

He turned from the window and winced. His rib cage ached. He hoped that Strecker had merely bruised his ribs and not broken any. The son of a bitch had gone King Kong on him, had actually slammed him against a wall and treated him like a punching bag.

Cannibal was a strong believer in violence. He considered pain the Great Persuader, and he felt no compunction about using it on someone half his size if a point needed proving. Even on someone like Mitch Nistler, an old friend.

As usual, the persuasion worked. After catching two cement-hard fists to the solar plexus and one more to the jaw, Mitch had agreed to *share* in Strecker's "good fortune," which meant becoming a partner, as Strecker euphemistically termed it, in the crack business.

Some partner: In reality Mitch would become a throwaway, a low-level courier of drugs and cash between Greely's Cove and Seattle. Every week he was to take a load of processed crack and cash (the proceeds from Strecker's retailing in Greely's Cove and surrounding towns) across the Puget Sound to an alley off Seattle's Pike Street, there to meet other throwaways who worked for Strecker's unnamed distributor. He would deliver the money and receive a load of unprocessed cocaine, which he would carry to an old house near his own place on the outskirts of Greely's Cove. There, in their newly outfitted "laboratory," Strecker and Stella DeCurtis would convert it to crack.

Mitch, of course, was not entitled to a percentage of the take, even though he would bear the lion's share of risk in transporting cash and drugs; his compensation would be a measly $250 a week, since he was a mere serf in the feudal world of cocaine peddling. Just as Strecker was a vassal of *his* lord, the distributor, who himself owed fealty to an even higher mandarin.

"Hey, what the fuck are you screamin' about?" Strecker had bellowed after hearing Mitch's complaint about the piddling money. "That's thirteen large a year, little man. You've never seen that much green in your whole life, I bet. And don't tell me you couldn't use it. How much is that old sleaze undertaker paying you, anyway? Eight grand a year, maybe ten, to sink your hands into dead people's guts? I'm more than doubling your income, you little shit. You should be kissing my ass with gratitude."

Mitch moaned.

Maybe Strecker was right. In some ways Mitch was as much old Matt Kronmiller's slave as he had been Cannibal's in Walla Walla. His job paid shit, a good share of which went back to Kronmiller as rent for this tottery old house, with its weed-infested yard, swayback roof, and clanking pipes. And when Kronmiller shouted, which was often, he jumped, just as he had jumped for Cannibal back in D Block.

Mitch still fantasized now and then about working hard and learning enough about undertaking to gain entry into a prestigious institution like the San Francisco College of Mortuary Science, but he knew in his heart that his job as Kronmiller's embalming assistant was a dark and certain dead end. He could never aspire to full membership in the profession, for he'd read in one of Kronmiller's textbooks that "practitioners of mortuary science," as they called themselves, must be super Boy Scouts—energetic, modest, cooperative, cheerful, brave, clean, reverent, neat, tasteful in dress, and the possessor of a strong face. *Christ almighty*, he often lamented, even the Boy Scouts don't demand a strong face! Mitch's criminal record alone, never mind his alcoholism and severely inferior face, shattered any hope for admission to a mortuary-science school.

Maybe he *should* be kissing Cannibal's ass: The extra money might get him out from under Kronmiller's thumb. By exercising a little thrift, he might be able to score a real apartment someday, a place with a telephone and a dishwasher, maybe even a hot tub. He might be able to unload his pathetic, rusting-out El Camino for a real car, something like a Camaro or a Trans Am. He might actually achieve a smidgen of respectability.

Oh yeah, respectability.

Who am I trying to kid? he asked himself while making his way painfully to the bathroom. Do you get *respectable* by being a throwaway in the crack business, by being so low on the totem pole that your arrest and cooperation with the police can't hurt anybody important, because you don't *know* anybody important? By earning $250 a week, helping to turn teenagers into drooling, twitching addicts? By letting yourself be terrorized into violating your parole rules and joining a criminal enterprise?

Oh, a few years of this, and I'll be up for president of the Rotary.

Mitch splashed his battered face with water from a corroded faucet, then stared at himself in the cracked mirror of his medicine cabinet. The face that stared back was in every way inferior: hooded, inert eyes; sunken, stubbly cheeks; colorless lips stretched taut over crooked teeth. In the thirty-three years he'd owned it, this face had disserved him amply. This face had been no ally.

Lindsay Moreland hated funerals, and she hated mortuaries. She wasn't wild about morticians, either. The trappings and rituals of funerals, tinged as they are with superstition and unspoken dread, grated against her rational view of the universe. The Chapel of the Cove was everything she hated about mortuaries. White antebellum columns. Gothic windows with panes of amethyst, ruby, and amber. Saturnine silence.

Matthew Kronmiller, Practitioner of Mortuary Science, epitomized the smoothly predatory undertaker, which was why Lindsay was glad she had refused to let her mother come along on this trip to the chapel. Nora Moreland would have been putty in Kronmiller's hands.

He was a potbellied, mustachioed man of seventy, whose demulcent voice flowed like oil, whose expensive chalk-striped suit had pressed-in creases that looked sharp enough to draw blood. His left eye was of glass, and he had longish, silver hair and hanging jowls that nearly covered his gold collar pin. His words carried the authority of a man who had staged thousands of funerals, who knew better than anyone what was "right and proper" in the handling of the dead. *Best not to argue*, the authoritative tone suggested. *Best to shut up and pay up*.

"You understand, of course, that even though Mrs. Trosper will be cremated, she will nonetheless require a casket," he intoned, folding his hands on the polished mahogany table of the elegant consultation room, gazing with his one good eye into Lindsay's face. "Many of our friends who choose cremation"—Lindsay noted his use of *friends* rather than *clients*—"find that casket selection is still very important, because it's the final opportunity to express love and appreciation for the departed in a material way."

And that "final expression" had better be a rich one, or you'll feel guilty for the rest of your life, Lindsay wanted to add. Or worse, the offended corpse might climb out of that cheap, uncomfortable coffin before it's cremated and crawl into bed with you in the wee hours, just to teach you a lesson. But she merely nodded, pretending to agree.

"And of course there's the matter of a vessel for the cremated remains, together with a suitable memorial," added Kronmiller.

"You mean an urn and a plaque?" asked Lindsay.

The old undertaker cleared his throat and smiled indulgently. "Yes, that's essentially what we mean, Miss Moreland. We're certain that you'll want to select these items very carefully. They are, after all, *forever*."

He rose from his padded chair and ushered her into the sumptuous selection room, where a dozen caskets stood on display like islands of comfort in a cool sea of voluptuous blue drapery and gray carpet. The caskets boasted wood and satin, or copper and velvet, all set off in the warm hues of life.

"A suitable casket for Mrs. Trosper might be this one," said Kronmiller with heavy solemnity, indicating a gorgeous hardwood model with white satin upholstery and brass handles. For a moment Lindsay's mind doted on the pleasant image of Lorna at rest in this work of art, comfortable at last in billowy white satin. But then she shook herself awake.

"How much?" she asked, interrupting the mortician's litany of this model's features.

"Only seventy-six hundred," assured Kronmiller.

Lindsay blinked and caught her breath. "No, I don't believe that one would be suitable at all."

"Oh, but it's such an elegant piece—"

"My sister was not an elegant woman, at least not in that way. The thought of burning a casket like this would've revolted her. She'd want something simple, unostentatious. Do you have anything like that?"

Within the next five minutes Lindsay had selected a gray model of light wood. Simple cotton upholstery instead of satin. Stainless-steel handles instead of brass. Three hundred dollars instead of seventy-six hundred. Five minutes more and she had chosen a small urn from a collection encased in glass, and a simple wooden plaque with a brass plate, upon which would be engraved Lorna's name, birthdate, and date of passing.

Mitch Nistler's El Camino swung off Sockeye Drive into the shaded brick access road of the Chapel of the Cove. Parked in the front portico of the white-columned funeral home, sheltered from the steady beat of rain, was a blue Saab Turbo that Mitch had never seen before. He continued around the side of the building to the employees' parking area, where sat Matt Kronmiller's brown Mercedes.

He let himself in through the garage and sidled between a pair of massive, sin-colored hearses. A few steps down an interior corridor brought him to the preparation room, which had tiled walls of apple green, a floor of immaculate white, and an array of glistening equipment that included two operating tables with "flush receptors" for draining away human fluids. A framed sign hung on one wall, a little reminder to promote reverence:

> "Regard Every Body As Though It Is Your
> Most Beloved Relative."

Taped to the frame of the sign was a note addressed to *M. N.* in Kronmiller's unmistakable bold cursive. Mitch's heart fluttered as he took it down and unfolded it, for this would surely be the old batfucker's final word to him, the long-anticipated walking papers. Mitch had played hooky the night before and had been late this morning, so the final word would come as no surprise, not after his many transgressions. That he had lasted six years was something of a miracle.

But the note did not contain the final word. Actually it was quite civil. Apparently written sometime the previous afternoon, it informed Mitch that Mrs. Lorna Trosper's family had called and specified cremation without open-casket viewing, making embalming unnecessary. Therefore, Mitch need not prepare the remains for embalming. He was off the hook. Kronmiller probably didn't even know that he hadn't shown up yesterday.

He closed his eyes and heaved a sigh of relief. For once in his life, the fates had favored him. He still had a job.

Voices came to his ears: Kronmiller's hushed baritone and the more direct contralto of a woman. Mitch slipped out of the preparation room and down the carpeted corridor, following the voices to the nearest of two slumber rooms, where many a bereaved family had beheld the cosmetic triumph of the embalmer.

Mitch grasped the handle of the service door that gave access to the slumber room and shoved it open a crack. Standing with Kronmiller was a young woman who seemed radiant in the pietistic light streaming through the Gothic windows. She had flaxen hair that swept back in a wave from a noble forehead, over the ears and down the neck almost to her shoulders. She had eyebrows thick with fine blond hair, deeply set eyes of startling size and blueness, and severe cheekbones that could have used a bit more flesh. Her body was lithe and tall, her shoulders square under a knitted pullover of bright green. She wore loose, pleated trousers of beige wool and sensible Reeboks on her feet.

Mitch thought her beautiful beyond belief and vaguely familiar.

"As I told you on the phone yesterday," the young woman was saying in a slightly irritated tone, "we don't wish to view the body, and we don't want a traditional funeral. One of Lorna's close friends has suggested a casual get-together in the park for anyone who wants to come, and that's what we've decided to do. We'll have some of her favorite music on tape, some light refreshments, and a little good, old-fashioned, heart-to-heart conversation. In other words, Mr. Kronmiller, we won't need your *slumber* room here, and we won't need your chapel for a service. All I want is for you to put the body in a casket, cremate it, and send me the bill. Can you do that for me?"

Kronmiller seemed nonplussed, which pleasured Mitch immensely, and after clearing his throat loudly, he said, "As you wish, Miss Moreland. We must caution you, however, that the weather this time of year can be very unstable, and a rainstorm could very well ruin your gathering in the park. Wouldn't it be more prudent to—"

"The park has a covered barbecue area, Mr. Kronmiller. I estimate that we could squeeze fifty to sixty people into it if we had to. Now, please excuse me. I have a crowded schedule this afternoon."

After signing the necessary release forms, Lindsay Moreland retired through an adjacent chapel with Kronmiller gliding after her, through the selection room with its rows of caskets, and finally out the front door of the funeral home to her Saab. Every step of the way, Kronmiller effused assurances that things would be done *exactly* as Lindsay had specified, that she was not to trouble herself in any way whatsoever.

Mitch was pretending to inspect the floor of the preparation room for dirt as his boss returned. Kronmiller had jettisoned his bedside manner and now wore a black scowl.

"What are you doing here on a Sunday?" he bellowed. "Didn't you see my note yesterday? And what the hell happened to your face?"

"Hi, Mr. Kronmiller," answered Mitch, reflexively touching the lip that Cannibal Strecker had fattened. "I just came by to see if you wanted anything done about the Trosper cremation."

The old man blinked with his good eye, and his wrinkled visage softened a bit. "Good God, some people don't know the meaning of the word *respect*," he growled, apparently having lost his concern over Mitch's lacerated mouth. "The woman who just left was Lorna Trosper's sister. Won't pay for a closed-casket viewing before cremation and doesn't even want a service in the chapel, for the love of Pete. A 'casual get-together in the park' is what she wants, with a 'little good, old-fashioned conversation.' That sure as hell isn't *my* idea of respect for the departed. It was all I could do to sell her a three-hundred-dollar box! I'm glad we don't get many of those, Mitch, because if we did, it wouldn't pay to turn on the lights in this place."

And you'd be forced to survive on your income property and your stock portfolio, thought Mitch. *Poor baby.*

"As long as you're here," said Kronmiller, "you might as well cremate her. Use display casket number nine, since we don't even stock those plain wooden jobs anymore. Then put the ashes in one of these." He handed over a slip of paper with the model of a "vessel" written on it. "I'll take care of the engraving on the memorial tomorrow."

He headed for the rear door, then paused and turned back to Mitch. "I'm going home to watch golf on TV. No matter what happens, don't bother me for the rest of the day, understand?"

"Yes, sir, Mr. Kronmiller."

The old man went out the door, leaving his assistant alone in the hushed funeral home, and Mitch set about his chore, feeling almost lighthearted.

Cremating a corpse is not hard work, and it requires few skills: Dump the body into a casket that's suitable for burning; roll the casket into the committal room, and rig it onto the catafalque, a mechanized slab that inserts the casket and remains into the retort; start a fire in the retort, which is no more difficult than turning on a gas kitchen range, and wait ninety minutes, checking the draft every now and then to ensure maximum temperature. The process reduces a dead body to about six pounds of ashes and bone fragments—"suitable for bottling," Mitch always said to himself with a laugh whenever he handled cremation chores.

Matthew Kronmiller owned one of the few crematories in the area, which he operated as a sideline to his funeral home, even though, like most funeral directors, he hated the very concept of cremation. Not enough profit in it. Unless of course the surviving family wants embalming and a traditional funeral before cremation. But these days more and more people were choosing *direct* cremation, forgoing the horrendous expense of showpiece caskets, embalming, and all the other costly malarkey commonly associated with American funerals. Kronmiller had installed his crematory as a hedge against this irksome trend, knowing that other funeral directors in the area would use his services when clients were "disrespectful" enough to demand cremation, direct or otherwise.

Mitch left the preparation room and went a few steps down the corridor, fingering the retractable ring on his belt and looking for the key to the padlock that secured the walk-in cooler. As he inserted the key, he caught a mental glimpse of himself astride one of Liquid Larry's bar stools, his hand wrapped around an icy mugful of triple threat, his brain awash in blessed fog. That's where he'd be in a couple of hours: astride that stool with nothing more on his mind than ordering his next drink and adding another thickness of foggy insulation against reality. *Fuck reality*, with its Matthew Kronmillers and Cannibal Streckers and *(Craslowe?)*, the real owners of Mitch Nistler. Astride that stool in Liquid Larry's, with eyes aglaze and jaw gone slack, Mitch Nistler would be nobody's slave.

In just a couple of hours—

Craslowe. Something writhed in Mitch's innards as he pulled the cooler door open. Cold, disinfected fumes crept out of the darkness and embraced him. His hand groped for and found a switch, and the dead-silent cooler filled with harsh light from a bare bulb.

Metal walls, close and gray. White-tiled floor. A trio of gurneys abreast, one of which held the sheeted body of a woman. A trace of smell that spoke of death, despite the aerosol disinfectant.

The *something* writhed again, but Mitch tried to ignore it. He took hold of the gurney and wheeled it from the cooler; and he nearly jumped out of his skin when the compressor kicked itself on, filling the cold air with an unfriendly whir. He hit the light switch and slammed the door home, shutting off the source of darkness and the whirring sound.

He pushed the sheeted cargo into the preparation room and parked it next to an embalming table, then readied the slings that were attached to the body lifter, an electrically run device that moved on tracks in the ceiling. Using the body lifter, one man could easily move the heaviest corpse from a gurney to the embalming table, and afterward from the table to a casket. Wonderful invention, the body lifter.

He drew the sheet off the gurney—

The writhing again *(Craslowe!)*. Mitch fought back a swell of nausea.

—exposing the pathetic, death-ravaged body of Lorna Trosper.

She lay on her back, naked. A bundle of beggarly clothes lay between her knees where the medical examiner had left it the previous day: threadbare jeans, wretched underclothing, a beige smock spattered and encrusted with water paint. Her facial skin was ashy white, her blond hair wild and stiff with dirt. Agonal dehydration had slackened her lips and loosened her facial muscles, giving her once-delicate nose a severe, pinched look. Her eyeballs had softened and appeared sunken. Her skeletal muscles had gone flaccid and had flattened under her body weight. On the undersides of her emaciated limbs and along the buttocks and back, the skin was a startling cherry-red—the mark of blood-pooling, which is typical of carbon-monoxide poisoning.

Mitch's nausea subsided a little as he gazed at the tragic, inert form that had been Lorna Trosper. Though filthy with its owner's neglect and wasted by the agonies it had suffered, the body was strangely beautiful to him. He knew now why Lindsay Moreland had looked familiar a few minutes ago: She shared her dead sister's beauty. And, contrary to what Matt Kronmiller had told him on the first day of his job, when the old undertaker had whisked the sheet off a gurney to expose an elderly man dead of a massive heart attack, Lorna Trosper's body was not "garbage."

"What you see here, Mitch, is nothing but garbage," Kronmiller had said, apparently relishing his new employee's unease over such close proximity to death. *"Let it stand awhile, and it'll start to stink, same as any other garbage. The man who owned it is gone, a mere idea, a memory. This heap of garbage contains no more of him than the dirty underwear he left on his bathroom floor. No need to worry bout sinking needles into it or cutting holes in it. It's useless to him and to everybody else."*

Mitch had not known Lorna Trosper personally. Occasionally he had caught sight of her as he ambled past the tiny gallery on Frontage Street, but he had never spoken to her, never even traded hellos. Yet he had admired her, had thought her the prettiest lady in Greely's Cove. He liked the way she held herself, so straight and confident, and the way she dressed, so casually grubby and unmindful of her own looks. When he dared to fantasize about having a woman of his own one day, he visualized not the spread-eagle sluts who adorned the pages of his porn magazines but someone like Lorna Trosper.

And here she lay, naked on an icy sheet of stainless steel, wrapped only in silence. Despite the body dirt, the signs of suffering, and despite the fact of death itself, she was still beautiful. She was *not* garbage.

Mitch's vision began to blur. The nausea sharpened again, and a ghastly stink flooded his nostrils and throat, seemingly welling up from his own gullet. He staggered against the gurney, jarring Lorna Trosper's body, flinching from a bolt of pain in his chest.

"Fuck a bald-headed duck, Cannibal must've really hurt me!" he wheezed, almost aloud. He righted himself and somehow managed to stand up straight on watery legs. He became aware of the darkness behind his eyes, blacker now than it had ever been, invading the edges of his vision, inflicting appalling glimpses into a deep well within his own brain, a well he had visited under the guidance of a doctor named Hadrian Craslowe. And hidden in that well, secure in its lair of bottomless darkness, was—*something*. Something or someone alive, alien and yet a part of Mitch Nistler.

The stink became a taste now—the same one he had suffered upon waking from yesterday's hypnosis session with Craslowe. It had gagged him then, had made him want to vomit. But now, vile as it was, the taste had a strangely clarifying effect. He saw things he had never seen before and possibilities that he had never dared contemplate.

Who owns Mitch Nistler? asked a voice from deep within the well.

Not Corley the Cannibal Strecker. And not Matthew Kronmiller. Not even Hadrian Craslowe.

Who holds the papers on Mitch Nistler?

Even with his newfound clarity he could not answer the question. But he now knew something better. The answer didn't matter. Just as nothing in Cannibal's world mattered. And nothing in Kronmiller's, either. *(Craslowe's?)* What mattered was the *hunger*.

His gaze floated over the dead form of Lorna Trosper and lingered on the cold, gray-white flesh of her face and neck; the bluish hillocks of her breasts with their flaccid, colorless nipples; the pitiable ridges of her rib cage and the sunken depression of her stomach and abdomen.

He stepped back from the gurney, breathing with great, spittle-laden gasps. *God, could I really do it?*

He was alone. Kronmiller would not come back, for he was glued to a television set at home, watching golf. The other three employees of the funeral home were family types, jealous of their precious weekends, and none would darken the door of the mortuary until Monday. Until tomorrow.

He had until tomorrow.

Mitch Nistler had assisted Matt Kronmiller in something like 500 embalmings over the course of six years at the Chapel of the Cove. He knew the procedures, the high and low drainage points on a body, the use of instruments like the motorized aspirator, the trocar, and the gravity percolator. He knew how to apply the various hardening compounds, sealers, and preservatives that embalmers use to guarantee a reasonable "viewing life" for a corpse. And he prided himself on his skill with the cosmetic dyes, humectants, and perfumes that render a corpse presentable, if not beautiful. Though he lacked formal training, he considered himself a good embalmer. He knew that he could make Lorna Trosper physically beautiful again.

But first things first.

A "cremation" must take place. The cremation of an empty casket. And the packing of ashes into the "suitable vessel" that Lindsay Moreland had chosen from Kronmiller's impressive selection.

No one would ever know the difference.

Mitch Nistler would have his woman, and she would give him what no living woman ever had.

7

By noon Carl Trosper was exhausted, both physically and emotionally. He and sixty other volunteers had spent more than three hours tramping through the thick undergrowth astride Bond Road, beating back the rain-heavy branches of sword fern and birch and pine, slogging through dank patches of tawny grass and climbing gingerly over fallen logs oozy with moss. They had scoured the ground for the smallest clue to Teri Zolten's fate: a scrap of clothing, a piece of jewelry, a billfold, or (God forbid) a bloody fragment of Teri herself. Pressing ever deeper into the woods they had filled the swirling, foggy morning with their voices, calling out Teri's name in the withering hope that she was near enough and well enough to hear. The voices that had sailed higher than all others, echoed most strongly and desperately through the tangle of trees and brush, had belonged to Sandy and Ken Zolten.

Shortly after noon Carl left the search party, thoroughly dispirited. He caught a ride back to the Old Schooner, where he went to the room that Teri had rented him the night before. After shedding his soaking clothes and taking a hot shower, he dressed in khaki slacks and a heavy Norwegian sweater, then went down to the parking lot and got into his rented car for the short drive to 116 Second Avenue.

The journey gave him little time to reacclimatize himself to his own private troubles, and too soon he was turning into the driveway of the little white bungalow that he and Lorna had bought just one week after their marriage. Too soon he was climbing the steps of the shaded front porch and pressing the doorbell button, hearing footfalls coming to answer. As the door opened he glanced around and noticed that among the cars parked out front was a flaming-red Jaguar.

Lindsay Moreland ushered him in without mentioning his abrupt departure from The Coffee Shoppe, though her blue

87

eyes glinted with assurance that their dealings were far from over. To Carl's surprise, the little house was abuzz with activity. Lorna's friends—a handful of watercolor artists, a poet or two, some neighbors—had turned up to help with the chores of cleaning and packing.

She shepherded him through the whirl of activity and introduced him stiffly to each one, raising her voice to be heard above the noise of a vacuum cleaner. Carl received condolences and warm handshakes, heard how much they would all miss Lorna, was promised help with any problem or chore that he might confront. They all seemed eager to show their love for the woman he had left more than eight years earlier.

Notable among the band of housecleaners was Hannabeth Hazelford. In place of her orange slicker and flowing silk scarves, she wore a blue jumpsuit and rubber gloves, but she still sported ridiculously heavy makeup and the blond Dolly Parton wig, which now sagged low on her forehead, slightly askew. She greeted him in her melodious British clip and shook his hand firmly, leaving cleanser suds in his palm.

"I do hope you're not put off that I organized this gathering," she said to Carl, blinking her luminous, turquoise eyes. "I knew that Lorna's closest friends would want to do *something* to help, if only to scrub the floors and carry out the rubbish. It certainly was not our intention to intrude into your hour of grief."

Carl gave a thin smile and glanced around at the busy people who manned mops, dust rags, buckets of suds, and scrub brushes. "I'm very grateful, Miss Hazelford—"

"Tut-tut, you've done it again! It's *Hannie*. At my age a woman requires no reminder that she's a dried-up old spinster."

Carl saw Lindsay Moreland roll her eyes and said, "I'm sorry, Hannie. What you're doing is really very nice. I appreciate it."

His former mother-in-law, Nora Moreland, came into the living room from the kitchen, wearing a bandanna around her head and a flowery apron spattered with soap suds. She made straight for Carl and, to his astonishment, hugged him hard.

"It's good to see you, Carl," she said with a slight quaver. "Lindsay tells me you plan to move back here and that you want Jeremy to live with you. Under the circumstances, I think you're doing the right thing."

"Mother," interrupted Lindsay, "the issue is far from settled."

Carl sensed a budding alliance with Nora, a woman he had never cottoned to. Nora had not deemed him a good match for her daughter because of his middle-class roots. Carl had thought her uppity and elitist, a country-club bitch who was preoccupied with scaling the higher reaches of Seattle's social scene. But now she was hugging him with genuine warmth and shared sorrow, reaching out to him through the bars of old animosities. Maybe he had been wrong about her. Perhaps she had changed. Or perhaps *he* had changed.

"Thank you, Nora," he answered, incurring a dark stare from Lindsay. "Having your support means a lot."

"No doubt you want to see your son," said Nora. "We gave him the job of cleaning his room, but he's probably finished by now." She nodded toward the short hallway that offered access to the bedrooms, the bath, Lorna's studio. One of the doors was closed: Jeremy's.

"How is he?" asked Carl, suddenly jittery about coming face-to-face with the issue of his own loins. "How's he taking all this?"

"Remarkably well, I'd say," said Lindsay. "In a way, Lorna's death may be a blessing for him."

"*Lindsay!* For the love of God, how can you say such a thing?" Nora was horrified by her daughter's remark. "How can losing his mother be a blessing to a thirteen-year-old boy?"

"You saw the condition of this place, Mother," said Lindsay. "It must have been hell living here. Lorna must have slowly lost all control of herself—changed into another person. She was never the world's best housekeeper, but my God, she cared about her furniture, her paintings. . . ."

"She was obviously very *ill*," said Nora, near tears.

"That's exactly my point, Mother. Jeremy watched her become someone he didn't know, someone who chopped up chairs and gouged holes in the walls. She even defaced her own paintings."

Carl's eyes darted around the room: There were holes in the plaster, as though made with a hammer, and pieces of dismembered chairs and tables stacked here and there, ready to be carted away. The sofa bed that had always stood near the picture window, now in the arms of two men who were easing it out the front door under Hannie's supervision, was a tatter of frenzied slashing, its stuffing leaking through its wounds in gobs. Heaped in the corners of every room were Glad bags jammed with refuse—much of it organic, judging from the ripe odor that hung amid the scents of cleanser and room deodorant. And stacked in low columns were the empty earthen pots that had housed Lorna's beloved plants—her artillery ferns, philodendrons, umbrella plants, the "green babies" she had nursed with unswerving devotion and even named, now yellowed and brittle and stuffed into cardboard boxes for disposal.

But most obscene, most heartbreaking, were the *paintings*: frames broken, glass smashed, paper ripped and defiled in a seemingly purposeful way.

"God, what would drive somebody to this?" breathed Carl, shaking his head, leaving unsaid his belief that Lorna could not have wreaked such travesties, especially upon the paintings.

"The same thing that drives a person to suicide," answered Lindsay with a hint of reproach in her voice. "My sister got sick, and her life became a hell. This *house* became a hell. That's what I meant when I said that maybe Lorna's death is a blessing for Jeremy: Their hell is finally over. At least we can be thankful for that much."

Hannie Hazelford interrupted with word that a neighbor had offered his pickup truck for hauling the slaughtered furniture to the county landfill, and she had authorized the job. The house would be virtually bereft of anything to sit on, sleep on, eat on. But not to worry: Hannie owned a shed full of perfectly serviceable furniture—surplus from the much larger house she had owned "out East" before moving to her comfortable Tudor-style cottage in Greely's Cove. She had ordered transport of the furniture from the shed to here, to be used as long as needed.

"Miss Haz—I mean *Hannie*, that's really generous of you," said Carl, intending to protest so lavish a favor, "but I couldn't let you—"

"Nonsense!" Hannie declared, assuming the ramrod posture that evinced British authority, the conquest of Hindu kingdoms, the victory at Trafalgar. "It's all oak—old but very sturdy, just the thing to stand up to whatever punishment a teenaged boy can dish out, I daresay. And quite presentable, too. You can't very well eat off the floor, now can you?"

"I guess not," allowed Carl, feeling foolish in the role of the taker of charity. "But I'll send it back to you as soon I've brought in some furniture of our own."

"Very well, then," said Hannie. "Let's get on with it. We've still much to do, much to do."

Yes, thought Carl, *much to do*.

Like quitting his job in Washington, D.C., and shipping his household goods west.

Like mucking through the process of probating Lorna's will (assuming she had bothered to write one), arranging to buy this house from the estate and disposing of her other property, what little there was.

Like setting up a law practice and starting a whole new life—or would it be a variation on an old life, one lost and terribly missed? Much to do indeed.

But the very next thing that needed doing involved walking a few steps from the living room into the short hallway and knocking on a closed door. *Jeremy's* door. Carl wondered why his guts were churning.

Lorna Trosper's body lay on the embalming table, damp and bluish under fluorescent lights. Mitch Nistler had lovingly bathed it, had gently lathered away the filth of its owner's neglect and the scum of the early stages of putrefaction. All odor had disappeared, save the clean smells of soap and shampoo.

He stood back from the table a moment and gazed upon her, liking what he saw, liking even more what he felt: a clarity that he had never known before, a sharpness of mind that seemed almost alien, a hungry sense of purpose that had completely eclipsed his native hesitancy. He knew exactly the order of the tasks ahead without even pausing to think through the process. For the first time in his life, he would work quickly and nimbly, using and relishing his new power over himself.

He went purposefully to the cabinets that lined the walls of the preparation room and gathered the instruments and supplies he would need during the embalming process. Bulb syringe, tubing, scalpels, trocars, cotton, hair dryer, many others, which he laid out on a rolling tray. He readied the percolator and the aspirator. He turned on the ventilation system with its overhead fan, covering the hush of the old funeral home with a low thrumming. He retired to the adjacent dressing room, where he assembled hairbrushes, combs, manicure set, cosmetics, and perfumes.

Having done all this, he stood a moment over the corpse, absently rubbing his latex-gloved hands against his full-length plastic apron, surveying Lorna Trosper's body as a sculptor might survey a shapeless mass of clay. There was beauty in this discarded assemblage of flesh and bone. Beauty waiting to be liberated. *He* would be the liberator. *He* would give purpose to something that others considered garbage.

The critical first step was draining away the blood. Mitch Nistler's hand closed on the handle of a scalpel, which he lifted to the chest of the corpse. With his other hand he marked a high drainage point, where he made a supraclavicular incision to locate and elevate the jugular vein. The blade slid easily through the cold flesh, and the cherry-red blood began to well out.

Carl knocked lightly on the bedroom door and leaned close to listen for an answer. The door opened, and his mouth went dry as he laid eyes on his son for the first time in nearly five years.

"J-Jeremy." His voice was hoarse, his throat choked with guilt. "Jeremy, it's me, your—your dad."

Was there an inkling of a smile in the lad's delicate mouth, the faintest glitter of satisfaction in those hazel eyes? Was his face too free of torment in the wake of his mother's tragic death? Carl banished such worries and stepped into the room, pulling the door closed behind him.

The boy stood chin-high to Carl, a shade taller than most thirteen-year-olds. Like his father he was long-limbed and lean, had the beginnings of a full-fledged "lantern jaw," the ancestral trait of the Trospers. The Morelands' genetic influence was apparent in the straight nose and huge, deep-set eyes. His longish, straw-colored hair bore a trace of Carl's reddishness but was closer to Lorna's unabashed shade of blond. He wore a freshly laundered sweatshirt of royal blue with *Nike* emblazoned on the front. It hung loosely on his bony shoulders.

"It's nice to see you, Dad," said Jeremy, issuing a perfect white smile. His smooth voice had not yet started its descent into the range of manhood. "I hope you had a nice trip."

Carl blinked and grew numb with shock: When last he'd seen him, Jeremy was scarcely eight years old and much smaller; but the *real* difference—the one that staggered Carl and sucked the breath from his lungs, the one that turned his legs to icy jelly—was not physical. The boy now had a *soul* that beamed forth through those deep hazel eyes. A soul where none had been before.

Carl's mind reeled through excruciating memories of a child-thing who stopped shrieking only to sleep, who endlessly squirmed and twisted and drooled; who dirtied his pants and smeared the furniture with shit, shattered television screens with his fists and threw himself down staircases; who defied a heroic legion of doctors to help or even explain how such a creature could be born of Carl and Lorna Trosper, two perfectly normal people.

God! What a purgatory this child had made for them—this animal who doctors feared would never speak; would never learn to care for himself; would forever be incapable of the tiniest, genuinely human expression—*this child who had no soul*.

The recollections flashed through Carl's mind like a slide show. The most painful was of the day on which he knew that he could take no more. Lorna and he had jousted wildly on the issue of institutionalization, Carl *for* and Lorna *against*. To closet their son in a state home, she had raged, would guarantee that he would never progress. To imprison him among psychotic strangers was unthinkable, not only because of the obscenities a young boy would suffer in such a place, but also because his only chance for a decent life lay with his family at home.

"Sure, it'll be hard for us! Sure, it means sacrifice! That's what moms and dads and husbands and wives are supposed to do—sacrifice!"

But Carl had had enough sacrifice.

He'd become interested in state and local politics, and had displayed a knack for campaign management and media relations while doing volunteer grass-roots work for some local legislators. A congressman from Seattle had noticed his successes and had asked him to quit his tiny law practice to become his legislative assistant in Washington, D.C. The job had been Carl's foot in the door, his launching pad to bigger and better things. Looking back, he knew now that the move to D.C. had offered more than excitement, importance and money, more than he would admit at the time; it had offered *escape*.

From Jeremy.

"You've grown a beard," said the boy. "It looks good."

Carl struggled for a reply, still shaken by the miracle of the new Jeremy. "I—I'm glad you haven't forgotten what I look like. It's been a long time."

The boy smiled again. "A kid doesn't forget what his dad looks like. You've gotten a little gray, I see."

Carl felt himself paling. Jeremy seemed too alert, too mature. This was a person transformed by an unknowable miracle into someone Carl did not know, a stranger he had never met before this very moment. Carl strongly doubted that the Jeremy of five years ago could have stored away the memory of his father's face; yet the new Jeremy remembered him beardless and without the tinges of gray over the ears.

"Gray hair happens to everybody, I guess," replied Carl unsteadily. "But *you*—you look great. You look—"

"I'm almost normal now," said Jeremy matter-of-factly. "Dr. Craslowe says that I might not even need any more therapy in a couple of years. He says I'm smart enough to be anything I want."

"I don't doubt that. I really don't."

"It's sad about Mom, isn't it?"

Carl coughed, cleared his throat, coughed again. "Yes, it is. Very sad." He put one hand on his son's shoulder and gazed deep into those incredible eyes. "Look, Jeremy, you and I are going to be together from now on. I'll be moving back here to Greely's Cove within the next couple of weeks. If everything goes all right, we'll be living right here in this house. You can keep up your therapy with Dr. Craslowe, probably even go to school, do all the things other kids do. I want you to know that—that I'll *be* here for you, and that I'll try to make up for—" Carl felt an ache in his throat and salty heat in his eyes. "For not being here when you and Mom needed me."

Jeremy moved closer to him, then closer still, then threw his arms around Carl's neck and pressed his cheek against his father's chest.

"That sounds good, Dad. It really does."

Carl hugged him back, forcing himself to forget that this boy was a stranger.

While waiting for the last few ounces of blood to drain from Lorna Trosper's arteries and veins, Mitch Nistler took a smoke break in his customary place: under the overhang of the garage entrance, where he could gaze out at the Puget Sound and breathe fresh, nonmortuary air. The afternoon sky hung in low, gauzy curtains that issued rain cold as gunmetal.

He finished his smoke and flicked the butt away, then returned to the preparation room, where the body waited. Cavity drainage was next on the agenda.

He picked up a trocar—a long metal rod, hollow and sharp on one end—and connected it with plastic tubing to the motorized aspirator. He marked a spot two inches above and left of Lorna Trosper's navel.

Mitch hesitated a moment: A trocar is the ultimate violator, a device that pierces the inner organs and sucks out their contents with motorized force, so unlike the quiet and passive process of arterial drainage, in which gravity does the work of removing blood. Though he had used a trocar countless times with the knowledge that the corpse certainly didn't mind, *this* time would be different. This time he would use it on his Lorna, and he thrilled to the lunatic fear that somehow she might *feel* the invasion.

The hunger rumbled inside him again, abolishing all hesitancy, and the demonic taste flooded his throat and mouth. His hands moved as if they had their own brains. He pressed the sharp point of the trocar into the tender flesh, and Lorna's skin gave way. Into her thoracic cavity it went, up and up through the lungs and finally into the heart. Mitch flipped a switch on the panel of the aspirator, and the machine started its work.

After emptying the heart he would withdraw the point and rotate the trocar to pierce the major vessels, where blood and other fluids might have pooled. Puncture, drain.

Then on to the small and large intestines, feeling his way, knowing with an alien certainty just where to shove the steel. Puncture, drain.

The liver would be next, then the stomach, the kidneys, spleen, pancreas, urinary bladder, and rectum. Puncture, drain. Puncture, drain.

And finally the nasal passages and upper respiratory tract, from which he would suck out all purge material. Then he would begin the real work, the artistic work that would transform Lorna Trosper's poor, defiled body into something beautiful, something that would bring joy again.

Night crept westward from the Sound onto the shore, bringing a chill that threatened sleet, and Police Chief Stu Bromton disbanded the search party because of darkness. The wet and bedraggled searchers tramped back to Bond Road with heads lowered, faces hanging with gloom. They boarded their cars for home, a caravan of defeated crusaders whose headlight beams danced forlornly against curtains of black rain.

After making certain that all the searchers had left the area, Stu drove alone in his police cruiser back to Greely's Cove and parked in the City Hall lot. The dispatcher, Bonnie Willis, glanced up through the steel mesh of her cage as he came through the heavy door, a stooped and slow-moving beast of burden. He shambled to a halt after letting himself into the inner sanctum.

"Any messages I should know about?" he asked, pocketing his keys.

Bonnie was finishing off a large order of Chicken McNuggets with sweet 'n' sour sauce.

"Ken Zolten just called," she said, chawing down the last morsel of an unfortunate bird. "He wants to know where you plan to start searching tomorrow and what time. I told him you'd call."

Stu ground his teeth. What good could possibly come from mounting another search? It would end as all the others had—in total, tormenting failure. The sheriff's office would call out its reserve search-and-rescue team; the National Guard would send a dozen volunteers; the Seattle PD would keep its bloodhounds on station for maybe three more days; and after several hundred man-hours of dogged slogging along forested roads and rugged beach, after poking into overgrown culverts and ditches until they could tramp and slog and poke no longer, this search too would peter out. There was, after all, a limit to what public agencies could spend on behalf of one little girl.

But it had to be done, of course. No one, least of all Sandy and Ken Zolten, could simply accept failure without making the effort. The search would be renewed and sustained to the very limits of funds and human muscles. Stu would lead it as he had led all the others, chalking up another grand goose egg for his fellow citizens to buzz about behind his back. No clues would be found, and the case of little Teri Zolten would enlarge the bloating list of unsolved disappearances.

Stu called Ken Zolten and, after outlining tomorrow's strategy, offered pat reassurances to the enervated, inconsolable father. The county forensics team had dusted Mrs. Solheim's Toyota for fingerprints and had sampled the stinking grime on the passenger's seat. Surely the crime-lab analysis would turn up *something*, and word would come back in a week or so. Teri's description had gone out over the Law Enforcement Telecommunications System, and by now every law-enforcement agency in the entire nation was on the lookout for her.

"We're bound to find her, Ken"—*sure we are*—"so try and get some sleep."

After talking to Ken Zolten he returned the half-dozen calls from the news media that had piled up since early afternoon, starting with the biggest outfits. Most wanted simple updates on this latest disappearance, but Seattle's KOMO-TV was planning a news special on the Mystery of Greely's Cove. They assumed he'd cooperate to the fullest. Of *course* he would, he told the eager female reporter who sounded like the owner of a fresh master's degree in broadcast journalism. Always glad to have help from the news media. Never can tell: a viewer might have seen something suspicious or recognize one of the missing and just might be able to blah blah blah.

He stood up from his cluttered metal desk and stretched. The wall clock said 9:45. His muscles ached from the rigors of an all-day tramp through misty woods, and his eyes were blurry. But he wasn't really tired—at least not tired enough to go home to Judy and the kids.

What he needed was a beer.

For the rare occasions that demanded a beer after work on weeknights other than Fridays, he kept a set of casual civvies in a metal wall locker in the squad room. He showered in the cramped stall at the rear of the squad room and changed into them.

Before leaving the station house, Stu locked the evening's paperwork in his office file. He was about to shove the drawer closed when his eyes fell on a folder newly inked with Lorna Trosper's name. Without knowing why, he opened it and perused the typewritten forms, all of which he had already studied in great detail. Investigative report. Coroner's report. Death certificate and medical examiner's findings. Tucked among the official documents was a rumpled slip torn from a notepad: Lorna's suicide note.

Stu had examined it at least twenty times, but now he studied it again, shaking his head. Legally, the note was the property of the decedent's heirs, inasmuch as the criminal justice authorities planned no autopsy or inquest. It did not belong to Stu Bromton. Yet he slipped it into the pocket of his light breaker, thinking to keep it if the rightful owners did not ask for it. He had, after all, loved Lorna Trosper as much as anyone. He had loved her from the very moment he laid eyes on her, back on that golden day at the University of Washington when Carl Trosper introduced his new girlfriend. Stu had continued to love her, even after she had started having an affair with that miserable profligate, Renzy Dawkins. The scrawly note, though nearly illegible, was the final fragment of the woman who had unwittingly lived at the center of his fantasies for almost fifteen years. As such, it was a minor, private treasure.

"I see you're headed out for a nightcap," said Bonnie Willis as her boss passed the dispatcher's cage. Bonnie, his one genuine ally in Greely's Cove, knew the meaning of the civvies.

"Yeah, to Liquid Larry's, I guess. I don't want to run into any of the city fathers."

"Good choice. You won't catch any of them in *that* place. What should I say if Judy calls?"

"Tell her the truth. If she doesn't like it, she can go home to Daddy."

Liquid Larry's was quiet, even for a Sunday night. A handful of patrons leaned against the bar, chatting, drowsing, or watching *Lifestyles of the Rich and Famous* on the color set that hung from the ceiling. Three or four others had clustered around the giant fish tank that stood against a far wall, oohing and ahhing and *Jesus-Christ*-ing over Liquid's prized fixture, an Oscar fish named Hammerstein. For one dollar, a patron could buy a live goldfish from the swarm that Liquid kept in a separate tank. The patron was then entitled to toss the goldfish into Hammerstein's tank, upon which the Oscar fish—a rotund, brownish predator the size of a man's two fists—would corner the terrified goldfish and wolf it down without ceremony. The bloody spectacle had great appeal to many of Liquid's regulars, and Hammerstein seemed forever hungry.

Stu slid onto a stool at the deserted end of the bar and ordered an Oly, which Liquid served in a frosted mug. Behind the bar were display cards of Bic disposable lighters, Bromo Seltzer packets, and air fresheners for the car. Sausages floated in huge cloudy jars, pickled eggs in clear ones. Lighted scenes of rippling waterfalls and dancing streams advertised Rainier and Olympia beer, while a less artful sign hawked chances in the Washington State lottery.

After draining his beer in three long slugs, Stu ordered another and contemplated having one of Liquid's infamous gut-bombs, a huge cheeseburger laden with mushrooms and fried onions. But he decided that he wasn't really hungry enough, which was strange, since he'd not eaten all day.

He resisted glancing up when the front door swung open, meaning to disregard the figure that sidled over and took the stool next to him. But the voice that ordered a beer could not be ignored. It belonged to Carl Trosper.

Stu swung around on his stool, grinning wearily. "This guy's money is no good, Liquid. Whatever he wants, I'm buying."

"Whatever you say, Sonny Butch," intoned the barkeep, placing a mug before Carl with professional reverence.

"Now, don't try to tell me," said Stu, leaning close to his old pal, "that you just *happened* to wander into this place."

"Okay, I won't," said Carl, sipping foam that stuck to his mustache, "because I didn't. I was getting a little antsy, so I called your house, and Judy said you were at the station. Then I called the station and your dispatcher said you were out on patrol. When I left my name and number, she said, *welllll*, maybe the boss would want me to know where he *really* is, since I'm the long-lost buddy he always talks so much about.

But I had to promise to buy her dinner if I ever spilled the beans that you were drinking alone at Liquid Larry's on a Sunday night. And that's the God's truth, Officer." He held up his right palm in solemn oath. "So how did things go today?"

Stu hung his head and shook it. "Not worth a damn. I was going to ask you the same thing."

Carl wiped the foam from his mustache, seemingly at a loss for an answer. A question instead: "Do you believe in miracles, Stu?"

"I don't know if I do or not. A year ago I would've said no. These days I'm not sure there's anything I don't believe in. Why?"

"Today I saw one, or at least the effects of one."

"You mean Jeremy?"

Carl nodded. "Lorna had written about his progress with this Dr. Craslowe, and naturally I was anxious to see for myself. But honest to God, I wasn't prepared for what I saw today."

"Yeah, I know what you mean. His progress has been pretty mind-boggling, all right."

"I'm still in a state of shock. I spent the whole afternoon with him, and I still can't make my hands quit shaking. Look." Carl held out his hand, and, sure enough, it trembled slightly.

"Don't worry, it's probably just exhaustion. All you need is a good night's sleep. By the way, where's Jeremy now?"

At home, Carl explained. With Aunt Lindsay and Gramma Nora. Sleeping the sleep of the innocent, while his father's out getting drunk with an old buddy. Carl related how Hannie Hazelford had outfitted the whole house not only with furniture to replace that which had to be discarded but also with kitchenware and groceries. How a dozen of Lorna's grieving friends had rolled up their sleeves and transformed the pigsty at 116 Second Avenue into a presentable home. How Lindsay Moreland had already made arrangements for Lorna's cremation and memorial service, and how he himself felt thoroughly useless.

"Lindsay and Nora are staying at the house?" asked Stu.

"They're using the room that used to be Lorna's studio," said Carl. "Hannie sent over a big double bed to put in there."

"How's the kid taking all this?"

"Fine—and I mean really *fine*. He seems totally unaffected, almost serene, and in a way, I think that's what's been bothering me. Maybe I'd feel better if I saw a little pain in his face. Anyway, Lindsay had an appointment this afternoon with Craslowe, but he called and asked to postpone it until tomorrow. I plan to tag along and ask some questions."

"So what happens after you've wrapped things up here—I mean, after the funeral and everything? What happens to Jeremy?"

Carl stared a moment at his old friend. Finally: "Stu, I'm moving back to Greely's Cove. Jeremy's going to live with me, and I plan to try my hand at practicing real law again."

Stu's mouth dropped open, and he nearly spilled his beer. "Are you serious? Tell me this is a joke."

"I've never been more serious in my life," answered Carl, smiling gently.

Stu took a long, deep breath and fixed his friend with a rebuking stare. "What in the hell do you want to do that for? You've got everything in the world going for you! You've gotten out of this fuck-stick town, you've *succeeded*—"

"That depends on how you define 'success.' "

"You're my definition, old stud. I mean, look at you: Rolex watch, two-hundred-dollar sweater, big job in Washington, D.C. Hell, you probably spend more on haircuts than I do on groceries."

"Yeah, but I also run myself ragged. I babysit self-important assholes who call themselves congressmen or congressional candidates. I write things for them to say, because most of them have never had an original thought in their lives. And every three months or so, I change women, just like I change the oil in my Porsche, even though I rarely have time to drive it. On top of all that, I drink too damn much."

"Sounds like heaven to me," said Stu, incurring a sad chuckle from his friend. "You've done everything you said you'd do when you left this shit-heap town. You've gotten what you wanted. Why throw it away now?"

"For Christ's sake, I became a lawyer because I wanted to help people. When the call from Washington came, I thought, 'Wow! Here's a chance to help people by the millions, not just in ones and twos.' What a joke *that* was. I was a lot happier helping people in ones and twos right here in Greely's Cove, and damn it, I want to do it again."

Stu Bromton drained his glass and bowed his head a

moment, looking almost prayerful as he thought. When he looked up again, his broad face was full of worry.

"I won't fault you for wanting to make a new beginning. I worry, though, about whether you've given it enough thought."

"Well, don't. I've been thinking along these lines for a long time. Lorna's death was just the catalyst that got me moving."

"I hope you don't think I'm off my knob, old stud, but is there any way I might convince you to make your new start somewhere else?"

"Somewhere else? You mean somewhere other than Greely's Cove?"

Stu nodded.

"I really don't think so," said Carl. "I want Jeremy to be near Dr. Craslowe until his therapy's finished. Besides, I'm known here. I used to practice here. People knew my family." He cocked his head and raised his eyebrows. "Why would you want me to go somewhere else?"

Stu had trouble getting the words out. Several times he opened his mouth to speak, then shut it again. Carl watched with morbid fascination as his friend worked up the courage to answer.

"It's just that things aren't so good here anymore," Stu said at length. "There's something bad here, Carl. I haven't figured out what it is, and maybe I never will."

"You're talking about the disappearances, right?"

"The disappearances are part of it. But there's something *else*."

"You're losing me."

"I don't know how to put this, and I hope you won't think I'm ready for the silly hatch—"

"I won't. You know me better than that."

"Okay, I'll blurt it right out: There's *evil* here. I can feel it. Sometimes I even think I can see it, sort of hanging in the air like it's not quite invisible. It does things to people, throws the normal rhythm of life out of whack. There's a kind of deadness in the atmosphere that wasn't here before. If I were you, I'd take my kid and get out of town, honest to God I would."

"I lied: You're ready for the silly hatch."

Despite himself, Stu laughed. "Get serious, would you?" he pleaded. "I'm worried about you moving back here, damn it. Greely's Cove isn't a healthy place these days."

"I'm sorry, Hippo," said Carl, clapping a hand on the big man's shoulder. "I didn't mean to laugh at you. But I think you're starting to feel the stress of these damn disappearances, which is only natural. My God, it's been happening for—what?—eight months. You're entitled to get a little silly." Carl's tone became that of the amateur shrink—he considered himself a good one. "You want to solve the problem, but the problem isn't cooperating. You're frustrated, you're tired. What you need to do is recognize that the problem won't last forever, that it'll go away someday. It really will, Stu. Whoever's doing these terrible things will make a mistake, and you or some other cop will nail him. At the very least, the guy will get scared and move somewhere else. Maybe we'll get lucky, and the bastard will suffer a fit of guilt and blow his own brains out."

"But I told you, it's not just the disappearances. There are *other* things."

"What other things?"

Stu Bromton stared into space a moment, worrying that he was about to betray an incurable lunacy. He glanced around to make certain that Liquid Larry was out of earshot, that another patron had not worked his way toward this end of the bar. Then he started to talk, keeping his voice low, his eyes averted from Carl's.

He talked about the *other* things, and Carl didn't laugh.

Encircled in the silent aura of pedestal floor lamps, Mitch Nistler labored over the corpse of Lorna Trosper. Except it wasn't really labor. His hands moved with a deftness he had never known before, as though he had spent his entire life mastering the skills of embalming. The smoothness of his motion, the certainty of his next move, and the precision with which he handled the instruments—all seemed beyond his normal capabilities.

This was not labor, or scarcely even work. This was love.

Occasionally, while watching his hands dance through the process of injecting embalming solution into Lorna's arteries, he would verge on asking himself *Just what the hell am I doing?* But the question never quite formed, because the *hunger* banished it before it could become a complete thought.

Always the *hunger*: cresting and breaking whenever any part of his old self began to stir, surging forth from that dark well in his mind, consuming and controlling him.

From that dark mental well came not only skill and dexterity and hunger but also knowledge. He wondered how he knew that the sacred profession of embalming, for example, began with the Egyptians in 6000 B.C., and how it came to be that he—Mitch Nistler, of Greely's Cove, Washington, twice-convicted petty drug pusher and menial servant of old Matt Kronmiller—could feel a kinship with the priests of the dog-headed god Anubis, the Divine Embalmer.

Kinship he felt, as though his soul had once lived in the body of a great practitioner of Anubis's art, as though he himself had launched countless human spirits on the 3,000-year "circle of necessity," completion of which allowed those spirits to return to their mummified remains and ascend into the eternal realm of the gods. Could it be that he actually remembered such things, that he had been one of Anubis's priests, that through some unknowable magic his own soul had broken out of the circle to survive an extra score of centuries?

Who owns Mitch Nistler?

He watched his hands as they finished the tasks of arterial injection, as they prepared the fluid for the next phase—cavity injection. The fluid must be an astringent, fast-acting preservative with a high formaldehyde content, augmented with phenyl, tanning agents, and odor suppressors. This he would inject into the body cavity to preserve the organs and give natural shape to the torso. After all, Lorna had given up so *much*—nearly a gallon of her blood to the flush receptor (virtually all of it), as well as the contents of all her major organs to the trocar and aspirator. The time had come to put something back: *formaldehyde,* the great preserver, the acrid-smelling stuff of embalming fluid, pumped in with motorized force through a trocar hole in the tummy.

Oh, the beauty of it.

When that was done, Mitch Nistler snapped off the injector, and its whine descended into nothingness, leaving only the hushed whisper of the ventilation system in its place.

On to the surface applications. Cosmetic dyes like red ponceau and yellow eosin, to banish the grays and blues and chalky whites of death, at least for a while. Humectants and oils to combat postembalming dehydration—sorbitol, dulcitol, glycol, and lanolin. And to counter the horrific chemical smells, perfumes—sassafras, lavender, and the oils of cloves and orange and wintergreen.

Then the final touches. Having decided against sewing shut the eyelids and jaw, he removed the body to the dressing room, where he lovingly washed, combed, and brushed its hair. Filed and lacquered its nails, both hands and feet. Daubed on sealing compounds to hide blemishes and bruises and discolorations caused by pooling blood. Applied facial makeup, eyeliner, mascara, and peach-colored lipstick to complement Lorna Trosper's radiant blond hair. All with love, with anticipation. And with *hunger*.

At last he stepped back from the gurney to behold the product of his labors in its wholeness. She lay on her back, naked, needing no clothing. Her skin was flushed and rosy, her face positively angelic. Mitch had taken great care in applying the makeup, lest he overdo it and fail to achieve the look that Lorna had had in life, of purity and wholesomeness. All flaccidity was gone, thanks to pressurized injection of embalming fluid, which had given her limbs and torso the firm, ripe look of a living woman. She seemed almost radiant.

Only touching her would dispel the illusion of life, for her flesh was dead-cold, but Mitch was prepared to live with this one small shortcoming. After all, never in his living memory had he touched a warm woman. You can't miss what you've never had, he told himself.

After wrapping Lorna Trosper's beautiful body in a clean sheet, he moved one of the massive black hearses out of the garage and drove his burbling, rust-cratered El Camino into its place. He then gently laid the body into the cargo bed of the half-car, half-pickup truck and covered it with a sheet of plastic to protect it from the rain. Back to its place went the hearse. The mortuary went dark as he shut off the last light. The garage door rattled closed, and Mitch Nistler, feeling both weary and exultant, drove away into the black night, bound for home with his woman.

8

That the sun shone on Greely's Cove seemed a small miracle after two days of gloom and sleety rain. Lindsay Moreland rolled out of bed, heaved open the bedroom window, and drank deeply of the crisp, winter air. She savored the miracle, small though it was, with its pine-laden breeze and dazzling patches of blue sky. A good feeling washed over her, and the dark age since her sister's death appeared to be on the verge of ending. Even so, she suffered a nibble of anxiety over being away from the brokerage on a Monday morning, and she thanked God for sympathetic associates who were willing to cover for her.

While her mother puttered over breakfast in the kitchen, Lindsay showered and dressed in a red cotton sweater and fitted oatmeal slacks. She topped off the outfit with a black linen jacket, simple brass bracelet, and earrings. Not in the mood for contacts this morning, she wore her horn-rims with the thin bows and larger-than-usual lenses, which her friends said made her look "bookish."

Nora presented her with a plate of French toast and a welcome cup of black coffee when she came into the kitchen. "Mmmhh," she said after the first bite. "No one does French toast like you, Mom."

"You can thank that Miss Hazelford person," said Nora, sipping from a coffee cup. "The woman must have spent a small fortune in groceries for this household. We could've had Tillamook cheese omelets or smoked salmon or even eggs Benedict, for that matter. But I know how much you love my French toast, so French toast it is. By the way, are the others stirring yet?"

"Not according to the sound of the rumbling snores coming from Carl's room," answered Lindsay. "Or the silence that seeped through Jeremy's closed door.

"It wouldn't surprise me," she offered, "if Carl's feeling a

106

little under the weather this morning. He didn't come in until two o'clock."

"I know," said Nora. "I was awake myself."

"I hope it wasn't because of my tossing and turning."

"Not at all. My head was just so full of thoughts and memories, so many"—her voice cracked ever so slightly, and her eyes fluttered, but she kept control—"so many questions. Even though most of her old things are gone, this house is still so full of Lorna. I don't think I could ever sleep well under this roof."

"I know what you mean. I'm glad that tonight's our last night here. There's no reason we can't go back home after the memorial service tomorrow."

After breakfast Lindsay placed a telephone call to her lawyer in Seattle, Denver Moreen, a trusted old friend who had handled the Moreland family's affairs for a quarter-century. All she wanted was some "quick and dirty" legal advice, she told him, on her chances of winning a court battle against Carl Trosper for custody of Jeremy. But like all lawyers, Moreen was wary of giving quick advice over the phone. He posed a dozen questions about Carl's moral and emotional fitness, finances, ability to earn a living, and the answers were hardly encouraging to Lindsay, the prospective litigant. Moral turpitude, Moreen explained, is difficult to prove in a custody case, even on the basis of expert testimony and documentary evidence, and nigh impossible with only hearsay and suspicion. After forty minutes of jawing, he offered the tentative conclusion that she would be crazy to challenge Carl over custody of the boy. Absent some unknown factor that would override all else that was known about him, Carl would win.

Lindsay thanked him, told him good-bye, and wandered back into the small kitchen to refill her coffee cup. Her mother had settled at the dinette table with the morning newspaper.

"I couldn't help but overhear," said Nora. "Denver wasn't very encouraging, was he?"

"No, he wasn't. In fact, he was downright discouraging, which makes you happy, I'm sure."

"Lindsay, would you please keep your voice down? I think Carl is awake."

"He's in the shower, and I don't care if he hears. There's no way I'll ever believe that he's fit to raise Jeremy."

"That's not for you to decide, is it?"

"Mother, there's nothing to decide. Look at his behavior last night: Lorna hasn't been gone two days, and he's out on the town, getting blotto with that police chief friend of his. You and Denver can say what you want, but that's not my idea of responsible fatherhood."

"Maybe I'm becoming weak in the head as I get old," said Nora, "but I'm not so sure I disapprove of it. I was tempted to do the same thing when your father died."

"You can't even handle one martini, Mother."

"That is hardly the point, dear. Now listen to me, because I'm about to give you some good advice—"

"I don't need any more advice."

"Well, listen anyway. As the contributor of half your genetic makeup, I'm entitled to give it. Let this *drop*, Lindsay. You can't accomplish anything by going to war with Carl. Oh, you can throw away hard-earned money on legal fees, and you can create lots of heartache and ill feeling, and you can probably alienate your nephew forever—which could very well happen if you pursue this insane notion of yours. Instead of fighting Carl, you should be trying to help him. Why not become an ally instead of an enemy? Do you really think Lorna would have given her blessing to a war between you and Carl over Jeremy?"

This last thought shook Lindsay, and her iron-woman bearing faltered. "That's not a fair question! Lorna wasn't herself during—"

"It *is* a fair question," insisted Nora. "Your sister was kind and decent. She lived to bring joy to others—in her art, her friendship, her generosity. She would have wanted nothing more than for us to help and love each other. The best way to keep her memory alive is to be like her, don't you think?"

Lindsay suddenly broke down. Tears gushed from her blue eyes, and her mouth contorted in a stifled sob. She had fought back this onslaught since that dark hour on Saturday morning when the coroner had called from Greely's Cove.

Nora rose and went to her younger daughter, now her only daughter, and wrapped her in motherly arms, cradled her head as she cried, daubed at her tears with wadded Kleenex. They huddled in a pair of dinette chairs, patting and stroking each other's heads until the onslaught finally subsided.

Red-eyed and stuffy-nosed, Lindsay said, "Oh, maybe you're right, Mother. I've been acting like a slug."

"No you haven't, dear," said Nora, caressing her daughter's blond hair. "You've been acting like your father, that's all. I've always said that you inherited his spirit."

"I'll back off over this custody thing," said Lindsay. "I'll even try to be helpful—really I will. But I'm going to stay on guard, Mother. If things start to go wrong for Carl, I'm going to be on hand to take care of Jeremy. Lorna would've wanted that, don't you think?"

Nora cradled her daughter's head against her shoulder again and sighed. "Yes, dear, you may be right. You just may be right at that."

Mitch Nistler woke from the deep sleep of exhaustion and, as usual, panicked. He was late again. The old Westclox alarm clock on his fourth-hand bed table showed 8:38, and dust-specked sunlight streamed through a grimy bedroom window. He should have been up and at work long before the winter sun had risen this far.

He climbed out of his lumpy bed with its tattered blankets and herded himself toward the bathroom, stepping awkwardly over a clutter of magazines, beer cans, and fast-food refuse. While urinating, he became aware of a strange new reality: He was not hung over. His head was clear and free of the familiar ache. His stomach was not threatening revolt. Tired though he was, he did not feel alcohol-sick, as he did on most mornings.

Then a dam burst in his head, and a torrent of memory surged into his consciousness. He saw his hand with a scalpel, poised above Lorna Trosper's naked body, saw the blade slicing through her cold, clean flesh, the cherry-red blood welling out. He saw himself shoving a trocar into her innocent heart and heard the whine of the aspirator as it sucked. He smelled formaldehyde and humectants and sassafras and lavender—

My God! Had he actually *done* it?

The rest came back to him in mental gobs, and he staggered out of the bathroom, clothed only in yellow-stained under-shorts, a gawky little man with fish-white skin and wild, frightened eyes. In the dead, dark hours of the morning he had transported the embalmed corpse of Lorna Trosper to this very house on the forested edge of Greely's Cove. In his tortured little mind, he had called it a homecoming.

Between the entrances of his bedroom and the kitchen stood a door that was peeling twenty layers of ancient paint. Beyond it was a narrow stairway to the second floor.

He pulled open the peeling door and trudged up the dusky, narrow stairway, dodging cobwebs. The stairs creaked and snapped under his meager weight. On the upper landing was a pair of doors, and beyond each a tiny bedroom. He halted at the top of the stairs, where dust and grime gritted against his bare soles. Until now he had never used the upstairs, because he had been too lazy to attack the clutter and filth that had accumulated there during past tenancies.

He went to the door on the right and shoved it slowly open, stirring the mingled smells of sassafras, lavender, and other perfumes that hung thick in the air. The corpse of Lorna Trosper, encircled in feeble sunlight that poured through a crusty window, lay on a dilapidated bed, still cocooned in the clean sheet that Mitch had expropriated from the Chapel of the Cove. With her golden hair splayed against the moth-eaten mattress and her satiny skin aglow, she looked every inch an angel.

Mitch's breath caught. He had embalmed and prepared many corpses during his tenure at the chapel, but he had never before succeeded in creating beauty like *this*. The tiny bedroom itself—despite the garbage heaped against its dingy walls—seemed a chapel, the old bed an altar. The perfumes that emanated from Lorna defeated the stink of dirt and neglect. Gazing upon her, scarcely daring to breathe or swallow, Mitch again felt justified for having taken her as his own. True, he had stolen and deceived. He had cremated an empty casket and packed its less-than-human ashes into a small jug that old man Kronmiller would unwittingly sell to Lorna's relatives as the real thing. He had stolen Lorna's body and embalmed it without the family's permission—itself a crime that could land him back in Walla Walla. But he was untroubled: No one would ever know what he had done. Lorna would be *his*—not forever, of course, because embalming is far from permanent, despite the crap that funeral directors give out to their clients. For a little while, at least, she would be his—until bacteria and insects started their hellish work in earnest.

He approached the bed and touched the cool white sheet that clothed her. He pulled it downward until an alabaster breast lay bare.

"I'm sorry that I couldn't give you better than this," he whispered. "I wish I could give you a castle. I wish—"

A small noise came from behind him, a tiny crack of ancient linoleum. He stopped breathing, eyes wide. *Just the old house settling,* he told himself. Old houses are full of tiny, unknowable sounds.

"I can't give you much," he said, gazing down again at Lorna's sleeping face. "I can only give you myself. You'll never know how much—"

The sound again—the creak-crack of brittle floorboards under shifting weight. A clammy chill enveloped his bare neck and shoulders, and he whirled around. His lungs heaved at what he saw, and his legs turned to ice water. Standing before him, smiling so tightly that all his perfect white teeth shone brightly, was a young boy, his huge hazel eyes gleaming with unnatural light.

Mitch choked on a clot of saliva, and he would have pissed himself had he not just emptied his bladder. He shook and shivered, and his hands flew reflexively to his crotch as he tried to hide his near-nakedness. His brain grabbled for any possible explanation of how this boy had gotten in, or who he was.

Who!

The recognition hit him. On rare occasions he had seen this boy around town, always in the shepherding company of his mother. Citizens had whispered behind their backs, clucking and shaking their heads, lamenting the fact that his mother had not put him away long ago. The boy was Jeremy Trosper. Lorna's son.

Jeremy had a wicked, wicked grin. And a crazy, inhuman glint in his eye. Mitch Nistler's world would come crashing down yet again, this time with brutal finality. Back to prison, for sure. With no chance of escape, because this little shit would go straight to the police, and—

"There's no need to worry about that," said the boy with a distinctly British accent, though Mitch had said nothing aloud; he'd been too terrified to speak. "You've done rather well, actually. I'm impressed; I really am."

With a little nod of his head Jeremy turned to leave, but he paused at the door to look back at Mitch, who stood frozen, except for his open jaw that quivered like a new leaf in a spring breeze.

"I meant what I said. Your secret's safe with me."

Then Jeremy was gone, leaving only the sound of creaking stairs behind him.

At noon Carl Trosper's former mother-in-law talked him into eating something, if only a small salad and a bowl of soup. A light meal usually helps a hangover, she declared, and he clearly needed help. Though four Excedrin and three cups of black coffee had dampened his gnawing headache, and a near-scalding shower had sweated out most of the evil humors he'd imbibed the previous night, he was far from a hundred percent yet. He suspected that his eyes looked like a pair of piss-holes in the snow. Maybe something to eat *would* help, he allowed, so Nora bustled off to the kitchen, eager to serve.

The three of them—Carl, Lindsay, and Nora—had spent several remarkably civil hours together in the living room of the little house at 116 Second Avenue, coffee-ing and convers-ing like mature adults about Lorna and Jeremy, reliving past joys and hardships, venturing hope for the future. To Carl's amazement and relief, Lindsay had lost her combativeness, having apparently given up her idea of challenging him for custody of his son. Though far from gushy in her endorsement of Carl's intentions concerning the future, she was nonetheless coolly conciliatory.

After Nora went into the kitchen, Lindsay offered to help Carl get control of the yard around the place, and he remem-bered that her hobby was gardening and landscaping. Lorna had always coveted her sister's way with green things.

"I don't know whether you've noticed," Lindsay said, "but the shrubbery is almost all dead—which is a little strange, since all the neighbors' yards are in good shape. I doubt we can save any of it."

Indeed, Carl had noticed the yellowing junipers and ragged spirea, once so lush and beautiful—special joys to Lorna. Even allowing for winter nakedness, the spirea looked withered and brittle, as did the lilacs that grew along the property lines.

"I'd appreciate your help," he said. "My thumb has never been very green. In fact, it's burnt umber."

"By the way, Carl," Nora called from the kitchen, "that son of yours is certainly getting his ration of sleep, isn't he?"

Carl glanced at his watch and decided it wouldn't hurt to check on the boy. He came back from Jeremy's room, looking unsteady.

"What's wrong?" asked Lindsay,

"He's gone," said Carl. "His bed is made—like it wasn't even slept in."

"I saw him go to bed last night," said Lindsay. "I even tucked him in."

"He obviously made the bed when he got up," said Nora, "though I'll admit it seems a little out of character for a thirteen-year-old boy."

"But when did he get up?" Carl asked, chewing on a thumbnail.

"Apparently very early," said Nora.

Just then the front door opened and Jeremy walked in, looking freshly scrubbed and well groomed, dressed as he had been the previous day in a Nike T-shirt and sweatpants. The only addition was a gray hooded rain parka of lightweight Gore-Tex. After hanging his parka in the entryway closet, he sat down in an armchair and crossed his legs.

"I hope I didn't worry anybody," he said with a trace of accent that Carl found strange. "I woke up early and couldn't get back to sleep, so I went for a walk."

"You mean you've been walking all this time?" asked Carl incredulously. "Something like five hours?"

"A little more than that, I should think," answered the boy, sounding very adult despite his smooth, childlike voice. "I was thinking about Mom, you see. She meant so very much to me, and walking just seemed like a good thing to do."

There it was, thought Carl: the evidence of pain he had yearned to see in his son. It would have comforted him had it not been delivered with such polished maturity, had it not seemed contrived. There was not a glitter of tears in the boy's hazel eyes, nor a hint of sorrow in his handsome face.

"Jeremy," he said, "I think you and I should have a little talk. Why don't we go to your room?"

Fifteen minutes later Carl returned to the living room alone, having closed Jeremy's door behind him. Nora brought him his soup and salad on a TV tray.

"Well, what did you talk about?" asked Lindsay.

"We negotiated a little agreement," answered Carl, talking around a bite of lettuce. "He's free to come and go as he pleases—during the daylight hours, that is—if he tells me where he's going. And if he has a change of plans after leaving the house, he's to call and let me know. We were both very reasonable, and he seems to accept the fact that I'm in charge." Carl looked pleased with himself, and he shoveled more salad into his mouth.

"Isn't that a lot of freedom for a child who's undergoing therapy?" remarked Lindsay. "Don't you think a tighter rein might be advisable?"

"Not until he demonstrates that he needs it. I keep trying to remember what I was like at his age, and I've got to admit that Jeremy seems a hell of a lot more sophisticated and mature than I was. My parents let me come and go pretty much as I wanted, so it seems only logical that—"

"But you were undoubtedly a perfectly healthy, normal child," protested Lindsay, "and you had both parents to look after you. That's a major difference."

"Good point," said Carl. "I should probably get Dr. Craslowe's advice on this thing, shouldn't I?"

"It certainly wouldn't hurt," said Lindsay. "You'll have your chance in an hour. Our appointment with him is at one-thirty."

The three of them chatted awhile longer, each glancing now and again down the short hallway at Jeremy's closed door. Carl caught himself doing it after noticing the others.

"He was reading when I left him," he volunteered, hoping to satisfy Nora's and Lindsay's curiosity about what Jeremy might be doing in there. "He says he's become quite a bookworm since he learned to read. Judging from the mountain of books in his room, I'd say that's an understatement. I wonder where he got them all."

"It's truly remarkable," said Nora. "You may have a prodigy on your hands, Carl. I just hope—" A shadow of apprehension darkened her face, and she left her thought unsaid.

At 1:15, Nora announced that Lindsay and Carl should leave

for their appointment with Dr. Craslowe at Whiteleather Place, and Lindsay volunteered to drive them in her Saab. After buckling herself into the driver's seat, she lamented the gathering clouds in the northwestern sky. The first tentative drops of rain were falling by the time they turned off Second Avenue onto Frontage Street.

"You must have had quite a blowout last night with your buddy, the police chief," said Lindsay as they headed south down the main drag, parallel to the shore. "Has the piper been fully paid?"

Carl smiled at this reference to his hangover. "We had a lot of catching up to do, and I'll admit that we caught damn near all of it."

Lindsay turned west on Sockeye Drive, and the village of Greely's Cove started to recede in favor of dense woods. A glance at Carl's disturbed face aroused her curiosity.

"You were saying?"

Carl felt an itch to share the things Stu had told him, if only to vent his own wild, inexact apprehensions and to check Lindsay's reaction against his own. How would she react, he wondered, if she heard that several of the missing citizens of Greely's Cove had paid visits in the dead of night to people they had left behind?

Like old Elvira Cashmore, for example, the aged widow whose lawn Carl tended as a boy. Scarcely two weeks after her disappearance, Sig Knutson, longtime Little League coach and Elvira's occasional escort to movies and picnics, called the police station at three in the morning, his voice quaking with fright. Elvira had just *visited* him, he croaked over the phone. She'd somehow managed to climb onto the roof of his garage, which offered access to his second-story bedroom window, and had thumped on the glass to wake him. Later, in an interview with Stu, the old boy said that Elvira had beckoned him to follow her, wanting him to join in what Sig thought was a "feast." Too, she had spoken of "dreaming"—at least that's what Sig *thought* she'd said, because he'd been too frightened to open the window in order to hear her clearly. He'd fetched a flashlight and beamed it against her face. Much of Elvira's cheek and neck were gone—bloody bones showing through scabby holes in the flesh; naked stems of arteries and veins, twitching with her heartbeats. And in her eyes, an unhealthy gleam that seemed *hungry*. Sig's hysterical screaming had driven her away.

Like Peggy Birch, the schoolteacher who disappeared in November and allegedly visited her husband, George, several weeks later in the blackest part of the night. The particulars of this visit were indistinct, since George had not called the police to file a report but had confided in a couple of friends the following day. Something about Peggy's visit had been extraordinary, although that was hardly the right word. The sight of his wife had turned George into a raving, jittering maniac. The following night he had loaded his old Remington shotgun, rammed the muzzle between his teeth, and tripped the trigger with his big toe, blowing most of his head off.

Like Wendell Greenfield, the fifty-one-year-old service-station operator who disappeared in October and visited his wife, Debra, on a dark November night. During a raging storm, yet. Pounding on the back door, insisting that she follow him somewhere, until she grabbed the family revolver from a kitchen drawer and scared him off. Most of the flesh of his right arm was missing, and his voice seemed to come from inside Debra's own head. Needless to say, she was frightened out of her ever-loving wits.

How would Lindsay respond to these things? Carl wondered. Would she simply dismiss them as the raving of grief-sick survivors? Or try to reconcile the similarities among the stories by calling them collective hallucinations or dreams? He wanted to know.

So he told her everything Stu had related the night before, quickly and matter-of-factly, omitting the florid adjectives that Stu had used. And he told her about his friend's creeping worry that something evil had settled in Greely's Cove, a *darkness* that "sort of hangs in the air like it's not quite invisible," a darkness that throws the local life processes out of kilter.

And he told her about Lorna's suicide note.

Stu had produced it from his jacket pocket shortly before they parted company the night before, just as Liquid Larry was throwing out all the other patrons in order to close for the night. Stu had planned to give the note to Carl all along, he'd said. He was certain that Lorna's suicide somehow bolstered his theory of an evil presence in Greely's Cove. Lorna had felt that presence, insisted Stu, and had been sickened by it. In some

unimaginable way, it had touched her and had made her life
unbearable.

Carl now pulled the note from his corduroy jacket, a
rumpled slip of paper with an uneven tear along the top edge.
The scrawled handwriting was barely recognizable as Lorna's.
He tried to read it aloud as Lindsay drove with both hands on
the wheel, her eyes locked straight ahead, her jaw set.

Tried to read it aloud. The terror of Lorna's final moments
must have wracked her limbs and set her body to trembling,
making writing next to impossible. The script contained a few
of her trademark loops and swirls, but other than these it
showed little of her artist's even hand. Mostly tremulous
streaks and smears, mere approximations of letters and words.

Ca—l—

Don't try t- love it. Itl- kill you, l—ke me. Ge—away.

Carl spoke the words that he thought he saw: "Carl: Don't
try to love it. It'll kill you, like me. Get away."

Lindsay should have responded predictably: *Something evil,
my foot!* Hallucinations and nightmares had obviously plagued
the survivors of Greely's Cove, as any rational, twentieth-
century adult could plainly see. The suicide note was the
product of a sick and tortured mind, a meaningless jumble of
half-formed thoughts and fears. Lorna herself had probably
hallucinated all kinds of threats, which is hardly remarkable for
someone who's sick enough to kill herself.

But Lindsay did not react as Carl thought she should. Her
face betrayed fresh misery at this small taste of the hell her
sister had suffered in the final moments of life.

Carl was slightly taken aback when she asked, "And just
what do *you* make of all this?"

He was about to say something, though he didn't know
exactly what, when a break in the undergrowth appeared on the
right side of the road. A wooden arrow, wobbly on its ancient
post, pointed north into the forest. Traces of white paint
applied decades earlier rendered the message: *Whiteleather
Place.*

They turned into the narrow, twisting lane, and the tires of
Lindsay Moreland's Saab crunched over a damp layer of
ash-colored rock chips. A canopy of mature deciduous trees
and conifers nearly choked off the daylight, forcing Lindsay to

turn on her headlights. The dense overhead network of needles and limbs, already saturated by the winter storm, issued huge droplets of water that splatted noisily now and again on the windshield.

"How much farther?" she asked.

"Just a quarter-mile," answered Carl, gazing out the rain-streaked window into the woody dusk. "You know, coming out here brings back a lot of memories."

"Familiar with this area, are you?"

"When I was a kid, my buddies and I used to play here. We built forts in the woods and attacked enemy convoys on this very road."

"Enemy convoys?"

Little boys' games, he explained. Guns, cowboys, army. This forest was among their favorite stomping grounds, for it had most everything that kids love: grand trees to climb, little bubbling brooks for wading in, frogs and snakes to capture, myriad clearings to explore, and a zillion hiding places for playing guns.

"Stu and I had a good friend who lived in the mansion, named Renzy Dawkins. His father was a big insurance executive, real hard-charger, who caught the ferry to Seattle every morning. When the weather was bad, we played in the mansion—if Renzy's mother was in the mood to put up with a lot of shooting, that is."

He made his hand into a "gun" and gave out an explosive sound from the back of his throat. Lindsay thought it sounded like someone who had swallowed a bug and offered that the boys must have driven Mrs. Dawkins crazy.

"She seemed willing enough to put up with us," said Carl, letting himself believe that Lindsay was warming to him little by little. "The Dawkinses were great people. They were firm believers in charity—even to the extent that they sort of adopted a poor family who lived over near the marina. Every month or so Ted Dawkins—Renzy's dad—would bring them a box of groceries and some clothes, a few other household odds and ends, maybe a little extra spending money for their kid. I can even remember their name: Nistler. Ted always said he felt better about giving directly to the needy, trying to make a difference in just one or two cases, rather than signing a check and handing it over to the United Way."

"Did it work? Make a difference, I mean?"

"That's debatable, I suppose. Mr. Nistler ran off one day, never to be seen again, and his son grew up to be a petty drug pusher. Landed in the joint, I hear. Maybe the United Way is the way to go after all. At any rate, it's the thought that counts, I guess—or at least that's what Lorna always said. She was very close to Alita Dawkins. They worked together on community projects, art shows, that kind of thing. You may not have known this, but Alita was sort of Lorna's strong shoulder while she was pregnant with Jeremy—even rode along to the hospital when she went into labor. During those last few weeks before the birth, I saw almost as much of Alita as I did my wife. It was like having a day nurse around."

As they rounded curve after curve, the tangle of undergrowth thickened along the road, and the forest seemed duskier and less inviting than Carl remembered it. Ragged clutches of holly and Scotch broom grew in profusion among the trees. Morning glories festooned the trunks, and the mossy bark had a sooty, brittle look that suggested sickness. Then the tangle suddenly gave way to a clearing that swirled with ground fog. The Saab passed unimpeded between two gateposts of crumbly, cinnamon-colored brick. The spiked wrought-iron gate had long ago rusted off its hinges.

Whiteleather Place loomed above its lake of fog, a Victorian relic that dated from the 1890s. Built of the same cinnamon-colored brick, it boasted an imposing, three-story tower at a front corner, with small dormers set into an elaborate roofline that rose to a needlelike lightning arrester. An enormous wooden porch with arched ceilings swept around the ground floor, sagging here and there under the weight of time, needing repair and paint. Terra-cotta inserts adorned the many gables and windows, though rain and wind had defiled their elegance, giving them the look of filigreed tumors. Attending the great house was a graveyard of madronas, now warped with decay, their gnarled and naked branches rising from the mist in a silent, frozen hosanna of death. The once-lavish shrubbery had become a chaotic wreckage of yellowed twigs that cowered in the undulating ground fog.

Lindsay parked the Saab in the circular drive, set the brake, and switched off the engine. She stared a few seconds at a tatterd gazebo that sat like a forlorn orphan in the yard, clothed in dead, crinkly vines.

"This place looks like something out of Edgar Allan Poe," she said, suppressing a shiver.

"It's really gone to seed since the old days," said Carl, "which is a shame. When I was a kid, it was a showplace." His eyes landed on Lindsay's face and narrowed. "What's this I see? A little case of the creeps?"

"Not a little one, a big one."

"You're ruining your tough-as-nails image, you know. You stockbrokers aren't supposed to have romantic streaks."

"It's not my image I'm worried about."

They got out of the car and trudged up an eroding flagstone walk to the porch, where a neat brass sign hung on a balustraded post: *Dr. Hadrian Craslowe*.

"It doesn't say doctor of *what*," observed Carl.

"If you're a patient, you're supposed to know."

They climbed the steps and paused in the dank shadow of the porch, where the air seemed ten degrees colder.

"Do you see a walk-in sign or a doorbell?" Lindsay asked.

Carl saw only a heavy brass knocker—a malevolent lion's head whose beard was the handle, which he gripped and let fall three times, generating cold thumps that hinted of dark secrets within. They waited, straining to hear sounds of someone coming to answer, shifting on their feet and glancing nervously at each other while pretending not to.

Without warning, the dual oaken doors swung open on croaking hinges, revealing a tall, straight-backed woman who looked barely thirty. She had sad almond eyes of deep brown, flawless olive skin, and raven-colored hair pulled back in a severe bun. She wore a floor-length skirt of charcoal wool and a funereal satin blouse with long, billowy sleeves. A bone cameo hung at her throat on a velvet band. "Yes?" Her tone was low, almost secretive.

"I'm Lindsay Moreland, and this is Carl Trosper. We have an appointment with Dr. Craslowe."

"Yes, of course," said the woman. "I am Mrs. Ianthe Pauling, assistant to Dr. Craslowe. Won't you please come in?" Carl thought her speech sounded English, though it lacked Hannie Hazelford's broad and lordly vowels. "The doctor will be with you momentarily," said Mrs. Pauling.

She took their wraps and ushered them through a dark foyer into a parlor lit by Tiffany gas fixtures that some previous resident had long ago converted to electricity.

"Please make yourselves comfortable," she said, indicating an antique sofa that stood on carved, clawlike feet. "Dr. Craslowe won't be long." She glided soundlessly out of the room, scarcely stirring the somber air.

"God, this place is like a museum," breathed Lindsay, surveying the ancient furnishings from her perch on the sofa. "There's a fortune in antiques in this room alone."

"No kidding," whispered Carl, gawking at the venerable nineteenth-century cabinetwork, the porcelain vases decorated with gold butterflies and enamel flowers, the woolen draperies that swept in elegant rolls from the lofty ceiling to the floor. "The Dawkinses never had anything like this. But then again, they had kids, and I'm told that antiques and kids don't mix."

"How long did your friends live here?"

Carl thought a moment, leaning back on the sofa and pursing his lips. "Renzy's parents were here about twenty-six years. Moved in when Renzy was in the first grade, as I recall. I can't remember exactly when Renzy moved out, but it must've been when he went off to college. His sister, Diana, was a year younger, and she stayed on, right up until Ted and Alita—" He broke off, clearly reluctant to go on.

"Until Ted and Alita what?"

Carl fidgeted in his seat, planted an ankle on a knee, and toyed with the laces of his deck shoes. "They committed suicide," he said with a little grimace, as though the words tasted bad. "Right here in this house, in fact. There's another parlor in the back, with a little alcove off to one side. They called it the 'prayer corner,' because it had stained-glass windows. That's where Renzy found them—both dead—and Diana was in one of the upstairs bedrooms, having something like a nervous breakdown. The story was that they ate rat poison or something. There was no suicide note, no evidence of any emotional turmoil, absolutely nothing that gave any clue about why they did it. Renzy'd been off sailing his yacht somewhere, and he was just dropping in to—"

"You're making this up," gasped Lindsay. Her face had whitened a shade, and her blue eyes were huge behind her horn-rims. "Tell me you're making it up."

"I wish I were," said Carl, staring at his shoelaces. "It doesn't feel good to talk about it right now, believe me. It just seems so senseless." He ran his tongue over his drying lips. "At the funeral, Renzy vowed never to set foot in this house again. As far as I know, he never did, and I suspect the place was vacant until Dr. Craslowe moved in. Maybe that explains why the grounds are in such bad shape. As for Diana, she never really recovered. The doctors all expected her to get better, but she never did. Last I heard, she was still in a private mental hospital up near Port Angeles."

Mrs. Ianthe Pauling appeared from the hall, her hands folded officiously over her stomach. "Dr. Craslowe will see you now," she said, stepping backward to indicate the way.

She led them down a long corridor hung with faded seventeenth-century landscapes to the rear parlor that Carl had mentioned a moment ago, the room where the Dawkinses had ended their lives by eating rat poison. On the outer wall of the room stood a massive stone fireplace with a mantel that matched the dark walnut wainscoting. A tentative fire cast dancing shadows. Heavy drapes covered the windows, effectively denying the daylight. Above the mantel hung a bank of framed diplomas. A luxuriant Persian carpet covered all but a narrow perimeter of parquet floor, which, Carl remembered, had been a source of special pride to Renzy's father, who never passed up a chance to remind guests that the inlaid cherry, oak, and birch had been imported from South America *(You just don't see this kind of craftsmanship anymore,"* he had often said with a satisfied smile). A pair of electric Tiffany lamps sat at opposite ends of a stately ebony table that in another century could have graced the dining hall of an Elizabethan castle, but which now served as a desk. Splayed here and there on its surface were thick, leather-bound books, presumably taken from the vast collection that crammed the shelves on the walls. Brooding, heavy-limbed furniture sat in clusters throughout the room, and in the corners stood porphyry busts of long-dead scholars, their faces somber under a thin layer of dust.

In the tiny alcove that the Dawkinses had called their "prayer corner" stood Dr. Hadrian Craslowe, hands clasped behind his back, his wispy white hair vaguely tinted by the feeble afternoon light that filtered through the stained-glass windows overhead. He stepped smoothly out of the alcove and smiled, his ancient dentures gleaming. He wore steel-rimmed glasses that exaggerated his watery gray eyes and a formless suit of dark tweed that gave no hint of the shape of the body inside it. With his large head slightly cocked, he reminded Carl of a kindly English lord who had graciously granted an audience to his tenants.

"Miss Moreland, Mr. Trosper, I'm Hadrian Craslowe. Won't you please sit down?" His voice flowed like the venerable Thames, deep and ageless and unhurried.

Since he offered no handshake, Lindsay and Carl smiled their hellos and obediently took their seats in a pair of brocaded armchairs that hunkered before the great table. The doctor settled into a massive black leather chair on the opposite side and leaned forward until his chest touched the wood, keeping his hands out of sight below the edge.

He nodded to his assistant, who waited wraithlike in the shadow of the doorway. "That will be all, Mrs. Pauling, thank you." She slipped softly away, closing the double doors behind her.

"Before we begin, allow me to offer my sincere condolences on the passing of Mrs. Trosper," he said in his sober, aristocratic English. "She was a remarkable woman, strong and loving. Her perseverance in seeking help for her son was truly inspiring. She was also an accomplished artist, I'm told."

"She loved all kinds of art," said Lindsay. "And all kinds of people, too." She cast a quick, sidelong look at Carl, one he disliked. "She'll be missed by all of us."

"Yes, of course she will, and not the least by Jeremy, I should think."

"As you well know, Dr. Craslowe, Jeremy is the reason we're here," said Carl, using the deferential tone he customarily reserved for senators and cabinet officials back in Washington, D.C. "Since he'll be living with me, I thought it wise to consult you about the care he'll need. I haven't been a hands-on father for a long time, and I need all the advice I can get."

Craslowe's craggy face produced a smile. "Naturally, I'll be happy to advise you in any way I can, Mr. Trosper."

"We also want to thank you," said Lindsay, "for all you've done. Jeremy's recovery has been a miracle, and I can't tell you how grateful we are."

Craslowe's smile broadened almost imperceptibly. "To be called a miracle worker is really very seductive, Miss Moreland, but it is a title I cannot claim. Jeremy's recovery is attributable to science, and there's nothing miraculous about it. Were this the fifteenth century and not the twentieth, I could perhaps get away with claiming to have worked a miracle"—he actually chuckled—"at the risk of being burned at the stake, of course."

"I don't know whether Lorna told you, but we took him to something like fifty doctors," said Carl, "and not one of them could even tell us what was wrong. We spent a fortune on clinical tests, not to mention airline tickets and hotel rooms, but it was all hopeless. We—"

"Yes, yes," interrupted the doctor, "Lorna described your ordeal in some detail, and I must agree that it was tragic, all the more so because it was needless." He leaned back in the huge chair, wholly serious now, looking very old and wise. "Had you known of our work in Europe, or if someone had referred you to the Zurich Mental Health Institute in Switzerland where I was practicing, you would have been spared considerable suffering, I daresay. We could have effected Jeremy's recovery much sooner."

"I know very little about psychology," said Lindsay, "and I'm not sure I'd even understand an explanation of how you did it, but I'm curious about why you succeeded when so many other doctors failed."

"I merely opened the right door, Miss Moreland. In deference to my copractitioners, I had the advantage of knowing which door to look for, owing to my considerable experience in such matters. You see, Jeremy's case is not totally unique—in fact, it is rather more common than most would expect. Why, scarcely two years ago in Switzerland, I attended a young German man who had much in common with Jeremy.

"He was nineteen years old and completely dependent on his family. He had never spoken a coherent word, never laughed or smiled, nor so much as shown recognition of a family member. He could neither dress himself nor attend to his sanitary needs, and at any given moment he would shriek meaninglessly at the top of his lungs, flailing his arms and feet, breaking furniture and such, frightening everyone around him. Like you and your wife, Mr. Trosper, his parents had consulted dozens of physicians and therapists, only to hear that the case was utterly hopeless. Most recommended institutionalization, of course."

Carl felt a little stab of guilt. Thank God Lorna had resisted his arguments for sending Jeremy to an institution. He listened with his head lowered as Craslowe went on.

"We effected his recovery through what we call channeled hypnotherapy, as we did with Jeremy. In all honesty, once the process was under way, the young man cured himself, just as Jeremy did. As is typical in such cases, we discovered that the subconscious had been assimilating knowledge throughout his entire life, that he actually *did* know how to speak and behave like a normal human being. All that was needed was to open the door through which this knowledge could flow.

"Today he is a productive laborer in a factory. He's learning to read, which should enable him to seek more responsible jobs in the future. His father wrote recently with news that he's even met a young woman and that they plan to marry."

Lindsay seemed fascinated. "Are you saying that Jeremy has been subconsciously learning things all his life, and that these things are just now coming out?"

"Precisely," said the doctor, "although Jeremy's case is extraordinary in one respect: The boy is probably an actual genius. His powers of deductive reasoning are truly enormous. I suspect that his subconscious mind, during the period of his emotional and mental disability, compensated for its lack of expression through intense intellectual growth, and that today—given the opportunity to vent itself at last—is doing so and is manifesting a prodigy. As you well know, the boy has taught himself to read in just under six months, and he is reading on a level that most adults would consider difficult. I find it all very exciting and a wonderful way to end a long, long career."

"But what went wrong in the first place?" asked Carl. "Why wasn't Jeremy able to relate to the world like other kids? This door in the mind, you spoke of: Why wasn't it open from the moment he was born?"

The doctor delivered his answer with sacerdotal reverence, drawing out his words and pausing occasionally in order to find those suitable for laymen's ears. He spoke of "baseline consciousness," that level of awareness at which every person begins life. Not all children begin at the same level, he said.

Some, like Jeremy, start life at a level that is barely conscious at all, and they do not progress to higher ones in the normal way.

Between the worlds of conscious mind and physical behavior lies a mental "frontier," which, wrote a neurosurgeon named Wilder Penfield in 1943, lies on the upper midsurface of each cerebral hemisphere of the brain—the "supplementary motor area," the master control center of all voluntary action. In Jeremy's case, Craslowe explained, the frontier was especially wide and difficult to cross, meaning that his intellect had virtually no control over his behavior.

"Even so," said Craslowe, "he had perfectly functioning senses. He could see and hear normally. He could touch and taste and smell. Through the senses, his subconscious intellect gathered knowledge of the world around him."

And this, thought Carl, explained how Jeremy remembered him beardless and without tinges of gray at the temples, even though they had not been together since long before Jeremy's recovery.

"Jeremy's problem was that he suffered a chronically altered state of consciousness, the reason for which we lack the means of knowing," said the doctor. "We simply used hypnotherapy to activate the proper neural events in his brain, then relied on his subconscious intellect to sort out the problem of controlling his actions and behavior."

"I see," said Carl, not quite honestly. "All this through hypnosis. I wonder why none of the American doctors suggested it."

"This sort of application is not highly regarded in the United States," answered Craslowe. "Oh, you'll find hypnosis being used by clinicians here and there to help people stop smoking or to root out the causes of various neuroses and psychoses, but seldom as an actual therapy. Most consider it the realm of nightclub entertainers, I'm afraid, even though it was used quite successfully as a surgical anesthetic here and in Europe during the nineteenth century. Physicians in India used it in this manner for hundreds of years before that."

"Then the American medical world should hear about Jeremy's case," suggested Lindsay. "Maybe it isn't a miracle, Doctor, but it's certainly a dramatic success. Who knows how many other people could be helped by the knowledge?"

Craslowe's liquid eyes widened and for the briefest moment seemed to become dimly luminous from within, which Carl assumed was a trick of the firelight. A burning log snapped loudly, and the air moved in a vague whisper.

"I fully intend to publicize this case, Miss Moreland, but in due time," replied the doctor evenly. "I'll grant that Jeremy's recovery has been dramatic, but there is yet more work to do. His therapy should continue for at least another year, possibly two, just to ensure that his mental processes do not lapse back into their old rut. They are like muscles that have been paralyzed for years. They require a regimen of proper therapy and exercise in order to develop normally. For this reason I intend to withhold publication of the case until we can be totally certain of long-term recovery. I hope that I can count on both of you to cooperate in this regard."

"We've agreed," said Carl, "that his therapy should continue for as long as you say."

"Good," said Craslowe. "And for my own humble purposes, I would beg you not to spread word of this case. You can be assured that I will publicize it at the appropriate time through the proper professional channels. Until then I would prefer not to be the focus of media attention and all the attendant speculation." He smiled in a way that Carl found unsettling. "Besides, I'm not at all good with reporters."

"I think we can agree to that," said Carl, forcing himself to ignore a tiny warning bell in the back of his mind. "But I'm curious about something else, Doctor: Jeremy seems to have an accent that comes and goes. I wonder—"

"Nothing to worry over, Mr. Trosper. The accent is English—rather like my own, I expect, since my voice has been the only one he's heard while under hypnosis. It's only natural that he would subconsciously imitate it, just as the average two-year-old imitates the speech of his parents. There's no doubt at all that he'll grow out of it as time goes on, especially after therapy is discontinued. By the time he reaches maturity, he'll sound exactly like a red-blooded American lad, and not at all like a crusty old Oxford professor, I can assure you."

Lindsay and Carl joined in a quiet little laugh that brightened the heavy atmosphere a shade.

Carl asked whether he, as a parent, should take any special

measures in raising the boy, in supervising and nurturing him, and on this point Craslowe was forceful.

"None at all, Mr. Trosper. In every sense Jeremy's everyday life should be totally normal. In fact, he's fully capable of handling more freedom than the average child of his age, given his intellectual endowment. It's imperative that he have the latitude to explore and experience the world on his own terms, for he's been deprived of the usual learning experiences of early childhood. He desperately needs the exercise of managing his own behavior and organizing his own responses to the situations of day-to-day living."

And what about schooling? Carl wanted to know.

The doctor recommended that Jeremy be kept out of school for at least six months. Time would be needed for testing to determine his academic level. Quite conceivably, he would need some special instruction. Despite his intellectual brilliance, he lacked much of the fundamental knowledge needed to mesh successfully with a formal curriculum. For the time being, Jeremy should be allowed to study on his own.

"I've already lent him many books," said Craslowe, "and he seems to enjoy them. A structured academic program is not a matter of pressing concern at this moment."

So that was where Jeremy had gotten the mountain of books in his bedroom, thought Carl. "Well," he said after a brief silence, "I think you've answered most of my questions. Unless Lindsay has some more . . ." Carl had developed an itch to leave this house, to be free of the brooding atmosphere that seemed to soak through his pores and stir up his nerve endings.

Lindsay had no more questions, and her taut face suggested that she too was anxious to leave.

"Well then," said Craslowe, gathering himself to rise out of his leather chair, "I'll assume that we'll carry forward the therapy as we have been doing since the beginning—twice a week, one o'clock on Tuesdays and Fridays."

As they all stood up, Carl caught a fleeting glimpse of the doctor's hands, which had remained out of sight throughout the entire interview. For the briefest moment, they were visible while en route to the small of Craslowe's back, where he clasped them away from view. Carl thought he saw dark velvet gloves. Maybe it was another trick of the dancing firelight that suggested an outlandish deformity, an abnormally long and snakelike finger. Carl's flesh grew prickly and cold, and he was glad that Craslowe did not offer to shake hands.

"Is this an appropriate time to make arrangements for payment?" asked Lindsay. "I know that Carl will be against this, but I'd like to help with the fees."

"Oh, I see that your sister didn't tell you," said the doctor. "I'm not charging for my services in this case. Having heard about Jeremy shortly after arriving here, I offered my help gratis. My reward has been the joy of having had a hand in Jeremy's rebirth as a normal human being, not to mention the intellectual fulfillment of success. Besides, I've always believed that no man stands as tall as when he stoops to help a child."

The double doors swung open, and the sad-faced Mrs. Pauling appeared with Carl's and Lindsay's coats.

9

Somehow, Mitch Nistler got through the day. If old man Kronmiller noticed that his assistant embalmer had shown up late for work again, he gave no clue of it, and Mitch was spared yet another harangue about his overall worthlessness.

Around midmorning a death call came in, so Mitch and another employee were dispatched in a hearse to bring the body in for embalming. Throughout most of the afternoon, he assisted his boss in the process of preparing and dressing the body for viewing.

When quitting time came at last, Mitch threw on his weather-beaten anorak and, grimacing against the cold rain, jogged across the rear parking lot of the Chapel of the Cove to his battered old El Camino. Once behind the wheel, he paused only long enough to light a cigarette and curse his worn windshield wipers, which merely channeled the water into distorting streaks on the glass. Seconds later he was on Sockeye Drive, headed not for Liquid Larry's, which was his nightly custom, but in the opposite direction, propelled by a craving far greater than his thirst for alcohol.

With one hand on the wheel, he rummaged through a clutter of wadded hamburger wrappers, empty cigarette packs, and beer cans on the seat next to him, until finding a much-used cassette. He shoved it into the stereo on the dash. The music of Twisted Sister, a raucous heavy-metal band, shrieked from the cheap speakers behind the seat. The driving bass tones thumped in his chest, and he began to feel vaguely good about things for the first time that day. Then the music died and the sick old cassette player coughed out the tape by the yard, issuing unnerving clicks and squeals.

"Fuck a bald-headed duck!" he spat, smacking the dashboard with the bottom side of his fist, killing the machine for good. The death of the music brought an aching quiet that left room in his mind for a legion of fears. Chief among them was Jeremy Trosper. How the boy had gotten into his house no longer mattered. Of far greater concern was *why*. Mitch wracked his brain for some explanation of how Jeremy could have know about the theft of his mother's corpse, or how he even could have known where Mitch lived.

Why would a kid track down the thief of his mother's body, and then content himself with protecting the thief's secret, as he had promised to do, instead of going immediately to the police and reporting the outrage? And wasn't this the same kid who everyone knew was a drooling, screaming basket case?

The memory of Jeremy's smooth, cultured voice and the evil glow in his hazel eyes gave Mitch gooseflesh. Crawling in his belly was the dread that he had become a helpless puppet who was dancing at the hand of some fiendish puppeteer, performing a play that he could never hope to understand.

Who owns Mitch Nistler?

He turned off Sockeye Drive, and his headlight beams flitted and jounced through the dark trees alongside Old Home Road, the muddy forest trail near which stood his pathetic little house, separate and apart from the mainstream of Greely's Cove. A smattering of decrepit clapboard shacks stood in clearings along the road, most of them deserted and overgrown with Scotch broom and holly. His was the third house off Sockeye Drive.

Mitch's breath caught like a chicken bone in his throat when he saw yellow light streaming through the grungy windows of his living room. Next to his rickety front porch sat a fat Chevy Blazer with bulging tires and gleaming roll bars, meaning that Corley the Cannibal Strecker had come to call. Disliking locked doors and lacking a scintilla of respect for anyone's privacy, Cannibal had simply let himself in, probably with a crowbar.

Mitch parked the El Camino and forced himself to walk into his own home, cringing at the thought of meeting Strecker and his horror-movie girlfriend again. As he gripped the broken handle of his front door, he prayed that Cannibal had not ventured upstairs.

"So, what do you think of the place, Marvelous Mitch?" asked Cannibal Strecker, sweeping a hammy hand through the air, indicating the shabby room, the ramshackle house, and presumably everything else in this dark corner of the woods. "I admit it's no Four Seasons, but it ain't a hell of a lot worse than the dump you live in, right?"

He clapped the hammy hand on Mitch's shoulder and barked a loud laugh. The little man wobbled and pretended to be amused.

At their "joyful" reunion on Saturday, Cannibal had told Mitch that they were now neighbors, which was true to the extent that Cannibal had bought a place less than a mile up Old Home Road from Mitch's own. The house was in appalling condition, but then Cannibal and his girlfriend, Stella DeCurtis, did not actually live here. They owned a "moocho lux" condominium in Seattle, Cannibal had bragged. They needed the house in the woods only as a laboratory to convert cocaine to crack. Though reeking with neglect and overgrown with moss and mildew, it had in great abundance the most desirable feature of any crack lab: privacy.

"Well," said Mitch, clearing a frog out of his throat, "it's nice, real nice. I like what you've done with it."

Cannibal ignored the sarcasm and grinned around a huge wad of bubble gum, missing nary a beat in his noisy chewing. Stella DeCurtis, sullen as ever, seemed to be pretending that Mitch did not exist.

"I really should be going now, Cannibal," Mitch added. "I've got things to do tonight."

Scarcely ten minutes earlier, immediately after he had arrived home to find Cannibal and Stella lounging in his living room with heads full of coke, Cannibal had herded him back outside and into the Blazer. Just a little tour of the lab and some neighborly hospitality, Cannibal had insisted—a little beer, a little whiskey, maybe a little hit of coke to put lead in the pencil. Much against his will, Mitch was dragged along, knowing it was pointless to let Cannibal have anything but his own way.

"Hey, I haven't finished showin' you around yet, Mitchie Witchie," protested Cannibal. "Come 'ere. You're gonna get a fuckin' rush out of this."

The big man pulled open the door of a fairly new General Electric refrigerator, inside of which was at least a case of Anchor Steam in bottles. Instantly Mitch's mouth was watering, and he was grateful to the god of beer when Cannibal tossed him one.

"I ain't showin' you the *beer*, little man," said a laughing Cannibal. "It's *this* I want you to see." He pointed to a pair of packages neatly wrapped in butcher paper and tied with kite string. "That's two pounds of crack, m'man, each worth seventy-five large on the street in Seattle. Me and Stella cooked it up this weekend."

Mitch guzzled half his beer, hoping that the tingling suds would dampen the hunger and the demon-taste, but they did not. The beer merely ignited pain in the torn flesh inside his mouth, Cannibal's handiwork of two days earlier.

"That's great, Cannibal, really great. I can see why you're getting rich."

Cannibal slammed the refrigerator door and moved over to a countertop.

"The beauty of it is that we did it with these."

He indicated four glass coffeepots like those found in cheap cafes and truck stops, a hot plate, and a pair of digital scales. Stacked nearby was an open case of baking soda. In a sagging cupboard sat rows of bottles with white labels marked "ETHER" in black felt-tip. Scattered over the countertops were clusters of little glass vials, measuring spoons, paring knives, and butane lighters.

"No fancy equipment or nothin'. Me and Stella have got this down to a science, Mitchie. I do the cookin', she does the dryin', and we both do the packin'." He nodded at a feeble-looking card table upon which sat plastic molds and packing materials, the final station in an assembly line that produced evil little chips of smokable cocaine.

"Like I say, Cannibal, it's great," repeated Mitch, worrying now about what the former secretary-general of D Block wanted from him tonight. "I always knew you were smart, and I knew you'd find a way to jackpot when you got out of Walla Walla. It looks like life is being good to you, and I'm glad, I really am. But hey, I've had a hard day, and I really need some Zs, man."

Cannibal's attitude suddenly changed. His blue-stubbled jaw clamped tight and his hazy, hooded eyes grew hard as ball bearings. He thudded across the room to Mitch, grabbed the little man's shirt, and forced their faces to within inches of each other. Mitch felt himself go numb with terror.

"Now you listen to me, Mitchie Witchie, and you listen hard. I'll let you go when I'm good and ready, and not until, you dig? You seem to forget that you and me are partners." The stink of Cannibal's breath flooded into Mitch's nostrils, gagging him, and for a horrible moment he feared he would vomit in Cannibal's face—which of course would mean the end of his wretched life, right then and there. "We've got responsibilities to each other, you and me. Just because you happen to be a little tired doesn't mean you can kiss off your responsibilities, hear what I'm sayin'? Am I getting *through* to you, little man?"

To get his point across, Cannibal shook him hard, and Mitch heard popping sounds in his neck. But he managed to nod his head. Cannibal smiled and released him.

"It's not like I don't want good things for you, Mitch," he continued, now smoothing the smaller man's shirt like a helpful big brother, still chewing his bubble gum loudly. "I'm payin' you good money for your help, and all I ask is that you do what you're told. That's your end of the fuckin' bargain—to do what you're fuckin' told. I've got a lot invested in this business, a lot of goodwill worked up with people, and I'm not going to let you queer it because you've got an attitude problem."

For the first time that evening, Stella DeCurtis took an interest in the men's conversation. She moved close to Mitch, a cigarette between her bony fingers, smelling heavily of costly perfume. Her colorless, coke-glazed eyes looked like plastic buttons set deep in a painted doll's face.

"There's something you should know, little slave boy," she said. "We didn't just *happen* to settle here. We didn't choose this place just because it's out here in the boonies, y'know. We chose it because of *you*."

Mitch's eyes widened and his throat went dry as sandpaper.

"Does that surprise you?" she went on. "I can't imagine why it should. You see, Cannibal remembered you from the joint. He knew you were a worthless little shitbag who'd never have balls enough to fuck us over. That makes you the ideal throwaway. You're cheap, you're gutless, and you're expendable. What makes it even better is that you live just up the road, so you're always within reach if we need you. How does that make you feel, slave boy?"

"Aw, c'mon, Stella, don't be so hard on the little puke," pleaded Cannibal Strecker with mock sympathy. "Underneath that sorry excuse for a chest beats a heart like warm oatmeal. Ain't that so, Marvelous Mitch?"

Marvelous Mitch gulped air and nodded.

"He'll do just fine, now that his attitude's straightened out," added Cannibal. "He'll carry our goods over to Seattle once a week, and he'll keep an eye on the road for us, just to make sure our arrangement with the local heat is working out."

"I—I don't get it," stammered Mitch. "I thought I was going to be a throwaway. Am I supposed to be a lookout, too?"

"Hell no," answered Cannibal, chawing his bubble gum with violent relish. "We just want you to check on this dump now and then when we're not here. All you have to do is give me a call if you see somethin' that looks like a narc pokin' around, so we'll know not to show up. We never store any drugs here, so if the place gets tossed we won't lose anything more expensive than a case or two of baking soda and a few bottles of ether—nothin' anybody could use to send us back to the joint with."

"What's this about an arrangement with the heat?" Mitch wanted to know.

Cannibal's eyes hardened into ball bearings again. "That's no concern of yours, little man. Let's just say that our associates in Seattle have worked out a deal with somebody who's important locally and that we'll hear about any under-cover jobs goin' down in the neighborhood. Like if the state and county decide to get tough on crack, or something equally wacko."

"That's enough, Cannibal," said Stella DeCurtis in a tone Mitch had never heard anyone use with the animal. "The little shit doesn't need to know anything about anything."

"I only told him that much so he can sleep nights," apologized Cannibal. "We don't want him goin' wild and paranoid on us, do we?"

"All he needs to know is that you'll rip his liver out if he ever crosses us or if he ever fucks up," said Stella.

"Hell, he already knows that, don't you, Marvelous Mitch? You've seen ol' Cannibal in action before."

Indeed, Mitch had. Better than most, he knew what this beast was capable of, and his hatred of him roiled in his guts like a nest of rattlesnakes. The day would come, he vowed silently, when he would be free of this monster, when Cannibal's ownership of Mitch Nistler would end. For the barest moment he thrilled to the vision of holding a large-caliber pistol to Cannibal's ugly head, of pulling the trigger and hearing the magnificent bark of fire and smoke, of seeing Cannibal's subhuman skull come apart and his brain spatter in all directions. The vision sweetened as he saw Stella DeCurtis kneeling at his feet, naked as a newly hatched crow, pleading for her worthless life, offering to fuck him and suck his cock, until choking on the muzzle of the gun and . . .

"Hell, what are we standin' around here for?" barked Cannibal, having regained his good cheer. "We've got work to do—miles to go before we sleep and all that good shit. We're due at eight, so we can't fiddle-fuck around any longer. Let's all have a little toot and hit the road."

Mitch came to earth hard. "What do you mean, hit the road? You mean *tonight*? What are we going to do?"

"You're going to make some money, Mitchie Witchie." Cannibal laughed. "Two hundred and fifty fresh little greenies—your first big run. And just to make things easy, Stella and I are gonna walk you through it, introduce you to the people you'll be working with from now on. All you gotta do is sit back and relax!"

So the three of them snorted perhaps eighty dollars worth of cocaine from the surface of a chrome-edged mirror that Stella DeCurtis produced from her alligator-skin purse. Cannibal then took the two neatly wrapped packages of crack from the refrigerator and zipped them into a large gym bag, which he ceremoniously turned over to Mitch. They switched off the lights in the sorry little house, locked it up with massive Yale padlocks, and boarded Cannibal's Blazer for the ferry ride across the Puget Sound. They nipped Jack Daniel's from a bottle under the seat, smoked cigarettes, and listened to country-western music on the stereo. But Mitch did not relax, as Cannibal had instructed him. Despite the booze and coke in his veins, the *hunger* was tearing him apart from the inside out.

• • •

They got off the ferry at the Seattle Terminal and took First Avenue northward through the heart of the downtown area to Pike Street. The evening was young, but a cold drizzle and a stiff wind off the Sound had thinned the traffic that usually swarms around Pike Place.

Cannibal Strecker turned into an alley just a block from the market, and Mitch squinted through foggy glass at the sights that crept by on either side of the truck. Huddled amid rusting dumpsters and mountainous stacks of plastic garbage bags, their backs propped against walls of sweating brick and cement, were the street people of downtown Seattle, the winos and bag ladies and shopping-cart jockeys, the child prostitutes already exhausted from a tough night on Second Avenue, and the wild-eyed addicts of heroin and crack.

At an intersection of alleys, Cannibal turned yet again and piloted the Blazer into an open area paved with broken asphalt and concrete. Once a parking lot, the site had been chosen for yet another office building, wherein lawyers and accountants would impress their clients with spectacular views of the Puget Sound. It was dark, but Mitch could see the looming abutments of an elevated roadway ahead, which he suspected was the Alaskan Way Viaduct.

Cannibal parked the Blazer next to an abutment out of the rain, and switched off the headlights. Darkness enfolded them, and Mitch fought the panic of instant blindness. After their eyes adjusted, the three of them piled out and lit cigarettes.

"Where the hell are they?" grumbled Stella DeCurtis. "It's almost eight o'clock, and it's colder than shit out here." She seemed worried about muddying her alligator shoes.

"Don't sweat it, Punkin'," said Cannibal. "They'll be on time. They always are."

And they were. Two cars arrived, a dark Caddy and a new white Corvette. The main man was someone Cannibal hailed as Laughing Luis Sandoval, the driver of the Corvette. From the Caddy stepped two bodyguards and a pair of "mules," couriers of crack to various retail houses throughout the Seattle metro area. One of the mules had a name: Dexter, the man whom Mitch would meet every Monday night in some horrible place like this to hand over crack and money and to receive unprocessed cocaine for delivery back to Cannibal.

Though the darkness denied Mitch a clear view of their faces—which was exactly why this spot had been chosen—he got from Luis Sandoval the impression of a small man not much taller than himself. A small man who dressed in expensive clothes. Who bathed himself in expensive scent. Who had battled his way up from some stifling Hispanic slum to become a mandarin of the crack trade in Seattle, Washington.

Beneath Sandoval's amiable Latin charm ran an icy current of threat: Notwithstanding his willingness to laugh and joke and call a stranger by name, as he did with Mitch, he would gleefully kill anyone who needed killing. Of that Mitch was certain.

After the introductions, Mitch handed the gym bag full of crack to Dexter, and everyone talked and chuckled and smoked cigarettes that glowed like little orange eyes in the dark. Money changed hands, hands slapped backs, and everyone was great friends. His business done for tonight, Sandoval said good-bye, but before climbing into his white Corvette he took time for a quiet word with Mitch.

"Welcome to our little band of bad guys, *amigo,*" he said, squeezing Mitch's arm. "I hope you're happy with us. Just remember who you are, okay?" A dim hint of a smile flashed in the darkness. "You do right by us, we do right by you. Otherwise . . ." He made a sound in the rear of his mouth that could have signified a throat being cut with a long, glittering knife, which Mitch supposed was strapped to his forearm in a quick-release scabbard. Then Sandoval laughed loudly, and everyone else did, too.

Everyone except Mitch Nistler.

It was late by the time Cannibal and Stella dropped him at his house near Greely's Cove. They thundered away in the Blazer, shit-brained with cocaine and whiskey, leaving him alone in the dark, cold rain.

He stood a moment in the quiet of the night, watching their taillights bouncing away through the trees, listening to the fading growl of the Blazer's V-8, and hating Cannibal and Stella with every calorie of energy he could muster. Then the hunger stirred, and the demon-taste bubbled up from his guts. His hatred of Cannibal and Stella faded in importance. He felt himself trudging along the weed-infested walk to his house, propelled by a sick urgency that part of him wanted to deny. He felt himself pushing open the front door, moving inside, not needing light.

Who owns Mitch Nistler?

He climbed the stairs in the darkness, arousing creaks and snaps from old boards. The hunger owned him wholly now, and he knew the uselessness of trying to fight it. Every muscle in his body, every bone, every fiber of nerve was under its control, and he was again the man he had been just twenty-four hours earlier—the master embalmer, the artist with certainty in his hands, the giver of beauty to dead and discarded flesh.

Dancing in his head were answers to great mysteries, solutions to ancient riddles and visions of magical faces and symbols. Flowing through him, coursing up from that vacancy in his soul, was the power of Anubis, the god of embalmers, whose red dog's eyes and slavering canine teeth flashed briefly in his brain like a lick of flame, followed by the scaly, horned head of the Lord of Misrule, who smiled horrifically, approving.

And swarming within the cloud were symbols he somehow recognized, that in defiance of any sane man's reason gave him power and urgency—the four Hebrew consonants of the Divine Name, the five-pointed star, the bronze hand, a multitude of others, all conjured from an ancient time when every breath of wind had a message, every tree and stone a soul. These were the ken of wizards and warlocks, of learned scholars who studied dark tomes—not of Mitch Nistler. He had never read such books. He had never studied the grand mysteries of time and death and magic. The knowledge could not have been *his*.

His head cleared when he came to the upstairs landing, and he stood a moment in the pitch blackness, listening to the pounding of his heart. From below came the labored sound of his old refrigerator kicking on, and from above, the patter of cold rain. His senses were incredibly alive, and for a moment he fancied that he could hear his own hair growing, that he could actually taste the odors of old cardboard and rotting wood.

He moved forward in the blackness toward the door he knew to be closed, needing no light because he could feel its location without touching it. Old hinges groaned and squealed as he pushed through into the cluttered bedroom. The cloying scents of the embalmer's perfumes filled his throat and lungs.

He knew exactly where Lorna Trosper lay, and he went to her. Snaking a gentle arm beneath her neck, he lifted her dead weight upward, and with his other hand he worked away the sheet in which he had wrapped her the night before. After letting the sheet fall to the floor, he stood upright, his hungry eyes round in the dark, his heart skittering, his chest heaving. Vaguely he became aware of his hands working again, this time on his belt and the buttons of his faded slacks. With pants and undershorts gone, he attacked his shirt, and it too fell away.

He stood naked in the dark. His hands went to his groin, and he nearly screamed with excitement and alarm: His cock was monstrous, twice as big as it had ever been, a sinewy rod of steel.

Who owns Mitch Nistler?

Down, down he went, until the skin of his chest touched the corpse's breasts. For an excruciating moment his heart cried out in revulsion, for they were not warm and silky as he had imagined a woman's breasts to be, but cold and vaguely moist, like latex filled with something went and spongy. His thighs found hers, and his cock played in the cold hair of her groin. He forced it into her, no longer expecting warmth and delight, wanting only depth. He achieved it. Just as his tongue achieved the depth of her dead throat after forcing her teeth apart with his own.

He tasted embalming fluid and sassafras and lavender and humectant.

He tasted the unthinkable slime of bacteria and fungus, already growing in the oral region.

He tasted the sickness of death as no man was ever meant to taste it, and his soul writhed in agony. His body squirmed and his hips jounced as he thrust his mindless cock into and out of that poor, dry vagina.

He came explosively, and thunder clapped in his head. With every spasm he screamed into the blackness, as if yearning to rouse the faintest whisper of response from Lorna's defiled corpse. He lay silent and spent, gasping, worrying insanely that he was smothering her with his weight. Rain fell, and somewhere in the night the refrigerator whirred.

Somehow, now that the hunger was gone, he managed to sleep.

10

Lindsay Moreland had insisted that the gathering for Lorna in Suquamish Park be neither a funeral nor a memorial service, but rather a simple coming together of friends and loved ones to comfort each other and to remember.

"An informal celebration of Lorna's life," she had called it, for this is what Lorna would have wanted in place of a lugubrious ceremony and tearful eulogies. Those friends who felt a need to make short speeches were certainly welcome to do so, and a few of them did. They remembered Lorna's loving nature, her willingness to involve herself in community projects, her hands-on support of the local arts, her unflagging readiness to do charity work even though she herself was far from well-off. Old Hannie Hazelford—shrivelled and tiny under full-length black velvet, outrageously rouged and be-wigged in blond—spoke of Lorna as a woman of great wealth, measurable not in money but in "richness of spirit," the treasure of love for her fellow humans, the riches of steady friendship.

Carl was glad when the speeches were over, for he had come dangerously close to tears more than once during the outpouring of love. He made his way to the fringe of the surprisingly large crowd that had gathered under the barbecue shelter, hoping that no one had noticed his fluttering eyelids. He edged into the tentative sunlight that poured between billowy gray clouds.

The morning had been cold and dank, and the meager warmth felt good on his shoulders. The music resumed, played through a sound system that someone had set up under the shelter and connected with a long cable to a utility pole nearby. There was Beatles' music from the *White Album* and *Rubber Soul*, salvaged from the stash of records that had somehow survived the terror of Lorna's final days. Crosby, Stills, Nash and Young came next, then Simon and Garfunkel.

The lump in Carl's throat grew hot and painful as he remembered younger times, loving times with Lorna. This was the music that moved her. And him, too. He wondered how he ever could have left her.

His eyes wandered over the tall cedars and pines of Suquamish Park, down the grassy hill that ended on a brief stretch of gritty beach and then beyond to the white-capping waves of the Puget Sound. Cormorants and gulls dipped and wheeled overhead, tankers and container ships lazed in the distance. A breeze stirred the rain-laden trees, producing a sibilant background whisper that could be heard between the gentle rock songs.

This had been one of Lorna's favorite places, where she had often set up her easel in quest of capturing its magic in watercolors, a retreat during those brief hours when some kind friend had agreed to look after Jeremy in order to let her savor a morsel of aloneness. Here she had allowed her mind to roll outward over the waves, or soar high into the billowing clouds. Here she had created beauty.

In better times Carl had often come here with her, for the park was only a five-minute walk from their bungalow on Second. They had strolled along the beach or eaten sack lunches on the picnic tables or lain hand in hand on a blanket in the grass, watching the sky as it sailed by. They had often joked about that summer night shortly after their marriage, when they had slunk into the park like a pair of randy teenagers, to shed their clothes and lie naked in the questionable privacy of a cluster of cedars near the shore. They had drunk cheap California wine and munched expensive Oregon cheese. They had fucked like a couple of insatiable hamsters. The odds were at least even that Jeremy had been conceived on that very night.

Carl tore his gaze from the clump of cedars—

—and it landed on Lindsay, who stood under the barbecue shelter where she shepherded well-wishers up to the long tables on which was spread a staggering array of casseroles, salads, home-baked breads and desserts, steaming coffee urns, and jugs of punch, all contributed by Lorna's legion of grieving friends. Since this was neither a funeral nor a memorial service but merely a simple coming together for an outdoor lunch on a Tuesday, Lindsay wore no mournful black but rather a green classic blazer over a white blouse and a green windowpane-plaid skirt.

For a blinding fraction of a second, Carl saw her cold-reddened cheeks as Lorna's, her grain-colored hair as Lorna's. The easy movement of her lithe frame, the way she tossed her head to banish stray hair from her eyes, the way she crossed her arms—all were Lorna's. Carl felt his face grow warm with new guilt. Even after the fraction of a second was gone, the tickling in his groin remained, and he knew that he was craving the body of his dead wife's sister.

Jeremy sat at a picnic table apart from the crowd, alone in the shadowy lee of the bandstand, dignified and somber in the dark suit that Carl had bought him earlier that morning in Bremerton. With his legs crossed and his arms folded, he looked very adult, very much in control of himself.

Carl experienced a minor flash of anger toward the milling crowd, simply because no one was taking any notice of Jeremy, the human being whom Lorna had loved above all others, the one who would miss her most. Why weren't people thronging around *him*, laying comforting hands on his shoulders and hugging him with shared grief, as they were doing for Lindsay and Nora Moreland, as they had done for Carl himself? He suspected that many citizens of Greely's Cove still considered Jeremy something of a freak, the product of an unknowable miracle, or at the very least a stranger whose beautiful hazel eyes seemed full of secrets. This was perhaps understandable. Best to leave the unknown alone, went the common wisdom.

Carl wanted his son's company and was about to move in the direction of the bandstand when Stu and Judy Bromton approached him. He had always thought them an odd-looking couple: Stu a mountain of rock-hard muscle and Judy a tattered sparrow of a woman. Their marriage had produced a daughter who was large and heavily muscled like Stu and a son who was tiny and mousy like Judy, exactly the reverse of what they had expected and wanted. More odd, however, was the mix of personalities: Stu was gregarious and fun-loving, ever ready for a good laugh; while his wife was quiet and retiring, always on the verge, seemingly, of taking refuge behind Stu's protective bulk. Judy and the Beast, Carl had always called them.

They all shook hands, hugged and traded the kind of smiles seen at funerals. They talked about how the weather was cooperating, the great turnout and the wonderful array of food. Close on the heels of the Bromtons were Stu's in-laws, Mayor Chester Klundt and his wife, Millie, handsomely attired in their most expensive Sunday clothes, in stark contrast to Stu's shabby suit and Judy's plain wool dress.

Carl soon tired of the small talk. The Klundts, who were born-again evangelicals, kept trying to steer the conversation to things Christian, which made Carl uneasy. He found himself moving backward, one step at a time, retreating. Before drifting away completely, he caught Stu's eye and winked, hoping to convey gratitude to his old friend for having interrupted the search for Teri Zolten in order to attend this gathering. Stu nodded and smiled a little, as though to confirm that he and Carl should get together again soon for some serious talk.

Carl found himself talking to Ken and Sandy Zolten, who—despite the burden of sorrow and fear they carried for their missing Teri—had come out to celebrate the memory of Lorna, their friend. Carl was moved. He fought hard to hold back tears, for their faces were slack with exhaustion, their eyes baggy and red. He astounded himself by hugging them both.

He made several circuits through the crowd, talking with old acquaintances from his youth and thanking Lorna's friends for taking time to show their love. The gathering began to thin as people headed for their cars, having dedicated a lunch hour to the memory of Lorna Trosper.

As he watched them go, he thought of what Stu Bromton had said Sunday night at Liquid Larry's: that a darkness had settled in Greely's Cove, hanging just beyond the limits of human vision, a kind of sickness that twisted and distorted the normal life processes of the community. He could not deny that there was something evil in Greely's Cove; one needed only to gaze into the ravaged faces of Ken and Sandy Zolten to become aware of it. Some maniac was abducting innocent people and doing God-knows-what to them. The community as a whole was sick from the "darkness," including Carl himself, even though he had only recently returned to the town. Stu's story about visitors in the night, along with the vagaries supplied by Lorna's suicide note, had momentarily sickened Carl's own mind, to the extent that he had imagined all kinds of unmentionable evil in the presence of Dr. Hadrian Craslowe, the man who had delivered his only son from a life of screaming insanity.

There was indeed something evil in Greely's Cove, but not the kind of creeping evil that Stu and possibly others imagined. There was a criminal here—a demented kidnapper who was, in all likelihood, a murderer to boot. His capture would cure the sickness, once and for all. Greely's Cove would return to normalcy, as would its people.

Having told himself this, Carl began to feel good again. He felt even better when his gaze alighted on a solitary figure who stood on the beach, clad in rumpled khaki trousers and a weathered aviator jacket—a slim man of his own age but slightly shorter, topped with a thick mop of coal-black hair that fanned in the brisk breeze. The man turned from the rowdy water to glance up the gentle hill toward Carl, and Carl's mouth dropped open.

Renzy! Carl raised his hand to wave, felt a flood of childhood joy, then raced frantically down the hill. Renzy Dawkins waved back and threw his arms open wide.

PART
II

Buried in every human mind is a remnant of the ancient time,
when the race was young—
a shadowy memory of the Old Truth in all its grand blackness.

—Shaun Richard Thompson

11

The Grand Island Courier
August 10, 1985

GRAND ISLAND, NEBRASKA (AP)—A psychic led police Friday to the shallow grave of Carolyn Hudsten, 30, the Grand Island housewife and mother who had been missing for nearly nine months.

Robinson Sparhawk of El Paso, Texas, directed officers of the Nebraska Highway Patrol and the Hall County Sheriff's Department to a wooded area near the Platte River south of Grand Island, where investigators found the body in a shallow hole covered with brush. The exact cause of death is uncertain, but Sparhawk has told police that Hudsten was bludgeoned to death with a baseball bat or similar weapon.

"I don't doubt that's what happened," said Lt. Joe R. Roberts of the Sheriff's Department. "I'm sure the coroner's office will confirm everything he's said."

Sparhawk would not comment to reporters, but others close to the Hudsten investigation say that the psychic visited the missing woman's home, where he received "impressions" from items that had belonged to her.

"I don't know how he does it," Roberts said of Sparhawk, "but I know that he's earned every cent we've paid him. . . ."

The Battle Creek Daily Journal
March 15, 1983

BATTLE CREEK, MICHIGAN (AP)—The search for Danny Markins, 10, ended Wednesday morning in an abandoned barn near Penfield, where state police and Calhoun County deputies found the body of the boy, who had been missing since New Year's Day.

Police won't say exactly how they knew where to find the body, but the boy's father, Andrew Markins, 36, told the *Daily Journal* that a psychic from El Paso, Texas, assisted with the case. As late as March 10, a state police spokesman had characterized the case as "verging on insoluble." . . .

The Atlantic City Herald-Dispatch
September 9, 1980

PORT REPUBLIC, NJ (AP)—The nine-week search for Tracy and Twyla Langfeldt, the twin 14-year-old girls missing from this small, suburban community since early July, ended Sunday, when investigators found their decomposing bodies in the basement of a west-side Atlantic City house.

Kidnapping and homicide charges have been filed against the owner of the house, James P. Walterheimer, who surrendered quietly to police at the scene.

Sergeant Harold Klemp of the New Jersey State Police said that investigators retained the services of Robinson Sparhawk of El Paso, Texas, a self-proclaimed "forensic psychic" who is well-known in police circles. After examining objects that the Langfeldt twins had owned, Sparhawk directed police to the Atlantic City neighborhood where Walterheimer lives and eventually to the suspect's house.

Investigators are now trying to determine whether Walterheimer could be connected to any of the other six disappearances of young girls from the Atlantic City area during the past year. . . .

For the second time in an hour Robinson Sparhawk's telephone rang, and as was his custom he let his answering machine kick in so that he could screen the call. Few things riled him more than telephone salespeople.

The voice that came through the machine at the sound of the tone was a welcome one, though it sounded nasal to his west-Texan ears. It came long-distance from New York City, sparking a vision of a bubbly woman who had lively dark eyes and a long black ponytail that should have been gray decades ago.

"Robbie, you old dog, I know you're there, so just answer the damn phone, okay?"

He answered. "Mona, darlin', how's my favorite witch?"

This was not an insult, because Mona Kleiman was indeed a witch, one of the few real ones in North America. She was also president of the National Society for the Furtherance of tne Occult Sciences, an organization that regularly featured Robinson Sparhawk as a speaker at its annual convention.

Mona was very well, thanks, and how about him, and what was he doing, and did he have time to talk?

"I'm finer than frog fur, darlin'. I'm just sitting here with Katharine in my sixty-foot double-wide, sippin' a whiskey in front of the picture window, watching the stars come out."

"Katharine? Who the hell is Katharine? Have you been holding out on me? Don't tell me you've finally taken my advice and gotten yourself a girlfriend!"

"Now don't go gettin' jealous on me, darlin'. She's an old buddy, that's all, with big pointy ears and four big feet—probably outweighs you by forty pounds."

"Are we talking about a dog?"

"Prettiest brown eyes you ever saw on a Great Dane, and smart as a whip. Ain't too many pooches big and smart enough to fetch an old cripple his crutches when he needs 'em, but I swear to God, Katharine can do it."

"Katharine the Great Dane. I don't believe it."

"Man's best friend—next to woman. Hey, how's this for a vision, sweet pea? Me and you gazin' at each other over a pair of candles at Clemenceau in uptown Manhattan, sippin' somethin' light and white, pushin' scallops into our faces and talkin' high-class shit. . . ."

"I'd love to be having dinner with you at Clemenceau right now, but there's this small matter of several thousand miles between New York and El Paso, and anyway . . ."

Anyway, Mona had not called just to chat. She was worried about him. Like all real witches, she had ways of knowing certain things, or at least feeling them, whether through tarot cards or trances or crystal ball–gazing, Robbie could not guess. The ways of witches were beyond him, as strange and confounding as his own gift.

"Are you working on anything right now?" Mona wanted to know.

"As a matter of fact, I am," he confirmed, stroking Katharine's massive head while she drooled on the spokes of his wheelchair. "Got a call from a police chief maybe half an hour ago, from some place up in Washington State—what the hell's it called?" He flipped a page on a legal pad that lay on the cluttered desk before him. "Here it is. Greely's Cove. Seems they've been having a run of disappearances up there, and the local boys are at the end of their rope. They mean to get themselves a psychic."

"Robbie." He listened to Mona clearing her throat. "Robbie, please don't think me crazy, but do an old friend a favor and lay off for a while. Don't take any new cases just now."

"Oh, but darlin'," he said, chuckling, "I *do* think you're crazy; always have. That's what I love about you: You're crazier than an old sow with a bellyful of month-old apple peelings. Why in the Sam Hill would you want me to sit on my hands when I could be doing something useful? And lucrative?"

Mona explained, or tried to. For the followers of the Old Truth, she said, this was a special time, the ancient Celtic season of Imbolc, which had begun on February 2 at midnight. The Crook of Leo, a millennia-old star symbol, was visible in the heavens, signifying the Golden Sickle used by the Druids to harvest mistletoe, and—

"Now, Mona, you know I don't hold with all that mumbo jumbo. I'm just a simple country psychic with legs like a pair of link-sausages. If I could handle a real job, I'd have one, like I've told you a jillion times. As it is, I'm barely making enough to keep Katharine in kibbles. . . ."

"Shut up and listen. It's a time of good things but also *bad* things, Robbie. There are forces abroad that can be—well, dangerous."

Robbie snaked a rum-soaked cheroot from his shirt pocket, which he licked and lighted. "Okay, suppose I swallow all that craziness: What's it got to do with me?"

"Whether you want to believe it or not, you're a very special person—"

"That's true. I'm handsome, urbane, cultured—"

"What matters is that you have the *Gift*. You're one of the few who have the natural mental ability to tune in on the spiritual energy of creation. It's a gift that makes you a very valuable human being, but it can also make you vulnerable, Robbie. Ever since the new moon rose ten days ago, I've been getting warnings about you, and I've been trying—"

"Warnings? From who?"

"You wouldn't understand. Just believe me when I say that you could be in danger if you open yourself—" She broke off, hesitating, as though arguing with herself over how much to reveal. "If you expose your sensitive mind to something really evil. Anyway, it's not forever. The season will pass, and when I get the all-clear, I'll let you know."

"You're serious about this, aren't you, darlin'?"

"I've never been more serious in my life."

Her tone became embarrassingly pleading, and Robbie got a vision of the pain in her eyes. This was most unlike Mona Kleiman.

"Okay, I believe you," he lied, blowing out cigar smoke that made Katharine sneeze explosively. "If you want me to give it a rest for a spell, that's what I'll do. But you've got to promise to make it up to me, hon." His lascivious smile was nearly palpable over the telephone line. In far-off Manhattan, an old witch giggled with relief.

They said good-bye, but not until Mona had extracted his promise to put in his customary appearance at the annual NSFOS convention, which was coming up in May.

After hanging up the phone, he swung his wheelchair around to face Katharine, from whose jowls dangled the glistening strings of drool that lovers of Great Danes call "hang daddies."

"Now, don't that knock the bung out of your pickle barrel," he said, massaging the area behind the huge dog's right ear. "It just goes to show you how a little old white lie can put somebody on top of the world again, right, girl?" Katharine licked her chops and whined as though she understood.

Robinson Sparhawk had no intention of turning down the Greely's Cove case. Police Chief Stuart Bromton had said on the telephone that the city council had appropriated five thousand dollars in order to retain him, and an ad hoc citizens' group had raised an additional five thousand as a reward for locating some or all of the missing people. Ten thousand dollars in all—nothing to sneeze at after the long dry period that he had just suffered.

Not that he needed a lot of money to sustain him. His mobile home was paid for, as was his VW Vanagon, which was outfitted with a power lift for his wheelchair and special controls that let him drive without need of his legs. His portfolio was healthy with mutual fund shares that were growing both in yield and capital value, which meant that his old age was taken care of.

Still, the extra money would be nice, though not as nice as the prospect of ending the boredom that always set in during periods of inactivity. He quit the wheelchair in favor of crutches and set about the task of packing for the long drive to Greely's Cove, Washington, which he had estimated, from a quick glance at the road atlas, would take three days. Whenever possible, he drove to his jobs, since traveling by air inflicted incredible hassles on a man with crutches and a wheelchair in tow. He detested being the object of the special attention that airline attendants lavished on him with smiling pity in their eyes. Thanks to his useless legs, a simple undertaking like visiting the airborne lavatory was an ordeal, especially when there was turbulence. But the best reason for driving was that Katharine could come with him, which was nigh impossible on airplanes.

While packing, he thought about Mona's warning and smiled to himself, but he failed to put it entirely out of his mind. She was, after all, more than a crackpot who called herself a pagan and a witch. She was a published scholar on the history of the occult, a sought-after thinker from whom serious historians often begged insights into the influence that followers of the Old Truth have exerted on history. She was as close to "legitimate" as any self-proclaimed witch could be, and a warning from her was not to be taken lightly.

This thought aroused disturbing recollections, ones he always shuffled to the back of his brain whenever they popped up, memories of those rare occasions on which he had gotten a psychic whiff of something "really evil," as Mona would have termed it. Throughout his career as a forensic psychic he had encountered much ugliness, to be sure—the grisly leavings of child-killers, kidnappers, and serial murderers. But this comparatively routine brand of evil paled next to the kind that caused his guts to churn and his head to ache, the kind he had sensed only twice in his life.

From his earliest memory, Robinson Sparhawk had possessed the Gift, even as a freckled west-Texas lad who played with marbles and slingshots. He had never claimed to know how it worked, but he had fairly strong ideas about how it did *not* work. Spirits and ghosts had nothing to do with it, and most assuredly the Gift did not come from Satan.

Several years ago a fat-headed Assembly of God minister from Phoenix had charged that Robbie was a "creature of the Devil," who was doing the Devil's work. Robbie had countered with the fact that he had spent his entire adult life in the service of the lawful authorities, helping them locate missing people and putting the minds of bereaved families to rest. Did that sound like the work of a creature of Satan? Robbie had asked.

God works in strange ways, the minister had pronounced piously, *and so does the Devil.*

During his early childhood the Gift had never seemed very important to him. He simply possessed the ability to know things that he had no business knowing, and that was that. If one of his brothers lost a sack of marbles or a priceless baseball card, Robbie could usually find it without really trying, merely by using a feeling that came over him when he concentrated on the lost object. While his father was away fighting the war against Hitler, Robbie always knew exactly when a letter from the European Theater would arrive at the family home in El Paso. And once, just before the polio struck in 1945, his family lost its beloved golden retriever, whose name was Spike, and everyone feared that dognappers had pounced and spirited Spike away forever. While holding the dog's leash in his hand, Robbie saw an image in his mind and ordered the family into the car. They motored outward from El Paso on Almeda Road, chasing a little boy's vision of flowing water and shady trees. They found Spike in Ascarate Park on the bank of the Rio Grande, gamboling like a pup and chasing grasshoppers, just as Robbie had pictured in his mind. Though Robbie had been in school when the abduction occurred, the family accepted his explanation that two men had coaxed the dog out of the yard and into a pickup, and that Spike had bolted away into the park when the abductors had stopped on their way out of town.

Not until the following year, however, as he lay on his back with his meaningless legs stretched out on sweaty sheets, the fever having finally burned itself out, did his mother come to him for a serious talk about the Gift—the same ability that her grandfather had possessed. And her grandfather's mother before him. And at least a dozen of the line before *her*.

Robbie must come to terms with it, his mother insisted. He must define its importance in his life and prepare himself for the trouble it could cause. The world was full of people who would readily ridicule and condemn what seemed out of the ordinary, or what they could not understand. He must steel himself against their cruelty. But at the same time he must recognize his responsibility to use the Gift for goodness. He must understand that *different* did not mean *bad*.

In the wake of that mother-son talk, Robbie's feelings about his unusual ability changed. In his child's mind he began to see the Gift as a substitute for his polio-ravaged legs—something he could stand on. Its importance grew as he discovered that he could use it to make a good living, that it exempted him from the study and the toil that the less gifted must suffer to ready themselves for day-to-day jobs. By the time he had established himself as a proven forensic psychic, he fully believed that the Gift would have become his staff of life even if he still had two good legs, despite what he had told Mona Kleiman and others so many times.

Life had been good, despite the loneliness. Robbie had long ago conquered any inclination toward self-pity. Though he had never overcome the longing to discover the joy of a woman's love, he had learned to relish living on his own. He liked his work, the satisfaction it gave, and the certainty that he was using the Gift for goodness.

He zippered shut the L.L. Bean bag that lay on his bed, having stuffed it with folded ranch-style shirts, faded Wrangler jeans, underwear, socks, and shaving gear. The sound of the zipper set Katharine to whimpering and whining with anticipation. She knew that it signified packing, and packing meant that a ride was in the offing. Next to chicken enchiladas, there was nothing that she loved better than a ride in the Vanagon.

"Take it easy, old girl," said Robbie, stooping from his crutches to scratch the underside of Katharine's muzzle. "We ain't goin' anywhere till sunup." Having administered a good scratching, he stood up again and wondered why he wasn't feeling his usual sense of exhilaration over the prospect of heading out for a new job. Had Mona's warning been that chilling?

Once again, unwanted memory stirred—a memory of something "really evil." It would not go away.

Four years earlier he had received a call from the Clinton County sheriff in tiny Keyesport, Illinois, which lay roughly fifty miles east of St. Louis. Four children had disappeared over the span of two months, three little girls and a boy, all between the ages of seven and ten. The sheriff's office lacked even the smell of a lead, so Robbie blew in to look things over.

While perusing some clothing that had belonged to the children, he received the definite impression that a body of water figured into the disappearances—which made sense, because Keyesport lay near a large one called Carlyle Lake. Still, Robbie was not getting his usual strong feelings, and this made him uneasy. It was as though some living presence had drawn a curtain of blackness over his psychic eyes.

He had told the sheriff that he wanted a boat, and the sheriff obliged with a nice big inboard-outboard, in which they motored away from the shore on a hot August afternoon. Robbie told the driver to halt about half a mile out, because he suddenly got the feeling that there was something important beneath the surface of the water, right there on that very spot. At the same time he felt a sick knot deep in his innards, a psychic anxiety that he had never felt before. The boat stopped, and he became dizzy. He made himself believe that it was only minor seasickness coupled with the effects of the engine fumes. A few seconds went by, and he felt vulnerable and exposed, yet he forced himself to lean over the transom and stare into the water.

What he saw turned his blood to sludge.

Later, when thinking about it, he could not say whether he had seen it with his eyes or with his mind, but regardless of how he saw it, he knew that it had awareness. It knew that he—Robinson Sparhawk of El Paso—was there in the boat. It knew why he had come. And it wanted him, just as it had wanted the children.

When he vomited into the water, the sheriff and his deputies assumed that he was seasick, since none of them had seen or felt anything unusual. They raced back to shore and delivered Robbie to a doctor. Robbie recovered quickly. He told the sheriff that he had made a mistake, that the lake had nothing to do with the disappearances—a lie that he hoped would save the lives of scuba divers who, if he had given the word, would have dived into the evil spot in Carlyle Lake. He could not bring himself, of course, to say anything about the insanity he had seen in the water.

And what, exactly, had he seen? he had often asked himself.

The answer defied words. An *evil*, more pure and potent than any mortal mind could ever imagine, an evil so intensely malevolent that it scorched his soul in the way liquid oxygen scorches bare skin—so cold that it was hot. He sensed it could do great harm, both physical and spiritual, that it could have eaten his soul.

But this time was not the first time. On one other occasion he had come face-to-face with the blackness, and the terror so numbed his mind that the recollections were now fuzzy and indistinct, for which he was thankful. On a few other occasions he had sort of brushed near it while poking into mysterious disappearances, and he had simply gotten the hell out—quit the cases with no discussion, no argument.

Meaning to get a good night's sleep and to leave for Greely's Cove with the rising sun, he pulled off his heavy jeans and boots and hit the sack. Katharine plunked her heavy bones down in her customary spot at the foot of the bed. Sleep, however, did not come easily.

Mona Kleiman's warning buzzed in his mind. Though he could not take seriously the Old Truth propounded by the pagan witches, he could not discount the reality of his own experiences. There *was* such a thing as evil, something far more potent than the human insanities that drove child-killers and serial murderers. It was evil in the atmospheric sense, a kind of cloud that hung around certain people, places, and things, something he could damn near smell.

Maybe the ways of witches were not delightful craziness after all, he worried. It was this worry that kept him awake into the small hours of the morning.

12

For Sandy Cunningham Zolten, the ten days since her daughter's disappearance had seemed like ten consecutive eternities. Each had ushered in a new brand of hell: pungent terror in the first days, with visions of the unspeakable agonies Teri might be suffering; then the progressive decay of all hope as Stu Bromton's search ground to a weary halt; and finally the bleak weight of numb depression, broken now and again by stabbing fits of self-blame.

I should never have let her go out! Sandy had screamed silently to herself at least a thousand times. *Big deal, if my daughter calls me an old witch behind my back! I should have played the wicked stepmother, the jailor, the uncaring old bag!* Teri would have been madder than a wet hen, of course, had Sandy kept her in on that rainy night, but this would have been a small price to pay.

"Are you sure you want to work the desk tonight?" asked Ken, having finished checking out the till of the Old Schooner Motel. His face had grown noticeably thin, and pouches had formed under his tired eyes. He had been burning his candle at both ends, participating in the search until it finally halted in hopeless failure, then running the motel virtually by himself. Yet he had managed to be on hand to comfort his wife in the dark hours of each waning hell.

"Yes, I'm sure," she answered, lighting a Merit. "I wouldn't be able to sleep anyway." She went to the tiny Sony color television set that sat in a corner of the alcove behind the front desk and snapped it on. Seattle's KOMO-TV was wrapping up the eleven o'clock news, so she flipped through the channels— *The Best of Johnny Carson, Night Heat, Nightline,* sappy old movies. Nothing seemed appetizing.

"If that's what you want, Sweets," said Ken, bending to kiss her cheek. "But come to bed at one o'clock, okay? If somebody wants a room after that, they can ring the bell."

He took his nylon parka from the closet and slipped it on, because a hard rain had been falling on Greely's Cove since early afternoon. Sandy noticed that his movements had lost their sureness, that his arms seemed laden with invisible weights of lead. *An old man's movements, an old man's arms*, she thought with a pang as he ambled toward the door. He was not yet forty, but the ten eternities had worked their evil magic on Ken, too.

"I'll be in at one sharp," she said. "If you're still awake I'll make us some hot chocolate."

He turned and smiled thinly, as she knew he would. "That'll be nice. I doubt that I'll be asleep yet."

"Kenny," she said, causing him to turn back toward her again, "we've got to start putting it together again, don't we?"

He nodded. "Yeah, I guess so."

He just stood there, his shoulders weary and hunched, like a servant waiting to be dismissed. God, how Sandy hated seeing him like this, and she knew that he was feeling the same about her. Their return to the routine chores of running the motel had been a purely physical thing, not as therapeutic as they had hoped it would be.

"We know what the outcome will be, don't we?" she said. "I mean, we shouldn't be kidding ourselves, should we? Our daughter is gone, and the sooner we accept that, the sooner we'll become real people again."

"Real people again," he repeated, and his eyes filled with tears. This was the first time Sandy had ever seen her husband cry, and the sight tortured her. He was crossing an emotional bridge that they both had prayed to be spared. "I'll make the effort if you will," he said, forcing the little smile again. "We'll do it together. We'll do it for each other."

"And for Amber," Sandy added, her vocal cords straining.

"And for Amber," he confirmed. "G'night, Sweets." He turned and moved through the rear door, heading across the parking lot and the alley toward their white stucco house with its five bedrooms and middle-of-the-line furniture—a house that had abruptly become too big and too quiet.

Sandy stepped into the tiny rest room of the motel office and repaired her makeup, which a flash flood of tears had savaged.

The image in the mirror told her that she, like her husband, had lost weight, but not in the right places—mostly in her face and neck, where the skin appeared slightly loose and sallow. Her green eyes, normally snapping with vitality, seemed hooded and dull, which no amount of eyeliner or shadow could cure. Only her flaming red hair, carefully combed and shaped around her once-plump face, had survived the ten preceding days unscathed.

She brewed a pot of coffee, then plopped down with a steaming cup in the armchair behind the desk. She gazed senselessly at the TV screen, scarcely noticing what program she was watching. Curiously, she felt a tentative sense of peace come over her. She and Ken had crossed an important line just now, merely by exchanging a few words. They had *accepted*. They had firmed up their alliance with each other. They had resolved to make a new beginning, though each would cling to a remnant of hope that Teri would someday come back to them. Hope and acceptance would survive side by side—a small, self-contradictory miracle that would enable the Zoltens to get back to the business of living.

Sandy must have dozed, for she suddenly became aware that the channel she had been watching was playing the national anthem in preparation to go off the air. A glance at the clock on the back wall of the motel office amazed her: It was 12:55. Her coffee cup, half-full and smudged with her lipstick, lay cold and untouchable on the desk next to her arm.

At least I got a little sleep, she remarked to herself, massaging her neck. *I needed it.*

She snapped off the television set and stood up, feeling a little uneasy in the thick silence that had descended with the ending of the "Star Spangled Banner." While stretching she thought she heard something, a fleeting crescendo of rainy sound, as though someone had briefly opened the rear door that led out to the parking lot. She stood still a moment, her elbows raised above her shoulders in the act of stretching. Her nose twitched with a faint whiff of something gangrenous.

Her eyes swept the small motel lobby, which was softly lit by a pair of table lamps at either end of a rather gaudy blue sofa. Nothing seemed amiss. End tables and padded armchairs sat in their assigned spots. A rack of travel brochures stood against the far wall, next to an Early American console TV on which guests often watched the *Today Show* while munching their complementary breakfast rolls. The only sound was the steady patter of cold rain and the buzz of the neon sign above the door, which rendered VACANCY in pink.

Something made Sandy move off the spot onto which she had been frozen, a nibbling apprehension that edged her through the waist-high gate at one end of the counter. She let the gate snap shut behind her and stood still, listening hard to the silence.

Another breath of that awful smell waved by her nostrils, and she wrinkled her nose: What on earth could it be? During the past two days she had scoured, vacuumed, dusted, or disinfected every inch of the lobby and office, needing physical work. The place had still smelled vaguely of Formula 409 when she came to spell Ken on the night shift.

Had she missed something? A barrel of rotting fish, maybe, or a closetful of dead cats? She tried to smile at the absurdity.

Her brain clicked into high gear: Stu Bromton's investigative report had included a reference to a "strong stench" in the car that Teri had been driving on the night of her disappearance. Also, the police had taken a sample of a slimy, moldlike substance on the passenger's seat and had sent it to a Seattle crime laboratory for analysis. The results were expected shortly. Had the stench in Anita Solheim's new Toyota been similar to the odor that now tickled Sandy's own nose? Or, by some unfathomable twist of cosmic reality, could it be the same one?

Sandy would have shaken off these incredible notions, blaming them on her battered emotional state, if the lights had not suddenly gone out.

Hannabeth Hazelford's cottage stood in the oldest residential quarter of Greely's Cove—a stately, woody neighborhood called Torgaard Hill. In the early days the Hill had been a bastion of old money, where sea captains and shipping executives had built dignified Victorian and Tudor houses with views of the Puget Sound. Hannie's cottage boasted a lavishly landscaped yard with towering cedars and sprawling madronas, beds of rosebushes and manicured clumps of azaleas.

At the tick of 1:00 A.M. on February 19, 1986, Hannie's place was dark, as was the rest of the neighborhood. This was a weeknight, and the modern-day residents of Torgaard Hill were either retirees or working people who needed their sleep. But Hannie was not sleeping. In a corner room of her quaint house, behind shuttered and curtained windows that allowed not a trace of candlelight to escape into the rainy night, she sat alone at a special table, naked and scrawny as an elderly reptile. Had any of her neighbors or friends been present, they would not have recognized her, for she was without her elaborate blond wig and turquoise contact lenses. She had washed away her thick makeup, having no need to hide the embrangled wrinkles and creases in her face. Her ancient skull was shiny and splotchy, only faintly haired with gauzy wisps of white. Clipped to her nose was a shiny set of pince-nez with thick lenses that magnified her watery eyes beyond grotesquerie.

On the ceiling was painted a huge seven-pointed star in white, the Kabbalistic symbol of the Divine Essence, and on the floor a five-pointed one in red, the Eternal Pentagram. In the center of the pentagram stood the table on waxen blocks that were inscribed with the long-forgotten letters of an ancient language. On the wooden table itself was yet another pentagram rendered in chalk around yet another waxen block. Resting atop this block was a small hinged box of glossy wood that contained a pewter mounting and a palm-sized disk of lustrous obsidian—a *scrying mirror,* a witch's tool that was nearly as old as Hannie herself.

Her dry lips, leathery with age and still bearing a smear of outlandish lipstick, recited the words of the old ritual. The words were all-important, the givers of power to the mirror, of sight to her eyes. Her bony shoulders twitched and swayed as she spoke, and her haggard breasts brushed over the cold surface of the table in short pendulum strokes. She leaned forward in her chair until her face hung directly over the obsidian disk, and her watery stare bore deep into the black surface, fetching out the images that floated there, absorbing the meaning and the truth that the old words had brought to life.

Suddenly she gasped and sat bolt upright, her teary eyes gleaming in the stuttering candlelight. She clapped an osteal hand over her mouth. Evil was afoot. Not the common, everyday sort of evil that generates familiar headlines, nor the kind that causes a desperate addict to steal a stereo out of a car, or the young father to break the skull of his infant daughter, or the congressman to vote for massive funds to build ballistic missiles while cutting off aid to the hungry and jobless. This was evil of a purer sort, the kind she had tilted with all her life, the kind that had drawn her to Greely's Cove—an evil of a species that human words cannot name.

Fighting nausea, she forced herself to peer again into the scrying mirror, to mouth the powerful words that would enable her to see the truth, or at least a portion of it. The *full* truth of evil, she knew, could never be seen, which was perhaps fortunate, for a mortal's eyes could not bear the whole of it.

The vision formed again, and Hannie knew instantly that her suppositions of the previous weeks had been wrong. The evil was stronger than ever. It was reaching out again to the realm of the normal, seeking yet another human life to scar with its evil. The trance deepened, and she saw the face of a friend, a weary one with wide, frightened eyes and hair of fiery red—the face of a victim.

Hannie tore herself away from the mirror, inflicting on her mind a brutal psychic wound that she could have avoided by taking time to recite the proper parting words. But there was no time. Already Sandy Zolten was feeling the icy tendrils of a predator, and the only chance of saving her lay in instant action. No time now for chants and ritual, no time for casting spells.

She darted from the candlelit chamber into her bedroom and snatched clothing from her closet, her blond wig from the headform on her dresser, underwear from her drawers. She stuffed her misshapen old feet into a pair of sneakers and threw on whatever she had in her hands. By the time she flitted out the door into the garage, where waited her Jaguar, she was wheezing and coughing from exertion, almost too dizzy to drive.

Sandy Zolten stood like a statue in the lobby of the Old Schooner, taxing her eyes against the darkness that had exploded so suddenly, a darkness that seemed to have weight and texture, that bore down on the muscles of her body like a velvet boulder.

A breaker switch or a fuse? she wondered.

Sparse ambient light filtered through the plate-glass windows of the lobby, meaning that the utility lamps and the all-night signs of Frontage Street were still burning. Not a general outage, then, but merely an overloaded circuit here at the motel. Strange. The Zoltens had never experienced any such problems before.

The thing to do, Sandy told herself, was to find the breaker box and flip the switches (Would it be *up* or *down*? She could never remember which way was *on*.), as any other normal, rational adult would do. If the breakers snapped off again, there was a wiring problem somewhere, or maybe something as simple as a pair of motel guests using their curling irons at the same time. But first she would need a flashlight, and she remembered that Ken kept one in a drawer under the counter. She turned to fetch it, and—

The *smell*.

It assailed her again, blasting into her nostrils and nasal passages, a stink that choked and gagged, that generated mental images of bloating corpses with maggots in their eyes. Sandy staggered against the near wall, her stomach lurching. Her mind whirled and swirled with a blizzard of dreads, vile images from childhood nightmares, visions of night things and unborn animals who could talk—

O God! The smell!

She collected herself and staggered forward, feeling her way through a blackness made worse by a torrent of stinging tears, to the drawer that held the flashlight. The drawer came easily open, and her hands rummaged through a clutter of pens, paper clips, and credit-card forms until finding the cool aluminum cylinder. She switched it on, and it became a glaring wand that cast dancing shadows across the counter, the ceiling, the walls.

Now be cool, she told herself, heaving in lungfuls of air. *There's absolutely nothing to be afraid of.* An overloaded electrical circuit was no reason for hysteria. So what if she had been overwrought and jumpy? Any mother who has suffered the loss of a child is entitled to a little fit of insanity now and then.

Back through the counter gate into the lobby. Back to the mouth of the short corridor that led to the rear door. Back through a tunnel of thickening stink that forced her to breathe through her mouth.

At the end of the corridor was a utility closet in which she and Ken kept cleaning supplies, the vacuum cleaner, the buffer—the home of the breaker box. She would open the door of the closet, shine the flashlight inside to locate the box, pop it open, and flip the switches. The lights would come on again, and the world would return to normal. Nothing could be simpler.

She completed the black pilgrimage from the front lobby to the closet door and beamed the light against it. Her hand gripped the knob so tightly her knuckles screamed. Something prevented her from twisting the knob and pulling the door open, something like fire bells and air-raid sirens and warnings from your mom never to get into a car with a stranger, something—

"Oh, Mother, what are you waiting for?"

Sandy Zolten's heart thundered at three times its normal rate, unleashing drums in her ears and cannon in her temples. Her flesh went cold.

Teri's voice—whether inside her head or on the other side of the door, she could not know. *Teri's voice*, clear and sweet, the voice of the happy little girl for whom she had sewn dresses and jumpsuits, given birthday parties, baked cakes, shed hot tears of anguish. Sandy wobbled, and her hand fell away from the doorknob.

"Well, if you're not going to open it, I'll do it myself."

The door opened, though untouched by any hand.

In Sandy's brain, as in the brain of every other human, was an emergency circuit-breaker that trips when the senses are flooded with a reality too vile to be admitted.

Her limbs went flaccid. The flashlight tumbled from her fingers and dropped onto the carpet, where it rolled between her feet. Her daughter stood in the rear of the closet amid shelves stacked with bottles of Formula 409 and rolls of paper towels, smiling so tightly that the whites of her eyes shone all around her incandescent pupils.

Sandy's mental breaker tripped. Her brain did not register the sight of Teri's mutilated face with its left cheek nearly eaten away, the stems of blood vessels pulsing through gaping bites out of her flesh. Or the cloudy reek that billowed out of the closet to enfold her. Or the grin that stretched Teri's lips gruesomely away from her teeth in a silent laugh that could not possibly have any love in it.

Sandy's mind substituted.

She saw what she wanted to see. Teri with healthy skin all aglow, not mottled and scabby and wet with slime. Not swollen and horribly ravaged by some hideous mouth equipped with flesh-eating teeth.

She saw her little girl having come home, and this was cause for tears of joy. No matter that Teri had chosen the dead of night, or that she was standing in a utility closet with fully six inches of thin air between her feet and the floor.

Sandy cried with happiness. And plunged into the closet. And embraced the gargoyle figure of her daughter, mindless of the vermin-infested, blood-stained field jacket. And the stink. And the unnatural light in Teri's eyes. Sandy blubbered insanely about taking Teri home, for her father and sister would be overjoyed. She would need something to eat and maybe a bath, and then a good night's sleep. Tomorrow she could tell them all what had happened and why she had been away, and the family would be whole again, and let's get *on* with it, *come on, baby* . . .

"That isn't why I've come back, Mom," said Teri, her voice rasping with phlegm.

Sandy paused in her joyful weeping, then pulled away from the embrace. She stared up into her daughter's wild eyes.

"Baby, what are you saying? I know why you've come back—"

"No, you don't. Mom, I've come back for *you*. I want to take you somewhere—somewhere wonderful! It's not far from here, and we can leave right now."

Sandy's mental circuit-breaker started to fail, and the truth of the moment began to trickle into her consciousness—slowly at first but more quickly with every passing second: mind-sickening spurts of sight and stench, then a soul-shattering debacle of horror. She saw the hell-thing that her daughter had become, smelled its evil odor, felt its demon gaze on her skin.

Sandy jerked backward and away, stumbling, flailing with uncooperative arms, only to hear the closet door slam shut behind her back, trapping her in blackness. How, then, could she still see Teri's eyes, as though the girl's head were a jack-o'-lantern?

She screamed from the depths of her being. Her own icy hands clawed her cheeks. She felt her bladder let go, and urine washed down the prickly skin of her legs. The green light of Teri's eyes floated nearer, as though suspended in their own evil stench, and Sandy groped insanely for the doorknob.

"Oh, Mother, don't *be* this way," said Teri, so near now that her gangrenous breath stung Sandy's face. "You're making it so much worse than it has to be."

This isn't my daughter! screamed Sandy in her heart. The muscles of her mouth were too numb to form words.

"But I *am* Teri," it said, having heard its mother's unspoken words. "Who else could I be?"

Several times Sandy managed to ram the door open an inch or so, but each time it slammed shut again, as though someone very strong was holding the knob on the other side, fighting her, forcing her to confront this obscenity that called itself Teri.

"Oh, that's real nice, Mom. An *obscenity?* Is that how you think of me?"

"Get away! Let me go!" Sandy struggled all the harder with the door. She felt the hell-thing's arms slide around her, felt its crusty hair settling against her own.

"Just listen to me, would you, Mother?" The gurgling voice became a little girl's. "I made the lights go off, because I wanted to talk to you. I wanted to see you and let you know that I'm okay."

Sandy fought the arms away, dashed herself against the door, felt it give a little. *"You're not Teri! You're not my—"*

"I want to share something with you, Mom. I can't force you to come with me—at least not yet—but if you won't come with me tonight, I'll be back in a few weeks, and I'll be so much stronger then. I'll be able to *make* you come then, if I want to. It's because I love you, Mom, that I'm here tonight: You're the very first person I came out to see."

From terror, from revulsion, Sandy's stomach erupted, and she felt gobbets of vomit wash over her arms and hands and feet. She sank to her knees, shuddering with every retching spasm, too weak to stand or fight.

"That's okay, Mom, just take it easy," said Teri with two voices, one inside her mother's head—the silky voice of a radiant and loving little daughter—and the other belonging to the bulk that floated down to snake its arms around Sandy's shoulders. "It won't be so bad, really it won't. We're going to a wonderful place, all dark and damp, full of little mice and rats and spiders, and—O God, it's great, Mom! The dreams are just incredible! You can go anywhere and be anybody, see and do things you didn't even know existed. I've already been to the castle of the Emperor Barbarossa, and I was a whore to his soldiers. God, I never knew that fucking could be like that, Mom. I've seen cave people and popes and—let's see—oh yeah! I've even been to a monastery in the tenth century. I'm not sure where it was—maybe Europe or somewhere—and I was a little boy who the monks passed around and tortured and stuff. It was great!"

Sandy's will stretched to the point of snapping. That she had clapped her hands to her ears mattered nothing: The obscenities that issued from the Teri-thing could not be shut out. The voices danced in her ears like crystalline music, and she sobbed until even sobbing became impossible.

"It's the *dreaming* that makes it all worthwhile, Mom, the *dreaming*. We can go now, you and me. We won't even have to walk—look! I can take us on the air! See how strong I am?"

Sandy began to ascend off the floor, out of the puddle of vomit into which she had crumbled. Her arms and legs flew out, and her hands grabbled for a hold with which to drag herself to earth again but failed. Her lungs managed yet one more cry of terror.

"See?" squealed the Teri-thing, like a child who has discovered an exquisite new toy. "All you have to do is let yourself go, Mother! I'll take us to the Giver of Dreams, and we'll go to the Feast. You'll love it, I know you will. Oh, you'll be scared at first, just like I was, and you'll fight and scream, but then all your strength will be gone, and the Giver of Dreams will take you just like he took me, and we'll dream together!"

Sandy Zolten's will snapped, which the Teri-thing knew instantly. The closet door swung open, and mother and daughter floated through it, out the rear entryway of the motel office, into the cold night and the relentless rain. Sandy Zolten was a limp rag of a woman who had given up her short fight for sanity, who saw nothing particularly outlandish about floating through the alleys and backstreets of Greely's Cove, bound in the viselike embrace of the Teri-thing.

They kept always to the deep dark, thumping now and again into dumpsters and utility poles, or—on the edge of the town, where civilization gave way to thick forest—butting into rough-limbed trees that bruised and welted Sandy's wet skin. She no longer rebelled at images of rats and Barbarossa's whores. She accepted as inevitable the inane truth that *this* should be her reward for suffering the sweet agony of birthing a wonderful little daughter, for sacrificing and worrying and praying and mucking through all the other ordeals of parenthood.

No, it was not particularly outlandish that she should be moving through the forest as though floating on a cloud, knowing vaguely that she was going to a feast, which seemed not altogether bad. She had vomited up her dinner, after all, and was feeling just a little hungry.

Hannabeth Hazelford's Jaguar swerved into the drive of the Old Schooner, where it braked to a halt with a screech of rubber on damp asphalt. She bounded out of the car, leaving lights on and motor running, and hustled to the front door of the lobby. All was dark, the neon sign and the interior lights dead, which she knew was not normal. She pushed through the plate-glass door.

The smell assailed her immediately, and her aged bones shuddered with an old familiar terror. The stink of the Giver of Dreams was unmistakable.

She moved toward a faint shard of light in the distant dark, a flashlight that lay on the carpet at the end of a short corridor, casting its beam in a parabolic arc against a wall. To one side a closet door stood open, and a little farther was another open door, which led out to the night.

"Sandy?"

Hannie heard her own voice, weak with age and fear, hardly the voice of the self-assured English gentlewoman she had taken to portraying.

"Ken? Is anyone here?"

Only silence.

She forced herself toward the light. Reached it. Picked up the flashlight with frail, quivering hands, and swept its beam around. A lake of vomit lay on the tiled floor of the closet. On the interior surface of the door were smears of filth and the marks of desperate fingernails.

Whoever had retched should have left foul footprints on the carpet, but there were none, and Hannie knew why: Whoever had retched had not *walked* away.

That tears flowed down her cheeks amazed her, because she had long ago assumed that her old eyes were no longer capable of weeping, that her soul had become calloused to the sorrows inflicted by the Giver of Dreams. She cried not merely for Sandy Zolten, but for the countless others who had suffered this abominable evil. For herself, too, grown old and weak—having become too willing to believe that the evil could simply run its course and wear itself down, that despite the symptoms so glaringly apparent in Greely's Cove, the evil might be dying.

As mortals die.

Her mind, still paining from the psychic wound she had inflicted upon it minutes ago with the scrying mirror, sorted through the realities that she had earlier avoided. The evil was growing stronger, maturing through its cycle of hunger and feeding, moving with practiced diligence toward the most unspeakable of its goals.

Reproduction.

The making of another of its kind.

Hannie Hazelford wept. For lost friends like Lorna Trosper and Sandy Zolten. For herself. For the people of Greely's Cove.

She let drop the flashlight and retreated to her car, knowing that she could do no good here.

13

Carl Trosper stood in the empty dining room of his Wisconsin Avenue condominium in Washington, D.C., watching two beefy men load the last of his household goods aboard a hand truck for transport to the moving van. A third man, the foreman of the crew, gave him some forms to sign—verification of destination, an insurance policy, one or two others—which he signed and handed back.

As the foreman closed the door behind him, Carl stood in the yawning silence of his home, his hands pocketed in grungy Levi's, lamenting the stark emptiness of the place. The walls were bare of his treasured books and beloved Matisse prints, now crated in cardboard and entrusted to people he did not even know. Gone were his Roche-Bobois leather furniture and Fisher stereo system, as were his television and VCR, his collection of antique chess sets and most of his clothes.

The home itself would soon pass from his ownership. The previous day a realtor had presented him a buy-sell agreement, which he had executed on the spot. The nation's capital would soon officially lose Carl Trosper as a resident.

He had flown back to Washington two days after Lorna's funeral, leaving Jeremy in the care of a committee: his old boyhood buddies, Stu Bromton and Renzy Dawkins, and his former mother-in-law, Nora Moreland, who had somewhat hesitatingly offered to stay with the boy in the Trosper bungalow on Second Avenue. Carl had verged on declining Nora's offer, for he had sensed her unease about staying in the house where Lorna had lived and died. More than once he had overheard her remark about not sleeping well there. But when it came down to brass tacks, he had little choice but to accept.

He had assured Nora that he would not be away for more than two weeks, that in his absence both Stu and Renzy would look in on Jeremy daily. As would Lindsay: Apparently in an effort to shore up the new spirit of détente she had effected with Carl, she'd volunteered to take the boy to his therapy sessions every Tuesday and Friday.

Two weeks. A fortnight. Half a month in which to clip the bonds to the city that had been his home for more than nine years.

Closing bank accounts, charge accounts. Filling out change-of-address cards. Cancelling utility service and memberships in the sailing club and health club and country club. Packing cardboard boxes with virtually everything he owned.

These were the comparatively easy things.

Not so easy was the confrontation with his colleagues at J. Howard Maynard and Associates, who had counted him among the strongest in their stable of high-horsepower political consultants. After hearing Carl's revelation that he intended to quit the firm and move back to the provinces, the senior partner had "gone ballistic" and rattled the windows of his plush office with his anger. How in the hell could Carl *do* this to them? he had demanded to know. The congressional elections were a mere nine months away, and the firm had accepted lucrative campaign-management contracts based on Carl's experience and brains, not to mention the assurance of his presence in the firm. Didn't he feel any sense of responsibility to his clients and colleagues? How in the fucking blue blazes did he expect the firm to fill his shoes on such short notice?

His carefully rehearsed answers to these questions had sounded shallow and unconvincing. His son needed him. For medical reasons his son needed to be in Greely's Cove—not Washington, D.C., the city that boasted the finest medical facilities in the world. But Greely's Cove, a foggy little backwater on the shore of the Puget Sound, where lived the only doctor in the galaxy who could help. Right.

Still worse had been his confrontation with Melanie Kraft, the chestnut-haired lawyer with whom he had shared most of his free hours during the three months before Lorna's death. Over drinks in a dusky cubicle of the lounge in the Hay Adams Hotel, he had told her point-blank that he was quitting Washington for the quietude of a cedar-shingle law practice in his old hometown. Their relationship—good as it had been— must end. Jeremy needed his father, and Carl himself needed the healing simplicity of Greely's Cove. There was atoning to be done. There were debts of guilt to be paid, old wounds to be mended. Could she understand this?

Yes, she could, and this is what made the confrontation all the more wrenching: She understood perfectly. With her brown eyes brimming, Melanie had agreed that Carl should do exactly as his heart dictated.

Thus it was over between them, without eruptions of venom or wounded pride. In the aftermath Carl felt hollow, having underestimated both the intensity of Melanie's love for him and its importance to his life, a love he had neatly rejected in order to pursue better things. This realization had a disturbingly familiar ring.

The telephone bleeped loudly, undampened by walls bare of drapes or books or furniture. He crossed to the nearest extension and picked up the handset.

"Carl, it's me," said Stu Bromton's voice in faraway Greely's Cove, where it was still morning. "Can you talk?"

"I learned at a very early age. What's up?"

"Carl, I think you better get back here as soon as you can."

"What are you talking about? It's only the twenty-first. I'm not due back for three more days, and I've still got a ton of stuff to do. I haven't even sold my Porsche yet."

"It's about Jeremy," said Stu, clearing his throat. "I've got him here at the station house, and unless you show up soon to take custody of him, the county juvenile folks are going to haul him over to the youth-detention facility pending court action."

Carl felt his face beginning to flush, and a pit formed in his stomach. "Detention facility? What in the hell's going on, Hippo? Is he under arrest or something?"

"He will be, unless I can sign him over to you, his new guardian, and real quick."

"Do you mind telling me what this is all about? Has Jeremy done something illegal?"

"That's a little unclear right now, but there's a possibility that he was involved in some criminal mischief. Remember those two assholes I told you about—the kids who were out with Teri Zolten's girlfriends on the night she disappeared?"

"I think so. Wasn't one of them the Tanner kid?"

"Kirk Tanner and Jason Hagstad, seniors in high school, a pair of little pukes with too much time on their hands and too much money to spend. We got Tanner on a drunk-driving charge that night, remember?"

"I remember. Are you telling me that Jeremy was involved with those guys?"

"From what I've got so far, it looks like they've been harassing the hell out of old Hannie Hazelford. Four nights ago they—"

"Hannie Hazelford? That cute little old English lady? Why would someone want to harass *her?"*

Stu Bromton made fidgeting sounds on his end of the line, as though he appreciated how absurd his story would sound. The facts were these: On the night of Monday, February 17, someone had slashed all four tires of Hannie's red Jaguar, which she had locked in her garage for the night.

On the following Wednesday, sometime shortly after midnight, someone had broken into the municipal vehicle park and stolen the city garbage truck, which happened to be full of garbage awaiting hauling to the county dump the next morning. After beating in the rear door of Hannie's boutique on Frontage Street, the thieves had shoveled the entire load of garbage into her stockroom, after which they fled in the truck.

And finally, that same someone had firebombed the front door of Hannie's cottage on Torgaard Hill at 2:00 A.M. on Thursday, February 20. Fortunately the bomb had been a crude Molotov cocktail consisting of a Gatorade bottle filled with gasoline and stuffed with a rag. Quick action by the fire department had prevented a really serious fire, but the damage had nonetheless run into the thousands of dollars.

"Hannie was lucky it was raining like a cow pissing on a flat rock, so the fire didn't really take hold," said Stu, "and fortunately one of the neighbors got a look at the perpetrators' car, which—"

"Let me guess: belonged to either Tanner or Hagstad."

"Kirk Tanner, to be exact," confirmed the police chief. "A black '67 Chevy. We even got the license number. I've had them in custody since this morning."

"And you think that Jeremy was somehow involved in all this madness?"

"All I know is what Tanner and Hagstad have told me," said Stu. "They've both confessed to the tires, the garbage, and the bomb, and they've both implicated Jeremy. They say that it was all his idea, and that he somehow made them do it."

Carl gave out a disbelieving, rebuking laugh. "And you believed them? For crying out loud, Stu, they're seniors in high school, and Jeremy's just a thirteen-year-old kid! Since when do seniors in high school let themselves be led around by a little boy?"

It did sound weird, admitted Stu, but Tanner and Hagstad had told the same story with minimum prompting, and separately.

A story about a tagalong kid they had met a few weeks earlier in the parking lot of Liquid Larry's bar. A kid who had approached their car as they were firing up their crack pipes, having just bought a couple of hits from someone named Cannibal. This kid had literally charmed his way into their company, with tales about strange powers and promises of awesomely good times. He'd made them feel things they had never felt before.

"I know it sounds incredible," said Stu, "but they both said it was Jeremy, the kid who used to be a retard, or words to that effect. And they described him right down to his sneakers."

Carl was incredulous, and becoming angrier by the second.

"Don't you think it's possible that they cooked up this tub of shit in advance, just in case they were caught? I mean, who better to blame things on than the weird little boy who everybody knows isn't all there?"

"Come off it, Carl, they had no reason to finger Jeremy. They were amply aware that they couldn't make things any better for themselves by blaming someone else, least of all a thirteen-year-old. Besides that, they were scared—"

"As well they should've been."

"Not scared of me, or the cops, or the system, Carl. They were scared of *Jeremy*."

"Jesus, Stu!"

"I mean it. I videotaped their confessions, and I'll play the tapes for you when you get here. You can see the fear in their faces, the way they were sweating and shaking. Jeremy did something to scare these two dirtballs to death."

Carl shook his head and groped for words. How could this be happening, just when he was on the verge of a new life, one full of goodness and decency and quiet fulfillment? What malevolent god had brewed up this heap of excrement to dump on his shoulders?

"What about Nora?" he asked. "Is she okay?"

"That's the other reason you need to come back, Carl," said Stu. "Jeremy's been driving her crazy. He's been refusing to do anything she says, stays out late at night, talks back. And he's been picking up stray animals—dogs and cats—and he insists on keeping them in the house. Plus—" Stu broke off, allowing a tense silence to endure.

"Plus what?" demanded Carl.

"She's scared, Carl. Jeremy's been saying strange things to her, like—well, I'd prefer that she tell you herself. The woman's close to a breakdown, and Lindsay's taking her back to Seattle today."

"So there's no one to take care of Jeremy?"

"He can stay here at the station house until you get here. Which I hope is soon."

Wonderful, thought Carl. My son is in jail at the age of thirteen, under suspicion of criminal mischief. His alleged coconspirators are scared to death of him, as is his grandmother. And from the sound of Stu's voice, so is *he*.

"Tell me this," said Carl in a flat tone that hinted of accusation. "You and Renzy agreed to help look after Jeremy while I was gone, right? Did you do it?"

"I've been stopping by the house every day, usually around lunchtime. A couple of times we went out to eat, and I even took him for rides in the police car."

"And how did he seem to you? Any signs of his being involved in a vendetta against Hannie Hazelford?"

"None at all, Carl. He seemed—well, he seemed fine. A little quiet, a little suspicious, maybe, but just fine. I got the definite feeling that he would rather have been with someone else, that's all."

"And what about Renzy? Did he notice anything?"

"You'll have to ask Renzy about that. I hear that he took Jeremy out to his boat several times, taught him how to tie nautical knots and read charts, all that sort of thing. Jeremy seemed to get a kick out of it, from what I gather."

Renzy Dawkins lived on a magnificent forty-two-foot Hinckley sloop that was permanently docked in Greely's Cove Marina, the final trapping of his patrician life. He had promised to take both Carl and Jeremy sailing as soon as the weather warmed and cleared, and Jeremy had seemed excited at the idea. Perhaps even as excited as Carl had been.

"Okay," said Carl with a tired sigh, "I guess you're right. I'd better get my ass out there. I'll call the airport and get on the first plane that has an open seat."

"Good. I'm sure that's what's best for Jeremy." Stu grew quiet again, and something in his silence suggested that Jeremy was not the most major of his troubles. Carl detected it.

"Is there anything else I should know about?"

"Yeah, I guess maybe there is. I don't know what's happening to this town, Carl. Everything is getting crazy and distorted." He coughed into the receiver, causing Carl to wince on the other end. "This thing with Jeremy is only the latest, and I have an ugly feeling in my guts that it won't be the last."

"What is it? What else has happened?"

"We've had another disappearance—this one ahead of schedule, not even two weeks since Teri Zolten. All the others were a month apart, and I'd let myself think we'd have some breathing room before we needed to start worrying again. That's funny, isn't it? A little breathing room until another citizen is wiped off the face of the earth!"

"God, Stu, I'm sorry." *He's snapping*, thought Carl. The sense of helplessness, the frustration, the gnawing expectation of another tragedy were getting to him. "Anyone I know?"

"I'm afraid so. Sandy Zolten. Happened Tuesday night, or maybe early Wednesday morning. In some ways it was similar to her daughter's disappearance. We found something slimy on the walls of a closet at the motel. . . ."

Carl's mouth went dry, and his bones went cold. He hardly heard the rest of what Stu was telling him, and he had difficulty keeping his grip on the telephone handset.

For Lindsay Moreland, the emergency could not have come at a worse time.

She had been wrapping up an important presentation to the senior partners of the brokerage firm on a new investment plan, one targeted at clients who had $100,000 or more to invest. The plan had generated spirited opposition from several of her colleagues in the firm, especially those who worshiped at the shrine of Paul Volcker, the Republic's white knight in the

crusade against inflation. It assumed that the economy would
shortly enter another inflationary period. Hence, it called for
eschewing bonds, collectibles, and commodities and, in their
place, emphasized resource mutual funds, franchise stocks,
and gold. Her boss had called the scheme "contrarian." But he
had allowed her this one chance to sell it to the brass.

"Miss Moreland," called a secretary from the rear of the
walnut-paneled conference room, "please excuse me, but
there's an emergency call for you on line five. The caller says
it's very important."

After muttering a painful excuse-me to the assembled
mandarins of the brokerage, Lindsay retreated from the conference room to her personal office, where she took the call
from Police Chief Stu Bromton. Five minutes later she was in
her Saab, pulling away from the parking garage of the glass
and steel skyscraper near Seattle's Pioneer Square, heading for
the downtown ferry terminal.

Destination: Greely's Cove.

Jeremy was in jail, of all places, facing charges of conspir-
acy to commit criminal mischief. Worse, Lindsay's mother was
virtually prostrate with nervous anxiety, in need of immediate
care.

Within the next two hours, Lindsay had transported Nora
from the little bungalow in Greely's Cove to the Moreland
home in Magnolia, a posh quarter of Seattle where many
houses boasted expensive views of the Puget Sound. The
family internist had administered a mild sedative, sending Nora
safely to slumber land.

Lindsay left the sleeping Nora in the care of a family friend
and headed back to Greely's Cove. Stu Bromton had said
something on the telephone about turning Jeremy over to the
county juvenile authorities unless Carl could return quickly to
take custody of him. This, Lindsay had told herself, could not
be allowed to happen. Jeremy's recent aberrant behavior
notwithstanding, he had special needs that she doubted the
county could fill. He was obviously still very ill and in need of
his family. The thought of locking him up in a county facility,
treating him like any other juvenile delinquent—even for a
short time—raised her choler. She vowed to prevent it.

Lindsay lost any annoyance over having been disturbed
while delivering an important presentation to her bosses: There

would be other presentations, other chances to show her mettle. What burdened her now was the collection of anxieties and worries she had acquired within recent weeks, all centering on Greely's Cove and Jeremy.

Since Carl had left for D.C., Lindsay had twice taken Jeremy to Whiteleather Place for his scheduled sessions with Dr. Craslowe—on Valentine's Day, which had been a Friday, and on the following Tuesday. In fact, she would have taken him there today, had the emergency not arisen, at one o'clock, same as always. She would have sat for ninety minutes in the funereal elegance of the dusky front parlor, endeavoring to read the latest issue of *Forbes* or *Town and Country* or *Gardening*, wondering just what the hell was going on in Dr. Craslowe's inner office, whether Jeremy was under hypnosis or merely having a therapeutic talk with his physician. Craslowe's assistant, Mrs. Pauling, would have glided into the parlor now and again to offer tea or coffee, and Lindsay would have declined without knowing exactly why.

The fact was, the house itself disturbed her. Something about it seemed unwholesome, aside from its neglected exterior and grounds. The very atmosphere seemed thick and oppressive, too quiet and too dark. Mrs. Pauling herself exuded a feeling of heavy despair, and behind her almond eyes was a wall of hopelessness like you would see in the eyes of a slave or an indentured servant, Lindsay imagined.

More disturbing was the recent change in Jeremy. Since Carl had left, the boy had jettisoned his elegant manners and replaced them with a sullen hostility. On the occasions when Lindsay had taken him to Whiteleather Place, he had sat silent in the passenger seat of her Saab, hands pocketed, face averted from her own, apparently contemptuous of her tries at friendly banter. If he communicated at all, it was in monosyllables.

Several times Nora had called on the telephone to allege that something was horribly amiss. Jeremy was blatantly defiant and disobedient. He came and went at all hours of the night and day. He had started a collection of dogs and cats, and he kept them in the house, but he wanted no part of their feeding and upkeep (these he left to Nora). And though he pretended no interest in the animals, much less affection, he had threatened Nora with some unspecified misery if she were to set them free.

That was not all.

Nora was convinced that Jeremy could read her thoughts, that he had the power to move physical objects without touching them. Lindsay had only chuckled. She had unconsciously chosen to believe that her mother was *not* going around the bend, that she was only sick with grief over the lost Lorna, that things would get back to normal with time. Besides, Lindsay had been up to her eyeballs in work on her presentation and had lacked the time and emotional energy to deal with her mother's wild fears.

Nora had come dangerously close to a breakdown. That morning, when Lindsay had arrived at the bungalow on Second Avenue, Nora had been a quaking, sunken-eyed shell of herself, full of wild stories about Jeremy's bizarre behavior.

"He stays in his room for hours at a time, reading those awful books, reciting incantations of some kind—"

"Mother, really. *Incantations?* Listen, everything's going to be okay. I'll take you home."

"Sometimes in foreign languages. And his voice changes, Lindsay. I know this sounds like lunacy, but you've got to believe me. It's almost as though there's someone else inside him!"

After helping Nora pack her things, Lindsay had gone into Jeremy's room to inspect his mountainous collection of books and had gotten a start. Strewn across his bed, heaped on shelves and piled in the corners, were old, musty volumes with worn leather covers and crinkly pages.

The Words of Power.

The Magic of the Dark.

The Protocols of the Magus.

Authors with strange names like Bishop Gerbert, Count de Saint Germain, and Albertus Magnus.

Some volumes even appeared to be in Old English, while others were in Latin, Greek, and Hebrew.

Lindsay was unable to believe that Jeremy could actually read the classical languages, but the very presence of the books detonated little sparks of apprehension. Why wasn't he poring over real kids' books about adventure on the high seas or exploits in outer space or fun with computers? Had *Craslowe* given him these musty tomes from long-gone centuries? Something about the situation seemed profoundly unwholesome, in the same way that Whiteleather Place seemed unwholesome.

The ferry sidled up to the dock at Kingston, which lay quaint and nautical in its blanket of fog. At its watery edge the marina was a forest of bare masts. Lindsay eased her Saab off the ferry and took the main drag south toward its intersection with Bond Road, past quiet shops and businesses that seemed to be hibernating until spring. Bond Road was slick with rain, narrow and walled with lush woods, a deserted corridor of gentle curves.

Ten minutes later she was on the outskirts of Greely's Cove, where the streets were dead but for a few slow-moving cars and a smattering of lonely looking pedestrians. Lacing the fog was a nearly palpable funk that seemed somehow corrosive, that negated the light of day. The storefronts looked comatose under a sodden blanket of winter gloom.

There was *darkness* here, Lindsay remarked to herself, and then she scolded herself for entertaining such an outlandish notion. Why should Greely's Cove be *darker* than any other foggy little town in this latitude?

City Hall loomed on her left, and she swung into its muddy parking lot, which was packed with cars. After finding an open spot between a Washington State Patrol cruiser and a news van from KIRO-TV in Seattle, she stepped out of the car, popped open her clear-plastic umbrella and strode toward the entryway marked "GREELY'S COVE POLICE DEPARTMENT."

The last people she expected to see tramping up the cement steps from the dungeonesque house were Dr. Hadrian Craslowe and Ianthe Pauling, both bundled in long dark coats. The doctor looked very English in a floppy tweed hat with a wide brim and an umbrella hooked over his arm. His hands were thrust deep into the pockets of his coat. Mrs. Pauling was dark and wispy at his side, silent as a shadow. The pair paused face-to-face with Lindsay at the top of the steps.

"Good afternoon, Miss Moreland," intoned Craslowe with a nod, and as usual he withheld the offer of a handshake.

"Hello, Dr. Craslowe, Mrs. Pauling," said Lindsay, fighting a crazy little urge to move away from the old man's looming figure. "I was just about to call you. I suppose you're wondering why Jeremy didn't keep his appointment today."

"I *was* concerned," said the doctor with an inappropriate

smile, one that appeared to torture his craggy face and stretch his brittle lips to the point of cracking. "I made inquiries, naturally, and learned that the police have arrested the lad. Mrs. Pauling and I came here in the hope that we might be of some assistance, or at the very least to prevent Jeremy from being sent to some detention facility for juveniles. That would be most unwise, in my view."

"That's why I'm here, too," said Lindsay. "Were you able to talk to Stu—er, the chief?"

"Oh, yes," said the doctor. "I explained to him Jeremy's circumstances and proffered my professional opinion that the lad should remain with his family. For the interim, I offered to shelter him in my home, where he could receive proper care until other arrangements are made."

Something about that suggestion made Lindsay uneasy. For that matter, Craslowe himself made her uneasy. She itched to tell him about the troubles that Jeremy had caused Nora, to ask him point-blank why he had given the boy a collection of books more suitable for a druidic priest than a modern thirteen-year-old.

She caught herself. This was, after all, the man who had worked a miracle, the man who had freed the consciousness and intellect of a hopelessly impaired child. Craslowe probably had good reasons for giving Jeremy those books, and if anyone could help the lad overcome his current behavioral difficulties, no doubt it was he.

"What did Chief Bromton say to that idea?" asked Lindsay.

"He explained that Mr. Trosper is en route from the East, and that the police would hold Jeremy until his father's arrival. I'm happy to say that the chief has agreed not to send him to the county juvenile facility."

At least *that* had been taken care of, thought Lindsay with some relief. Even so, she did not like the idea of Jeremy being held here at the police station, alone and without friends or family. If Stu would not release him to her, then she meant to stay with him until Carl arrived, whenever that might be.

"I'm grateful for your help and concern, Doctor," said Lindsay. "After we get things straightened out here, I want to get your advice about a few things."

"Yes, yes, of course," said Craslowe. "You're no doubt speaking of Jeremy's recent behavioral difficulties—"

Does this guy read minds? Lindsay wondered. Dr. Craslowe had the unsettling habit of answering questions before they were asked, of allaying fears before they were expressed.

"—which, I can assure you, are not cause for undue worry. You must remember that he's crowding the learning experiences of an entire childhood into a very short period. It is hardly unexpected that he should experience some frustrations, or that these should manifest themselves in mildly aberrant behavior. To be sure, there will be difficulties, Miss Moreland, but with proper care and therapy we can overcome them. Of this I am certain." Craslowe nodded at Mrs. Pauling, who unhooked the umbrella from his arm and popped it open.

Lindsay wondered if Dr. Craslowe ever used his hands. It occurred to her that he always kept them out of sight, either pocketed or tucked into the small of his back.

"So, if you will excuse us, Miss Moreland," said the doctor, nodding once again, smiling his dry smile, "we must be going. Other patients, other problems, you know. Good day."

"Yes, of course. Thanks again, Doctor. Mrs. Pauling." She returned the nod and watched as the pair hurried through the rain to their car, a boxy black Lincoln parked at the far end of the lot. As they moved away, she remarked to herself how sad Mrs. Pauling looked.

Inside the station house pandemonium reigned.

The vaultlike foyer was jammed with newspaper and television reporters, who were armed with pencils and spiral notebooks, sound equipment, Minicams, and blinding flood-lamps atop long poles. Sandwiched among them was a handful of private citizens who craved nearness to the action, who relished the big-city attention being lavished on little old Greely's Cove even though it was for the wrong reason. Tucked away in a rear corner of the foyer, tiny in the midst of the press of shoulders, stood Hannie Hazelford, in her blond wig and orange raincoat.

Police Chief Stu Bromton presided from the safety of the steel-mesh enclosure that separated the herd from the inner sanctum, sipping now and again from a Styrofoam cup that Officer Dean Hauck kept filled with coffee. Resting on the counter of the enclosure window was a thicket of microphones into which he droned nonanswers to the reporters' urgently

shouted questions about the tenth disappearance of a citizen of
Greely's Cove. Massive though he was in his immaculate
police uniform, the very image of strength and controlled
authority, Stu's broad face was haggard and weary. Pouches
bulged beneath his bloodshot eyes, and the burning television
lights gave his skin a sickly pallor that did not go well with his
freckles.

The news conference was coming to an end, and Stu was
glad. He had deemed himself the wrong man to go in front of
the cameras, simply because the Washington State Patrol,
having finally decided that the Greely's Cove problem war-
ranted its undivided attention, had effectively coopted his
authority over the investigation.

Earlier that day, the troopers had descended in force with
forensic teams, helicopters, canine units, and four-wheel-drive
Jeeps. They had fanned out over the rolling woods and rocky
shore in an all-out effort to find *something*—if not an actual
body, a fragment of a lead, anything at all that they could call
progress. But since Stu had been the pivotal figure in all the
previous investigations, the media had naturally gravitated
toward him once again, and the mayor had pressured him to
grant the reporters' urgent requests for an on-camera news
conference, if for no other reason than to assure local citizens
that their city government was not sitting on its hands.

So Stu had held the conference. And displayed photographs
of all the missing. And pleaded for help from anyone who had
information. And carefully withheld any mention of the
physical evidence collected thus far: mere smudges of stinking
slime and mold found inside the Toyota that Teri Zolten had
apparently been driving and also in a broom closet of the lobby
of the Old Schooner Motel, from which her mother, presumably, had disappeared.

Stu also withheld mention of the fact that the city council
had agreed—over the mayor's strident objections—to retain a
forensic psychic named Robinson Sparhawk, whose arrival in
Greely's Cove was expected shortly.

Not a very satisfying news conference all in all, and the
dissatisfaction was clear in the faces of the reporters as they
packed up their equipment and filed outside. No leads, no
suspects, no bodies, not even any plausible theories.

To hell with them, thought Stu, watching them go, hearing

their grumbling. They would never have believed the truth anyway. How do you tell someone, least of all a mob of copy-hungry newshounds, about a *darkness* that you can't see or touch but can only feel? And how do you explain your certainty that it has corrupted the life of a sleepy little town, that it has spirited away ten of its citizens to black oblivion and caused the suicides of two others, that it's alive and festering and corroding the natural balance between good and evil?

Right, Chief. And what century are you from?

To hell with them, and to hell with Greely's Cove. Very soon Stu Bromton intended to put his failures behind him. He took a small comfort from the vision of himself on a sun-drenched beach in some faraway southern clime, free of the nightmare he had endured for the past nine months. He meant to disentangle himself from his unattractive wife and his pathetic children, leaving them in the care of his shitbag father-in-law who would see that they lacked nothing. He would rent a nice little apartment with a view of surf and subtropical sky. He would play the futures market and Wall Street, and he would make a fortune in the coming bull market. To show that he was not a consummate jerk, he would set up trust funds for his wife and kids. And someday he would be able to shake hands with Carl Trosper as an equal, not as the fuckstick police chief of the old hometown, or the boyhood pal who couldn't cut the mustard in law school.

All he needed was the grubstake, and it was not long in coming, thank God. If he could just hang on for seven or eight more months, if he could just survive the blackness a little while longer . . .

The last of the news media filed out the door, and Chester Klundt clapped him on the back.

"Well, Chief," said the mayor, leaning close to his son-in-law's face, massaging the muscle of his shoulder, "the council members and I have to be going. I just want to say that you did a fine job with those folks"—he nodded toward the outer door, which was about to slam closed—"and that if you need anything, you know where to get in touch."

"Thanks, Chet," said Stu, leaning away from the mayor's rank breath. "I'll keep you posted."

"Just one more thing, son," whispered Klundt. "Millie and

I want you to know that we're praying for you. We're expecting a miracle, Stu, and you should, too."

Which did not surprise Stu, of course. On the rear bumper of the Klundts' Eldorado was a sticker that said: *"EXPECT A MIRACLE!"* And on the trunk lid was the universal badge of evangelical Christians—a chrome outline of a fish.

"I appreciate that," lied Stu.

The door of the foyer swung open again. Lindsay Moreland strode in and smiled a hello at Hannie Hazelford, who had not yet forsaken her post in the corner. Stu edged away from the mayor toward the window of the mesh enclosure.

"Looks like I've got some other business to handle right now, Chet. We'll take this up again later, okay?" Chester Klundt smiled beatifically and uttered a God-bless-you before heading up the backstairs to his office on the floor above.

Lindsay approached the window of the enclosure and wriggled out of her white raincoat, which she draped over an arm. She wore a black-knit cardigan dress that had bold horizontal stripes in white. Her earrings were bright red porcelain that matched her bracelets. She carried a red leather shoulder bag.

How different she is from her older sister, thought Stu. Though blessed with Lorna's bold blue eyes and lustrous, grain-colored hair, the same delicacy of face and build, she lacked Lorna's softness. Lindsay was hard and all business, a real ball-buster.

"Afternoon, Miss Moreland," said Stu, leaning on the counter. Though he had known her for nearly two weeks and had seen her often since Lorna's funeral, he still could not bring himself to use her first name. "Did you get your mother taken care of?"

"Yes, I did," said Lindsay. "I appreciate your getting in touch with me."

"No problem. By the way, how is she?"

"The doctor says she'll probably be all right. Nervous exhaustion, stress. I should never have let her try to take care of Jeremy alone."

"No question about it, that kid's a real handful. Would you like to see him?"

"I would, thanks."

Stu signaled his dispatcher, Bonnie Willis, who pressed a

button on her desk, producing a loud buzz that disengaged the lock on the front door of the steel-mesh enclosure. Lindsay entered the inner sanctum of the station house and followed the hulking police chief into the squad room, where stood a knot of Greely's Cove policemen, sheriff's deputies, and blue-uniformed State Patrol officers, smoking cigarettes and chatting quietly. Off the squad room was a short hallway that led past a cramped detainee cell barely large enough to accommodate a bunk, an open toilet, and a sink. Its massive steel door stood open.

"Even though Jeremy's in custody," explained Stu as they walked, "I don't see any reason to lock him up in there. I'll let him sit in my office or the squad room, where he can read or watch TV."

They entered Stu's cluttered office, which boasted the same gray tile floors and institutional green walls that afflicted the rest of the station house. Stu's secretary, a jowly woman of fifty who sat at a typing desk across from the chief's slightly larger metal one, scarcely looked up from her word processor as they came in.

Jeremy sat in a metal side chair, neither reading nor watching TV, but leaning back against a wall, his hands pocketed and his face blank. He wore a faded jean jacket over a blue soccer pullover, jeans that matched the jacket, and white Nike shoes.

"You have a visitor, Jeremy," said Stu, laying a heavy leg across the corner of his desk. The boy raised his hazel eyes and smiled sweetly.

"Hi, Jeremy," said Lindsay, moving close, glad for the smile. The boy looked so small and innocent, so incapable of fracturing another person's reason and injecting insane notions into that person's mind, as he had apparently done to Nora. His handsome face radiated his mother's goodness.

"Lindsay, it's good to see you," he answered in his slightly British accent. "It's really quite boring here, and frankly I'm anxious to leave."

Lindsay returned his smile. "The chief has probably told you that your dad is on his way. When he gets here, you'll be able to go home. Isn't that right, Chief Bromton?"

"That's right. It might be late tonight, though. Catching a

plane out of Washington, D.C., on short notice can be tough, I hear."

"The sooner, the better," said Jeremy. "I'm certain that he will straighten out this mess. It's all been a terrible misunderstanding, you know."

"I'm sure it has been," said Lindsay. She turned to Stu, whose face had darkened with worry. "Chief, could we talk alone for a moment?"

Outside the closed door of the office, Lindsay asked Stu whether there was any chance on God's green earth that he would release Jeremy to her custody. She would take the boy home to the bungalow, she promised, and would keep him there until Carl had returned. She gave her personal guarantee that there would be no trouble and that Jeremy would appear in juvenile court whenever his case came up. Surely the chief could see that keeping him here was serving no one's interest.

"I'm afraid that's impossible, Miss Moreland," said Stu, barely concealing his annoyance at her demand that he bend the rules of the juvenile justice system. "I had to talk like hell just to keep him out of the county lockup. The prosecutor's office has stipulated that he be released to Carl, and *only* to Carl. I'm sorry, but that's the way it is."

Lindsay's eyes flashed and her face hardened. "But you can't possibly believe all this crap about criminal mischief, can you? He's just a little *boy!*"

"Not just any little boy," interjected Stu. "There are two high-school kids sitting in the county jug right now—a pair of real winners named Tanner and Hagstad—who've sworn that Jeremy Trosper conspired with them to hurt Hannie Hazelford, that he somehow made them do it."

"You can't possibly believe that!"

"Listen, we're not talking about harmless Halloween pranks here, Miss Moreland. What they did was malicious and life-threatening. They firebombed a house, for Christ's sake, and they swear that Jeremy was involved. Besides, it doesn't matter what I believe. If you knew what I *believe*, it would curl your hair. All that matters is what the prosecutor's office thinks, and what they can prove in court."

"Well, I can see that you're not going to give an inch on this," said Lindsay icily. "You've got the badge and the gun, and I don't have any choice but to do things your way."

"Like I said, I'm sorry. I didn't write the rules."

"At the very least, let me stay here with him."

"Miss Moreland, I'm not so sure that's a good—"

"Look, you've been very nice about not locking him up in that—that *vault,* there, but even so, he's just a little boy. He's entitled to have someone from his family with him. As you well know, Chief Bromton, Jeremy is a child with special needs. He's been undergoing therapy—"

"I know all that."

"—and he's just lost his mother. He needs someone close by who loves him and has his welfare at heart. I'm sure that even you can understand that."

"Miss Moreland, this is a police station. In case you hadn't heard, we're running a search for missing people here. I'm up to my ass in State Patrol, county mounties, reporters—"

"And western civilization will collapse if you let me stay here with my nephew, is that what you're saying? For the love of God, Chief, show a little human decency!"

Stu Bromton gnashed his teeth and clenched his fists, but somehow he managed to smile. He resolved not to let this woman drive him to an outburst of anger, not with so many people around to watch. In a shouting match with Lindsay Moreland, it would be *he* who would look like an ogre, not Lindsay. Besides, he had stood his ground against her on the issue of releasing Jeremy, so perhaps it would not kill him to let her remain with the boy in the station house.

In a gesture of magnanimity that amazed himself, he even offered her a cup of coffee.

14

At the Chapel of the Cove, another week of ghoulish business ended. The giant grandfather clock, which presided over the sumptuous front waiting room, lugubriously bonged the hour of five. Matthew Kronmiller's employees donned their raincoats and rubbers and filed out the back door of the funeral home, happy to have shed the burden of another workweek and eager for a quiet weekend with their families and friends.

The last to head for the back door was Mitch Nistler, who, even though he had no family and no friends, was equally grateful for the bonging of the big clock. He had nearly reached the door when Kronmiller's deep voice caught him from behind.

"Mitch, I'd like to see you for a minute. In my office."

Mitch stopped dead and stood still as a statue for a full five seconds, his hand frozen in its reach for the door handle, his weary eyes clenched. *What now?* he wondered. He knew that no other death calls had come in, that no funerals were scheduled for the weekend, that no bodies were waiting to be embalmed. *What does the old fart want with me now?*

Matthew Kronmiller had seated himself behind his cumbrous cherry desk and folded his knotty hands on the leather blotter before him. Resplendent in his dark vested suit and his shirt of puritanical white, he had the air of a grand inquisitor who was waiting for the next hapless heretic to be dragged before him.

Mitch approached the desk and stood with his hands clasped obeisantly over his fly.

"What can I do for you, Mr. Kronmiller?"

The old man stared silently at him for a moment, and Mitch had trouble—as he always did—looking his boss straight in the eye. Kronmiller's left one was of shiny glass that never made

191

real contact. The right one, however, had a mean, eaglelike look that made Mitch uncomfortable.

"I'm afraid the time has come, Mitch," intoned Kronmiller in his sonorous undertaker's voice, "for you and I to have a parting of the ways."

So this is it, thought Mitch. It's finally happening. The balloon's going up.

"In the past few weeks your work has been most unsatisfactory," continued Kronmiller, his gaze passing from Mitch's down-turned face to the gold pen and pencil set on his polished desk. "You've been walking around in a fog. You're late for work all the time, and your appearance—well, I mean, *look* at yourself, Mitch."

Which was something Mitch had been loathe to do recently. His clothes were dirty and wrinkled, because he'd been unable to scrape together the energy to wash them. He knew that his eyes were hollow and reddened, owing perhaps to the fact that he could scarcely ever sleep anymore, which made him appear totally dazed during the daylight hours. He had lost weight that he could not afford to lose, giving him a gaunt look that was even worse than normal. Worst of all, however, were the *sores*: the fiery, rufescent rash around his mouth, the lurid pimples on his cheeks that festered and ran, the splotches of scabrous inflammation on his neck and hands.

"It's clear as the nose on my face that you've been drinking again, and drinking hard," said Kronmiller, scratching his full white mustache as though the very sight of Mitch made him itchy. "And as you well know, you and I made a bargain about six months back. You were supposed to get help with your booze problem, and in return I'd give you another chance to keep your job. I even set you up with a counseling program that Dr. Craslowe was nice enough to provide free of charge. But you didn't take the agreement very seriously, apparently."

Mitch started at the mention of Craslowe, and he glanced up at his boss. "I haven't been drinking, Mr. Kronmiller," he muttered weakly. "And I *have* been taking our agreement seriously. Up until a few weeks ago, I'd sort of been tapering off"—oh, this sounded wonderful—"and just last week Dr. Craslowe told me I didn't have to come back for any more hypnosis."

Which was only partially true: Craslowe had abruptly told

him that hypnotherapy could not work unless the alcoholic patient was totally committed to changing his behavior, that even though hypnosis could induce revulsion to alcohol, a determined alcoholic could overcome that revulsion and continue to drink.

Or some such garbage. The bottom line was that Craslowe no longer wanted him as a patient.

"I haven't had a drink since—" Mitch thought a moment, biting his lip. When had he taken his last drink? Monday, February 10, the night he made his first delivery of Cannibal Strecker's wholesale crack to Seattle. The same night he—

"I haven't had a drink in eleven days, Mr. Kronmiller, and that's God's truth."

Kronmiller's face hardened, and he shook his head, wagging his hanging jowls.

"What do you take me for, son? Do you think I rode in on the last truckload of melons? My God, you look like death warmed over. You look sick."

You'd look sick, too, if you'd been fucking a corpse, thought Mitch with a sudden, welling hatred for this man.

"A booze-hound kind of sick. You don't wash, you don't keep yourself up, you walk around like a goddamn zombie. The long and the short of it, Mitch, is that I can't keep you on. I can't send you out on calls, looking like you do, and on top of that, you're having a negative effect on the other employees. You're bad for morale."

So just like that, you're turning me out! After six years of working for pigshit, putting in long overtime hours when none of the other employees could be torn away from their precious families; studying and watching and learning in order to become a good enough embalmer to handle even the toughest jobs alone, *you're turning me out!*

"I want you out of here, Mitch. Today's your last day. And as for the house I've been renting you, that's another matter I want to discuss. I went over there yesterday just to check on things—"

Mitch's knees suddenly weakened, and he feared that he might topple onto the plush carpet. His head buzzed with dizziness, and his stomach lurched. *Kronmiller had gone to the house, invaded his privacy!* Had he also gone *upstairs?*

"—and I barely got in the front door when I was hit by a

smell I couldn't believe. Worst thing I've ever smelled in my life—and I'm a practitioner of mortuary science, for crying out loud. I had to turn right around and leave."

Mitch fought to steady himself. To stop the room from swimming, he concentrated on the framed Kiwanis awards that hung on the paneled walls, the diplomas and business licenses, the pictures of Kronmiller pumping some congressman's hand.

"I don't know what you've done in there, Mitch. Either you haven't emptied the goddamn garbage for two years, or you've got a dead cat under the floor. If I didn't know better, I'd swear it smelled like a human body. Anyway, I want you out of that place. I've decided to fix it up, maybe sell it. Just to show you that I'm not a complete asshole, I'll give you another month rent-free. On top of that, I'll give you an extra month's salary, so you'll have something to live on while you're looking for another job. But thirty days from today, I want you gone, understand? And I want the house clean and smelling decent."

So Mitch Nistler turned around and walked out of Matthew Kronmiller's office as quickly as his tired, sickness-ravaged body could carry him. The rear door of the grand old mortuary closed behind him for the final time. He scarcely glanced back at the place as he wheeled his wheezing, grumbling El Camino out of the parking lot.

As he drove west on Sockeye Drive through darkening rain, he became aware of a yawning feeling of emptiness, a sense of rootless vacancy. For the past six years he had been Kronmiller's assistant embalmer—a distasteful job, but one that had given him an identity. At times he had intensely hated the job and had wished for something—*anything*—else. He had deeply resented the feeling of being owned by Kronmiller-his-boss, Kronmiller-his-landlord, Kronmiller-his-teetotalling-conscience. But an ex-con with Mitch Nistler's lack of job skills really could not afford to be choosy. A job was a job.

Now that he had joined the ranks of the unemployed, he lacked even the identity of Kronmiller's assistant embalmer.

But his sense of vacancy went deeper.

The blackness that had lurked behind his eyes, the hunger that had bubbled up from the well of emptiness in his soul, was gone. It had driven him to steal a corpse, embalm it, and take it for his *wife*, God help him. For seven consecutive nights he had lain with it, making cold love to it, pretending that it was still Lorna Trosper, despite icy flesh and the stinging vapors of embalming fluid. Then, as suddenly as it had come, the hunger had disappeared, leaving him with a rotting corpse in his upstairs bedroom and fiery sores over most of his body.

He had nothing now. Nothing but a prison record, an unspeakable sickness, and slavery to Cannibal Strecker. Thirty days from now he would not even have a place to live.

By the time he arrived at the sorry little house in the woods Mitch Nistler was weeping bitter tears that stung the inflamed edges of his eyes. He could not shake off the crawling sensation of having been used—by Strecker as a throwaway in the crack trade and by Kronmiller as a virtual indentured servant for six years. And by something *else,* too—some force that had invaded his reason and given him hungers that no man should feel. Having used him, having gotten what it wanted, the force had simply left him, cast him off like a worn-out tool.

The stink hit him as soon as he opened the front door. It was a fulsome stink now, noxiously sweet and laced with the sulphurous rankness of bacteria and fungus, the reek of the dead.

Poor Lorna, Mitch moaned to himself. She had been so beautiful. She had been *his*. He had restored her beauty for a short time and had lavished his love upon her, hoping against hope that the evil magic that had given him his hunger would intervene against the ravages of decay. But it had not intervened, and Lorna had become ugly, as all the dead eventually do, no matter how skillful the embalmer. Her stench permeated the house.

The time had come, he knew, to put her to rest. He would find a spot for her in the woods—a leafy, quiet place, where birds sang and the rain brought flowers, where she could slumber forever in the cool ground.

He tossed his raincoat onto a dusty armchair and fumbled through the cluttered old bureau in the living room until finding the flashlight that he kept there for emergencies. He had never bothered to screw a bulb into the socket on the ceiling of the upstairs bedroom, for what he had done in that room had never required light. After switching it on and slapping it against his palm several times to produce a feeble blade of yellow, he opened the door onto the stairway and trudged up the groaning steps.

The stench grew thicker the higher he climbed, forcing him to breathe through his teeth. Aside from the creaky protests of the old stairway, the only sound was the thrumming of rain against the sagging roof above his head.

Mitch entered the bedroom where the corpse of Lorna Trosper lay and swept the light over the decrepit bed that he had shared with it. As he drew closer, his eyes widened, for something was not quite right. The white sheet in which he had wrapped the body, now dingy and stained with the emissions of putrefactive organisms, lay crumpled at the foot of the bed. The body itself, which he knew he had wrapped in the sheet before he had last left it, lay on its side, naked.

This could not be. When leaving her, he had always wrapped her in the sheet, thinking it somehow improper to leave her naked and exposed to the air. Moreover, he had always left her on her back, with her arms folded over her chest. Now the body was on its side, facing away from him, its arms splayed.

He drew closer still and shone the light directly onto the skin of Lorna Trosper's torso. Irregular patches of green covered the nape of her neck, her back, and her buttocks, consistent with what Mitch knew of the putrefactive process. With some reluctance he gripped her arm, and, fighting his newly acquired revulsion at touching dead skin, pulled her onto her back. Now that the embalming solution had begun to dissipate through her flesh and evaporate into the air, her breasts had become flaccid, her eyes sunken, her cheeks hollow and saggy. The superficial veins of her neck and arms appeared as dark lines through vaguely translucent skin. Her face had taken on that disturbingly blank look of the dead, and the cosmetics that had once rendered her beautiful had begun to cake and rot and peel.

But most confounding was the obvious bulge in the abdomen. Within eight to ten days after death, an unembalmed body begins to bloat, Mitch knew. The linings of the stomach, the large and small intestines, and other organs produce gas as they decompose, and the gas causes severe distention of the abdomen.

But this body had been embalmed and injected with a solution rich in formaldehyde, which should have slowed the process considerably. If the abdomen was bulging with gas, then the fatty tissue under the skin should also be infiltrated with gas, blistered here and there with eruptions. Judging from the condition of the skin, that process would not be apparent for days yet, possibly even weeks.

And why had the body been moved? *Who* had moved it?

Tremors of apprehension rattled through him. He had not been sleeping during the past week because of the noises that seemed to come from this room at night—creaking noises, squeaking noises, the thumps and bumps and scrapings of something moving around in this room. But, of course, nothing had actually been moving in this room, for there was nothing here but a corpse. Corpses don't move.

Do they?

Cowering under his filthy blankets in the downstairs bedroom, Mitch had told himself that he was hearing the wind, the rain, the settling of old and rotting wood that probably warned of the day when this sorry old house would collapse altogether. Still, sleep had eluded him. He had wondered whether the wind could cause the noisy springs of this old bed to squeak, a sound he had experienced often enough during his "marriage" to Lorna. Or whether the rain could simulate the scraping of feet on the floorboards of this room. In the dark of night, surrounded by the stillness of the woods, all manner of explanations had seemed possible, even the most horrific.

Someone has been here, Mitch concluded. Someone had come and taken the sheet off the body, and for some unknown reason rolled it onto its side. Could the culprit have been Lorna's son, Jeremy, who had once before invaded the moldering privacy of this room, frightening Mitch nearly to shitting himself?

He shuddered at the memory of the boy, with his wild, light-filled eyes and his demented grin. He thrilled again to the fear that this horrible child would betray the secret of his crimes, sending him back to prison, where he would be even lower than child molesters on the social ladder of inmates.

It *had* to be Jeremy. The boy had come and tampered with his mother's body. There could be no other explanation. Corpses don't move around by themselves, and they certainly don't become—

Don't even think it! Some things are just too—

Pregnant.

Mitch's heart thundered in his chest like a kettledrum, and he knew that he could not wait another minute to dispose of Lorna Trosper's stinking remains. If Jeremy were to tell the authorities what he had seen here, then they had better not find anything incriminating when they came searching. With a little luck, the cops would think that the boy was still brain-sick, and they would leave Mitch alone with his other miseries.

He set aside the flashlight and bent low to lift her off the bed, trying to remember where he'd last seen the rusting old shovel that had once leaned against his rear stoop, covered with spiderwebs, apparently left years ago by the previous tenants. Cringing against the smell, he slipped an arm underneath her neck, telling himself that he would burn the shirt he was wearing after finishing the chore of burying Lorna, for it would be stained with mold and slime.

The corpse opened her eyes.

As though to protest the move.

As though to warn Mitch Nistler away.

He let her drop back onto the bed. He ran, his mouth agape in terror. Out of the stinking bedroom. Down the rickety stairs and out the living-room door into the night rain, screaming from the depths of his soul.

15

Conditioned to the urgency of a ringing telephone, Carl's body moved without need of mental commands. He followed the sound out of the bedroom and into the hallway, and from there to the living room, where his eyes finally opened fully.

The ringing stopped.

Jeremy stood next to the telephone, which sat on the heavy oaken end table that Hannie Hazelford had lent, holding the handset to his ear.

"Good morning, Dr. Craslowe," answered the boy in his smooth, cultured voice. He had apparently gotten up some time ago, for he was fully dressed in corduroy jeans and a Seattle Seahawks' jersey with the number ten on both the front and back. "Yes, of course he's here. I'll get him."

Jeremy smiled cheerily and pushed the handset toward his father, who was clothed only in his boxer shorts, still fighting off sleep.

"It's Dr. Craslowe, Dad. He would like a word with you."

Carl padded over to the table and took the phone. *How did he know it was Craslowe?* Carl wondered, feeling goosefleshy in the chill morning air. Jeremy had answered the telephone as though he knew who was calling.

"This is Carl Trosper," he muttered in his sleep-heavy voice, glancing at his Rolex. Seven in the fucking A.M.; not even light yet. He wrestled away images of jetliners, airline attendants, and maddening lines at airport check-in counters—images that just eight hours earlier had been real—and forced himself to concentrate on the voice in the telephone.

"Mr. Trosper, this is Hadrian Craslowe. Please forgive my calling at this appalling hour. I felt as though I should talk to you as soon as possible."

"It's okay, Doctor. What can I do for you?"

"Naturally, I want to know how things are with you and your

199

son. I only just spoke with Jeremy, and he certainly sounded all right, but I thought it best to talk to you."

"Everything seems to be under control," said Carl. Jeremy appeared at his side with a thick terrycloth robe, having fetched it from his father's closet like a loving son. Carl wriggled into it and smiled his thanks to the boy, who quickly pocketed his hands in his jeans and smiled back. "I wasn't able to catch a direct flight from D.C., so I didn't get into town until after midnight," Carl told Craslowe. "I rented a car and went straight to the police station to pick up Jeremy."

"And how was he?"

"Sound asleep in Stu Bromton's holding cell. He certainly wasn't hurting for company: Both Lindsay and Stu were there with him, drinking coffee and trying to make conversation."

Carl had been gratified and pleasantly surprised to find his former sister-in-law on the scene, and more than a little touched by this expression of her concern. He had been truly surprised, however, to see old Hannie Hazelford in the parking lot of City Hall, hunched over the wheel of her red Jaguar, waiting in the dark for God only knew what. He had toyed with the idea of approaching her with apologies for whatever involvement Jeremy might have had in her recent troubles but decided to put off the chore until he had gotten a decent night's sleep and could talk like a sane man.

"I myself saw Miss Moreland earlier in the day," said Craslowe. "She seems to feel a genuine love for Jeremy. Is she there now? She mentioned that she had something she wanted to discuss with me."

"I offered to put her up in the spare room, but she was anxious to get back to Seattle," Carl answered. "I expect she'll check in later today." He hoped she would.

"Did the police chief have any more news regarding the charges against Jeremy?"

"Not much. He did venture a guess, though, that the county would decline to prosecute, given the past records of the guys who implicated him. I'm no criminal lawyer, but I'd say he's right. Both have a history of alcohol and drug abuse, and if you ask me, their testimony isn't worth much."

Carl left unsaid the fact that Stu had insisted on showing him the videotapes of Kirk Tanner's and Jason Hagstad's interrogations. Unnerving as the tapes had been, Carl could not

believe their tales about Jeremy's strange powers or the control
he was able to exert over them. Clearly they had been under the
influence of drugs at the time of their interrogations, despite
what their blood tests had shown.

"Mr. Trosper, I should very much like to see the boy—
today, if at all possible," said the doctor. "As you know, he
was unable to keep his appointment with me yesterday.
Undoubtedly he has suffered considerable stress during the past
several days, and I think it best if I have a look at him.".

That sounded reasonable, so Carl agreed, and they set a date
for nine o'clock.

"You needn't stay here during the therapy session," added
Craslowe, "for we may not finish until noon or so. I'm sure
you'll understand that I want to be very thorough, given the
circumstances."

"Of course," said Carl. "I have some errands to run
anyway."

So, at the stroke of nine o'clock on Saturday morning,
February 22, 1986, Carl Trosper dropped his son at Whiteleather Place. Father and son parted on the best of terms, their
faces full of hopeful smiles.

Some errands to run.

A million things to do at nine o'clock on a foggy, drizzly
Saturday morning in Greely's Cove, Washington, U.S. of A.
People to see, places to go, money to spend.

Except that Carl could not think of a single thing that needed
doing as he drove his rented Chevrolet away from Whiteleather
Place, other than the urgent task of escaping the hulking
mansion with its dead and dying trees, its sagging timbers and
rusting gate. Whiteleather Place was a sepulcher of forgotten
boyhood secrets, not a comfortable place. In another age its
halls had resounded with the joyful sounds of little boys'
games—his own laughter, and Renzy Dawkins's and Stu
Bromton's. But now silence reigned. Silence and shadow. And
the verity of Renzy's parents' suicides. Not a comfortable place
at all.

He drove back toward town on Sockeye Drive and missed
the turn onto Frontage Street, so thick was the fog. He turned
south at the next intersection, cursing, intending to round the
block in order to head home for some much-needed sleep. But

a street sign caught his eye, and he slowed to a crawl. This was Marina Street, which led downhill to a little spit of land that jutted into the water. At the end of the street lay Greely's Cove Marina, where Renzy lived aboard his yacht.

On impulse, Carl drove on, feeling a need to see his old friend, even at the cost of rousting him out of the sack. Renzy had never been known for his early risings, especially on weekends.

The street descended past a huddle of low shops and houses to a gravel parking lot. At one end of the lot was a corroding aluminum shed, warped so badly by time and wind that its yawning door would not close. Inside was Renzy's most prized possession, other than his yacht: a 1954 Buick Roadmaster convertible, a ruthlessly green classic with leather upholstery and chrome-spoked wheels. Carl parked next to the shed, zipped up his nylon jacket against the chill, and made his way toward the water.

Blanketed in cottony fog, the marina materialized around him like an ill-remembered dream. A dozen long docks clung to tall, pitch-blackened pilings that loomed out of the lapping water like giant toothpicks. Bobbing in the slips were perhaps seventy pleasure boats of every description.

He ambled up and down the docks until he found a boat that could belong to no one but Renzy Dawkins: a majestic forty-two-foot Hinckley sloop with *Kestrel* stenciled across her stern. Carl scanned the graceful craft with a sailor's loving eyes. *Kestrel* was visual poetry, even at rest in her slip. She had powerful lines meant to rhyme with winds and tides and currents. Her deck was custom-laid teak, whitened by sun and salt. A gleaming chrome helm wheel stood on its post in her cockpit, inviting a helmsman's caress. With her mainsail neatly stacked on her boom under bright blue canvas, her halyards and sheets coiled into figure eights and tied with hanging knots, and her genoa tightly furled on her headstay, she seemed only to be sleeping.

Carl stepped over the lifelines, swung onto the deck, and knocked on the teak boards that covered the companionway. To his surprise, the boards immediately lifted away, revealing Renzy Dawkins's smiling face.

"Will wonders never end!" said Carl, reaching down into the companionway to shake Renzy's hand. "I would've bet a hundred beans that you were still in the fart sack, sleeping off a hangover."

"Well, if it isn't the Bushman, back from the decadent East! Come on down, damn it. You're right about the hangover, by the way. I was just in the process of fixing it. I'd be happy to fix yours, too, if you've got one."

Renzy had called Carl "the Bushman" ever since their high-school days, when Carl—the head photographer for the school newspaper—had perfected the technique of photographing female cheerleaders at the very instant when they were kicking their highest, capturing on film glimpses of their "bushes" around the edges of their satin panties.

"No hangover today, but I'll take some of that coffee I smell," said Carl, thumping down the companionway ladder into the teak- and cherry-paneled saloon.

Renzy ducked into the galley and poured a mug of black coffee, which he laced heavily with Courvoisier. He handed the mug to Carl, who was lowering himself into a settee.

"Zounds!" exclaimed Carl after taking a sip. "What did you do—throw a shot of coffee into the cognac?"

"Shut up and drink it," ordered Renzy, sitting down opposite his visitor. "Good for the glands. Puts hair on your man-thing."

At just under six feet tall, Renzy Dawkins was slightly shorter than Carl and nearly the opposite in complexion. His long hair was thick and coarse and nearly black, combed straight from his high forehead. His green eyes attested to his mother's "black Irish" heritage, as did the heavy stubble that gave his angular jaw a bluish look. His face was permanently wind-browned from many days at sea, and his hands—which seemed always to be in motion, either torturing a hank of rope in the practice of nautical knots or rolling burnt out cigarette butts into little balls that he eventually flicked away—had the leathery look of a sailor's. He wore a dark red sweater of raw wool over tacky beige trousers and frayed leather Topsiders.

"This is some boat, my friend," said Carl, taking another jolt of the spiked coffee and glancing around the elegant saloon. Adorning the glossy teak bulkheads was a collection of ancient ferrotypes, all with nautical subjects: old schooners and clippers under billowy sail, long-dead skippers and traders, panoramic views of nineteenth-century harbors. "If I had something like this—not to mention your money—I'd be out on the blue water somewhere, probably heading for Papeete or Bora Bora."

Renzy laughed loudly then grew abruptly silent a moment. "No, you wouldn't, Bush," he said. "You'd be right here in Greely's Cove, same as I am, same as you are right now." Then: "Speaking of *money* . . ." He jumped up from his seat and went to the navigation station, where he pulled open a drawer and fumbled through books of charts, compasses, and grease pencils. He returned with an envelope, which he tossed into Carl's lap.

"It's all there—seven hundred and fifty dollars, cash-money. Old Subarus just aren't worth a grand anymore, Bush."

During Carl's absence in Washington, D.C., Renzy had handled the sale of Lorna's old station wagon, the one in which she had killed herself. Carl had been glad to have his help in the matter, for he doubted that he could ever have brought himself to touch the car, much less drive it.

"Thanks, Renzy. I'll drive into Seattle next week and put this down on another car. I can't drive a rental forever, I guess. Anyway, I appreciate your help with this thing."

"No sweat, amigo. Sign this title transfer and drop it in the mail to Olympia, and you're all set. I'm just sorry I couldn't get the grand you wanted. Hey, what do you say we have a little toast?"

"I've already had breakfast."

"Not that kind of toast, ass-breath. *This* kind." Renzy held his coffee cup in the air. "To new beginnings!"

"To new beginnings!" said Carl, raising his cup.

They both drank. And Renzy refilled Carl's cup.

"Since you've already had breakfast," he said, "I won't offer you any. You wouldn't like what's on the menu, I'm sure." He had returned from the galley with a giant bag of Whoppers malted milk balls, which he began to crunch down vigorously after taking his seat.

"Very nutritious," said Carl, snickering.

They bantered for another half-hour, catching up on old times, remembering past faces and places and friends and enemies. They had not really gotten an opportunity to talk since Lorna's memorial gathering in the park.

"So what have you been doing with yourself for the past six

years?" Carl wanted to know. "I've only gotten vague details from Stu, and you yourself really didn't tell me much before I left for D.C. What has your life been like?"

"Very good lately. I've been doing what I do best—nothing. Oh, I've done some offshore sailboat racing, a lot of cruising— both on and off the water." He threw a lewd wink at Carl. "Tried my hand at teaching philosophy in a community college in California, but it didn't work out. Even wrote a pornographic western novel that nobody wants to publish. In short, I haven't contributed much to the world recently."

"Well, you're probably wondering why in the hell I'm here at this ungodly hour," said Carl, feeling warm with the glow of cognac and liking it. "Would you believe that I just needed a little good, old-fashioned friendship?"

Renzy smiled and popped a Whopper into his mouth. "That's what I'm here for. I may not be good for much, these days, but if it's good, old-fashioned friendship you're after, I'm your man."

"It's about Jeremy," said Carl.

"I'm not surprised."

"I just dropped him at Dr. Craslowe's. Have you heard the latest?"

Indeed, Renzy had. The story of Jeremy's arrest and his alleged involvement in the harassment of Hannie Hazelford had spread throughout the village like wildfire. But Carl's revelations about Jeremy's treatment of his grandmother seemed to take Renzy completely by surprise. Carl recounted to him what Lindsay had revealed in the wee hours of that very morning in the station house of the Greely's Cove Police Department: the collection of stray animals, the nighttime escapes from the house on Second Avenue, the verbal abuse, the "mind-reading," the incantations and the array of mysterious books in the boy's room.

Most troubling to Carl were Jeremy's sudden and complete changes of personality. With Nora he was a little hellion, and with Lindsay or Stu a sullen mope. But with Carl he was cheerful and considerate, a loving son.

Kirk Tanner and Jason Hagstad had described him during their police interrogations as a kind of mesmerist who could plant urgent desires and schemes in their minds.

"You should've seen those guys on the videotapes," said

Carl of Tanner and Hagstad. "Scared shitless, both of them. Whenever Stu asked them to describe exactly how Jeremy forced them to do what they did to Hannie, they started sweating bullets. Their faces turned white, they started shaking and blathering about spells and spirits. . . ."

"But you said yourself they were on drugs, right?"

"The cops gave them blood tests, which were negative."

"Hell, that doesn't prove anything. If they're chronic crack users, their brains are full of bruises, and they can be totally wigged even if they don't have it in their blood. Trust me, Bush: I know about these things. Crack is cocaine, and cocaine can eat up your mind, make you see and feel things that aren't there."

"That's what I've been telling myself," said Carl. "And that's what I intend to tell the prosecutor if he presses the case against Jeremy."

"Good man."

"Did you notice anything wrong with Jeremy when you were with him?"

"He seemed perfectly normal to me. His attitude was downright sunny, in fact."

Carl got up to stretch his legs and wandered around the wood-paneled saloon of the boat, absently eyeing the brass-framed pictures that hung on the bulkheads. One, a ferrotype hazy with age, wrinkled and cracked here and there beneath its protective glass, was a portrait of two men. On the left was a grizzled seaman dressed in the dark, bunchy uniform of a ship's captain. On the right was a taller man with a long face, wearing a somber suit and thick, steel-framed spectacles that exaggerated his watery eyes. Something about the taller man's face disturbed Carl, though he could not say what it was. He leaned close to the bulkhead and studied the picture closely.

"Who's this?" he asked Renzy. "Looks kind of familiar."

Renzy's mood seemed to darken just a little, as though a cloud had scuttered over the sun, except that the sun was irrelevant here in the saloon of the *Kestrel*.

"That, my friend, is no one other than the redoubtable Captain Tristan Whiteleather," he said, "the builder of White-leather Place. That picture was taken in 1895, according to the writing on the back. I'd show you, except it's screwed to the bulkhead and I'm too lazy to dig for a screwdriver."

"Where did you get it?"

Renzy hesitated, as though sorting through discarded memories.

"My parents' estate," he answered finally. Carl winced. "There was an old trunk in the basement of the house, full of documents and files that had apparently belonged to Whiteleather. After Mom and Dad—" He stammered and cleared his throat, causing Carl to regret having noticed the picture at all. "After they died, I donated it to the Greely's Cove Historical Society but kept out a few things. This was one of them."

"I'm sorry, Renzy," said Carl. "I didn't mean to rip open—"

"Hey, don't worry about it. I'm a big boy now, and I can talk about it without choking up—most of the time." He took a drag on his cigarette. "Remember that old vault in the basement of the house, the one my father always told us to stay away from?"

Carl remembered. Renzy's father had adamantly warned the boys never to play near the locked steel door in a dark, musty corner of the basement of Whitcleather Place. But, of course, they *had* played near it, had tested its massive lock and pressed their ears against the cold metal, listening for hints of the creeping dangers that surely lay on the other side.

"The trunk was next to it, along with a lot of other junk from the last century. There's a rumor among the local history buffs that Whiteleather had built a secret passage off the vault, but nobody has been able to figure out whether it really exists. Anyway, thc whole question became moot when I sold the place to Mrs. Pauling. I doubt whether she and Dr. Craslowe would let anybody poke around in the vault, secret passage or no secret passage."

"What about the other guy in the picture?" Carl wanted to know. "Was he a friend of Captain Whiteleather's?"

Renzy narrowed his eyes on the picture. "There was a name written on the back along with Whiteleather's, but the ink was faded out, like somebody had spilled coffee on it. All I could make out was the word *merchant,* which I suspect is what the guy was. The picture was taken in Sumatra."

"As in Southeast Asia?"

"For all I know, it could have been Sumatra, Okalahoma," said Renzy slyly.

"But wasn't Captain Whiteleather one of those dauntless traders who plied the South Seas?"

"That's what the legends say. And he must've made a handsome living at it, too. The mansion he built is certainly no shack, as you and I well know."

Renzy retreated to the gallery to fill their coffee mugs yet one more time. "What do you say we get down to serious business?" he said, after returning and handing over Carl's mug. "First thing we've got to worry about is getting you back into the groove here in good old Greely's Cove. Let's see, your living arrangements are taken care of, right?"

They were, answered Carl. He and Jeremy would live in the bungalow on Second, where Carl and Lorna had begun their married life. The red tape of probating Lorna's estate was a mere formality.

"Good," said Renzy. "Now, what about a law office? You can't nail your shingle to thin air."

True. Carl's plan was to convert Lorna's gallery on Frontage Street, which entailed yet more red tape in probate court—a hassle, but not an insurmountable one. Lorna's remaining inventory of paintings, sculptures, and art supplies would have to be auctioned off, a task that Carl did not look forward to. Then carpenters and painters would have to be brought in to undertake the necessary remodeling.

Renzy offered to ramrod the auction, to lend his hands and talents to tying up all the other loose ends.

"You said you wanted a little old-fashioned friendship, didn't you?" he said, countering Carl's protest over imposing his burdens on someone else. "Besides, I have nothing but time until the weather clears up. You can repay me by serving as first mate on a long cruise to the San Juans. We'll shanghai that kid of yours and teach him how to sail, so you and I can sit down here in the saloon and drink. Maybe we can even coax Stu along, provided we can load enough beer aboard. Sounds good, doesn't it?"

It did sound good. But Carl wanted more from his new existence than relaxation, he told Renzy. He intended to involve himself in worthy projects and causes, visiting old people in rest homes, perhaps, or volunteering to help teach illiterate adults to read. He wanted to give something of himself to the community, as much to set a worthy example for his son as to find self-fulfillment.

"Good God!" exclaimed Renzy. "You might even set a good example for *me*! You'd better watch out, though: If you do too many good things around this town, someone might try to get you back into politics."

"Never! I'm through with politics forever."

"Never say never, Bush. The fact is, this town could use a new mayor."

"Would you stop? The thought of going into politics makes me nauseous, and besides that, we have a perfectly good mayor."

"Yeah, if you like Bible-thumping bigots. Chester Klundt is one of those unctuous types who thinks that anyone who disagrees with him is an apostate of Hell or an agent of Moscow. We need to be rid of him, and you just might be the man."

"Renzy, for the last time: I'm not going back into politics!"

"Not even if there's an honest draft?" Renzy's face beamed as he needled his old friend. "Hell, I'd run your campaign for you. I can see the slogan now, plastered all over town on billboards and telephone poles, on bumper stickers and yard signs: *Carl Trosper: Flexible but Not Flaccid.*"

Suddenly, Carl could not hold back the giggles, and they squirted out between his scowling lips. Seconds later he was laughing loudly with Renzy, feeling better about himself and the world than he had in weeks, or maybe even months, or maybe even years.

16

Robinson Sparhawk finished his Belgian waffle in The Coffee Shoppe of the West Cove Motor Inn, gathered up his metal crutches, and hobbled back to his room. Katharine welcomed him as though he had been away for a decade and not a mere forty-five minutes, dancing around the room with worshipful joy, making great thuds on the carpet.

"Calm down, darlin'," Robbie told the Great Dane while scratching the area between her pointed ears. "You didn't really think you'd been abandoned now, did you?" She jiggeted her tail and raised a paw to shake hands, telling him that this was exactly what she had thought.

After putting on his sheepskin jacket with the white-fleece lining, a garment he seldom if ever needed in El Paso but that he kept for winter trips to northern climes, Robbie hobbled to the mirror and checked himself for presentability: Except for his puny, link-sausage legs, he didn't look half-bad for fifty-one. His salt-and-pepper hair was still thick and wavy, his jaw still square, his brown eyes bright and lively despite the squint lines at the corners. Like most west Texans, his face was sun-bronzed and healthy-looking. He straightened his string tie with its slide of hand-tooled Mexican silver and headed for the door, ready for a day's work.

"Now, be a good girl and heel," he ordered Katharine, "and don't be slobbering on the carpets, damn it. I had to talk my ass off to get you in here, told all kinds of lies about how clean and quiet you are."

The huge dog whimpered and fell in beside him, a model of good behavior.

The parking lot of the West Cove Motor Inn was a dreamscape of fog—not Carl Sandburg's fog on cat's paws, but a grainy and coarse-textured cloud that lay heavy on the land. Robbie made his way carefully to his Volkswagen Vanagon, which he had parked in a space reserved for handicapped people, and waited while Katharine did her morning duty in the shrubbery that bordered the lot.

After letting her into the van through its cargo door, he undertook the task of positioning himself in the driver's seat. A push of a button activated a motorized lift that rotated a wheelchair and lowered it to street-level from its spot behind the steering wheel. Robbie sat down in the chair, pushed the button again, and rode upward and into the cab of the van, where the chair locked into place. On the steering wheel were two movable grips—one for the throttle and another for the brakes—which let him drive solely with his hands, since his feet and legs were virtually useless. These expensive modifications were a gift from the International Association of Chiefs of Police in recognition of Robbie's long and illustrious service to the criminal justice system, a gift that he could never have afforded to give himself and one that provided a measure of freedom that he otherwise could only have dreamed about.

Robbie started the engine. In accordance with the desk clerk's directions, he went south on Frontage Street toward City Hall and the Greely's Cove Police Department, driving at a snail's pace through the drizzly fog, past storefronts and shops that would have looked at home in any small American town. Something in the atmosphere disturbed him: an arctic silence that seemed unnatural even on a sleepy Saturday morning, an insulating numbness that voided the sun, the sky, even the hush of the tart breeze.

He thought of the island in *The Tempest*, of the beastlike Caliban's lament in Act II: "All the infections that the sun sucks up from bogs, fens, flats . . ." He cut himself off upon discovering that he was reciting the lines aloud.

Infections. The town was a capsule in a dream and, like Caliban's island, saturated with a feeling of enchantment. An *island:* the thought made him uncomfortable.

Tucked away in the bowels of City Hall, the police department had all the trappings of its counterparts throughout small-town America, except for its lack of a wheelchair ramp alongside the damp concrete steps that descended to its main entrance. The heavy door was yet another barrier to be surmounted, and he nearly lost his balance as he heaved it open. With Katharine at his heel, he approached the walk-up window and waited for the dispatcher to finish on the telephone. A musty, basementlike smell hung in the air. Taped to the colorless plaster walls were posters that pleaded for support of the local police, vigilance against neighborhood crime, contributions to the March of Dimes.

"How-do, sweet thing," said Robbie to the dispatcher after she hung up the telephone, "my name's Sparhawk. This here's Katharine"—Bonnie Willis rose from her seat to peer over the counter at the huge dog who stood at Robbie's side—"and we're here to see the police chief. I think he's expecting us."

Bonnie's eyes, apparently, had never beheld a canine of Katharine's proportions, for they grew big as half-dollars.

"Oh, you must be—" She sat down again. Did the rules allow dogs in the station house? Or small horses?

"I'm the psychic y'all sent for. And don't worry about Katharine—friendliest little old pooch you ever saw."

Bonnie ushered man and dog into the squad room, where a grim-faced Washington State Patrol sergeant and a pair of official-looking civilians were hunched over a table. None of the three gave more than a quick glance at the visitors. Splayed before them were topographical maps that flopped over the edges of the table, leading Robbie to suppose that they were coordinating the search for the town's missing citizens. The dispatcher disappeared briefly through a door at the end of a short hallway, then reappeared to motion Robbie in.

"Mr. Sparhawk, I'm Stu Bromton," said the mountainous, blunt-featured man who rose from his desk in the tiny office. "Welcome to Greely's Cove. This is Officer Dean Hauck, sort of my right-hand man."

Robbie leaned on his right crutch and shook the offered hands, grinning from ear to ear. "Right pleased to meet you both. This here's Katharine, named after Katharine Hepburn, prettiest woman alive except for Miss Willis here, whose first name I'm sad to say I don't know."

Bonnie Willis fingered her plastic name tag and blushed hotly while Stu introduced her. "I'll get some coffee," she said, after shaking Robbie's hand, and hurried out. Officer Hauck positioned a chair for Robbie in front of the chief's desk, and all three sat.

"Mind if I stink up your office?" asked Robbie, pulling a rum-soaked cheroot from his shirt pocket.

"Not at all," said Stu. "Maybe it'll deaden the taste of the coffee." Robbie chuckled and wondered aloud why the worst coffee in the continental United States was found in police-station houses. Hauck jumped from his chair to fetch an ashtray.

"I hope you'll forgive my informality," said Stu, alluding to the stained sweat suit he was wearing in place of a police uniform. "Just got back from my morning run. I was about to hit the shower when you got here."

"You run in this pea soup?" asked Robbie, lighting up. "Sounds like a good way to get hit by a truck."

"If I didn't run, I'd weight about six hundred pounds," said the chief. "It's also a good way to unwind, burn off a little anxiety. God knows I've got enough of *that*."

Robbie nodded with sympathy and decided that he liked Bromton. Here was a strong man who was not afraid to admit his weaknesses, and he had a sense of humor to boot.

Bonnie administered coffee, and the men got down to business. After going over the terms of Robbie's payment in return for services, Stu recounted with more detail than Robbie needed the tragic story that had begun in June of the previous year, nearly nine months past, a story of people who simply vanished on a monthly basis—normal, everyday people who had lived quiet, unremarkable lives. Good folks, all of them: high-school kids like Jennifer Spenser, Josh Jernburg, and Teri Zolten; an old widow like Elvira Cashmore, who had left a rhubarb pie in the oven; hardworking, salt-of-the-earth citizens like Monty Pirtz, the disabled Vietnam vet, and Wendell Greenfield and Peggy Birch and Elizabeth Zaske. The most recent disappearance, that of Sandy Zolten, had occurred a mere ten days after her daughter's.

"I don't think I'm overstating the situation when I say that you just might be our last hope," concluded Stu. "The State Patrol is on the scene in force now, but they haven't done any better than we have, and quite frankly, Mr. Sparhawk, I don't expect them to."

"Not being one to stand on ceremony, I'd appreciate it if you'd call me Robbie," said the psychic, "and if you don't mind, I'll call you Stu."

Then he fell silent, gazing into space while stroking his chin, thinking. The worming anxiety that he had felt during the drive from the motel worsened: This case was unnervingly unique. In all the other serial murder cases he'd undertaken, there were rigid patterns. The victims of homicidal sex maniacs, for example, were all of the same sex, had the same color hair, or were of the same age or build or occupation (prostitutes, notably). Their killers kept to an unbending routine that had major motivational significance. Not that Robbie ever brought these patterns into play: He merely used feeling—not rationale or deduction—in locating bodies or material evidence. His psychic gift did not require reasoning.

That this case apparently had no discernible pattern to it, except for the monthly regularity of the disappearances—and even this pattern had recently fallen apart—bothered him. Patterns, after all, lead to explanations that normal men can understand. Sexual and mental derangement, schizophrenia, and all the other psychoses that drive child-killers and rapists and ax-murderers are explicable, if no less heinous. But this case had no pattern, suggesting that there may be no reason for the tragedies other than pure evil.

An old witch's warning rang in his mind.

"So where do we start?" asked Stu, sipping his coffee. "How do you usually approach these things?"

"Normally we start with the physical evidence," answered Robbie. "I take a look at it, paw through it, if that's possible, and wait for the feelings to hit me. If there's no physical evidence to speak of, then I ask for items that belonged to the victims, and I go through the same routine. Simple as that."

Dean Hauck, who had been sitting quietly, as though waiting for an opportunity to fetch more coffee or to empty Robbie's ashtray, spoke up for the first time.

"I've been doing some reading about your cases, Mr. Sparhawk, and I've gotten a pretty good idea of what you need. For the last couple of days I've been collecting things that belonged to the missing people—clothes, jewelry, tools, stuff like that—and I've stored them in the evidence locker. Would you like to see them?"

Robbie smiled at the young cop and said, "Sounds good to me, son. Stu here told me on the phone that it was your idea to give me a call. That so?"

"Yes, sir. I first heard about you at the law-enforcement academy. You're pretty famous, you know."

Robbie's smile broadened. In Hauck's young, earnest face he saw competence and dedication, the makings of a police chief someday, maybe even a politician.

"Let's start with any evidence found at the scenes of the disappearances—assuming you found some."

"There isn't much," said Stu. "All we have is some kind of gooey slime that was on the seat of a car, the same stuff we found later on the walls of a closet in the motel office, where Sandy Zolten was last seen. We sent it to the crime lab in Seattle, and they sent it back with a short report. Why don't you bring it in, Dean? It's in the refrigerator."

Officer Dean Hauck leapt to the errand.

He returned shortly with a pair of petri dishes in one hand and a sheaf of papers in the other: the physical evidence and the report from the crime lab. Robbie suffered a minor thrill of apprehension as Hauck set the petri dishes on the desk before him. What was it, he wondered—the first inkling of psychic impression, even before the lids were off the petri dishes? This seemed unlikely. He bent over the dishes, and Hauck offered him the lab report.

"Do you mind reading it to me, son?" he asked the young cop. "I left my specs in the van."

Hauck read aloud from the neatly typewritten forms.

" 'Subject: semisolid, moldlike substance taken from passenger seat of automobile belonging to Mrs. Anita Solheim of Greely's Cove, Washington,' and it goes on about the dates, locations, and everything. Here we go.

" 'Sample contains several varieties of live Schizomycetic bacterial colonies of filamentous and single-celled bodies, of the kinds associated with the putrefactive process in postmortem vertebrates, particularly mammals; sample also contains several varieties of Mu—' " Hauck stumbled over the tough scientific jargon. " 'Mucoralic fungus (mold) consistent with organic decay; also traces of soil, soft-wood fiber, water and human blood. Though the analysis proved inconclusive with respect to the origin of the sample . . .' "

Robbie peeled away the cellophane tape that held the lid to one of the dishes, then removed the lid and set it down. Inside was a moist, brownish-green substance that looked as though it had been scraped from the bottom of a septic tank. Suddenly his eyes blurred, and his stomach wrenched. A dull, hot ache spread from the base of his skull to the back of his eyes.

"'. . . Its components compare positively to known substances found on the clothing of deceased human remains. The results of the analysis do not rule out, however, that the sample could have come from an injured or dying vertebrate, the condition of which would accommodate the specified organic and inorganic materials and specimens.'"

The sick knot in Robbie's guts was the one he had felt years before while looking over the transom of a boat into the water of Carlyle Lake, near the innocent town of Keyesport, Illinois, where something not so innocent had taken away three little girls and a little boy over two months' time. Where Robbie had been drawn to the water—to a feeling of freezing, stinking blackness.

The feeling washed over him now, spiking his head with pain. *It knew why he had come. And it wanted him, just as it had wanted the children.*

Just as it had taken the citizens of Greely's Cove.

The petri dish fell from his hands. Robbie convulsed and shuddered in his chair. Before Stu Bromton or Dean Hauck could move to help him, his stomach erupted, and he vomited his Belgian waffle and morning coffee all over his hands, his lap, the surface of Stu's desk. Katharine yipped and whined with fright. Hauck just managed to throw an arm around Robbie's shoulders to stop him from careening off his chair to the floor.

In the emergency room of the tiny but well-equipped hospital in Poulsbo, Washington, which was only a short drive northwest of Greely's Cove, a young physician named Heinecke pronounced Robinson Sparhawk healthy, if empty of stomach. Food poisoning was the tentative diagnosis. Heinecke suggested a day of rest, plenty of liquids, and call-me-in-the-morning-if-you're-not-better. Stu Bromton drove Robbie and his dog back to their room at the West Cove Motor Inn.

"We'll keep your van at the station house until you're well enough to pick it up," said Stu, after helping the psychic onto the queen-size bed and stacking pillows for him to lean on. "I'll drop by for you in the morning."

"I'm well enough *now*, God damn it," said Robbie, lighting a cigar. "You heard the doc: It was only a little food poisoning. I reckon I should stop rooting around in garbage cans. Anyway, I sure appreciate all the trouble you boys have gone to."

Stu drew a chair up next to the bed and sat down, which Katharine took as an invitation to lay her chin on his knee. He scratched her ear while she drooled on his sweatpants.

Robbie studied the police chief's face and got a nibbling psychic signal, the kind he sometimes felt after a blast of sensation like the one that had flattened him a few hours earlier. A strong experience often left his mind bruised and overly sensitive, enabling him to pick up snippets of other people's thoughts and emotions.

"I get the definite impression that there's more to this business of vanishing people than you're lettin' on. Like maybe you haven't told me the whole story."

The way Stu dropped his stare confirmed Robbie's suspicion. "I should've known better than to try to hold out on a psychic," he said in a feeble attempt at levity.

"Honesty's always the best policy, Bubba. But you have a right to your secrets. You don't need to tell me why you're so dang unhappy with your life, or about why you wish you never got married. I don't need to know why you think you're a lousy cop, or any of your *other* secrets—" He broke off, aware that he was jabbering his thoughts to the open air, distracted by a mental whirlwind of fears. Stu sat limp in his chair, open-mouthed.

"Look," said Robbie, his voice heavy with apology, "I wasn't really reading your mind. Having a strong psychic experience is sometimes like getting a cut on your arm: The meat around the wound is tender and real sensitive to the air. Right now my mind is open to things it doesn't normally feel."

"Like other people's thoughts?"

"Not whole thoughts; just feelings, really. Your mind is no open book, Stu, and I wouldn't read it even if I could. You've got your secrets, and I've got mine, and that's the way it stays, okay?"

Stu got up from his chair and wandered to the window, where he stared a moment into the gray distance, his thumbs hooked into the waistband of his sweatpants, his face tight with trouble. "You're right, I didn't tell you everything there is to tell about the disappearances," he said, speaking to the window. "I didn't tell you that I've had reliable reports that some of the missing people have made visits around town, always at night, or that they've tried to make their friends and relatives follow them somewhere. I didn't tell you that one of those visits actually caused someone to blow his own head off with a shotgun. . . ."

Or that he himself had suffered a growing, clawing awareness of something poisonous in the air of Greely's Cove, a cold presence that hung just beyond the reach of human eyes. But he told Robbie now, and Robbie listened while trying not to think about what had overloaded his psychic circuits at the station house, or what had invaded his mind years ago on Carlyle Lake near the little town of Keyesport, Illinois.

"So that's the whole of it," said Stu, talking to the sweating glass of the window.

But not quite, thought Robbie: There was the matter of *another* secret, more intensely personal and in its way darker, crouching in the cellar of Stu Bromton's mind. The police chief apparently meant to keep it there, safely out of sight.

"I'm sure you can understand why I didn't want to say anything about this in front of Dean Hauck," Stu was saying, turning now from the window and forcing a small laugh. "If it got out, the city council would probably start involuntary commitment proceedings on me. I may have a loose lug nut or two, but I'd like to stay out of the state home awhile longer, if that's possible."

"You don't have any loose lug nuts, son. What you have, I suspect, is a smidgen of the Gift, like a lot of other people do. It's more common than you think. Everybody, to some degree, can sense strong thoughts and emotions, and you'd be surprised at how many folks can even see a little way into the future, if the conditions are right. Others have what your pointy-headed intellectuals call 'strong intuition,' which is really just a watered down version of what I've got—I call it the Gift. It's nothing to get lathered up over, believe me."

"I'm glad to hear that, but it doesn't really help me, Robbie. I need to know what this thing is and how I can fight it. Or at the very least, I need to know if I'm licked before I start."

"I wish I could help you, Stu, I really do, but I'm afraid this thing's a little out of my league."

"What? I don't understand. You got some kind of psychic impression from the lab samples, didn't you?"

"I never said that."

"You felt something that left your mind sore and tender enough to pick up my thoughts, right?"

"That doesn't mean I—"

"Don't bullshit me, Robbie! If you know what this thing is, tell me! I've got to know! If you don't know what it is, then do whatever it takes to find out!"

"Can't do that. I'm sorry. I have a policy on things like this, a very simple one: I leave them alone."

"Why? I thought you were in business to solve crimes and locate missing people. That's why the city council appropriated the money to bring you in, for Christ's sake!"

"You wouldn't understand if I told you."

"Oh? What makes you think so? Try me."

Robbie clenched his fists and swore silently. "I'll tell you, God damn it! If you have to know, it's because I'm *scared*— scared pissless, as a matter of fact. I've come up against something like this once, maybe twice before, and it scares me right down to my boot heels, scares me so bad I upchuck and pass out. Satisfied?"

Stu stood a moment at the foot of Robbie's bed, a swaying hulk that looked ready to topple in defeat. His face sank, and his brow darkened. "I'll send someone over with your van this afternoon," he muttered sullenly. "I expect you'll want to be leaving as soon as possible." He left the room without saying good-bye, a man whose burden had just become heavier.

17

Mitch Nistler awoke with cramps in his muscles and an ache in his skull, his cheek resting against rough wooden floorboards. More than a minute passed before he overcame the numbness of his limbs and managed to sit upright. Another full minute dragged by before he was able to make sense of his surroundings: He was sitting on the rickety, rain-soaked porch of Cannibal Strecker's crack house, his back propped against the locked door. His trousers and shoes were caked with mud, his shirt ripped and sopping from a panicky romp through wet foliage, his face and hands welted from searing twigs and nettles.

He could not remember ever being this cold. His chest felt tight and his throat raw, and he worried about having caught pneumonia.

"Fuck a bald-headed duck," he wheezed, gathering himself to stand up.

He staggered against the splintery doorjamb as the horrors of the previous night trickled back into his head. *The corpse of Lorna Trosper had opened its eyes.* Terror had gripped him, causing him to drop the body and flee into the cold night, like a man with demons on his heels. The fog had engulfed him, and he had crashed headlong into the forest, colliding with rough tree trunks, sprawling countless times over fallen logs. He had somehow clawed his way back to Old Home Road and followed the road here, to the tottering old house that Strecker had acquired and converted to a crack laboratory, wanting only to put distance between himself and the horror in his upstairs bedroom. He had collapsed in the shelter of this front porch, exhausted and near insanity. How long he had slept he could only guess.

He coughed and raised his wrist to look at his watch, only to discover that he had lost it, along with his glasses. Though the fog had begun to lift, the sky was yet a gauzy gray that blocked out the sun. Was it morning or noon, he wondered, or would it soon be night again?

God forbid that night should come again.

The sound of an approaching engine came through the mist—the powerful, huffing engine of a truck making its way over Old Home Road toward the crack house. Mitch pressed a palm against his forehead to fight dizziness, to force himself to think straight. It would be Strecker and his horrible girlfriend, Stella DeCurtis, coming to brew up another batch of crack. Mitch didn't need this: How on earth would he explain why he was here—or his battered appearance?

He needed to get away.

He launched himself down the crumbling cement steps toward the thicket that bordered the yard, stumbling repeatedly, and lurched past the rusted shell of an ancient Dodge that was nearly hidden by a thatch of man-high weeds. Beyond it was a tall pine with dark branches, surrounded by thick clumps of holly and sword fern. He hunkered down in the foliage and waited, scarcely daring to peer around the rough trunk of the tree. Strecker's black Blazer wheeled into the yard and halted next to a pile of derelict kitchen appliances.

More sound—another engine, this one belonging to a car that was jouncing up the road behind Strecker's pickup. *Who could it be?* Beyond this point Old Home Road was impassable to anything but a full-fledged off-road vehicle, meaning that someone must be visiting Strecker's crack house.

The car—a nondescript Pontiac sedan that was four or five years old—halted, and a big man got out, a man who was actually bigger and more powerful-looking than Cannibal. Mitch craned his neck to see over the tops of the holly branches at the base of the pine tree behind which he cowered.

Strecker and Stella DeCurtis piled out of the Blazer and approached the man. Strecker had a large brown envelope in his hands. They talked for a few minutes, and their conversation seemed anything but jovial. Corley the Cannibal laughed nervously once or twice and chewed his bubble gum with rapid, pumping strokes, then handed the envelope to the visitor, who turned and headed back toward the Pontiac.

Recognition dawned in Mitch's eyes like the setting sun. The man was none other than Stu Bromton, chief of the Greely's Cove Police Department.

The Pontiac's engine started. The car backed away, made a loop, and headed in the direction from which it had come. Strecker and Stella ambled back to the Blazer and gathered up armfuls of packages and sacks—the makings, Mitch supposed, of another batch of crack. They disappeared into the house and locked the door behind them.

Mitch sank against the wet bark of the pine. His mind lumbered through the meaning of what he had just seen.

Weeks ago, as he was about to embark on his fledgling career as a throwaway in the crack business, Strecker had alluded to "an arrangement with the local heat." Strecker's associates in Seattle had worked out a deal with "someone who's important locally," in order to be warned against any undercover drug operations mounted by the county sheriff or the State Patrol. Mitch now knew who that someone was. Police Chief Stu Bromton had driven out to the crack house, using his personal car and dressed in civilian clothes, in order to receive his payment and to notify Strecker of any potential danger from police investigators. Mitch wondered how much Strecker and his pals were paying Bromton—a hell of a lot more, no doubt, than they were paying Mitch.

The cold was becoming more than he could bear, a painful cold that gnawed at his bones and made him shiver uncontrollably. Knowing that he must get warm or become ever sicker than he already was—to the point of dying, maybe—he slunk through the trees alongside Old Home Road until Strecker's crack house was safely out of sight.

He had no choice but to brave his own house again, to confront and face down the horror that waited there. His rational mind told him that what he had seen the previous night could not have possibly happened, or if it *had,* that it was explainable in comfortable terms. Corpses *do* open their eyes, after all, and not because they are coming back to life, but because of muscle reflex. Mitch himself had seen it happen before, and he knew that it was no cause for terror.

As he trudged up the road, he struggled to keep certain thoughts out of his mind, certain memories of sounds in the night, noises of someone moving around in his upstairs bedroom.

18

Lindsay Moreland spent the afternoon with her mother at the family house in Magnolia. She would have stayed overnight had Nora not insisted that she was feeling more herself again and that she was certainly no invalid who required around-the-clock care.

"I feel so silly," Nora said, somewhat unconvincingly, "having let a little boy get the best of me like that. Anyhow, I'm fine now, and there's absolutely no reason why I should ruin the rest of your weekend. Go home, Lindsay."

So after a brief argument, Lindsay headed for her restored Georgian house in Seattle's gentrified Capitol Hill, visualizing a mountain of put-off laundry that needed doing and office paperwork that needed catching up on. After arriving home, she placed yet another call to Carl Trosper in Greely's Cove (she had called twice during the day but had gotten no answer), and this time Carl was at home. Jeremy was fine, he reported, safely in bed after a full day. Dr. Craslowe had called early that morning, asking to see the boy, and Carl had dropped Jeremy at Whiteleather Place for a therapy session that lasted nearly four hours. Afterward, father and son had driven into Seattle with an old pal of Carl's, Renzy Dawkins, to return the car that Carl had rented the previous night at the airport. The three had taken in an early movie and a seafood dinner at McCormick's, then driven back to Greely's Cove in Renzy's classic Buick—a regular boys' night out.

"My biggest problem at the moment is the collection of animals," said Carl with a little laugh in his voice. "I've got your basic menagerie here: three adolescent dogs and two kittens. It seems my son can't resist picking up strays and bringing them home."

"I know," said Lindsay. "I saw them when I picked up my mother. What do you plan to do with them?"

223

"Well, I can't keep them in the garage, that's for sure. It's animal-shelter time, I'm afraid, but the place is closed until Monday morning. First thing on my list for tomorrow is to pin Jeremy down on which ones he wants to keep. I'm drawing the line at one dog and one cat, even though I've never been what you might call a cat-lover."

"Seems fair. Sounds like everything is under control."

"So far, so good. I'm finally beginning to feel really good about things. I still have a few loose ends to tie up in D.C., but I think I can do it by phone. As soon as this nonsense with the county authorities is cleared up, we'll have clear sailing."

Carl's cheerfulness was infectious, and they ended their conversation on a high note. Lindsay promised to drop by later in the coming week with some houseplants and some sketched proposals for landscaping, since she had promised him she would help restore the neglected and dying yard around the little house on Second Avenue. A house just isn't a home without lots of greenery, both inside and out, she reiterated. Carl said that he looked forward to her visit.

After hanging up the telephone, she sat awhile in her orderly study, absently fingering the telephone cord, thinking. Maybe there was hope for Carl after all. Though she still doubted that a person could change his basic nature overnight, she was willing to concede that she may not have seen Carl's true nature during the years before Lorna's death.

The doorbell sounded, and Lindsay suffered the small fear that some acquaintance had dropped by with thoughts of dragging her out for a late-night drink—one of the guys at the office, maybe, who had screwed up the nerve to try his luck with her one more time, or a pair of female pals who felt she was working too hard and not playing enough.

The last person she had expected to see standing on her porch was the risible old Englishwoman, Hannabeth Hazelford. "Hannie—I mean, Miss Haz—I mean *Hannie*. What a surprise!" Lindsay remembered that Hannie always insisted on being addressed by her nickname, which for some reason always seemed hard to do.

"I do hope that you'll forgive this intrusion," said the old woman. "I realize that it's very late, but I really must speak with you. May I come in?"

Though she stood with head held high and chin thrust out in

the aristocratic manner that sometimes made her the butt of jokes among the blue-collar types of Greely's Cove, she seemed somehow unsteady, which was definitely out of character. Her turquoise contact lenses could not hide an urgency in her eyes.

"Of course you can come in," answered Lindsay, pulling the door open wide. "I was just about to make a pot of coffee. Or, if you'd prefer, I'll make tea."

Hannie came inside and shed her orange raincoat, uttering more apologies and redundant thank-yous. Lindsay took her coat to the closet and tried not to stare at her guest, whose appearance was the definition of eccentricity. Hannie's blue-and-green paisley frock hung in billowy folds on a frame that seemed tiny and ancient and brittle, a frame that moved as though the joints needed oil. Tied around her waist was a silken rope of bright red, and around her neck hung a loose scarf of a florid print. Most remarkable was her face, a raddled webwork of wrinkles under cakey makeup, topped with the familiar blond wig that often seemed slightly askew, as it did now.

"So," said Lindsay, after seeing that Hannie was seated, "will it be coffee or tea?"

"Have you any gin?"

Lindsay held back a snicker and asked how Hannie would take it. "Straight up, and only a small amount, if you please."

Lindsay went to the liquor cabinet in the kitchen and poured a generous ounce of gin into a tumbler, after which she started a pot of coffee for herself. The chores gave her time to recover from the shock of finding Hannie Hazelford at her door and to run through all she knew about the old woman, which was not much. She had been acquainted with her only casually for the past few years, and then only through Lorna, whose watercolors Hannie had bought and encouraged. Hannie apparently had money. She owned a beautiful old cottage on Torgaard Hill, drove expensive English cars (that she could drive at all seemed incredible at her advanced age), and generally lived far better than was attributable to the income from a sleepy little boutique on the main drag of Greely's Cove. Lindsay had always been entertained by the fact that the operator of a women's shop, even one that sells cheap goods, should dress so atrociously.

"I want you to know how sorry I am," said Lindsay, presenting the tumbler to her guest, "for the trouble you've just been through. I really hope that my nephew wasn't involved with it."

"Thank you for your concern," said Hannie. "Fortunately, no lasting harm resulted, only inconvenience and some minor expense."

She took a tentative sip from the tumbler and grimaced approvingly. "I must say, I find your home very attractive and tastefully furnished. Do you live here alone?"

"Yes, I do. I'm glad you like it." Lindsay sat in the chair opposite.

"I've always admired Georgian homes. I see that you share my taste for your sister's watercolors."

She nodded at the far wall, on which hung a cluster of Lorna Trosper's paintings—traditional still lifes of fruit and pottery, all laced with colors that complemented the warm tones of the throw rugs on the floor and the cushions on the sofa.

"Lorna had such remarkable range, don't you think? Landscapes, still lifes, portraits—she was equally at ease with all of them. I consider myself fortunate indeed to have acquired a collection of her work, which I shall always treasure."

"She gave me these for my birthday several years ago," said Lindsay, trying not to show her raging curiosity over why Hannie was here on a cold, wet night. "There's another set on the wall of my study, if you'd care to see them."

"Perhaps later." She sipped her gin again, then closed her eyes a moment, waiting for the alcohol to flow into her veins, as though she needed its blunting effects. "Tell me, Lindsay," she said after a long moment, "do you consider yourself a religious person?"

The question took Lindsay aback, and her blue eyes widened. "Why, no. Not really. Why do you ask?"

"Do you believe in God?"

Lindsay took a deep breath and leaned back in her armchair, knitting her fingers on her lap and assuming the contemplative pose that she often used with clients at the brokerage. "Not in the sense that many people do," she answered noncommittally. "My family went to church regularly when I was a child—Episcopalian—but we were never really very spiritual. Oh, we believed in Christian goodness—human kindness, decency, honesty. But church was more a social thing for us, and I fell out of the habit as I grew up, even though I've tried to hold on to the values."

"If you don't believe in God, say so."

The hint of sharpness in the old woman's tone irked Lindsay. "Very well. I don't believe in God. Is that what you wanted to hear?"

A smile pulled at the corners of Hannie's withered, painted lips. "I only want the truth, child. I must know where you stand."

"I'll admit it: Religion offends me. I don't need it. I happen to believe that the universe has an orderly beauty that isn't improved by wild-eyed notions of gods and devils who can move the stars around, or cause storms, or interfere in our lives."

"I see."

Hannie dropped her watery gaze to the tumbler of gin that she cradled in her bony hands, and Lindsay noticed for the first time the large ring that adorned one of her twiggy fingers. She strained to make out the silvery shapes that some long-dead smith had pounded and etched into the metal, shapes that age and wear had obscured: the hooked head of a shepherd's staff, linked and entwined with a serpent and a lion's face.

"I've come to talk with you about Jeremy," said Hannie, looking up at last. "I must say that this will be difficult, considering your beliefs about God and creation— or, rather, your lack of them. Nonetheless, I sense in you a great love for the boy, as well as a fundamental goodness, which together make you a potential ally, a strong one."

"An ally? I don't understand."

The old woman straightened in her chair, and her stare hardened. "Lindsay, your nephew—Jeremy—has fallen victim to a very old and potent evil, one that ordinary human beings cannot possibly defeat on their own. It is a conscious and conniving evil. It eats both flesh and souls, and it has powers that mere words cannot describe. I believe that there is yet time to undo the harm that has befallen Jeremy, but we must act quickly and decisively. We really cannot afford to waste precious hours in the debate of things spiritual. I must have your assurance that you will do exactly as I say."

Lindsay groped for words that would not come, for an

answer that only evaporated the very instant it reached her vocal chords. How does a sane, rational person respond to such lunacy? she wondered.

"An *evil*, you say? What could possibly make you think that?" Too late she realized her error, for she was only encouraging the ravings of an obviously very sick old woman.

"I have a great deal of experience in such things," replied Hannie. "I know the signs, the symptoms. You yourself may have noticed some of them, for you have spent time with Jeremy, but given your background, your upbringing in this age of arrogance and skepticism, you could not be expected to recognize them for what they are."

Lindsay took a slow breath and exhaled, determined now to choose her words carefully. "Hannie, I want to help you. The best way I can do that, I think, would be to find someone who knows about the things you must be feeling, a professional. Now, I know several good doctors who—"

Hannabeth Hazelford's laughter suddenly poured out of her, a brittle peal that hung sadly in the otherwise still air of the parlor. Lindsay endured it with a patience that surprised herself, lowering her eyes against Hannie's unfailing stare, awaiting the ebb.

"Forgive me, child—I'm not laughing at you, only at the irony of being patronized by someone so young, so inexperienced." The laughter resumed briefly, more indulgently now, with a hint of real humor this time.

"I didn't meant to patronize you," said Lindsay.

"No, of course you didn't. I'm not offended, really I'm not. But neither am I—how do you young people put such things?—*batty*, or *loony*. I don't have a *screw loose*, Lindsay. Do me the honor of forcing yourself to believe, if only for a moment, that I am not insane."

"I'll try."

"Very good. Now, where was I? Oh, yes—the signs, the symptoms." Hannie grew serious again. "Have you noticed in Jeremy any odd behavior of late—any manifestations of extraordinary abilities or long periods during which his mood seems very dark?"

The question loosed a chill that crept down Lindsay's spine into the small of her back, causing her to squirm. She thought immediately of the troubles her mother had endured at Jeremy's hands, of Nora's allegations that he seemed able to read her mind, to move things without touching them.

"Or has he shown an especially keen interest in the occult?" pressed Hannie, leaning forward slightly in her chair, staring hard into Lindsay's eyes. "I'm not speaking of those horrible films that children watch these days, the ones with *Halloween* in the titles, or those awful paperback novels about demons and vampires and all such rubbish. I speak of the *real* occult, Lindsay, of old books and charms, of rituals—"

"I really don't see what we're accomplishing here," said Lindsay, not liking the direction the talk was taking. "You obviously know as well as I do that Jeremy has been behaving strangely. But you must also know that he's been a very sick little boy throughout most of his life, and that kids with his particular kind of sickness—"

She heard herself regurgitating Dr. Hadrian Craslowe's explanation of Jeremy's recent troubles, employing lofty terminology like "mildly aberrant behavior." Something about the explanation seemed hollow and rote even to herself.

"You're deluding yourself, my child," said Hannie. "You are shaping the facts to fit your own beliefs about reality; rather like trying to force square pegs into round holes. But don't be angry with yourself—it's a natural human failing, as old as time itself, the source of history's most delightful myths and legends, I might add."

"Hey, wait a minute," said Lindsay, annoyed now. "*You're* the one who's been talking about the occult, about some kind of ancient evil that eats flesh and souls. *I'm* the one who's trying to be scientific."

"There-there, my dear, don't be angry. I'm only trying to help you see that there are possibilities outside the realm of what you think of as truth. Surely you won't deny that there's such a thing as the mythology of science, a body of beliefs based on the rather arrogant assumption that everything *real* can be seen, or touched, or heard, even measured or counted. The high priests of this myth, the scientists and engineers, have declared that there is no such thing as an unseen truth, that everything outside the scope of mankind's senses is unreal. Their god is technology, which they say will eventually enable mankind to see and measure even the tiniest particles, the very smallest bursts of energy, to know nature's darkest secrets."

"I won't deny that there's such a thing as scientific myth, but since it makes sense to me, I won't deny that I believe in it, either."

"No, I don't suppose you will. But since you are an educated, rational woman, consider this: Your twentieth-century science cannot possibly explain what has happened to your nephew."

"That's not true, Hannie. There's a perfectly rational explanation—"

"*Listen* to yourself, child! You're saying that science can explain how a thirteen-year-old boy, one who has been severely impaired from birth, unable to speak or dress himself or even go to the toilet on his own, can suddenly become an articulate, well-spoken person who reads and reasons in the abstract—almost overnight! And you're saying that science can explain his ability to penetrate other people's minds, to read their thoughts and plant schemes for doing mischief, to *use* people—"

The old woman had apparently heard the yarn spun by Kirk Tanner and Jason Hagstad, thought Lindsay, the outlandish allegation that Jeremy had somehow forced them to dump garbage into the stockroom of Hannie's boutique, slash the tires of her Jaguar, and firebomb her house. But had she also gotten wind of the torture that Jeremy had inflicted on Lindsay's mother, of the fact that he had stockpiled in his room a veritable mountain of musty old books about the occult?

"Listen, Hannie," said Lindsay, interrupting, "those two boys who tried to harm you are known drug users, chronic juvenile delinquents—hardly reliable witnesses. They've obviously lied about Jeremy's involvement—"

"There you go again!" exclaimed Hannie. "You're trying to shape the facts to fit your own notions of what's real and what's not. But suppose you're correct, that those two boys are lying: Wouldn't you think that they'd be able to manufacture a better excuse for doing what they've done, than trying to pin the blame on Jeremy, a mere child? And why would they direct their mischief at *me?* I've lived in Greely's Cove for more than six years, and I've never had any trouble of this kind. Why should Jason Hagstad and Kirk Tanner suddenly take it into their heads to inflict misery upon *me*, someone they've never cared the least about in the past, someone whom they may not even have known existed until recently?"

"I don't know," replied Lindsay, "but I'll bet you have a theory on that."

"Hardly a theory, dear girl. The fact is, Jason and Kirk feel no hostility toward me whatsoever, and they never have. It's *Jeremy* who hates me, who wants me gone from Greely's Cove. He used the two older boys as tools with which to direct his hatred, knowing the inadvisability of doing it himself. After all, he had no wish to be caught and punished, no wish to—"

"*Jeremy?* Do you know what you're saying? Why on earth would Jeremy want to hurt you?"

"He knows who I am, Lindsay. He knows that I represent a threat to him in his present state. The trouble he caused was a signal to me, a demonstration of his powers, a message that I should leave him alone with his evil designs."

Lindsay discovered that she was gripping the armrests of her chair so tightly that her knuckles hurt. "You need help, Hannie," she said as gently as she could. "You're living in a world that doesn't exist, one full of fear and hallucination. I'm certainly no expert, but I consider myself your friend, and I want to help you find someone who can—"

"You promised that you would drop your silly misgivings about my sanity, if only for a little while!" barked Hannie, this time with no trace of joviality. "Kindly be true to your word, at least until you've heard me out!"

Lindsay started and shrank back into her chair, biting her lower lip. "Very well, I'll hear you out—"

"Your nephew is not the only victim of the evil," said Hannie, draining the last of her gin. "It has defiled the whole community of Greely's Cove. Twelve innocent people have fallen prey to its hunger thus far, perhaps more. Scores of others have suffered the grief of losing loved ones—"

"Are you actually saying that Jeremy has been responsible for the disappearances?" asked Lindsay, unable to restrain herself. "Do you realize how absurd that sounds? For the love of God, Hannie, he's just a little boy! He's been sick most of his life! Now he's better, and he's getting better all the time. A sane person couldn't possibly believe that Jeremy was involved with the disappearances. Besides that, you don't have your facts straight: Ten people have disappeared, not twelve."

"I'm counting all the victims I know of thus far," answered Hannie icily, "including Jeremy himself and——" She faltered, and her turquoise eyes seemed to glaze for a moment. "And Lorna, your sister."

"Oh, he's responsible for Lorna's death, too, is he? I suppose he drove his own mother to suicide, or maybe even murdered her. Is that what you're saying?"

"Not *Jeremy!*" spat the old woman. "The evil inside him! The personality that you know as Jeremy isn't Jeremy at all. His body and mind are only the shell, the vehicle!"

"This has gone far enough, Hannie. I feel sorry for you, I really do, but I feel sorry for myself, too. I've just lost my sister, and for the past week my mother has been teetering on the brink of a nervous breakdown. I've offered to help you, and I meant it, but I refuse to sit here and listen——"

"You *must* listen, Lindsay! I beg you to think of your nephew, of your sister, and to love them as you have always loved them——"

"My sister is dead!"

"Dead, yes, but not beyond harm. If you ever loved her, if you love her still, you will force yourself to hear me. There are powers afoot in this universe that your sophisticated scientific mythology can never explain, for which death and time are not barriers, but only tools. I know of such things, Lindsay, for I am among the last of an ancient Sisterhood that possesses the skills and knowledge of the Old Truth. There may yet be a way to help your sister and nephew, both of whom need our help desperately, but first you must hear me, and then you must believe me, and then . . ."

The raddled old face faded to ashen, took on a reptilian texture that the layers of makeup could not hide. Hannie actually shivered.

"And then, you must do *exactly* as I say."

Against her good judgment, and fighting back the urge to show the old woman the door, Lindsay Moreland listened. She listened in stunned silence without interrupting, for more than an hour.

19

The night was far from over.

Robinson Sparhawk sat on the bed in his room at the West Cove Motor Inn, elbows propped on his knees and face buried in his hands, arguing with himself as he had been doing throughout most of the afternoon. Katharine the Great Dane lay curled at his feet, sometimes raising her head to stare at him with regretful eyes, now and then whining in sympathy.

Robbie let his hands drop into his lap and gazed into the huge dog's face.

"Man's best friend," he murmured, as much to himself as to Katharine. " 'Cept your best friend ain't much of a man, is he, girl?"

There was a sadness in the way he cuffed her ear. She felt it and acknowledged it with a whimper and a lick.

"Yeah, I know," said Robbie, as though the dog had replied in English, "I'm a good dude, in spite of the yellow streak up my back, right?"

He gathered his crutches from the floor beside the bed and hobbled into the bathroom, where he splashed his face with cold water and gargled with Scope to banish the mouth-funk of the cheroots he had smoked all day and into the night. The psychic sickness that had swept over him that morning at the police station—the nausea that had landed him briefly in the emergency room in Poulsbo—was long gone. Physically he felt himself again, but emotionally, spiritually, he felt leprous and weak and small. He felt ashamed.

"It ain't right, high-tailin' it away, leavin' these folks to cope with it alone. And besides that, I'm not sure I can live with myself if I run away again. I've got to take a stand, Kate, to show some *guts*. . . ."

Talk is easy, talk is cheap. Talk takes no courage. So

Robinson Sparhawk acted, pretending that he possessed the heart of a lion, the courage of a young bull.

Five minutes later he was showing Katharine into the cargo hold of his VW Vanagon, which Stu Bromton had sent over from the police station early in the afternoon. Then came the ritual of boarding the vehicle himself, pushing buttons to activate the motorized lift, settling his crippled body into the wheelchair, riding it up and into the cab, locking it into place.

He started the engine, flicked on the headlights and wipers, and maneuvered the van out of the motel parking lot and onto the main street of Greely's Cove. He turned left, heading south toward Sockeye Drive.

"You must think I'm plumb nuts, huh, Kate?" he remarked, not taking his eyes from the deserted street ahead. "Since when do we go lookin' for trouble, is that what you're wondering? And what're we gonna do with it when we find it?"

Not *if* we find the trouble, but *when*.

Robbie's fists tightened on the wheel as he fought back a resurgence of dread. From the very moment he had pulled the lid off a petri dish at the police station, the Gift had been in high gear, purring like a well-oiled engine, pumping steel-hard images into his brain. He saw a hulking Victorian mansion, amorphous in its shroud of forest fog—a dead place, guarded by trees with twisted, seemingly arthritic limbs. A tortuous road wound through dank woods until ending in a clearing, at a rusted-away gate with posts of crumbly brick—the threshold of Whiteleather Place. Yes, he even knew the name. And he knew where it was, knew how to get there.

"Funny, ain't it, girl? A man gets into his fifties before he wakes up and sees that he's missin' a big piece of himself." He gulped, almost dropping the burning cigar from his clenched teeth. He was talking again, talking; trying vainly to distract himself from the terror of the thing from which, as a matter of policy, he had always run; trying to convince himself with out-loud words that he had manly guts.

But the effort was failing. The fear was winning.

He halted at the lonely intersection of Frontage Street and Sockeye Drive, signaling a right turn but not yet turning. He listened to the swipe of the wipers and the whir of the defroster, staring through the windshield at the conical shafts of his headlights in the miasmal fog.

His gaze drifted leftward to an island of electric light that seemed to float in the algid darkness: the dim bulk of City Hall, lit feebly by a trio of arc lamps atop utility poles. In the bowel of that building was the headquarters of the Greely's Cove Police Department, a musty, cement-smelling place, where perhaps even now—at this very moment, conceivably—sat Chief Stu Bromton, alone behind his paper-strewn metal desk. Robbie visualized the big man's haggard face, saw the scars of shattered hopes in his sleepless eyes, felt a tweak of guilt.

"Goddamn it, Kate, I can't run out on these people," he muttered through his teeth, "not this time. For once in my life I've got to face up to—"

Face up to what?

Facing him now, in the fifty-second year of his life, was the unclean *something* that he had glimpsed years ago while leaning over the transom of a boat on Carlyle Lake—the same black threat, perhaps, that Mona Kleiman had called from New York to warn him about, a hungry life-force whose essence had poured forth from a smear of slime in the bottom of a petri dish.

"Okay, no more talk. We're gonna make the crossing, girl, you and me together. If we get through it with both halves of our asses together, fine and dandy. If we don't, what the hell? At least we'll go out in a blaze of glory."

Katharine whimpered her agreement and lay down on her blanket in the rear of the van. Robbie completed his right turn onto Sockeye Drive and drove gingerly through the night, humming with a lightheartedness that he did not feel, keeping his eyes peeled for a sign that said *Whiteleather Place*.

Mitch Nistler lay between his grungy sheets and trembled in the darkness of his bedroom, while the rattletrap refrigerator in the kitchen filled the house with a grinding whir. Often he had cursed that sound when it had awakened him in the night, and just as often he had vowed to start putting aside booze money for a new fridge—a nice quiet Westinghouse that did not vibrate and ruckle the floorboards whenever the motor kicked on.

But tonight he welcomed the noise and prayed that it would never end, at least not until the sun had risen safely.

As though his prayer had been heard in hell and not in

heaven, the motor kicked off, leaving an inane silence in which seconds became centuries, every wheezing breath an avalanche, each heartbeat a sledgehammer. He waited, hoping that the stirrings above his head had ended—or better still, that they had not really happened at all, that the scrapes and thumps and gurgling moans had only been figments of his own sick imagination. The silence grew, got heavier, blacker.

The sounds started again.

Mitch's teeth clamped down on his tongue, igniting coppery pain and drawing blood that he tried not to swallow. He battled the urge to leap wildly from his bed and flee the house as he had done the previous night, after the bloating corpse of Lorna Trosper had opened it eyes and stared squarely into his own.

After he had awakened on the porch of Cannibal Strecker's crack lab, cold and quaking with fever, the need for food and warmth had been critical. He had forced himself back into his stench-filled house, and even managed a hot shower and a bowl of Dinty Moore's before collapsing in a heap onto his sorry bed. While drifting into croupy sleep he had vowed to deal later with the swelling monstrosity in the upstairs bedroom, as soon as he had mustered both the strength and courage—to bury the thing, burn the sheet that had surrounded it, scour the floor onto which it had leeched filth, air out the place.

Afternoon had become night and with night had come the sounds again, just as they had been coming every night for the past week, nudging Mitch out of torpid sleep. The sounds were so real, so immediate, so close.

Lorna Trosper could not be *alive*, much less pregnant with his child. He had embalmed her, for God's sake! The noises from above could not possibly be those of a woman giving birth. A woman needs nine months, say the laws of nature. But suppose—just *suppose*, for the sake of argument—that Lorna had been pregnant *before* she killed herself. . . .

Madness, carped the rational side of Mitch's brain. She *had* killed herself, and even if through some unholy miracle she had failed but had merely inflicted on herself a coma deep enough to fool a medical examiner and a mortician, Mitch had finished the job she had started, had drained away her blood and injected her with a potent formaldehyde solution, had punctured all her vital organs with a trocar and sucked out their contents. *Nobody could possibly live through that!*

No doubt about it, Lorna Trosper was dead, dead, *dead*. And dead women don't get pregnant or thrash about on squeaky old beds, or pace the creaky floors, or moan and groan with the pain of labor.

Or scream.

Which someone or something did in the upstairs bedroom, searing Mitch Nistler's soul, freezing the breath in his throat and jelling the blood in his veins—a mind-shattering scream that shredded the velvety blackness, a razor-sharp keen of agony and terror.

He bolted from his bed and clambered on watery legs out of his bedroom, flailing wildly against the smothering dark; he collided painfully with a doorjamb and knocked a rickety bed table to the floor; he grabbled his way like a blind rodent in flight from a monstrous black cat.

Groping and thrashing, pursued and surrounded by the hellish scream, he lunged into the pitch blackness of the living room and careened over his battered old armchair, sprawled on the floor, and scrambled crablike toward the front door, wanting only to be away, away. Suddenly the screaming ended, and just as suddenly his head crunched against unyielding wood—the door, much closer than he had supposed. His mind exploded in a fountain of sparks that cascaded and whirled behind his eyes. He bounced downward. Somehow he rolled to his front and planted his palms on the dirty floor, struggled to regain his sense of up and down, to gather in his stuttering limbs.

A light came on.

Yellowness, filtered through a dirty lamp shade, invaded his swimming brain and inflicted another dose of terror. Seated on the tattered sofa was Jeremy Trosper, angelically blond and bright-eyed, as serene in the muddy lamplight as he must have been before the light snapped on, unruffled by the scream that just seconds earlier had reverberated through the house. Mitch gasped and sank back to the floor, horrified by the glint of relish in the boy's eyes, the power and control in his face.

Whole minutes passed while Mitch teetered on the edge of a swoon, as half-remembered images flitted into and out of his head.

Anubis, the god of embalmers, with the head of a dog and horrible red eyes.

Mitch himself, an artist of the silvery scalpel, a master embalmer and priest of the god.

A submental cavern, cold and black and stinking, where Hadrian Craslowe was the host, the hypnotist, the server of an unholy feast.

The images evaporated, and he managed to right himself finally, to lean his back against the wall and face the insanity on the sofa. Another shuddering minute passed as his eyes digested the rest of the scene, for he was without his glasses, which added the handicap of nearsightedness to dizziness and terror.

Jeremy had not come alone. In his lap lay a mound of orange fur, scarcely bigger than a man's two fists—a kitten. Next to him on the sofa lay another one, silvery gray and slightly larger, curled close against his blue jeans. On the carpet at his feet sat three dogs, all nondescript mongrels, none of which looked fully grown. The animals seemed strangely lifeless and inert, as though drugged, and Mitch got the feeling that they were incapable of movement on their own, of even breathing without Jeremy's permission; that the silken creature on the sofa held them in an unseen grip.

Suddenly Mitch felt totally bloodless, too exhausted to flee whatever atrocity lay in store, beyond caring what else might happen to him. His head lolled and thudded against the ragged wallpaper. He closed his eyes in resignation, waiting like a condemned criminal for the whisper of the ax or the surge of 50,000 volts or the first sweet whiff of cyanide.

Jeremy spoke at last, ending the heavy silence.

"There now, that's the spirit. You'll feel much better in a moment, believe me, and we'll be able to get on with our business."

The boy's oddly deep voice and aristocratic British accent sent another tremor of fear up Mitch's spine: Jeremy could actually hear his thoughts.

"You really should take better care of yourself, you know. That's a nasty rash you have, and I'd say you're on the brink of pneumonia, from the sound of that cough."

Mitch had not realized he was hacking up thick phlegm, or that his breathing was a continuous, whistling wheeze. These were discomforts that paled next to the realities of the screamer upstairs and the smiling boy who sat a few feet away, surrounded by entranced animals.

But just as Jeremy had promised, Mitch *did* start to feel better, having settled deep into resignation and given up the fight against the madness that was loose around him. Somehow he managed to speak around his bitten tongue, to coax words from the chaos in his head.

"What's happening here—to me? Why are you—*doing* this? Why—"

"Oh, come now, Mitchell, you can't possibly be that thick! Surely you must have some idea of what all this means. After all, you've been groomed for this moment since your early boyhood, just as I have—or shall I say *prepared,* since the term *groomed* seems somewhat inappropriate for a creature such as yourself." The boy giggled at his own wit. "You should consider yourself fortunate to be a part of it—if you don't mind my saying so—inasmuch as this is a very historic occasion. Only rarely are all the conditions right: the proper season, the new moon rising precisely six days after the start of Imbolc, all that sort of thing."

"I don't understand. I—"

"No, I don't suppose you do. I sometimes overestimate people, as I have you. Still, you've performed rather nicely in a difficult role—that much I'll give you. Only a few hundred men throughout the whole of human history have succeeded in doing what you've done, which is something you can take pride in, I should think."

"The body," croaked Mitch, motioning feebly toward the ceiling, "the one upstairs—your mother. What I did to her—is that what you're talking about?"

"Ah, the truth dawns!"

"But I didn't mean to—I mean, I didn't really want—"

"Oh, but there's no need to apologize, dear boy. You did exactly what you were supposed to do. Thanks to you—"

A sound interrupted, a mewling whine that came from overhead, causing Jeremy to glance toward the ceiling and Mitch's flesh to crawl. It had a babyish ring, but it was grossly unlike any human baby's cry that Mitch had ever heard.

"You'll be happy to know," said Jeremy, grinning broadly now, "that your involvement is nearly at its end. Even so, you can still be of use for a little while longer, and how well you perform your assigned tasks could determine whether you live or die. I assume that you wish to go on living."

At this point Mitch was uncertain whether life held any appeal for him, whether an existence filled with lunatic horrors was preferable to whatever lay beyond death. What was life to a man who had done the things he had done, been what he had been? The likelihood of ever smiling again seemed slim, and slimmer yet the prospect of putting behind him the memories of the past weeks and months, of living down the guilt for the obscenities he had committed.

Jeremy, of course, caught these thoughts as though Mitch had spoken them aloud. He answered them, betraying anger for the first time. "I'm through coddling you, Mitchell. Now listen carefully to what I say, because it's important."

The mewling whine came again from above, louder this time, more demanding. Jeremy paused to appreciate it, then continued.

"The most loathsome thing about the human animal, Mitchell, is its conscience. Think about it: Man arrogantly assumes that his conscience sets him apart from all other living things, that it gives him the ability to declare what's right and wrong for all creation and everything in it. He presumes to know the difference between good and evil, saying that conscience is the source of that knowledge, all the while conveniently ignoring the fact that no two men can agree on such matters. As for yourself, you would do well to ignore whatever feelings your conscience gives you and accept yourself for what you are. If you do this, you may yet have a chance at some semblance of a life. Are you listening to me, Mitchell? Can you grasp what I'm telling you, or is it over your head?"

"I'm not sure," wheezed Mitch, blinking tears away. "Accept myself for what I am, you said. Just what am I, anyway?"

"Oh my God, lad, must we go into that? You're what you are: a human reject, a mistake. Even your parents wished that you had never been born, but surely you've surmised that by now. You're unschooled and stupefyingly ignorant. An alcoholic. An ex-convict. A grimy little functionary in Corley Strecker's cocaine enterprise—what your fellow criminals call a *throwaway,* if I'm not mistaken. You have no job, no prospects, you're ugly to look at, and you're covered with sores from having slept with a dead woman. No one will ever love you, Mitchell, because you are quite simply one of your race's truly unlovable specimens."

Mitch's chest heaved, and his throat felt as though he had swallowed a hot ball bearing. "You're right—I'm all those things," he managed. "So tell me, why should I want to live?"

The boy ascended from the sofa, bearing the kitten in his arms, and glided close to where Mitch sat on the floor. He bent low and spoke directly into Mitch's face, slowly, deliberately, giving punch to each word.

"For the simple reason that you have something the vast majority of your brothers and sisters lack: a true purpose—*my* purpose, Mitchell. Serve that purpose and you will survive—even prosper, I can assure you. Bury your sorry excuse for a conscience, accept what you are, and you will have a life that you want to keep—not like you've always wished for, perhaps, and certainly not like the others of your kind, but a life nonetheless. Fail me, and I promise you a death that's horrible beyond words, beyond your worst nightmare."

A third time the whine sliced through the night, rising both in pitch and volume until it pained Mitch's eardrums, an insistent, demanding screech that raised the hairs on his neck. Jeremy's face broke into a demonic grin. He stood upright, rose well off the floor to hang unsupported in the air, and turned slowly to face the door that gave onto the stairway. He began to move toward it, but en route he paused to look back at Mitch, his eyes glowering with hot glee.

Mitch cowered, not believing what he saw, wanting desperately to scrabble to his feet and bolt through the front door, but lacking the strength to do anything except sit transfixed and helpless.

"It's time for my new brother's first feeding," said the boy, cradling the kitten in his arms. "This will be your job for the next few weeks, Mitchell—a simple one that should give you no trouble."

He reached for the doorknob with a hand that seemed overly large and somehow deformed, like Hadrian Craslowe's hands, which Mitch remembered from the rare occasions he'd glimpsed them. The door opened, and Jeremy tossed the limp but seemingly conscious kitten onto the stairs, then pushed the door closed again. The screeching from above immediately subsided, giving way to thumps and scrapes that suggested movement across the splintery floor to the stairway.

Robbie braked to a halt just inside the deteriorating gateposts of Whiteleather Place, switched off the headlights, and stared through the bleary windshield at the mansion, a dinosaurian hulk whose one yellow eye—a porch light—peered weakly through the secretive fog. Though dark and indistinct, the very sight of the place caused his guts to cramp, and he farted loudly.

"Catch that one and paint it green," he said aloud, possibly to Katharine but more probably to himself, a locker-room quip dredged up from his boyhood.

The huge dog was unimpressed by this little show of juvenile bravado and said as much with a nervous whimper. Robbie had read somewhere that dogs have much stronger psychic powers than most humans do, and he half-believed this, having occasionally noticed that Katharine seemed to know what he was thinking. Sometimes she grew excited and joyful before he even suggested a ride in the van, while he was still only *thinking* about making an offer. He wondered now whether she sensed the threat nearby, as he himself did, whether her canine nerves were throbbing with psychic warning.

Robbie's own nerves were not in the best of shape. Every sixty seconds or so he asked himself just what the hell he was trying to prove (and to whom?), driving out to this horrible place in the forest, braving fog and drizzle and slick roads in the black of night.

Why not do the sensible thing and notify Stu Bromton that the answers to the riddles of Greely's Cove lay here, at Whiteleather Place, and let the wheels of the criminal justice system roll? Robbie was no cop, after all, and was ill-equipped to deal with even the least-dangerous felon, much less what lay in the house. He had no gun, no knife, not so much as a nightstick or a pair of handcuffs, though he doubted that such utensils could be of much use tonight.

Yet, he felt a strange tingling of power that he relished, a sharp sensation of being alive and in control of himself, having bested the dread that had paralyzed him earlier. He had discovered and experienced the truth of an old axiom: that courage is not the absence of fear but only the ability to beat it.

He was afraid, more so than he could have dreamed possible, but he was no longer a slave to fear, no longer a quivering little varmint who scuttered for a hole at the first sign of trouble. He was standing up to the dread, staring it straight in the eye and daring it to do its worst.

Which it probably would.

"Well, this is it, old girl," he said, shutting off the engine. "No sense puttin' it off any longer."

Katharine whined disapprovingly, as though to ask *why*?

"Good question. I'm not sure I know the answer. Maybe I've got somethin' to prove—to myself, if nobody else. Or"—he stumped out his cigar butt in the ashtray—"maybe I'm just curious."

Or just stupid. Some guys, he reminded himself, confuse stupidity with bravery, and history is littered with their broken bodies.

He opened the door, letting in a fenny night smell, and lowered himself to the ground, cringing from the electrical noise of the wheelchair lift. After alighting, he stood and leaned against the van, then collected a pair of metal crutches from their holder behind the driver's seat—the ones with the broad, flat rubber tips, which were useful on soft ground. He buzzed the chair back to its place behind the wheel, shushed Katharine's whining, and nudged the door shut as quietly as he could, locking it.

With his first hobbling steps toward the dark house came an overwhelming sense of aloneness, a feeling of naked exposure and vulnerability that nearly drove him back to the protective steel shell of the Vanagon and the loving company of Katharine. But he fought it and plodded on, keeping to the edge of the circular drive, carefully planting the rubber tips of his crutches onto the rock-chipped surface and testing for traction before swinging his weight forward, step after cautious step. Though the rain had stopped and the fog had begun to thin, his eyebrows and lashes were already picking up wetness from the humid air. The cold lay heavy against his face. He saw and heard no sign of life in or around the house that loomed ahead, except for the lonely light that glimmered under the arched ceiling of the enormous wooden porch—a beacon, it seemed, to warn away the foolish and unwary. Still he kept on, straining his eyes to glean details in the dark, drawing ever closer.

He became aware of the state of decay around him: the deadness of the trees with their twisted, holly-choked limbs. The tangled and brittle wreckage of shrubbery. The warped and sagging timbers of the porch that swept around the mansion.

Hanging in the air was the reek of rotting bark and noxious weeds, mingled with a hint of putrescence. More troubling than these physical sensations, though, were the psychic alarms that were clanging in his head, the equivalents of pulsating lights and blaring Klaxons.

He shook off the warnings, surprising himself with a display of renewed courage. He was crossing thresholds tonight, discovering new things about himself. He was not a spineless coward after all. His mind was no longer closed to the realities of the unseen world that his witchy friend, Mona Kleiman, endlessly spoke of. Robbie marveled now that he could have denied those realities, that he had gotten a small taste of them years earlier at a place called Carlyle Lake and still dismissed Mona's wisdom as the fanciful drivel of a sweet old crackpot.

He halted before the steps that ascended to the great yawning porch and gazed upward at the massive oak doors, wondering whether his newly found courage was strong enough to propel him up the steps. Briefly he considered going around to the rear of the house and testing the back door, with the rationale that slipping in from the rear might be wiser than a frontal attack. That idea caved in, however. The thing that waited inside was already conscious of his presence; of this Robbie was certain. A sneak attack was out of the question. Here, at least, he had the smirchy glow of the porch light, which seemed preferable to the darkness that lay outside its reach. Here, at least, he would be able to *see* whatever menace lay in wait.

He undertook the chore of climbing the steps—no small one for a man on crutches, bigger still for a man whose withered legs could support his full weight only for a few seconds at a time. It was a chore that required concentration, timing, and planning. He counted the steps as he went, bending his knees to plant his feet firmly on the step above while the tips of the crutches remained on the level below, then tilting his weight forward and raising the crutches to follow—one: regain balance, lean forward again, raise feet, repeat; two—and yet again.

Five.

Six.

And finally, eight, the last step, which placed him inside the maw of the porch, with its arched ceilings and warped terra-cotta filigree.

The air was inexplicably cold. He stood a few paces from the oak doors, staring into the hard, scowling eyes of a tarnished brass lion's head, the door knocker, feeling as though he had set foot on a distant planet.

Suddenly a shroud of blankness fell over his psychic senses, like a stage curtain crashing down. His stomach lurched and his mind swirled. He staggered backward, barely catching his balance to prevent a headlong plunge down the stone steps that he had just climbed. He steadied himself against the balustrade and took deep breaths to quench the dizziness, to regroup.

Something was fighting him, something that possessed enormous psychic power—the evil beyond the door, no doubt, the conscious life-force that had detected his presence. It had sent out a blast of energy meant to thwart Robbie's own Gift, to numb him and render him defenseless.

Defenseless.

His mental gears rolled furiously. The blast that he had just felt had surely been an act of defense, which meant that the evil that lay beyond the door felt threatened somehow—that's right, *threatened*—by an aging cripple who carried nothing more lethal than a set of car keys. Could this mean that—

The overhead porch light blinked off, plunging him into blackness. The cold air stirred and penetrated his sheepskin jacket to his flesh, inflicting a chill that set his teeth to chattering. Yellow light spilled from a widening crack between the two oak doors, now groaning on their hinges, separating and pulling inward, setting free a vaporous stench that choked him.

The image behind the door was worse than anything Robbie had ever imagined, more foul than the human carnage left at the scene of any crime he had ever helped solve. Nominally, it was a man—or once had been—seated in an electric wheelchair very much like the one Robbie himself owned. It wore a filthy Army-issue T-shirt of olive drab, shredded with holes that betrayed the savaging its body had endured. The bones of its legs poked through the tattered remains of blue jeans, bare of meat but for sinewy ligaments. Likewise its arms and hands had suffered the feasting of some unthinkable carnivore. Worst of all was its face, half-gone above a neck that itself sprouted stalks of quivering veins and arteries—a face that half-grinned with fungal bone and half-sneered with the remains of cheek and lips. Its eyes were wide and lunatic, brimming with an inner light and beaming lascivious glee.

Incredibly it was alive and capable of speech, which was the grandest possibly obscenity.

"Hi there, Robbie. Welcome to Whiteleather Place." Its voice gurgled and rasped, yet poured forth with alarming strength. "Monty Pirtz is the name, and I'd shake hands with you, but"—it chuckled appallingly—"I don't have much of a hand left to shake. Why don't you come in and take a load off?"

Robbie swayed on his crutches, sick with revulsion. The name, Monty Pirtz, sounded familiar.

"Well, it should sound familiar," said the thing in the wheelchair. "I'm one of Greely's Cove's missing citizens, remember? The Vietnam vet who ran the appliance-repair shop on Frontage Street. I was brought here by Jennifer Spenser— little high-school girl who used to drop into my shop most every day. She's a cute kid . . . uh, *was* a cute kid, I mean—felt sorry for me, my being crippled and alone and all, thought I needed company. Always bringing me snacks and stuff to read. When she disappeared, I thought the fuckin' world had ended, know what I mean? But then she shows up at my bedroom window one night, and—hey! You don't want to hear about all that, I'm sure. Come on in, damn it!"

Paralysis seized Robbie as Monty Pirtz's wheelchair came to life with an electric hiss and moved forward, shortening the distance between them, heightening the stench.

"Hey, I know what you're thinking," said Pirtz, "which, by the way, you've probably already guessed by now—but there's really nothing to be afraid of. A little pain, a little—uh, unpleasantness, as Hadrian calls it, but after that it's great, believe me. Besides, you're in no position to—"

"*Stop!*" screamed Robbie, not with a scream at all, but more of a croak. "I'm not going anywhere with you!"

"Oh, but you *are* coming with me, Robbie. You don't have a choice. You see, I've got power now, and I can make things happen. I can make you—"

"No! You can't make me do anything!"

"You'll thank me when it's over, dude. After you've had a taste of the Feast, and you've had all those wild and beautiful dreams, you'll wonder how you ever lived without it. You'll live for the chance to go out and bring somebody new in, just like I do."

The chair drew within inches of where Robbie stood, and he gagged from the stench of the monstrosity that sat grinning before him, all damp with mucilaginous slime, the handiwork of the evil that he had dreaded for so long. Gone now was the intoxication of newly discovered courage.

"You and I got a lot in common, Robbie," it said, raising a nearly fleshless talon. "We both know what it's like to be crippled, to be on the outside looking in. I guess I was a little luckier than you, though, because I didn't lose my manhood until I got to Vietnam—little place called Phuoc Hiep, about ten clicks northwest of Cu Chi. Stepped on a fuckin' booby trap and ended up in this fuckin' chair. On the other hand, maybe you were luckier than me, because you've never known what it's like to take a woman's nightie off and run your hands over her tits and feel her legs open up. I've known those things, and I've have to live without them. I—"

"Shut up! Get away from me!"

The talon closed around Robbie's wrist and tightened horribly.

"I can promise you that you'll know the good things, dude, all the good things you've ever dreamed of. You'll know women, all kinds of women: fat ones, skinny ones, old ones, young ones, from every time and place in all of history, Robbie. You'll know what they feel like, what they taste like. You'll know what it's like to stick your cock in one and cut her throat at the same time, how it feels to—"

Robbie choked back the bile gorging in his throat and tried vainly to wrest free of the thing's grip, which only tightened. A frenzy of thoughts whirled and collided in his brain. Somewhere amid the stream of his overloaded senses the Gift glimmered feebly, a remnant of the psychic power that only moments ago had blinked out under a thick, damp blanket of defensive energy. The evil had been *afraid* of him, had felt threatened.

"You'll know what it's like to run again, Robbie, to jump and dance and climb mountains. The Giver of Dreams will let you have any body you want, go anywhere in all history. Think about all you've read, Robbie, all the times and people and places that you've visited in your books, the great thinkers you could meet and talk to."

The energy that emanated from the Pirtz-thing was brutal and strong, far stronger than the faint inklings of the Gift. Robbie felt himself sinking, giving in.

"Come to the Feast, Robbie, and know what it's like to be rid of those sorry excuses for legs you've got, what it's like to fly!"

Robinson Sparhawk felt the vitality rushing out of him, leaving a yawning and hungry void. The talon-grip tightened yet more, loosing raw pain that washed up into his shoulder, his chest, his whole being. In his heart he said good-bye to the world as he had known it, to Katharine the Great Dane, his friends in El Paso, Mona Kleiman—

"Monty, no!"

A woman's voice rang out from somewhere in the dim background, jarring Robbie from the torpor. He tore his eyes from the nightmarish face in the wheelchair and stared into the yellow rectangle of light beyond the oak doors. A woman in black stood there, her fingers thrust into the depths of her raven hair, screaming as if all creation were ending.

"Monty, let him alone! There's no further need!"

The talon-grip weakened ever so slightly, and the Pirtz-thing wriggled around in its chair to face the woman in the doorway. "Who are you to say that there's no need?" growled the creature malevolently. "I need to dream! If I bring him, the Giver might take me again!"

"No, he'll *never* take you again, Monty!" she answered. "You're going to die soon, can't you see that? He doesn't need you anymore, and he doesn't need this man. For the love of God, Monty, let him go. Let him go!"

Summoning strength that he did not know he had, Robbie twisted free of the creature's grip, leaving a bloody scrap of his skin in the thing's bony fist. As the creature turned back toward him, Robbie loosed a bolt of will, scarcely knowing how he did

it or where it came from, knowing only that it was a facet of the
Gift. Never in his life had he moved objects without touching
them, as some claimed to be able, or gazed into the future or
communed with the dead. He had doubted that such abilities
were even real. Still, he knew that at times he could catch
pieces of someone else's thoughts or feelings, and he had
sometimes suspected that his own Gift went deeper than he
knew, that he had abilities he had yet to perfect or even
explore.

In the terror of a life-and-death struggle, every creature
summons power and ability that it does not normally use, and
such power is sometimes awesome, if not supernormal: Wit-
ness the well-publicized case of the hysterical young mother
who lifted the front end of a Cadillac to free her trapped child
and simply tossed it aside. That is what Robbie did, throwing
out a blast of energy like a man-sized chunk of concrete, which
struck the Pirtz-thing in the chest and heaved it backward.

Robbie held it at bay while he struggled down the steps,
while he hobbled at full speed over the rock-chipped drive
toward his van, scarcely hearing the chasing hiss of an electric
wheelchair. Somehow he managed to dig his keys out of his
pocket, open the van, clamber insider without benefit of the
power lift, fend off Katharine's frenzied welcome and excited
kisses, start the van, and careen around toward the road over
which he had come.

The work of driving, of keeping the roaring Vanagon out of
the ditch and on the road, momentarily distracted him from the
task of throwing concrete slabs of will to hold back the
Pirtz-thing. It caught up to him on the foggy road, an uncanny
apparition of a manlike creature in a wheelchair, keeping pace
with the van as it roared and lurched down a forest road at fifty
miles per hour. It drew up beside the driver's window and
glared in fiendishly, hungrily. Robbie drove on with his
bleeding hand. Katharine yelped and growled and barked. Not
until the Vanagon turned onto Sockeye Drive did the thing fall
behind, having given up its hope for another Feast, another
dream.

PART
III

Awful is Winter's setting sun,
   When, from beneath a sullen cloud,
He eyes his dreary course now run,
   And shrinks within his lurid shroud.
                              —Ann Radcliffe

20

Sunday morning broke wet and misty, the start of another week of winter on the Puget Sound. For Carl Trosper it was the beginning of a new life in Greely's Cove.

He swung out of bed with gladness about his prospects and eagerness to tackle the chores of settling into that life, of making a home for his son and a law practice for himself. In less than two days Washington, D.C., had already become a distant memory, a rapidly fading past that seemed irrelevant to the here and now, like a soldier's suppressed recollections of a combat tour from which he had, through some miracle, returned safely.

En route to the bathroom Carl paused briefly before Jeremy's closed door and considered waking him, for it was after eight o'clock and a full day was in the offing. But then he decided, what the hell? Let the kid sleep awhile longer.

With a light heart he breezed through the morning routine of the "three eshes"—shit, shower and shave—and dressed in Levi's, boat shoes, and a bulky oatmeal sweater with frayed cuffs, an old favorite that he had brought in a suitcase from the East rather than send it by van. He brewed a pot of coffee and sat with a cup near the living-room window, gazed out at the drizzle, and mulled the day ahead.

First thing on the agenda: Prod Jeremy to decide which two of their resident menagerie he wanted to keep—one dog and one cat, tops. Though the bungalow had a fenced backyard, it was hardly big enough for one dog, not to mention three. The remaining cat and two dogs, regrettably, would go to the animal shelter on Monday, a thought that disturbed Carl slightly. All five of the animals got along well together, were good-natured and cute, and he was already becoming attached to each of them. That Jeremy had proved unable to resist picking up strays and bringing them home was oddly comforting, even though the boy seemed totally disinterested in them now, which Carl assumed to be merely one of those notorious adolescent phases.

Next thing on the agenda: grocery shopping, and picking up household odds and ends: cleansers and sponges and Brillo pads, a mop and a broom—things that old Hannie Hazelford had overlooked in her outfitting of the house weeks earlier.

And after that, the big one: the task of inventorying Lorna's gallery on Frontage Street, cleaning it out, gathering its wares and fixtures for storage and auction—a massive job that Renzy Dawkins had offered to help with, as had Jeremy. Not fun, surely, but neither would it be an ordeal, for this was part of the new beginning that Lorna herself would have endorsed and encouraged. No sense in putting it off.

A full day indeed, and the morning was fast slipping away. He drained his coffee cup, rinsed it in the sink, and went to the door that separated the garage from the kitchen, meaning to herd the three young dogs into the backyard for their morning "hot and steamies." Then he meant to rouse his son and get things rolling.

He pulled the door open, fully expecting a rush of puppyish energy to come bounding into the kitchen. He stood still a moment, surprised by the quiet.

In the garage sat Renzy Dawkins's classic Roadmaster convertible, which Renzy had insisted lending him until Carl got a car of his own. Along the wall lay a jumble of rakes and hoes, a lawn mower, a nest of garden hoses, and Lorna's ancient Gitane bicycle. On the floor near the door were three pans mounded with Purina Dog Chow and a fourth one, smaller, heaped with Tender Vittles for the kittens. A plastic bucket filled with water sat nearby, and, like the pet food, it was apparently untouched.

The garage was empty of life and sound, and Carl suddenly became intensely conscious of the fact that Lorna had died here, having locked herself in the rusting Subaru wagon that she and he had picked out together and bought long before he'd graduated to Porsches. He suppressed a shudder and whistled into the blank atmosphere of the garage, then clucked his tongue and made kissing noises in the hope that the animals were only hiding, perhaps sleeping, on the other side of the

Buick. But they were gone. No amount of whistling could coax them back from nonexistence.

"No need to worry about them, Dad," said Jeremy from behind him, having slipped soundlessly into the kitchen. Carl nearly jumped out of his skin. "I knew how busy you'd be for the next few days, so I took care of them. A trip to the animal shelter won't be necessary now."

Carl collected his wits, pushed the door closed again. He turned toward his son, who was leaning against the counter with his hands pocketed in bulky white safari pants. He looked like any other towheaded teenager of the American Eighties, but something in that smile—as well as his mature, slightly British speech—insisted that he was anything but common.

"Hi," said Carl, a little unsteadily. "I was just about to get you up."

"Well, here I am," answered the boy with a shrug. "Shall I make us some breakfast? You look famished."

Carl took a step forward, scratching his short beard and frowning.

"Jeremy, what did you do with the animals?"

"Took care of them, like I said." He busied himself with fetching pans from the cupboard, eggs and juice and muffins from the refrigerator.

"Yes, but what did you *do* with them? They were in the garage when we turned in last night."

"I—uh—I set them free. You said that this house was too small for a passel of dogs and cats, remember? Freeing them seemed preferable to sending them to the shelter, where they'd probably be put to sleep. I thought they deserved a fighting chance."

"But I told you we could keep a dog and a cat. Wasn't that the deal?"

"I decided that I really don't need any pets after all. How do you like your eggs?"

Once again Carl endured the sinking feeling that his son was a stranger—or, worse, a stranger that he could never truly know, a creature of a different species. But he had heard other fathers voice the same lament about their teenagers, and from this he took a small comfort.

"Never mind the eggs, Son. I want to know what you did

with the animals. I want to know where you took them, and why. *Look* at me, Jeremy."

The lad turned from the counter and stared hazel bullets at his father, sliding his hands into his pockets again. "Very well, I shall *look* at you," he said in a tone that Carl found unnerving. "I set the animals free, as I said before. I did so because I wanted to spare you the inconvenience of transporting them to the animal shelter. What more do you want me to say?"

That this was a lie was evident in the opaqueness of Jeremy's face. Carl felt the first sparks of paternal anger. A good father does not allow his son to lie to him, and Carl meant to be a good father, starting this very moment.

"I want the truth, Jeremy," he replied sternly. "I'll always be on your side no matter what happens, no matter what you do, but the one thing I won't stand for is lying, not to me or to anyone else. Do we understand each other?"

Jeremy smiled again, but not with boyish openness this time: It was a cynical smile more befitting an old man who had known his share of trouble.

"So it's *understanding* you want, is it? Then understand this: I have my own life to live, and I shan't accept your intruding into my private affairs. I'll play this little father-son game so long as it suits my purposes, and not a minute longer. You would do well to remember that, *Dad*."

Carl was flabbergasted by the retort, by the boy's snide emphasis on the word *Dad* in particular. This was a side of Jeremy he had not seen before: defiant, hostile, even threatening. The abrupt turnaround in his son's attitude was like a bucket of ice water thrown in his face, and Carl could well understand why Nora Moreland had been unable to cope during her stay in this house.

"Better cool your jets, big guy," said Carl, planting his fists on his hips, determined to reestablish his fatherly authority. "I won't have you talking to me that way, not ever. Maybe you think you can get away with bullying your grandmother like you did, but don't try it with me. This isn't a game we're playing here—"

"Oh, isn't it? But I thought that's what pretending is—a game. I pretend to be your loving son, trotting along at your feet and playing the role of obedient teenager, while you pretend to be the all-American dad, wise and nurturing—all for appearances, of course. It just so happens that the arrangement suits me for the time being, since someone my age can't very well be out on his own, now can he?"

A tincture of rage and confusion colored Carl's cheeks as he fought down the wild urge to slap Jeremy's face. "Jeremy, what's gotten into you?" he asked pleadingly. "Why are you acting like this?"

"How do you want me to act? Like a little boy, perhaps? Shall I go out and buy a Michael Jackson album, or stand around with my friends in the parking lot of a shopping mall, bouncing a Hacky Sack off my foot? Or maybe I should try out for track or baseball, or start hanging out at video arcades. Would any of those make you happy?"

"Look, I'm not trying to be an asshole. I just want to know what's wrong, that's all. Maybe I can help—"

Jeremy laughed loudly, causing Carl to flinch. "You want to *help*, is that it? Well, don't try to help *me*, because I don't need it. Help yourself instead. You're the one who came back with a head full of notions about starting a new life and becoming a real father, without the slightest idea of what any of that means. You saw yourself as the kindly mentor of a stereotypical pubescent brat, whom you would teach and guide and mold into a younger version of yourself, doing all the fatherly things that you assumed were expected of you: fishing, sailing, bicycling, spending *meaningful* time together—all your ideas, not mine."

What kind of kid talks like this? screamed a voice in Carl's mind. Prodigy or not, this was hardly the speech of a thirteen-year-old boy, especially one who until six months earlier had been incapable of uttering a single human word. Even more wrenching was the realization that Jeremy was speaking the truth.

"J-Jeremy, listen to me," said Carl, immediately regretting his weak tone. "You and I—we've got to—we've got to have some kind of understanding, if we're going to live together and—"

"Did you say *if?* Is there any question about whether we're going to live together?"

"Let me finish, God damn it!"

"What's the matter, Old Carl? Having second thoughts about things?"

The boy's voice had suddenly deepened to the elegant baritone of Carl's own father. It lacked any trace of British accent and now had the same mocking inflections that Carl's father had used when teasing or scolding.

"That'd be just like you, wouldn't it? Bail out the minute the sledding gets a little tough! Maybe you're just not cut out for this home life after all, this father-business, the small-town lawyer. Maybe you really do belong in the fast lane, Old Carl, where you don't have to go to all the trouble of loving anyone but yourself."

Carl put a hand on the refrigerator to steady himself and tensed his muscles to dampen the shudder that was rippling through his body. How Jeremy could have known about the voice of his dead father and its alter-ego role in his mind was a chilling riddle. But more chilling still was the boy's flawless impersonation. Carl's father had died long before Jeremy's birth, so the boy could not possibly have known what his grandfather's voice had sounded like.

"Jeremy, listen to me. I'm not going to run out on you, never again. When your mother and I split up, it wasn't because—"

Because of what? He caught himself on the verge of telling the lie again, the one he had told to so many people over the years: that Jeremy had not been the reason for his and Lorna's breakup. He resolved to stick to the truth, as he admonished his son to do.

"Jeremy, you're my son, and I love you. I'm going to be here for you—"

"Oh, stop deluding yourself," said Jeremy, spitting the words. The British accent was back, stronger than before. "You don't love *me*, you love an *idea*: the idea of being a father, of having a son, of living a pure and wholesome life in good old Greely's Cove, just as Lorna would have wanted. You're totally out of touch with reality, *Dad*." The boy moved close to his father and stared boldly into his face with those hard, knowing eyes. "You haven't a clue about what I really am, or for that matter what this town is, or even what Lorna was. Suppose I were to tell you that your wife—my mother— had been fucking your friend Renzy Dawkins for the past year, right up until she killed herself. Or that your old chum Stuart Bromton has been taking bribes from a drug dealer, and that he plans to run away from his home and family as soon as he's collected enough cash. If I were to tell you these things—"

Carl quailed and paled, battling the desperate impulse to slam his fist into his son's smooth jaw.

"—you wouldn't believe me, would you? How much less would you believe the truth about *me*? The simple fact, *Dad*, is that the truth doesn't fit your tidy ideas and images, so you choose to discount it. Well, no matter. The games you play with yourself are of no concern to me. I'll even play along, if that's what you want. Just don't try to put a leash on me. As I said before, this arrangement suits me for the time being, as long as you don't intrude into my personal affairs."

Carl suddenly felt very sick. The stories told by a pair of teenaged thugs, Jason Hagstad and Kirk Tanner, about how his son had somehow forced them to commit acts of terrorism against old Hannie Hazelford no longer seemed outlandish. Jeremy was capable of incredible mental cruelty; that much was clear. He knew exactly which buttons to push.

A dark certainty took shape in Carl's mind: The challenge of raising this boy, of loving him and salvaging him from the sickness that had afflicted him since his birth, would be far greater than Carl had ever dreamed or feared. The new life would not be an easy one.

"Jeremy," he said heavily, trying to keep his eyes from welling with tears, "if you wanted to hurt me, you've succeeded. I'm not saying I believe everything you've said, but what you said still hurts. The fact is, you *are* my son—and God damn it, I'm going to love you even if it kills me. I may never be able to understand you, and the day may come when I can't even control you"—the glint in Jeremy's eyes suggested that the day had already come—"but I'm always going to love you."

He couldn't say any more, not just yet. His vocal chords ached.

For a few seconds Jeremy's face hardened rebarbatively, twisted and contorted as if in pain. Whether the pots and pans on the counter actually vibrated, or whether the kitchen utensils in the cupboards and drawers actually rattled and clattered, Carl did not know or really much care. Later he would tell himself that he had merely hallucinated. Jeremy's scowl softened, and the hard gleam fled his hazel eyes. He was suddenly a little boy again, gazing with dejection at his feet, perhaps feeling ashamed for the monstrous things he had said. The transformation was immediate and complete.

"I don't want to build a prison around you, Jeremy," said Carl, regaining his voice and assuming that his son's silence was an opening. "What matters to me most is your happiness, that you have a chance to grow and become whatever you choose. It doesn't worry me that you're not like other kids, because in many ways you're better than most other kids— smarter, more mature, capable of greater things, probably. But even so, Jeremy, you need somebody like me, somebody who cares about you and can provide the things you need, keep you on course. Can't you see that? You need a father, and I'm the guy."

The boy raised his gaze into his father's face, and at that very moment Carl knew fully what fatherly love was all about— selfless and steady, given without qualification, total. His own father must have loved him like this.

"I'm sorry, Dad," said Jeremy softly, sounding almost like an American boy now. "I shouldn't have said the things I did. I hope you'll forgive me."

Carl forgave him wholly, wrapped his arms around Jeremy's shoulders, and hugged him hard, ignoring the tiny apprehension that his son's contrition might be an act, a conniving and well-calculated charade.

"I forgive you, Jeremy. I just hope you can forgive *me*. Maybe it's time for us to get all our forgiving out of the way and start over again. How about it?"

Jeremy returned the hug, keeping his hands well out of sight behind Carl's back.

"Sounds good," he said. "A new beginning, right?" He even sniffed, like one who was himself on the verge of crying.

Lindsay Moreland heard the electronic buzz of a ringing telephone on the other end and waited impatiently for her mother's doctor to answer.

"Esther, this is Lindsay Moreland. Sorry to bother you on a Sunday, but I really would like to talk to you."

"Oh, I think I can manage a few minutes for a valued

customer like you. I was just about to leave on a little bike trip, but it's started raining again, and these old bones are getting sensitive to wet and cold. I don't mind putting it off, believe me. So, how's your mother?"

"Fine, fine. In fact she's almost back to her feisty old self. I'm at her house now, and she sends you her best."

"Good, I'm glad to hear that, and tell her thanks. I still want to see her, though, as soon as she can manage it."

"Don't worry. I'll have her in your office within the week. What I called about—well, actually this is a little hard."

Indeed it was. The previous night she had sat up until the wee hours, listening to the demented ramblings of Hannie Hazelford, a certifiably whacko crone who actually believed in witchcraft and demons. Lindsay had endured patiently, had quietly disbelieved Hannie's insistence that Jeremy Trosper had caused the suicide of his mother and that the boy's therapist was really an ancient sorcerer who served a flesh-eating demon.

Lindsay's patience had crumbled when Hannie had started in about how Lorna's corpse must have been stolen, how Craslowe had somehow arranged for it to be fertilized with the flesh-eater's seed in order to bear its offspring. How even now Lorna was hanging in some unspeakable state that was a combination of life and death. Hannie, who fancied herself among the last members of an ancient Sisterhood of witches, had tried to enlist Lindsay's participation in some execrable ritual aimed at destroying Craslowe and his creature.

And this is when Lindsay had thrown her out of the house.

"Lindsay, what is it?" asked Dr. Esther Cabaza. "Are you still there?"

"Uh, yes, I'm still here. I was just thinking . . ."

About Hannie's parting words, uttered desperately as Lindsay was hurrying her out the door, threatening to call the police if she didn't leave quietly, to summon the men with white coats. *"But surely you cannot believe that your nephew is just a sick little boy! Surely you can't believe the rubbish that Hadrian Craslowe has told you—"*

"I'm sick of listening to this insanity, Hannie! You need help—professional help—and I'm willing to help you get it, but I won't sit and listen to any more of this—"

"But you can prove it for yourself, girl! Check up on

Hadrian Craslowe, and try to verify his credentials! Try to corroborate all that he has told you! And if for some reason you still don't believe me, look at his hands, if you can! And Jeremy's hands, too! By now the boy will have started to—"

"Get out, Hannie! Get out of my house right now!"

"His HANDS, Lindsay! Look at the boy's HANDS!"

"I'm sorry, Esther, this may sound absurd, but I need to know how to go about checking on the bona fides of a local shrink, a clinical psychologist. My nephew is a patient of his, and I was just thinking—"

"Hey, it's not absurd. More people should do that kind of checking—not just on their shrinks but on all their doctors. A lot of grief would be saved. What do you need to know? Certification, schools attended, that kind of stuff?"

"Right. Who do I call?"

"The state board of clinical psychologists is your best bet. They can give you all the poop on the status of his license, the schools he attended, even his test scores, if you need them. Who is this guy, if you don't mind my asking?"

"Not at all. His name is Hadrian Craslowe, practices in Greely's Cove. He's English, apparently went to Oxford and even taught there. He also has said that he's practiced at some big mental-health outfit in Switzerland—Zurich, I think."

"Ummm. His being a foreigner might complicate things a tad. Say, Lindsay, why don't you let me check into this for you?"

"Esther, no. You're busy enough as it is, and I couldn't ask you to—"

"You're not asking; I'm offering. Listen, until last year I served on the state board of medical examiners, and I know some of the folks on the shrink board. I can pull a string or two and get a first-rate vetting of this guy for you, probably in about one-fifth as much time. How do you spell his name, anyway?"

Lindsay spelled the name, wondering if she herself needed psychiatric help.

21

Police Chief Stu Bromton cruised by Liquid Larry's roadhouse and pumped the brakes when he spotted a Volkswagen Vanagon with Texas plates in the lot. He made an abrupt turn, parked next to the van, and went inside.

Robinson Sparhawk sat alone at a corner table, well apart from the boisterous Sunday-afternoon crowd, nursing a double shot of whiskey and a short beer on the side. Clenched in his teeth was the well-chawed stump of a cheroot, which appeared to have gone cold and smokeless. His metal crutches leaned against a nearby chair.

As the police chief drew closer, he noticed the haggard expression on Robbie's face, the drained and bloodshot eyes, and for a moment he imagined that the psychic's hair was a shade grayer than it had been yesterday.

"Knock me over with a feather," said the big man, pulling up a chair and sitting down. "I thought you'd be long gone by now. Mind if I join you?"

"Not at all, seein' as you already have. Can I buy you a drink?"

"Sure," answered Stu, throwing a wave at Liquid Larry, which meant that he wanted the usual—a draft Olympia, which was okay, since he was technically off duty and dressed in civvies. "But don't let me tie you up. It's almost three o'clock already, and you'll probably want to get rolling, right?"

"Not today, Bubba. I got me a date with a bottle of Wild Turkey, and I mean to sit here and get pleasantly shit-faced, or get my sorry ass thrown out by that big old boy behind the bar, whichever comes first."

"Sounds like a ton of fun. Where's your dog?"

"Out in the truck. Seems animals ain't allowed in this place."

"Not the four-legged kind, anyway," said Stu, eyeing the

263

white tape around Robbie's left wrist. "What happened to your arm?"

Hesitation, a deep breath, a quick concoction of a passable nonanswer.

"Cut myself last night," said Robbie, studying his shot glass. "Not really deep, but deep enough to send me back to that emergency room in Poulsbo. Cute little nurse wrapped it up for me." Then, to change the subject: "Y'know, I thought I'd pretty near seen most everything there is to see in this old world, until I laid my eyes on this place."

He nodded toward a mob of young working-class males who had gathered around the pair of fish tanks against the far wall. One of them stuffed a dollar bill into a coffee can that wore a crudely lettered sign: "VICTIMS—1 BUCK." Then he fished around in the goldfish tank with a long-handled net until snagging a squirming victim and, with a beery chuckle, flipped it into the neighboring tank, where lurked Hammerstein, the flesh-eating Oscar fish. The predator quickly cornered the panic-stricken goldfish and gobbled it. The spectators laughed loudly and dug for more dollars.

"Folks in this town sure must be hard up for entertainment," said Robbie.

Liquid Larry appeared at the table with a mug of beer, which he placed before Stu. "Want me to tab that for you, Sonny Butch?" he asked.

"Take it out of this," said Robbie, pulling a five from the stack of long green underneath his ashtray, "and pour me another Turkey when you get the chance."

Liquid Larry made change and retreated to the bar.

After sipping his beer, Stu said, "Thought you might be interested in knowing that I got a call from a concerned citizen this morning, man named Dr. Hadrian Craslowe. Says you showed up at his front door late last night."

Robbie said nothing and made a production of lighting a fresh cigar.

"He also said that you scared the living bejesus out of one of his resident patients," Stu went on, "guy in a wheelchair. The doctor's assistant described you right down to your fancy belt buckle and your van, too. Care to tell me about it?"

"One of his resident patients, huh?" Robbie harrumphed and

sucked smoke from his cigar. "So, did this Craslowe fella swear out a paper on me? Is that why you sniffed me out?"

"No, nothing like that. He *was* concerned, though, and, being a doctor, was worried that you might need some help. You know how doctors are."

The barkeep returned with another Wild Turkey for Robbie, collected more cash, and left again.

"I really did think that you'd already headed for home," continued Stu, "but I called the West Cove to make sure and discovered that you hadn't checked out yet. Since you weren't in your room, I just started cruising around town, figuring you'd turn up sooner or later. I'll admit I was a little surprised to find you in *this* place."

"Closest thing to a Texas watering hole I could find. So what's the upshot of this Craslowe business?"

A roar of laughter rose from the lumpen crowd near the fish tanks as Hammerstein dispatched another hapless goldfish. Stu waited for the noise to die down.

"What were you doing out at Whiteleather Place, Robbie? I've got to ask —you know that. Is there something out there I should hear about?"

Robbie shut his eyes a moment and fingered the turquoise slide of his string tie. The lines that scored his sun-browned face seemed deeper than they had yesterday; he looked older. A sip of whiskey now, another pull from his cigar, and he was ready. "No, nothing that should concern the police," he said.

"Pardon me if that's a little hard to believe," said Stu in a low voice. "Yesterday you got knocked flat on your ass by a—a—*feeling*, some kind of psychic signal or whatever it is you get, and you told me that you steer clear of things like this. You were scared, man, and you were going to hit the road first thing today. Then I find out—".

"Now hold on, Bubba. I never said I got any kind of feeling."

"That's bullshit. You as much as admitted it yesterday in your motel room."

"I never said it had anything to do with your missing folks."

"For the love of God, Robbie, will you quit jacking me around? Put yourself in my shoes for one goddamn minute and tell me what the hell I'm supposed to think: I present you with evidence taken from the scene of a crime, and you get so sick that you blow chow all over my desk. You tell me later that the *thing* you felt, whatever it was, is something you never mess around with and that you plan to leave town in the morning. Then I find out that you've driven out to Whiteleather Place, of all places, after midnight, through fog and rain, to harass the assistant of one of the town's leading citizens, not to mention a patient of his. *Then* I find you here, drinking your brains out like you're trying to get ahold of yourself or maybe forget something ugly. So tell me what I'm supposed to think."

"I can't tell you what to think, Stu. All I can tell you is that there ain't any police business out at Whiteleather Place."

"Then what kind of business is it?"

"Something I've got to deal with myself; nothing that a cop can do anything about. Do yourself a favor and let it go at that. You'll thank me someday, believe me."

Suddenly Liquid Larry was back at the table. "You Mr. Sparhawk?" he asked. "Telephone call for you."

Robbie frowned with bewilderment, wondering who in the world could know that he was exercising his elbow at *this* particular establishment. He had told no one that he was coming here.

"Be right there," he replied to Liquid Larry while reaching for his crutches. He left Stu at the table and hobbled to the end of the bar, where the telephone waited.

"This is Sparhawk."

"Mr. Sparhawk, you don't know me," said an aged-sounding Englishwoman on the other end, "and I do hope you'll forgive this intrusion, but I really must talk with you—personally and privately, the very soonest."

"Ma'am, can you tell me who you are and what this is all about?"

"Yes, of course, I'm sorry. I'm Hannie Hazelford, and I live here in Greely's Cove. I want to discuss what happened to you last evening at Whiteleather Place."

Robbie's hands went cool and numb, and he began to feel slightly dizzy.

"You are an extraordinarily courageous man, Mr. Sparhawk, and you have gifts that are much needed here. You are just the sort that I can use. Can you come to my house, perhaps within the hour? We really mustn't lose a minute."

Robbie cleared his throat, hemmed and hawed. Other than a

name, he had no idea who this woman was, or whether he could safely discuss with her the ordeal he had undergone the previous night.

"Ma'am, I'm not so sure—"

"I can well appreciate your misgivings, but do put them aside for the moment. Even though you're a good man, and a strong one, you cannot possibly defeat this thing alone. You need allies, Mr. Sparhawk, as do I, so let us forge our alliance and do what must be done. Now, I live at Three Almdahl Circle, which is on Torgaard Hill—it's a Tudor cottage with an entrance blackened by fire, a recent misfortune that looks more serious than it was. Please be here as soon as you can. And feel free to bring your dog, inasmuch as I get along very well with animals and enjoy their company."

"Uh—well, all right, I s'pose I could make time. I'll be there as soon as I can, Miss uh—Missus . . ."

"Please call me Hannie. Everyone does."

"Fine. One thing, ma'am: How did you find out about what happened to me last night? For that matter, how did you know to find me here?"

"Mr. Sparhawk, I really *am* surprised at you, someone with your unique abilities and powers, asking such a question! Have you never heard of a scrying mirror?"

Robbie had not.

"Well, you have now, and you'll even see one when you get here—one of the few still in existence. Far better to demonstrate than merely tell you about it, don't you think? Now do hurry, Mr. Sparhawk, because we haven't much time."

So Robinson Sparhawk did as he had promised and hurried away, leaving a frustrated and bewildered police chief at Liquid Larry's to nurse his beer alone.

22

By midafternoon on Monday, Lorna's Little Gallery on Frontage Street had become a nearly vacant storefront with featureless walls and bare floors. Carl Trosper, his son, and Renzy Dawkins had slaved throughout half the previous day and most of the present one, boxing and crating the artifacts of Lorna's modest but loving enterprise: fixtures, paintings, posters, art supplies. They stacked them in the rear stockroom that fronted the alley. Later that week, hired movers would cart off the goods for storage until Carl could arrange for an auction.

Jeremy had proved himself an energetic and cheerful worker. He had shown none of the hostility or cruel astuteness that had so unnerved his father on Sunday morning. Around three o'clock they broke for Diet Cokes that Renzy had brought in a cooler from his boat, and Carl remarked that Jeremy looked a little tired—not surprising for a boy who had worked as hard as he had for the past two days.

"Why don't you knock off," suggested Carl to his son, "maybe walk home and watch a little TV? Renzy and I can finish up here. You know what they say about all work and no play."

Home was only a few blocks away, as most places were in tiny Greely's Cove.

"I guess I do have some reading to catch up on," said the boy with a grin, sounding almost like a normal American kid. He wiped his brow with one of the bulky workman's gloves that he had worn all weekend. "See you around dinner, then?"

"Around six," confirmed Carl. "And don't cook anything. I'm taking you both out for dinner. It's the least I can do for a faithful pair of draft animals."

After Jeremy had gone, Renzy lit a cigarette and smoked contentedly for a few moments, pacing lazily around the empty cavern that had been Lorna Trosper's store.

"Know what, Bush? I need a get-rich-quick scheme, something that'll get me back into the swim when my money runs out—which will be soon. What do you think of this? Genital cosmetics. I'm talking about a new rage here, a whole line of nicely packaged blushes, conditioners, liners, and scents for discriminating consumers of both sexes. It would be easy to do: Just adapt a bunch of existing products and launch them with a punchy ad campaign. Hey, are you listening to me?"

Carl was listening, but not closely. His gaze was far off, his face etched with worry, as it had been throughout the past two days.

"Sorry. I guess I'm a little preoccupied. Putting all this stuff in boxes, piling it up to be sent away—it's like we're getting rid of the last traces of Lorna. After the carpenters and painters are done, you won't be able to recognize this place. There won't be anything left of her."

"Yeah, it's sad. I feel it, too, but I keep reminding myself that this is the way she would've wanted it, and then I feel a little better. Are you sure there's nothing else eating you?"

"It's nothing, really. Unless you count the fact that virtually everything I own is in a moving van somewhere, probably overturned in a ditch in Kansas or Nebraska, buried in the snow until spring."

"For Christ's sake, your stuff will get here okay."

"Then there's the two hundred pounds of legal paperwork I've got ahead of me concerning Lorna's estate. I have to buy a car, furniture for the house and this place, law books, office equipment, hire a secretary—"

"It's Jeremy, isn't it?" said Renzy, his sea-weathered face growing serious. He dropped his cigarette butt on the floor, stepped on it, and drew close to Carl, who was staring downward in silence. "What happened, Bush? I thought everything was copacetic with you guys."

"I suppose it won't do me any good to keep it in. Yesterday morning he and I had a set-to over the dogs and cats he'd collected. Sometime Saturday night—after we'd gone to bed—or maybe even early Sunday morning, he got up and took them somewhere. Says he set them free, because he couldn't stand the thought of sending them to the shelter. Wanted to save me the work of taking them there. Or something like that. Wouldn't tell me where he took them or the real reason he did it. Then, when I pressed him on it and started giving him a lecture about truth and honesty, he—" This was difficult, and Carl's dry throat forced him to take a gulp of Diet Coke. "He *changed*. I don't know how to explain this without sounding like a stark-raving madman, but he *changed*, Renzy. . . ."

Renzy Dawkins listened quietly to the rest of the story, occasionally picking at his bluish stubble or absently practicing bowlines and hitches with the short hank of rope that he carried in his khakis. Carl left nothing out—not even Jeremy's spiteful tale about Lorna and Renzy, or the one about Stu Bromton being a crooked cop who took bribes from illegal drug dealers.

"And it was like he was inside my head, Renzy, like he knew exactly the right buttons to push in order to get my goat and cause me the greatest possible pain. How in the hell he was able to imitate my father's voice—even use Dad's kind of language—I'll never know. I'm not even sure I want to. And then, just as abruptly as it started, it was over, and he was back to his lovable self, apologetic and considerate, even cheerful."

"The same kid we took out on the town Saturday night."

"And the one we've been working with for the last two days. I keep thinking about what Dr. Craslowe said: that Jeremy's been through a hellish ordeal for the past thirteen years and that we've got to expect his attitude and emotions to swing back and forth as he goes on with his recovery, but that doesn't explain some of the *other* things."

"You don't really think Jeremy can read minds, do you? Is that what you're driving at? Listen, Bush, the kid is world-class perceptive—that much is certain—and it's the combination of his perceptiveness and intelligence that makes you think he's reading your mind. It's an illusion, a trick that he sets you up to play on yourself."

"What about Dad's voice?"

"That's an easy one. If you could hear a recording today of what Jeremy said to you—in what you thought was your dad's voice—you'd say that it doesn't sound like him at all. If the language was similar, it was probably because you talk that way yourself, and Jeremy was only imitating *you*. You heard what you heard because your imagination was running wild, and you were in a state of shock over all this sudden hostility. The kid doesn't read minds, Bush. Nobody does."

"Okay, maybe I buy all that. It still doesn't explain the

hostility, or the obsession with keeping a part of his life private from me—his personal affairs, he calls them."

"Good God, why is *that* so surprising? You were an only child yourself, Bush. If you'll think back a minute to when you were a kid, you'll remember you owned a part of the household, almost like a little fiefdom, that was all *yours*—separate and apart from the world of adults—and you didn't have to share it with anyone. You had no brothers or sisters—remember?—nobody who wanted a piece of it. You had *your* room, *your* toys, *your* clothes, and you learned very early what it means to have a personal life, one that belongs to you and nobody else. Why shouldn't your kid want the same thing?"

"And the hostility?"

Renzy undid a sailor's knot in his hank of rope and poked it into a hip pocket, holding back a moment, thinking. Finally: "I don't know the answer to that one. I could hazard a few more guesses, but good God, I'm no shrink. My opinion on that score wouldn't be worth much, I'm afraid."

Carl patted his friend on the shoulder. "No matter. You've been a help, Renzy; more than I can tell you. It's good to have an objective view on things like this, especially from someone who cares. Know what else? I appreciate your friendship, all you've done: lending me your car, helping me get this place in shape, not to mention letting me cry on your shoulder. I'll make it up to you some day."

"Does that mean you'll become a partner in the genital cosmetics business?" asked Renzy, grinning slyly.

"Let's not get carried away with this friendship thing," answered Carl with a mock frown that he could not hold for long, and they both laughed.

"What do you say we kick this job in the ass, finish it, and get ready for a nice quiet dinner at the Moorage? Crating the rest of this stuff won't take more than half an hour, and after that, all we have to do is scrub the floors and wash the windows. Another couple of hours and we'll be out of here."

"Carl," said Renzy somewhat hesitantly, dropping the nickname he'd pinned on his buddy when they were boys, "I have something to tell you. It's not easy—I mean, it's about something that Jeremy told you yesterday, the part about Lorna and me—"

"Don't worry about it," said Carl, about to lug a box to the back room. "I didn't believe him for a minute. He was only trying to hurt me with a lie. I probably shouldn't even have told you about it."

"That's the problem: He wasn't lying."

Carl straightened and stared wide-eyed at Renzy, wondering if he had heard correctly. "You mean—you and Lorna?"

"I'm afraid so. I should've leveled with you long before this, but I—well, I wasn't sure what Lorna herself might've told you. Besides that, I—"

"She never mentioned it to me," said Carl, feeling a little numb. He kneaded the back of his neck, then pocketed his hands and let a few more long moments drift by. "Were you in love with her?"

Renzy nodded, his green eyes sad. "You can understand that, I hope. It wasn't what you could call a storybook romance; in fact, we were in the process of breaking up when she—when she died. For a few horrible days afterward, I worried that maybe she had killed herself because—uh, because—"

"Because of the breakup?"

"Something like that, I guess. But the fact is, Carl, she wasn't madly in love with me, not like I was with her—at least not during those last few months. We started off like gang-busters, had about six months of that old I'm-in-love-and-the-whole-word-is-wonderful feeling. We kept things pretty private, which was my idea, since I'm just one cut above the town drunk on the social register around here. *That* distinction, by the way, belongs to Mitch Nistler. Remember him from the old days? Weird little guy with thick glasses who nobody could stand?

"Anyway, I don't think Lorna even told her mother and sister about us, which suited me just fine. We saw each other whenever we could, which wasn't all that often, because it wasn't easy to find someone to take care of Jeremy, even for a few hours. Then, after a while, Lorna started getting depressed, becoming afraid of things she wouldn't talk about, withdrawn. I almost felt like I didn't know her anymore. She shut me out, along with everything and everybody else, and it became clear that our relationship wasn't going anywhere. So—shit, you can guess the rest."

"You hadn't been planning to marry her?"

"I was on the brink of asking her a couple of times, but I never did. What could I have given her? Or for that matter, what could I have *been* for her? Here I am, running out of money, no real prospects—Christ, she was entitled to better than that. Besides, I always had the feeling that she had never really gotten over you."

Carl wandered over to the crate on which he had set his can of soda and took a long sip. "I suppose that should make me feel a little better, but it doesn't," he said, bleeding inside.

Renzy lit another cigarette. "Remember her memorial service, when I was just sort of standing on the beach, not getting too close to the crowd in the park? If you hadn't caught sight of me out there, I probably wouldn't have come any closer, because I was feeling so guilty. I felt like I had done you shit, Carl, and I was scared of talking to you. On top of that, I didn't want to run into Stu Bromton, not just then."

"Why not? What's Stu got to do with all this?"

Renzy blew out a lungful of smoke, staring at his old friend in disbelief.

"You mean you don't *know*? After all these years, you really don't know? Carl, listen: Stu has had it bad for Lorna ever since you first started taking her out back at UW. He never tried to horn in on you, because you and he were friends, and he knew he wouldn't have gotten to first base anyway, not with you around. After your divorce he actually made a few clumsy moves in Lorna's direction, but hell, he was the chief of police and the son-in-law of the mayor, so he had to watch his step. Needless to say, his efforts sort of fizzled."

"*Hippo* in love with Lorna? God, I feel like I'm dreaming. *You* I can understand, Renzy, but Hippo—"

"His marriage to Judy is a cruel joke," Renzy went on. "He hates her—actually *hates* her—and I don't doubt he hates his kids, too, along with his whole damn life, probably. This thing about the missing people has turned him into a grade-A basket case, which is understandable, I guess. The man is not a happy camper, Carl, and he's especially unhappy with me: thinks I'm a profligate jerk and a bum—which of course I am, but that's beside the point.

"When I first starting seeing Lorna, Stu and I were still friendly, and I let on to him what was going on between her and me. Real mistake, that was. I found out that he'd never gotten over her. He damn near demanded that I stop seeing her, got insanely jealous and predicted that I'd be a disaster for her. I haven't given up on the idea of salvaging my friendship with him, but even so, I'm sure he thinks I had something to do with her suicide. So you can see why I wasn't anxious to run into him at the memorial service."

"Yeah."

"I needed to tell you about this, Carl, because I value your friendship, and I want things to be on the up-and-up between us. I also want you to know that I'm sorry."

Carl smiled faintly, sadly. "No forgiveness needed. Lorna and I were divorced, a condition I brought on myself. I don't have any right to feel hurt, and certainly no right to be pissed off at you. I was just a little—surprised."

"You're not going to rip my arm off and beat me to death with it?"

"Not hardly. Who would I get to take me sailing in the San Juans?"

As evening fell, the drizzly mist floated eastward across the Puget Sound, driven by a sharp winter breeze that left a scatter of forlorn stars above Greely's Cove. Carl and Renzy finished their work at the storefront on Frontage Street and ambled back to the bungalow on Second Avenue, chatting quietly as old friends do, often slipping into a private jargon of their boyhood that an outsider would have found unintelligible. Carl grew quiet as they neared the little house that squatted dark and silent between the tall pines in the front yard.

"Something's wrong," he said, as they turned onto the walk that led to the porch.

"No kidding," replied Renzy. "Your yard looks like a fucking biological warfare experiment. What's happened to the shrubbery, for cripes' sake? The grass is half-dead, and even those old pines are turning yellow."

"That's not what I mean. If Jeremy were here, like he's supposed to be, there'd be some lights on." Carl dug for his keys as they clomped onto the porch, unlocked the door, and pushed it open, only to be greeted by darkness and silence.

Just as Carl had feared, Jeremy was gone.

Robinson Sparhawk sat quietly in the stuttering candlelight

and tried not to watch Hannie Hazelford disrobe, though she clearly suffered no compunction over doing so in the presence of a man she had met only one day earlier. Nakedness was a requirement of the business she was about, a very serious business that allowed for no squeamish modesty.

Robbie tried to concentrate instead on the mysterious paraphernalia of the small room: the incredibly old-looking tomes that lined the walls on sagging shelves, the ornately carved wooden table that stood on waxen blocks at the center of a pentagram inscribed on the floor, the murky bottles and jars that sat in clusters atop musty cabinets and bureaus (most were full of vile-looking liquids and powders and chips and chunks of things he dared not even guess about).

But try as he might, he could not resist staring at the spectacle of Hannie's nakedness as she peeled off the last of her clothing. Her leathery breasts hung flat against her sunken chest, pendulous and long empty of flesh. Her rattleboned arms and legs were so spindly that they appeared near breaking. The skin of her misshapen torso hung in droopy folds and creases, giving the impression that her organs were rolling around loose inside.

Off came the blond wig, revealing a nearly bald and spotted skull that looked too ancient to house a living brain. Lastly, she removed her turquoise contact lenses and replaced them with a pair of silvery pince-nez that perched crookedly on the bridge of her nose, enlarging her filmy eyes beyond absurdity.

Naked but for her pince-nez and shiny witch's ring, she sat down at the table and opened the hinged wooden box that lay before her on a thick block of wax, inside which was the instrument that she had reverently shown Robbie the previous day—the scrying mirror. Its round obsidian surface and pewter mounting gleamed softly in the candlelight.

"I'm quite ready now," she said, glancing up at Robbie. "I must warn you that I may behave strangely, once the scrying begins, and I may even appear to be in some distress. But under no circumstances should you try to help me or even communicate with me. Any interference by you could be extremely dangerous to us both. Is that understood?"

"Quite," replied the Texan, imitating her British manner. "I'm s'posed to sit here and watch, nothing else."

"Very good. I must warn you, too, that you yourself may be

affected, owing to your own considerable psychic ability. You may see unsettling images, feel forces around you, but you must take great care not to unleash any of your own psychic energy, no matter how frightened you become. My scrying spell will protect us both, unless of course you interfere, either psychically or physically, which would be akin to battering down our defenses from within."

"Don't worry, Hannie," said Robbie. "I'll hold myself back, no matter what happens."

Hannie then leaned forward until her senescent face hung directly over the scrying mirror, but with her eyes closed, her bony hands alongside her head with palms facing downward and fingers pointed stiffly toward the lustrous disk of obsidian. Her old lips, wiped clean of lipstick, began to move. From her mouth issued low, sibilant words that Robbie had never heard before—a language as ancient, he imagined, as the human species itself. After seven repetitions of a long phrase, she broke into heavily accented English that was very unlike the modern British dialect she normally spoke, grammatically familiar but hard to understand because of its singsongy, weirdly modulated tones and exaggerated diphthongs.

Was this the English of centuries past, Robbie wondered, perhaps spoken in the manner of Shakespeare or Henry VIII, from an era when Hannie Hazelford was already one of the oldest humans alive?

> *Mother under the Sea, with whom Woman is One,*
> *In the fullness of Lammass now having begun,*
> *Using Mugwort, Plantain and an herb called Stime,*
> *Have I proffered a Plea and uttered a Rhyme. . . .*

She began to rock back and forth in short, rhythmic jerks, eyes suddenly open wide and fixed upon the disk. Robbie detected the papery sound of her nipples brushing the wooden tabletop. Gone now was any doubt in Robbie's mind that everything Hannie had told him was anything but the awful truth.

Throughout the previous afternoon and deep into the night, from the very moment he had been summoned to this cottage, he had listened to her dark story while sitting in her comfortable parlor and sipping tea from a Wedgwood cup that Hannie kept perpetually full, munching little cakes that she brought from her cupboard until he could not eat one more bite. They'd graduated eventually to gin, which Hannie seemed only too happy to pour, until Robbie had become so tipsy that he could not possibly have driven back to the motel. He'd had no choice but to let her put him up in a spare room.

With the coming of morning, the telling had resumed, over breakfast and continuing through midmorning coffee, then over lunch and afternoon snacks and finally supper, interspersed occasionally with her interrogating him thoroughly about his ordeal at Whiteleather Place.

That he had stayed so many hours with this queer old crone in her little cottage, listening raptly to her words like a newly initiated disciple at the feet of a wizened holy man, would itself have seemed incredible, had not her words given him answers to the dark questions that had plagued him since an episode years ago at Carlyle Lake. Having recently met the thing that called itself Monty Pirtz, Robbie had needed those answers more desperately than he had ever needed anything in his life. Hannie had supplied them. In addition, she had been hospitable and kind.

She radiated a feeling of power and, more important, of *hope,* to which Robbie felt himself drawn—power against the evil that had nearly consumed him on the front porch of Whiteleather Place, and hope that there was some way to defeat it, kill it, cleanse the earth of it.

With these Nine Herbs, which are Three times Three,
And the power of the Words, which comes from Thee,
I shall loose this Charm into the World of Light
To guard me from harm and to save me this night
From Craft of vile Creatures, whose Names Thou dost know,
And to grant me Thy Favor, O Mother Below. . . .

She lapsed again into the old tongue that would have sounded like gibberish to Robbie, had it not been so fulsome and rhythmic, so alive with power. His crutches lay across his lap, and he discovered that he was gripping one of them so tightly that his hands ached. He wished that Katharine were with him, sitting beside his chair with her massive head resting comfortingly on his knee, and not locked away in the spare bedroom as Hannie had insisted. Dogs, the old witch had explained, are psychically sensitive and easily frightened by the energies released during a scrying session. If a huge dog like Katharine were to go berserk during the session, the result could be disastrous.

Hannie fell silent at last and leaned forward to stare closely into the black surface of the mirror, a hunkered caricature of the ancient hag, her face twitching and contorting in the dancing candlelight. Robbie stared at that face, scarcely daring to breathe and feeling the first tentative tingling of his own psychic nerves.

It was happening now, whatever it was, this business of scrying, by which Hannie had learned of his nearly catastrophic meeting with Monty Pirtz two nights ago, by which she had located him on Sunday afternoon at Liquid Larry's. For a seasoned practitioner like Hannie, the scrying mirror was a window into time and space, through which she could locate and observe the doings, comings and goings of others—past, present, and future. With it she could track the forces of the unseen world.

Yes, the Old Truth was real—of that Robbie was certain beyond any flittering doubt. He felt ashamed for having so neatly ridiculed Mona Kleiman's attempts over the years to make him see this. But now he had come face-to-face with it—if one could indeed say that Monty Pirtz had a *face*—and he had taken Hannie Hazelford's crash course on the subject. He had become a true believer.

Hannie Hazelford was more than a thousand years old, one of the last members of the Sisterhood of Morrigan, an order dedicated to ridding creation of the kind of evil that had invaded Greely's Cove. At Whiteleather Place, somewhere in its black lower echelons, lived a specimen of that evil, guarded and served by a sorcerer whose name was Hadrian Craslowe, himself old beyond belief. The evil had reached out into the community of Greely's Cove in order to feed, to strengthen itself on the provender of human flesh, to procreate and inflict another of its kind upon humanity. It had commandeered the body, mind, and soul of a tragically impaired little boy named Jeremy, subjected him to execrable ceremonies and rituals in order to transform him into a steward, like Craslowe. Jeremy would serve the newborn offspring, just as Craslowe served *his* master.

Sickened as he had been by the story, Robbie would not have dreamed of refusing Hannie Hazelford's plea for his help. Though newly converted to the Old Truth, and lacking even the status of a rank novice in its practices, he could be a valuable ally to her. He did, after all, possess the Gift. While facing the Monty Pirtz–thing and struggling to free himself from its clutches, he had discovered a new dimension of that Gift, a new power that he could use to defend himself and other innocent humans from the predatory evil of Whiteleather Place. He was no longer an aging, helpless cripple.

Their first goal, Hannie had declared, must be to find and destroy the newborn, and the key to accomplishing this, she'd been certain, was Jeremy. This would be no small undertaking, because although Jeremy was a mere slip of a boy, he already possessed awesome powers that Craslowe had transplanted into him from his own feral mind. Jeremy, no doubt, had driven his own mother to suicide, using those powers to stretch her sanity beyond the snapping point, subjecting her to hair-raising demonstrations of his evil magic, planting abominable thoughts and urges in her mind. He had become a dangerous creature in his own right. Hannie had concluded that the safest way to locate him and track him was through the scrying mirror, hoping that he would lead her and Robbie to the newborn.

Suddenly the old witch began to tremble. The table rattled, causing the pewter candle holder to vibrate against the wooden surface. Robbie stared at her and wondered if she were in pain, whether his imagination or a trick of the candlelight was giving a soft, greenish glow to the Kabbalistic symbols carved in the block of wax, upon which the scrying mirror sat. Low coughing sounds came from Hannie's throat, and her body stiffened.

Robbie himself felt a tremor of psychic energy, and within the space of three heartbeats his mind was aswirl with images. At the very center of the gestalt display was Jeremy, and someone was with him, someone very old. On the periphery were fixtures like candles, heavy books and ponderous furniture that Robbie had never seen before. He knew that this was Whiteleather Place. The old man at Jeremy's side, who Robbie could sense was Craslowe, was talking, giving advice, issuing warnings. Somewhere in the distance Robbie got an impression of someone searching, someone who was near panic, whose heart was full of dread, and Robbie's mind was drawn to him. It was Jeremy's father, Carl, whom Robbie had never met except in the story told him by Hannie. Carl, too, was with someone else. In an old car. They were cruising the dark neighborhoods of Greely's Cove, searching for Jeremy—but for different reasons, it seemed, although Robbie could not be sure, because the focus of the scrying rippled and the scene was beginning to move. Something was happening. . . .

23

Mitch Nistler parked his old El Camino next to Cannibal Strecker's Blazer and trudged through the sharp night air to the front door of the crack house. He knocked tentatively on the splintery wood and waited for the door to open, which it did. But not until a dingy curtain had moved aside briefly in one of the front windows.

"So, it's you," said Stella DeCurtis, who was spiderlike under a sleeveless jumpsuit of leathery black. The flesh of her arms was nearly as white as her fissile hair. "Well, don't just fucking stand there. You're letting all the heat out." She turned and wandered back toward what had once been the kitchen of the tiny house but had since become the production room of a crack factory. Mitch followed, pulling the door closed behind him. Corley the Cannibal sat in a plastic lawn chair with a beer in one paw and a cigarette between his lips, watching the *Bob Newhart Show* on a portable TV. An electric space heater glowed nearby.

"It's Mister Wonderful," said Stella, by way of announcing Mitch, "on his weekly mission of mercy." She plopped down in an empty lawn chair and lit a joint.

"Hey, what's happening, Marvy Mitch?" bellowed Cannibal, popping his chewing gum loudly. "Want a beer or some—"

His stony eyes grew large as they took in the sickly condition of Mitch Nistler, who stood small and stoop-shouldered under the glare of the bare bulb in the ceiling, looking fishy-white and dazed.

"Jesus H. Christ, what happened to you? Go a couple of rounds with a cement mixer or something?"

"I haven't been feeling very good lately," answered Mitch, coughing painfully. "I don't know, maybe it's the flu."

"Well, you look like a scoop of shit. Maybe you should

knock off a few days' work, rest up, maybe even see a doc about that fuckin' rash all over your face. I can't afford to have my main mule rotting away before my very eyes!" Cannibal thought this worthy of a belly laugh.

"That's something I need to talk to you about, Cannibal," said Mitch when the laughter had stopped. "As of last Friday, my job was history. I've been fired. On top of that, my old boss is also my landlord, and he's throwing me out of my house— says he wants to fix it up and sell it. He wants me out within thirty days."

Mitch studied the worn linoleum and scuffed at it sullenly with the sole of his shoe, hating himself for the fact that he had even come here, for the fact that he was cowering before this felonious slimeball like a slave before his master. The horrors he'd undergone during the past weeks, particularly in the past few days, had not freed him of Strecker, had not changed the fact that he was still Cannibal's throwaway, and this angered him.

"I guess it means we're going to have to split the sheets," he continued, glancing up first at Cannibal and then at Stella. "I'm going to have to leave town, get another job somewhere. There's nothing for me around here, that's a cinch."

Cannibal rose out of his chair, went to the fridge, and pulled out a brew, which he tossed to Mitch.

"Hey, little man, let's not give up so easily. You've got friends, remember? If you ask me"—which Mitch had not, but this mattered little—"you're better off without that stinking job. I mean, who in the hell wants to pump blood out of dead bodies for a living anyway? And it's not like you don't have any cabbage coming in—as long as the crack market holds up."

"But I can't stay in this town," Mitch protested. "Nobody would rent to me, not after Kronmiller throws me out. He knows everybody in Greely's—"

"I *said* you've got friends, Mitchie, and one of them is *me*. I'm not going to let you get thrown out in the street." The big man took the final swig of his beer and crushed the can with one hand, then arched it into a cheap plastic garbage can that stood in a far corner.

"Y'know, this is funny. Me and Stella were just talking to Luis"—the mere mention of Laughing Luis Sandoval, the crack baron, caused Mitch to blanch—"about how good business has been. There's thousands of little high-school pukes out there, even *junior*-high pukes, who can't seem to get enough of our product. We sell out our whole fuckin' inventory like three hours after it hits the streets, and the very next day it's a mob scene of pukes, hittin' on us for more—no matter that half their crackhead friends are lying sick somewhere."

This was so funny that Cannibal had to laugh again, but he recovered quickly.

"The bottom line is this: We've got to step up production, maybe double or triple it. That means we're talkin' two, maybe three trips a week into Seattle for you. We're also talkin' serious cabbage, Mitchie. With seven hundred and fifty a week you can live anywhere you want, you get my drift? And you can use this place until you get something better."

A wave of despair swept over him as Mitch glanced around at the little kitchen with its glut of drug paraphernalia. Accustomed though he was to living in a dump, this place would be a new low. His guts jittered as he remembered the conditional promise that Jeremy Trosper had given him on Saturday night, which seemed a horrific millennium past: *"You will survive, even prosper."* Fuck a bald-headed duck, was *this* what the kid had meant by surviving and prospering? Living under the thumb of Cannibal Strecker, putting up endlessly with insults and abuse, dancing to a maniac's tune and enduring the contempt of that she-snake, Stella DeCurtis? *"Fail me, and I promise you a death that's horrible beyond words, beyond your worst nightmare."*

It was this final thought that brought Mitch back to earth. He had other obligations tonight and little time to engage in fruitless argument with Cannibal. There was *feeding* to be done.

"Well, I—uh—I guess my problems are solved," he said, causing Cannibal Strecker to grin hugely. "I should probably start packing up my stuff, get ready to move in and all that."

"Yeah, the sooner the better," said Cannibal, clapping his slave on the shoulder. "But first things first. You've got a delivery to make."

He turned as though to head for the refrigerator, then whirled with bullwhip speed and drove a hammerlike fist into Mitch's midsection, plunging the little man against the wall with a bone-jarring thud and knocking his beer can to the floor, unopened. Mitch's eyes nearly bulged out of their sockets as he went down, crumpling forward into a fetal ball. He landed on the nasty linoleum, where he writhed and choked and yawned for air, certain that at last he was dying. Strecker's mighty hands found wads of his jacket, hoisted him back up, and slammed him into the wall again, detonating a blast of pain in his spine.

"Cannibal, no!" screamed Stella DeCurtis from across the room, and Mitch could scarcely believe that she was intervening to spare him more agony. *"For shit's sake, don't touch the filthy little faggot! Do you want to catch whatever he's got?"* So much for that idea. *"I'm warning you, Cannibal, you can forget about stuffing your chubby in me unless you put him down, and I mean right now!"*

Cannibal was breathing in adrenaline-charged huffs, chewing his gum at four times his normal speed, obviously enjoying what he was doing. He continued to hold Mitch against the wall.

"I'm just making a little point here, that's all," he said breathlessly. "I'm just sort of whatcha call *underscoring* to my little buddy here that I'm in charge of his future. I don't want him getting any strange and wonderful ideas about running out on us or thinking that he has any say about anything. I want him to stay conscious of how important it is to keep us happy."

"You've made your point," said Stella. "Now put him down and go wash."

Cannibal released his hold on Mitch's jacket. Mitch wadded into a ball again and slid down the wall to the floor, drooling saliva and trembling uncontrollably.

"Come on, get up," said Cannibal. "You ain't hurt. In fact, you better get used to this, because I aim to plant one on you every so often just so you appreciate the nature of our relationship. You hear me, little man? You understand what I'm saying?"

Mitch groaned an acknowledgment, for he had not quite started to breathe again. His chest was a bonfire of pain. Finally he was able to climb back up the wall, to stand against it, to move crazily toward the doorway.

"Just a fuckin' minute," barked Cannibal. "Aren't you forgetting something?"

He strode to the refrigerator, withdrew the two packages for which Mitch had come, and zippered them into a gym bag, along with half a dozen envelopes full of cash. Then he crossed the room and stuffed the bag into Mitch's arms.

"Have a nice trip, and don't get mugged in Pike Place, okay? And try not to slobber on the bag."

The last thing Mitch heard as he staggered painfully out the front door of the crack house was the sniggering laughter of Cannibal and Stella, and he vowed again that someday, some-day *soon* . . .

The scrying ended, and Hannie Hazelford muttered the long and redundant phrases that shut off the flow of energy through the obsidian disk, allowing her mind to disengage gently. Robinson Sparhawk's mind also disengaged, and he leaned back in his chair, crutches across his lap, his face slick with sweat. His hands ached from gripping the crutches, and he felt as though he had spent the preceding hour in a sauna.

Hannie immediately set about the task of dressing.

"Ordinarily I'd offer you a gin and tonic," she said, pulling on a billowy, flowered smock, "because it's just the thing after scrying."

Robbie was struck by her matter-of-fact tone: She could have been talking about a lively round of shuffleboard or badminton.

"Unfortunately, we haven't time, I'm sure you'll agree." She paused a moment while hoisting up her pantyhose. "You *did* connect with the scrying, didn't you?"

"Oh, I connected, all right," answered the psychic, mopping his brow with a sleeve. "I saw Jeremy Trosper, Hadrian Craslowe, a lot of other things I'm not sure I can talk about yet. You weren't kiddin' around when you said it could get a little scary. Hell, I almost turned tail a couple of times, I don't mind telling you."

"Yes, I quite understand. There's no need to be ashamed. You were subjected to forces and phenomena that until recently you had not dreamed could exist. You've fared remarkably well, if I may say so."

"What's the next step?"

"That should be obvious, shouldn't it? Jeremy left White-leather Place and went to that awful little house in the woods."

"Yeah, I reckon I know where it is."

"I know *exactly* where it is, and I fancy that I know who lives there: a most unfortunate little man, named Mitchell Nistler. Something of a misfit, I'm told, an ex-convict and an assistant embalmer, widely regarded as the town drunk." She sat down again and started levering her misshapen old feet into a pair of Birkenstocks. "But of course he no longer lives alone. You felt the other presence there, didn't you?"

"I think so. I felt something, that's for sure—kind of like what I felt the other night at Whiteleather Place."

"Indeed. What distresses me, though, is that I never thought to consider Mitchell Nistler a likely paternal surrogate until now. I must be getting old and senile."

"You're what, darlin', only about a thousand or so?"

"Advanced enough to be considered a spinster, it seems." She removed the pince-nez and undertook to install her contact lenses.

"Let me see if I have this straight," said Robbie. "The steward—in this case Craslowe—snags himself an unsuspecting male adult, hypnotizes him—"

"Hypnosis is not the proper term. *Entrancement* is much closer."

"Okay, entrances him, and then forces him to eat the flesh of the Giver of Dreams. With the proper rituals and magic and so on, the unsuspecting male is then the carrier of the creature's seed. He's able to sire another Giver of Dreams, that right?"

"That's exactly right, but only with the corpse of a suicide. The rituals give to the unfortunate man most unwholesome desires—"

"I hope to shout. He actually wants to make love to a dead body?"

"Yes. You must remember that he has communed with the Giver of Dreams in the most hideously intimate way—has actually eaten its flesh—and his mind and soul have combined with the creature's. This man is in every sense a victim, perhaps as pitiable as the corpse herself. Quite often such a man is cursed from boyhood, selected by the steward and his allies as a target, subjected to charms and magic that result in his growing up to be an opprobrious and maladjusted citizen, easy prey for the steward later on. Stewards themselves often begin life in a similar way: Their mothers have been cursed or charmed just before giving birth, so that their sons are like Jeremy was—physically healthy but empty shells, open receptacles into which mature stewards can pour their own personalities and knowledge."

"Is that how Craslowe started out? Someone charmed him before he was born?"

"No, not at all. Hadrianus Craslovius was an alchemist in southern Europe about the time of the First Crusade, traveled mainly throughout Italy and the Balkans, performing minor feats of thaumaturgy. Somehow he stumbled upon a body of ancient writings that were Egyptian in origin—mostly having to do with the cult of Anubis, the Egyptian god of death and embalming. He immersed himself in them and discovered truly powerful magical secrets. He became a potent sorcerer and, like many who achieve great power, began to thirst after even more—in this case, power over death. It seems that he accompanied the crusaders to Antioch, for the writings had told him that a certain high priest of Anubis was entombed there, and buried with him was the secret of resurrecting him. I don't know whether Craslovius was aware that the priest would arise as a Giver of Dreams or that he himself would be cast in the role of steward. All I know is that this is what happened: that Craslovius awakened an evil from deepest antiquity, and that both he and that evil have survived to this day."

Robbie shuddered even though Hannie had covered this material earlier in great depth. Maybe it was her offhanded, almost casual delivery that made it so chilling, even the second time around. A mere week ago he would have laughed himself to tears, having heard this tale about ancient magic that enabled a man to live thousands of years, that required human flesh for sustenance, that needed the corpse of a suicide to bear its offspring. But a week ago he had not met Monty Pirtz.

Having dressed fully—blond wig, makeup and all—Hannie bustled around the cluttered chamber, collecting samples of this and that from vials and jars on the shelves: liquids, powders, and dark chunks of something or other, which she stashed in a bulky leather pouch she had taken from a hook on the wall. She turned and tossed to Robbie a small earthen jug, not quite fist-sized, that was stoppered with a dark cork, painted with words that might have been Hebrew.

"I must ask you to fill this with urine," she said. "And do hurry. We haven't much time."

"With *urine?* What the hell for?"

"A charm, of course. It will give you some protection in the event you need it."

Robbie gulped, and his stomach did a flip-flop. The Old Truth certainly had its disgusting aspects. As he hobbled on crutches to the bathroom, he worried about whether he could work up a good piss, but he managed, then hobbled back to Hannie's chamber and handed her the warm jug.

"Really, such a face, Robbie," she said about his scowl. "If *this* disgusts you, wait until later. You'll be positively mortified!" Robbie got the impression that she was enjoying his discomfort, despite the deathly seriousness of the business at hand. "Now," she said, "I'll need a short lock of your hair, a clipping of fingernail—"

"A lock of my hair? Now hold on, darlin', I just got it cut last week. I'm very sensitive about my hair."

Hannie held up an extraordinarily old-looking pair of scissors, and her hard expression gave no hope that she would be dissuaded from taking a chunk out of Robbie's mane.

"Small price to pay," she said archly, "for immunity against demons and familiars, wouldn't you say? Also, I'll need a small quantity of your blood."

"Is this when I'm supposed to be mortified?"

"Oh, heavens no! This is *nothing!*"

She went to work on him—first on his head, from which she snipped hair, then on the index finger of his right hand, from which she clipped a crescent of nail, and then on his right forearm, in which she made a rather deep and stinging incision with a long, bone-handled knife. She directed the blood into a pewter bowl.

Having collected hair, nail, piss, and blood, and having cleansed and tightly wrapped Robbie's wound, she set about brewing the charm—uttering old words and mixing things into bowls and jars, crushing and grinding and pulverizing, even doing an absurd little dance around the table. Robbie watched and tried not to be woozy. Abruptly it was over, and she poured a sample of the mixture into a tiny glass vial, placed the vial into a small skin pouch on a leather thong, and slipped it around Robbie's neck.

"There now," she said, with a twinkle in her turquoise eyes, "this will protect you from the minor forces. They're seldom lethal, but they can be troublesome and hurtful."

"What about yourself?" Robbie wanted to know. "Don't you need some kind of protection, too?"

"Not to worry—I possess power of my own. One doesn't serve a thousand years as a witch without picking up a few tricks, you know." She donned her orange slicker and gathered up the large pouch that contained the odds and ends she had collected earlier, then headed for the door.

"What's all *that* stuff?" asked Robbie, hobbling along behind. "You fixin' to cast another spell or somethin'?"

"In a sense, yes. These are the items we need to kill a newborn offspring of the Giver of Dreams, provided it hasn't yet matured to—" She fell abruptly silent and busied herself with turning out lights, checking the locks on the doors, and digging for her car keys.

"Matured to *what?*" pressed Robbie, distressed by her apparent reluctance to say more on the subject. "Are you sayin' that the thing can grow to a point where we can't kill it? Is that what you're sayin', Hannie?"

"I've said no such thing. Now kindly go into the garage and make yourself comfortable in my Jaguar. It's high time we were on our way." Robbie did as he was told, feeling as though he had little choice in the matter.

From his vantage point, Stu Bromton watched the red Jaguar roll out of the driveway and head down the hill toward the heart of the village. He was parked in his old Pontiac at the mouth of the service drive that divided Hannie Hazelford's land from the estate of which it had once been part, hidden in the deep shadow of a high hedge that ran along the property line. Behind him, against a sky that was bright with a full moon, loomed the proud Tudor manse that dominated fashionable Torgaard Hill—now an apartment house peopled mainly with affluent retirees who treasured their views of the Puget Sound and the village below. Most of the windows were still lit, but a few had already gone black, and the others would have done so by nine o'clock. Old people usually hit the sack early—unless they happen to be Hannie Hazelford.

Stu swung out of the service drive after the Jag had gone

about two blocks. He followed it toward Frontage Street, where it stopped for the traffic light and made a right turn. Stu did likewise, maintaining his distance behind it and taking care not to betray his presence. At the end of Frontage Street, the Jag signaled right and turned west onto Sockeye Drive, causing Stu to slow and allow it to gain another quarter-mile of distance. Sockeye Drive was dark and nearly deserted of traffic. His headlights in Hannie's mirror would have been a tip-off.

Something strange was going on; of that Stu was rock-solid sure. Just a day earlier, on Sunday afternoon, Robinson Sparhawk had received a telephone call from Hannie at Liquid Larry's and had driven immediately to her cottage to meet with her, leaving Stu by himself at the bar. Robbie had denied him even the semblance of an explanation before leaving, and he'd seemed ruffled, like a man who was wrestling with some colossal problem.

Whether the subject of Hannie's call was the reason for Robbie's discomfort, Stu did not know. Maybe it was the mysterious encounter with one of Dr. Craslowe's patients at Whiteleather Place the previous night. Stu *did* know, however, that Robbie had received a strong psychic impression from the smear of slime that was evidence in the investigation of Teri Zolten's disappearance, even though Robbie staunchly refused to admit it. And although the psychic had vowed to leave the Cove—apparently out of fright—something had caused him to change his mind, to pay a nocturnal visit to Whiteleather Place and generally start behaving strangely.

Stu himself itched to have a look-see around Whiteleather Place—not because he suspected Dr. Craslowe of any connection with the disappearances, but because the area surrounding the estate was fairly remote and heavily timbered. A homicidal kidnapper would find no shortage there of places to hide his victims. Maybe Robbie had gotten a psychic feeling about the area and, after deciding for some unknown reason to poke around the place himself, had run into one of Craslowe's patients. Such an encounter could indeed be frightening, both to Robbie and the patient, especially on a black, foggy night.

Earlier in the day, Stu had talked to the county sheriff's office and suggested another sweep in the vicinity of Whiteleather Place, only to be rebuffed: The area had already been

thoroughly searched on two previous occasions, it was pointed
out to him. Resources were scarce, and overland searches of
rugged, heavily vegetated terrain were costly and exhausting.
Helicopter fuel wasn't cheap, and neither were the man-hours
of pilots, ground-pounders, and dog-handlers. The State Patrol
and the sheriff's office had concluded that the key to solving
the disappearances lay not in sweeps of forest and shore but in
good, old-fashioned police work. At the conclusion of the
search currently under way, the National Guard, the pilots, and
the dog-handlers were to be sent home and replaced by a team
of special agents from the FBI.

Thanks, Stu, but we're handling this now, so . . .

So kindly get out of our way. Better still, make yourself
scarce.

Which should have suited Stu just fine, in view of the fact
that his days as the chief of the Greely's Cove Police
Department were numbered. He would soon be free of the
petty local politics and the inane little rituals it demanded.
The stroking and flattering. The pretense of being interested in
the suggestions of some dipshit city councilman. The charade
of cooperating with other jurisdictions. By the end of the year,
he planned to have amassed some $50,000—ten months' worth
of payments from Luis Sandoval's drug cartel—in addition to
his own meager savings from his pathetic salary. More than
enough to finance a suitable southern exile.

Happy a prospect as this was, Stu yearned to possess just one
more prize in addition to his freedom: He wanted to go out in
a thunderclap of success. He wanted the denizens of Greely's
Cove to lament his departure, to remember him with admiration as they chatted about local politics over dinner or drinks,
to hearken back to his tenure as the "golden days."

Stu wanted to be the one who solved the woeful mystery of
the missing people of Greely's Cove, not only to sop up the
glory that it would bring, but also to salve the emotional sores
that it had inflicted on him. He had imagined an invisible cloud
of evil hanging over the town, had believed the whispered
rumors of missing people who visited friends and loved ones in
various states of dismemberment and decay, had even let
himself conclude that Lorna Trosper's suicide was a symptom
of the "sickness" in the air. In short, the case had driven him
nearly insane. The healing salve would be the discovery that

there were plausible, real-world explanations for the madness afoot. He *needed* those explanations; he meant to get them and regain his mental health.

Stu had driven by Hannie Hazelford's house half a dozen times since Sunday afternoon and had seen Robbie's Vanagon in the drive each time, causing his curiosity to build like steam in a pressure cooker. What connection did Robbie have to that funny old Englishwoman, Stu wondered, and why had he stayed in her cottage so damned long? And what in the hell were they *doing* in there, anyway?

At the close of his shift, Stu decided to watch Hannie's house, believing that Robbie would have to leave *sometime*. A hunch suggested that the psychic's stay at the cottage had something to do with his extraordinary Gift. If that was so, Robbie's next move would be a significant one, a move that could well involve his reason for coming to Greely's Cove in the first place: the disappearances. If the hunch was right and Robbie was to make such a move, Stu Bromton wanted to know about it.

Hannie slowed the Jaguar to a crawl and steered off the pavement of Sockeye Drive onto a rutty strip that led deep into a wall of timber, past a rotting wooden sign announcing Old Home Road.

"It won't be much farther now," she said to Robbie, who sat in the right-hand bucket seat, his stare frozen forward.

"I know," he said tensely. "I can feel it. Hell, I can almost *see* it." He pawed inside his jacket for a cigar, then decided against having one. "This place where Nistler lives—it ain't very far from Whiteleather Place, is it? Mile and a half, maybe two?"

"Not far at all," answered Hannie. "As you perhaps surmised during the scrying, distance means little to Jeremy. He's already progressed beyond needing his feet for transport, or wheels either—just one of the little advantages he has over us."

"But I thought you witches were supposed to be able to fly, too. How come we're not ridin' your broom, instead of this here twelve-cylinder rocket?"

"Some witches have been known to fly, though not actually on brooms. I've done it myself, but I've found that it requires more magic than it's worth—saps energy that could be better used for other things. Besides that, it's cold in the wintertime."

"I guess Jeremy wouldn't agree with you," said Robbie. He fell silent again, watching the jouncing shadows cast by the headlights in the trees.

"Your Gift has become very strong, hasn't it?" remarked Hannie. "That often happens to people like you, after they've undergone the kinds of things you have. They discover powers and capabilities that have lain dormant all their lives. Sometimes those powers can be a mixed blessing."

Robbie merely nodded. His senses now were full of Jeremy Trosper and the newborn thing that a dead woman's body had borne, a thing closely related to the feculent presence he had felt at Whiteleather Place. Both were near, very near.

"I have often envied people with your Gift," Hannie went on, "and have often wished I possessed it myself. It would make things so much simpler for someone in my line of work. You see, even though I command considerable powers, they are powers outside myself. They come from words and the magic they invoke. Oh, I've become quite good at using the forces available to me, but how much simpler life would be if I could know things by merely feeling them, or influence events with my mind, as you now can. Magic is useful, Robbie, and frequently there is no substitute for it, but it requires so very much knowledge—much more, really, than the vast majority of people could ever hope to learn in a lifetime. And concentration, too, and discipline. That's why there are so few real witches and warlocks anymore, so few sorcerers. Magic requires sacrifice."

They emerged into a clearing, on the far edge of which, at the end of a muddy drive, stood the house where Mitch Nistler lived—dark and lonely and tumbledown, a sorry place, even in the filtering light of a silvery full moon. Hannie braked, turned toward the shoulder of the road, and halted. She shut off the engine and doused the headlights.

"Before we go any further," she said, "I want to express my gratitude to you."

Robbie ran his tongue over his lips, which had become as dry as the skin of a rattlesnake. "Gratitude? For what? I haven't done anything yet."

"I'm grateful for your courage," said Hannie, "and for your

willingness to help me. Your Gift will provide me with an additional set of eyes and ears—powerful psychic ones that can warn me of any lurking dangers. Without your help, it's doubtful whether I could succeed in what I'm about to do. I can't thank you enough, Robbie."

The Texan squirmed inside his heavy sheepskin jacket, which was becoming hot and sweaty. He itched to get on with things. "Well, I'm glad to do what I can," he said finally. "So, what do you say we get started? What's first?"

"I must celebrate a short ritual," answered Hannie, reaching into the rear seat to retrieve the bulky pouch she had brought along. "Then, of course, we must enter the house." She began rummaging in the pouch, locating certain objects and putting them in order.

"But Jeremy's in there," said Robbie. "I can feel him. I thought you said he was dangerous."

"Oh, he *is* dangerous, no doubt of that, but he is no Hadrian Craslowe, fortunately; at least not yet. Properly prepared, I can deal with him."

"And what if Mitch Nistler comes back while we're—uh—while we're doin' whatever it is we're going to do?"

"He will be no problem whatsoever, of that I can assure you. Now, if you will please assist me . . ."

She withdrew from the pouch a small earthen dish, into which she poured something, and handed it to him. In the moonlight streaming through the windshield, Robbie saw that it contained a mossy wick that floated in what looked and smelled like animal fat.

"Kindly set that afire, if you please," she instructed, and Robbie dug into his pockets for his butane lighter. He was about to flick the lighter when a torrent of psychic dread gushed over him, fluttering his heart and knotting his stomach. His hands began to shake, and his spine felt as though it had turned to mercury. This was not Jeremy he felt, and neither was it the newborn. This was something more ancient, more powerful by far, a presence that had communed so often with Hell that it carried Satan's stink. It was very close.

This was *Craslowe*.

A muscle spasm caused Robbie's thumb to tighten on the lighter, and the flame leapt upward from the tip, flooding the interior of the Jaguar with yellow light.

"Good heavens!" said Hannie, having glanced up into Robbie's petrified face. "What is it, man?"

"It's—I think it's—" His throat felt tight and cold, his vocal chords frozen, and he fought for a breath that did not want to come. "I think it's Craslowe. He's close, Hannie."

"Craslowe! But why would he be—good God! He must have detected the scrying, perhaps even our identities and plans. He must have known that we'd come here and try to—" She broke off and began stuffing back into the pouch the objects she had taken from it only seconds earlier. "We mustn't stay; not just now. We aren't prepared to face Hadrian Craslowe tonight."

She threw the pouch into the rear and twisted the ignition key, giving life to the huge twelve-cylinder engine. She flipped the headlight switch and—

Robbie felt himself screaming. Illumined by the powerful glare of the Jaguar's headlamps was the being he knew was Hadrian Craslowe, clothed in a baggy tweed suit and hanging unsupported in thin air, upside down, his inverted face only inches from the front grille. Craslowe's arms were spread wide, as were his massive, taloned hands, as though to embrace the pair who huddled before him. The index finger of each hand was easily twice the normal length, topped with a long, hooklike nail. On his face was a lascivious grin that made Robbie's guts roil, and from his baneful eyes beamed a light that was nearly blinding.

Hannie slammed the gear-selector into drive, cramped the steering wheel to the right, and gunned the engine, throwing mud and gravel into the air. The Jaguar swung sideways, filling the night with a lusty roar. The seconds dragged by as the car careened around to face the direction from which it had come, then straightened out and accelerated toward the wood line and the intersection with Sockeye Drive.

Robbie still held the flaming lighter, which was becoming hot, then performed an actual feat of will to relax his hand and let it snap off. He wondered why he had not caught fire, since the liquid fat in the dish had spilled over his lap, his hands, his jacket, thanks to the bucking of the car over the uneven road. But this was a minor concern, because from the corner of his right eye he caught sight of the horrible, teratoid face of Hadrian Craslowe, only inches from his own on the other side of the window glass, grinning obscenely, wantonly, gleeful with evil.

The Jag was rumbling down the road far faster than any man could run, and it was weaving and bouncing over ruts and potholes, coming close to ditching now and again as Hannie fought the wheel and held the throttle down. But here was Craslowe on the other side of the glass, his arms spread wide and his fingers coiling and uncoiling, not running beside the car or even holding fast to it, but *flying* alongside.

"*Hannie!*" screamed Robbie, and his voice died in a gag.

The old woman glanced to the right and grimaced fearfully, tromped the accelerator harder, and began to chant in that ancient language at the top of her lungs as the car lurched and heaved down the road.

Robbie cowered from the face outside the glass, strained against the seat belt, and screamed and choked and fought to keep from pissing himself. Above the roar of the engine and Hannie's shrieking chant came a groaning, moaning growl—it *had* to be coming from Craslowe's mouth—that burrowed into his skull, into his sanity, where it erupted like a volcano of hideous promise and threat:

You cannot seek to destroy my handiwork and live. You cannot spy upon me, come prowling around my servant and the object of my demon-love, and live. I will cut off your testicles with a red-hot knife; I will tear out your organs, one by one, while you still live; I will burn out your eyes and tongue; and I will force-feed you a dead man's shit before giving you to the Giver of Dreams. . . .

Suddenly there was heat on Robbie's chest, and it quickly became searing. It scorched his shirt and filled the car with an acrid, dizzying smoke, making him writhe and claw wildly at the pouch around his neck. The charm that Hannie had given him for protection against "minor forces"—the ones that could be "troublesome" and "hurtful"—was throbbing and growing hotter by the second. The pain was excruciating. Just when he was certain that he was about to burst into flame, the vial exploded, shredding its skin pouch and spattering its horrid contents all over his front, his face, his hands. The heat, mercifully, was gone.

But Hadrian Craslowe, sorcerer, steward of the Giver of Dreams, was not. His lurid face was less than an inch from the

window, contorted with that slavering grin, and his body was
twisting and his arms flailing like the wings of some wicked,
reptilian flier. The wind stream was whipping at his dark
tweeds. He planted a horrible hand on the glass, and to
Robbie's stark terror, the glass began to fizzle and melt.

Hannie turned her attention away from driving—which itself
could have been disastrous—and leveled a bright-eyed stare at
the thing that glided mere inches from where Robbie sat. Her
chanting grew louder. Her face and eyes were luminescent.

Somehow the Jaguar stayed on the road. A blast of bluish-
tinged energy rushed past Robbie's face from Hannie, and he
felt more than saw it impact against Craslowe, saw the
abominable form falter briefly away from the window. Another
blast came, and then another, and Craslowe fell out of sight,
just as the Jaguar dashed out of the woods to shoot headlong
onto Sockeye Drive, where it whirled with a screech of rubber
and a scream of brakes, before Hannie got it under control
again.

Stu Bromton, warned by the oncoming roar of a huge
engine, plunged into the thicket at the side of Old Home Road
and flattened himself against the bark of a pine as Hannie
Hazelford's Jaguar thundered by, a bright streak of headlamps
and bloody red taillights. He stood still a moment, catching his
breath in the inky blackness, listening to the diminishing roar
and wondering just what the hell was going on.

Why Hannie and Robbie had driven from town to Old Home
Road, he could not imagine. The fact that they had done so was
more than a little unsettling, because the only two inhabited
houses out here belonged to Cannibal Strecker and Mitch
Nistler, neither of which should have been of any interest to
them. Hannie and Robbie had sniffed at the edges of the local
crack industry, perhaps without even knowing it, and this gave
Stu a case of ants.

Having seen Hannie's Jag turn onto Old Home Road, he had
hidden his Pontiac in the trees near the intersection, pocketed
his police-issue flashlight, and started trudging toward Nistler's
house on foot. He certainly could not have followed in the car
without giving himself away, since Old Home Road came to a
virtual dead end at Cannibal Strecker's crack house. Casual
traffic was nonexistent, and any passing car would have

attracted attention. He had walked less than two hundred yards before he heard the sound of the approaching Jag and saw the first glare of its headlights, before he realized that it had reversed its direction and was fleeing toward him at high speed.

Yes, *fleeing*. Lurching, swerving, thumping over ruts and watery potholes, barely staying on the road as it bore down on him. Stu had just managed to hide himself before the car was past him.

He picked his way through damp foliage back to the road and stood a moment in the bright moonlight, thinking. Mitch Nistler, he knew, was away from his house, because this was Monday, and Monday was delivery day. After carrying a batch of Cannibal's crack to Seattle, Nistler would return with a load of unprocessed cocaine and drop it at the crack house farther up the road. But that would not happen until much later. Cannibal Strecker and his appalling girlfriend were undoubtedly waiting at the lab this very moment, probably drinking and toking and snorting themselves blind. It seemed unlikely that Hannie and Robbie had gone to the crack house, quite simply because there had not been time. The road beyond Mitch Nistler's hovel had deteriorated badly, even worse than this stretch, and Hannie would have been forced to drive at a crawl to keep from high-centering the low-slung Jag. She and Robbie would just now be arriving at Strecker's place, Stu figured, had they been headed there.

So they had stopped at Nistler's, but only briefly.

Why?

Stu decided to have a look. After a brisk, ten-minute hike—which, because of the fulgent moon, had not even required his flashlight—he stood before the front door of the rickety, neglected house that Nistler called home. The surrounding weeds were nearly shoulder-high, the yard was a nest of refuse and abandoned appliances, and the windows were stygian maws.

How could anyone actually live here? Stu wondered.

As he placed his foot on the first step of the porch, his eyes caught a flicker of movement behind an upstairs window, a trace of greenish light that had the indefinite quality of an old-fashioned, radium-coated watch dial. He put it down to a prank of the moonlight, for clearly nobody was home. The muddy drive was empty of Nistler's old El Camino.

The lock on the front door was broken, apparently having been recently forced with something like a crowbar, or so suggested the splintery marks on the wooden frame. The door swung easily open.

He stepped into the blackness of the house and immediately choked on the thick, putrescent stench that descended on him. He fought to keep his lunch down, drew a handkerchief from his pocket, and pressed it over his mouth and nose. *It smells like a body,* he said to himself.

Unwholesome, worrisome thoughts flashed into his head, scenarios in which Mitch Nistler was the perpetrator of the spate of evil doings in Greely's Cove, the kidnapper and killer who abducted innocent people and snuffed out their lives, who stashed their bodies in the closets of his sorry little house in the woods, or in the cellar or under the floor, or maybe even sewed them into the furniture. But that couldn't be, Stu reassured himself—not Mitch Nistler, whom he had known since boyhood. The guy was weird, no doubt of that, and was certainly not the type you'd want your sister to marry. But he was no homicidal kidnapper, no malicious blood-fiend. *Was* he?

Stu snapped on his flashlight and waded deeper into Mitch Nistler's abode, sweeping the beam over the beggarly contents of the living room, moving into the reeking kitchen where the refrigerator suddenly kicked on and nearly scared him shitless, into the main-floor bedroom with its pestiferous bed and sheets. Amid the squalor he saw nothing that accused Nistler of kidnapping or murder, nothing to indicate that Hannie Hazelford and Robinson Sparhawk had been here. And certainly nothing that explained their hasty retreat from the place.

Then he heard a sound overhead, the crack of old flooring and something that sounded vaguely slithery. He moved out of the bedroom and beamed the light against a warped and splintery old door that he assumed led upstairs. He pulled it open.

A moment earlier he would not have believed that the stench could have gotten worse, but now it was indeed worse, an egregious vapor that stung his eyes and soaked through his handkerchief to torture his nostrils and throat. It was the reek of dead things, of moldering flesh and decaying bones.

He lowered the handkerchief and stuffed it into a pocket, letting his hand fall onto the handle of the Smith and Wesson nine-millimeter pistol that hung in his holster. As he stepped onto the creaking stairway, he wondered why his instincts were raising such a ruckus, why a part of him wanted to turn and run away from this house, to sprint fiercely toward Sockeye Drive and his waiting Pontiac. He fought those instincts, wrestled them back into their holes, knowing that, having come this far, he could hardly run away without first finding answers to his questions. He climbed the stairs, step after creaking step, until he stood on the upper landing.

A few feet ahead was a door that stood partially open, a thin rectangle of scant moonlight that filtered through a dirty window in the bedroom beyond. He pushed through the door, following the flashlight beam into the bedroom, trying not to think about the smell. He stepped on something that seemed fleshy and soft, yet somehow brittle. He lowered the beam and saw that he had crushed the head of a dead cat, or more likely a kitten, judging from its size.

Rats must have gotten to it, he told himself, for much of its flesh was gone, and its orange hide was splayed open, ripped to shreds. He swallowed a clot of spit and kicked the lifeless animal aside, hoping that he had found the source of the stench, though he doubted it.

Movement. To his right. Barely a ripple in the blackness on the fringe of the flashlight beam.

He swept the circle of light across the floor to the far wall and nearly choked at what he saw: a dog, or what had once been a dog. It was a small, dark animal, leaning against the musty wallpaper, lacking its eyes and much of its snout—for that matter, a good share of its body. The hide had apparently been ripped backward from its neck, or so suggested the raglike train of bloody fur that hung from its hindquarter onto the floor. There were gaping holes in the muscle tissue of its shoulders and torso, through which hung tatters of arteries and veins. Incredibly, it was still alive.

Sweet Jesus, rats didn't do that!

He could not have heard the sounds behind him, the scuffing and slithering, the pops and snaps of the old wooden floor under moving feet, so thunderous were the heartbeats in his head. He swept the beam forward again, toward the bed that stood beneath the moonlit window. A body lay on that bed. A woman's body, naked and entangled in a crusty sheet.

It was oozing filth onto the mattress, which in turn was oozing filth onto the floor. The flesh was greenish and blistered, spotted with bacterial decay, the limbs splayed over the bed. Mercifully, its face was turned toward the wall.

He moved toward it—one step, then another, not liking the thoughts his mind was weaving, not liking the familiar blond tone of the hair that hung in webby festoons from the body's head. Another step, and he was *loathing* now the insane suggestion taking shape in his brain. He stooped over the thing, directed the light into its face—

Her face.

Lorna's face—still recognizable, despite the discoloration and swelling, despite the work of bugs and fungus and maggots. But just barely.

Revulsion shook him, and rage that someone had thus defiled the remains of the one woman he ever really loved. Stu pressed his hand to his mouth, struggled to keep breathing, promised himself that he would not lose his wits and go crashing down the stairs into the night, fleeing.

Revulsion, rage, and certainly *fear,* yes. *What kind of idiot,* screamed a voice in his soul, *would deny that there was something to fear here?* Something that did unspeakable things to harmless little animals? That stole the body of a young mother? That stank the very stink of Hell? Who could deny—

"*Those are intelligent questions, Chief Bromton,*" said a deep voice from behind him. Stu would have gone for his Smith and Wesson had he been able to move a muscle. But as it was he could only stand like a figure carved in petrified bone, bloodless and white. The world was ending, of that he was sure, for it could not go on in the face of madness like this.

"You may turn around now, if you please."

Somehow he did. And the world did not end.

A pair of figures stood in the darkness near the door, one tall and old, the other shorter and young. Stu found the strength from somewhere to raise the flashlight and direct the beam onto their faces.

"I'm glad you're here," said Dr. Hadrian Craslowe in his House of Lords voice, with his steel-framed spectacles throwing back the light and his dentures flashing with every grinning word. "It's always nice to have someone with whom to share a secret, especially if that someone can be trusted to keep it."

Stu lowered the light a little, beamed it onto Jeremy Trosper, then back to Craslowe. He searched for his voice. His body felt leaden, as though at any moment it might crash through the floor to the living room below. At last: "I guess you have me at a disadvantage, Doctor." Not bad at all; his voice was a little thin, a little squeaky, but it didn't quiver or crack. It hadn't shamed him. "Maybe you can you tell me what's going on here."

"I hardly think that's necessary or even advisable," said Jeremy, sounding like an Oxford prodigy. "You wouldn't like it."

Understatement of the fucking century, thought Stu. This was the body of Lorna Trosper, the boy's own mother, lying here in bacterial filth. Any possible explanation of *that* would certainly be outside the bounds of *liking*.

"What are you doing here?" Stu demanded of Jeremy, feeling a little stronger now, more aware of his status and authority. "Why aren't you home with your dad?"

"Ah, those questions aren't nearly as intelligent as the earlier ones," intoned Craslowe reproachfully, "the ones about *fear*. You were right, Chief Bromton, to suspect that there was something to be afraid of here."

Stu felt an unholy tickling in his guts. He had merely *thought* those things, not spoken them aloud. "Suppose you tell me what it is," he managed.

"It is what humans have always feared," answered Craslowe, "from the time before they were even humans. It is the same fear, I suspect, that a small herbivorous animal feels when it gets the scent of a predator, the instinctual dread of tearing claws and teeth, the terror of being eaten. Man was also once a prey animal, you know, the staple of cave bears and saber-toothed tigers, other carnivores. Today, in every human mind, lurks a remnant of the old fear of claws and fangs, of being caught and eaten, a racial fear that dates back to the era when man himself was prey."

"You haven't told me anything," said Stu, wondering if he had the strength to unholster his pistol, if need be. "Something is very wrong here, and you know what it is."

"*Wrongness* is a matter of definition," said Jeremy, smiling hideously.

"The boy is quite right," said Craslowe. "But on to other things, for the moment. I said that I was glad you dropped by, Chief Bromton, and I am. You see, now that each of us knows a little something of the other's secrets, we can be useful to one another."

"I don't follow you. All I know is what I've seen here."

"And that should be quite enough, I daresay. I must have your assurance that you will say nothing to anyone of what you've seen, and further, that you'll endeavor to keep Hannabeth Hazelford, together with her crippled Texan friend, away from this house and my estate at Whiteleather Place. The rewards for your cooperation in this regard will be substantial, I assure you."

"What in the hell are you saying?" asked Stu, becoming increasingly angry. "Are you trying to bribe me?"

"Yes, as a matter of fact, that's precisely what I'm trying to do," answered Craslowe, his aged eyes glinting. "But more than that, I'm also threatening you, Chief Bromton, make no mistake about that. You see, should you fail to do as I ask, I shall ensure that the entire world learns of your—ahh—*arrangement* with Mr. Corley Strecker and his esteemed associate, Mr. Luis Sandoval. I doubt that this knowledge would set well with the county sheriff's office and the Drug Enforcement Administration. I understand that they take a dim view of fellow law-enforcement officers who throw in with the purveyors of illegal drugs. And prison, I'm told, is especially unpleasant for a former policeman."

Stu felt the room whirling. He wanted to shout something like *You could never prove it! You don't have any evidence!* But that seemed so feeble, so pitifully theatrical, and for all he knew, maybe Craslowe *did* have evidence. The mere suggestion that he was an evil cop could be disastrous, particularly if it had the ring of truth. Discovery of Strecker's crack lab, right under Stu Bromton's nose, would supply that ring. He wanted to struggle, to avoid going down without a fight, but all that came out was, "H-how in the hell did you know?"

"Oh, I make it my business to know everything," said Craslowe merrily. "You don't live as long as I have without picking up a variety of useful skills." In his watery, insanely lit eyes was a power that Stu could not doubt was capable of seeing into the deepest reaches of a man's mind and soul. No one could keep secrets from Hadrian Craslowe.

"You're a lucky man, you know," continued the doctor. "Had you blundered into this house merely one day later—say tomorrow night instead of tonight—we most assuredly would not be having this conversation."

From somewhere behind him came the sound of slithering, scuffing movement, the moist sounds of ripping flesh, chewing, swallowing. Stu's skin began to crawl, and his jaw began to quiver.

"It would be best for you to leave now, Chief Bromton. But before you go, let us shake hands on our agreement." Craslowe glided, not walked, the short distance to where Stu stood. "You will protect me, Chief Bromton, and I will protect you. We will advise each other of any move against the other, isn't that right? And just as important, we will keep silent about each other's secrets. Is it a deal?"

Craslowe withdrew his right hand from the pocket of his tweed suit jacket and extended it into the glaring cone of Stu's flashlight. Without glancing downward, Stu gripped that hand with his own, shook on the deal, and plunged briefly into insanity.

24

Mitch Nistler accomplished his rendezvous with Luis Sandoval's courier in the dark belly of downtown Seattle and returned on a ferry across the Puget Sound to Cannibal Strecker's crack house, bearing a fresh load of unprocessed cocaine. The night was very starry and cold, the full moon still high in the western sky.

"Good job," said Cannibal, after examining the contents of the gym bag. "Me and Stella'll get right on this shit and have it turned into crack by tomorrow night. Be here by eight o'clock to pick it up, okay?"

"You mean I'm making another run tomorrow night?" asked Mitch weakly.

"Like I told you before, we're stepping up production. We're gonna be making two, three, maybe four deliveries a week. What's the matter, don't you understand the King's fucking English?"

Mitch forced a smile in order to head off another explosion of Cannibal violence. His hand went to his bruised and aching ribs and rubbed them. "It's just that—well, it's—"

"It's just fucking *what*?"

"I'm just a little worried, that's all. Making so many trips—well, it could be dangerous, man. I don't want to get ripped off, or busted."

"What the hell are you complaining about? You're getting paid, aren't you? Besides, Stella and me are the ones who gotta stay up all night, workin' our butts off to get this stuff converted. Do you hear *us* bitching and whining? Shit, I'm gonna have to drop a hundred bucks worth of meth just to stay awake tonight."

The big difference, thought Mitch, is that you're the one who's becoming a millionaire, not me. *I'm* the one who gets to put my balls on the block, take all the risks, for a paltry two hundred and fifty dollars a load. *I'm* the one who'll end up with a knife in my guts, bleeding to death in some dark alley, or sitting in a steel-walled closet in Walla Walla, nursing my bloody asshole after the wolves have had their fill of me.

"Sorry," he said. "I guess I was worrying over nothing. I'll be here at eight o'clock."

"Goddamn right you will. Now get out of my face; I got work to do."

Mitch's stink-filled house seemed deserted when he arrived home, black and silent like a grave, but he knew that it was not deserted. Grateful as he was for the silence, he worried that it might not last long. Before leaving for Seattle earlier in the evening, he had served up the last remaining dog to the newborn, in answer to the mewling scream that had come from upstairs, a savage and infantine demand for food. Thus far, it had consumed one kitten on Saturday night, the second kitten and one of the three dogs on Sunday. The final two dogs had met their end today.

Each time the screaming started, Mitch had lugged one of the stuporous animals to the mouth of the stairway, opened the door, and heaved it inside, then quickly slammed the door in order to spare himself the gruesome spectacle. Until Mitch had carried them to their hideous fate, none of the animals had moved an inch from where Jeremy had left them, or had begged to go out or to be fed, or had even touched the water pan that Mitch had set before them. The job of feeding the newborn disgusted him, and he felt for the poor, entranced beasts who were its meals. But more troublesome was the question of what food he would provide when the screaming started again.

"That is indeed a problem you must deal with," said Jeremy Trosper, giving Mitch a horrible fright. The boy had appeared silently at the door of the bedroom and had spoken just as Mitch was about to turn off the light and collapse in exhaustion.

Mitch stared openmouthed a moment and sat down on the bed to collect himself, not having guessed that Jeremy was on the premises. He considered saying something, then thought, what the hell? The kid can hear my thoughts; why bother talking?

"True," said Jeremy, moving into the room and alighting on

the bed next to Mitch. "I know everything you're thinking, so you needn't ever try to hide anything from me. As to the matter at hand, I am obliged to tell you that my brother, the newborn, no longer requires small animals for food."

Mitch felt a tide of relief. Thank God for small favors.

"What it requires now," said Jeremy, his hazel eyes sparkling, "is something a little richer, something with a little more meat on the bone. Are you following me, Mitchell?"

Oh, indeed Mitch was following him, and his throat was aching, and his chest was paining, and he was desperately trying not to cough up the fire in his lungs, and his tender soul was demanding to know when this fucking nightmare would end. *Something a little richer, with a little more meat on the bone.* Not canned stew, then, and tuna salad was out.

The newborn needed people. Human flesh. And Mitch was expected to procure the entrées.

"It won't be long," assured Jeremy, "before the question of food will take care of itself. A victim, you see, is not totally consumed in one sitting but is allowed to go on living for quite some time, allowed to absorb some of the Giver's powers and abilities, to dream the most exquisite dreams. And, of course, to recruit others like himself. The victims—oh, I detest that word, Mitchell; let's call them *dreamers*—the *dreamers* will provide all the food that the Giver needs. But until our newborn is mature—which won't be very long, considering the rate at which it's progressing—it needs your help. You must procure its first several *real* meals."

Mitch wheezed and sobbed, and he wondered if anything in his world would ever get better, or whether he was doomed to commit deeds ever more vile. The most loathsome aspect of his existence was that he had no choice but to do everything demanded of him, from stealing a corpse to carrying crack to—*God, this has to be the end of it!*

Slow murder.

"My advice to you," said Jeremy, "is that you install a strong padlock on the stairway door, one that you can lock from the outside. You and I will each have a key. Best to do this early tomorrow, don't you think?"

Mitch nodded, bit his rashy lower lip, and just managed to hold back a flood of enraged tears. Jeremy rose from the bed to head for the door.

"I know that I can count on you, Mitchell," he said with a confident smile. "I know that you appreciate your obligations. You *will* find a meal for my brother, and you will do so before the full moon wanes, which means that you have one more night. After tomorrow night, Mitchell, it will be too late, so please don't waste any time in this matter—for your own sake."

With that he turned and glided out of the room. A moment later Mitch heard the front door close.

25

The golden rays of morning flooded through Carl Trosper's window and fell across his face, waking him. He rolled to his side and turned his back to the sun, craving the blankness of the dreamless sleep that he had sampled only in fits during the night. But awareness won out and wrested him away from his pillow, forcing the day upon him. He poked his feet into a pair of slippers and wrapped himself in a terrycloth robe, then steered himself into the hallway, where he lingered before his son's closed bedroom, worrying. Hoping. Dreading.

He twisted the knob and pushed open the door, saw Jeremy mounded over with blankets in his bed and breathing in heavy, regular cycles. Carl's innards relaxed a little.

Beyond the window of Jeremy's room was a yellowing spirea that should have been atwitter with morning birds proclaiming a new day. But the spirea was dead and empty.

He stood a moment longer, scanning the stacks of musty tomes that lay around Jeremy's bed, on shelves, on the little writing table that Carl had long ago expropriated from the freshman dorm at UW—books with unsettling titles like *The Magic of the Dark* and *The Protocols of the Magus*. For Christ's sake, where were the posters of rock stars and NFL quarterbacks, the fold-out from *Sports Illustrated*'s swimsuit issue, the catcher's mitt and the football, the plastic models of the F 16 and Ferrari Testarossa, the butterfly collection, and all the other appurtenances of a red-blooded American boy's bedroom? Carl could have accepted that his son had too recently awakened from his sickness to appreciate the trappings of normal boyhood, if not for those eerily unwholesome, inexplicably worrisome, fucking *books*.

Yes, Jeremy had come home, but not until midnight had come and gone.

And not until Carl and Renzy Dawkins had frantically

telephoned every friend and acquaintance in Greely's Cove, including Hadrian Craslowe out at Whiteleather Place, to ask if they had seen him or knew where he was.

And not until Carl had called the local police, only to hear that Chief Stu Bromton was not available. (Besides, a person isn't officially missing for the first forty-eight hours, the dispatcher had said, absent some clear evidence of foul play.)

And not until Carl and Renzy had boarded the Roadmaster to cruise the moonlit streets for hours on end, creeping up and down alleys, circling the parking lots of every fast-food place in town, scouting school yards and playgrounds and video stores, reconnoitering parks and shoreline, climbing out of the car now and again to call his name into the darkness.

And not until Carl and Renzy had gone back to the bungalow on Second Avenue, exhausted and fevered with worry, defeated—

—had Jeremy come home. Looking no worse for wear, a smile on his beautiful face. A shrug in his shoulders and hands in his pockets. Ready for bed.

Carl had been too weary, too thankful that his son was safe, to stage the battle that must eventually erupt, a battle for explanation, for understanding and authority, for mutual respect—for all the prizes over which fathers and sons go to war with each other. Better to sleep awhile, to regroup. There would be time enough later for battle.

Renzy, bless his soul, had offered to stay the night in the guest room, just in case Carl needed his help and support. So they had all three hit their respective sacks with a minimum of fanfare and the thin pretense that everything was fine, that the universe was spinning along safely on its designated course.

And suddenly, morning.

"It's about time you got up," whispered Renzy from behind him, and Carl pulled the door closed softly.

"Hell, it's only a few minutes after sunup," he replied. "If I thought I could sleep, I'd go back to bed."

"Yeah, but its winter, and sunup comes late in the winter, in case you hadn't heard. It's after seven already. You should be out there grabbing the world by the balls, shaking it around. Why can't you be more like *me*?"

Carl came close to laughing at this, despite his weariness and distress over Jeremy. Carl was glad that his old friend had stayed over.

"In case you're wondering," said Renzy, who was dressed and ready for the day, "I used your razor, your soap, and your bottle of good-smell. But don't worry, I didn't use your toothbrush. I've got to draw the line somewhere."

"I hope you didn't use all the hot water."

"Forget about the hot water, because you're not taking a shower yet. I've got omelettes going in the kitchen. Take a whizz and pinch a loaf if you have to, and then report for breakfast."

Which Carl did. Though he wasn't really very hungry at first, the omelette tasted great. After the first bite he dug in and kept digging until he had devoured it, along with two slices of buttered toast and three cups of strong coffee. He and Renzy had missed dinner the previous night.

"My secret," said Renzy after breakfast, lighting a Marlboro and leaning back from the table, "is mayonnaise—about a tablespoon whipped in with the eggs. Gives the omelette a nice, creamy texture, don't you think?"

"Someday you're going to make someone a great wife," said Carl.

Renzy sipped his coffee and sucked a drag of smoke. "I hate to say this, but it's not going to be *you*, Buckwheat. I never date people who already have kids. Speaking of kids, how long do you plan to let yours stay in the fart sack?"

"Until I can't put it off any longer. I haven't yet decided what I'm going to say to him."

"Mmmh. Want to rehearse something?"

"I haven't figured anything out yet. All I know for sure is that I miscalculated somewhere along the line, that I came back here with all kinds of rosy visions about being a father and having a son, and now all those visions are in the toilet."

"So what did you expect?" asked Renzy, serious now. "A perfectly normal pubescent kid? I've told you before, Bush, and you've said it yourself: You can't expect Jeremy to be like other kids, given his history. And you can't expect yourself to be the good old all-American dad, given yours."

But his expectations weren't the problem anymore, Carl insisted. He had lived long enough to know that expectations were the main ordeal of life—giving them birth, coping with them when they don't turn out, coping with them when they *do* turn out. The problem was—

He didn't know. Something to do with those damnable books in Jeremy's room. Or the boy's capacity for maliciousness. Or his uncanny ability to get inside someone else's head. Something horrible was happening to his son, Carl was sure, and he meant to find out what it was.

They sat in silence for a full minute, listening to a fresh pot of coffee perking. Renzy rolled his depleted cigarette butt into a little ball and hooked it into an ashtray. Carl rose from the table and paced the floor.

"After we went to bed last night," Carl said, "I couldn't sleep for shit, so I got up and stared at the sky through the window for half an hour. The stars were out, and I tried to find the constellations and remember all their names. I thought back to when I was a kid, about fourteen—and you might remember this, too, because I'm sure we talked about it—I read that the light from those stars has been traveling a long time before it ever reaches the earth. Years, hundreds or thousands or even *millions* of years. Ever since then, whenever I've looked up at the stars, I've always wondered if they're still there—I mean, really *there*. Why couldn't they have just given off their light and winked out, like somebody flipped off the switch? Or gone supernova or something? It might be millions of years before anyone would ever know about it here on earth, because the light would just keep on coming, even after its source was dead."

"Seems to me I do recall you talking about some sort of garbage like that," said Renzy, arching one eyebrow like John Belushi.

"Why is it garbage, Renzy? We see the light from the stars, but it's light that was made long before any of us was born, most of it before there were even humans on the earth. The point is, what we see may not really be there. Maybe there's nothing at all where once there were stars. Or maybe there's something *else*."

"I'm getting the message: You think there's something more going on with Jeremy than what you think you see, or what you've been told."

"Give the man a cigar."

"And you intend to find out what that something is, right?"

"Bingo, you win a side of beef."

"And just *how*, pray tell, do you intend to do this?"

Carl sat down at the table again, folded his arms and leaned on them, studied the sleeves of his terrycloth robe. He hoped that what he was about to say would not sound wild.

"Craslowe. It all has something to do with Craslowe, Renzy. I can't tell you how I know this, but he's hiding something from me. I'm going to find out what it is, and I'm going to start today."

A flicker of shadow crossed Renzy's green eyes as he lit a fresh cigarette.

The telephone call from Dr. Esther Cabaza came just as Lindsay Moreland was wrapping up a meeting with a new client, and she waited until the young man was out the door of her office before picking up the phone.

"Esther, hello. Sorry about the wait."

"No problem. How's your morning going?"

"Fine, so far—great, in fact. My first client of the day was a nineteen-year-old security guard who just won two million dollars in the Washington lottery. He wants to give a third of it to the Cystic Fibrosis Foundation, another third to a shelter for the homeless, and the rest he wants to invest with us. Can you believe it?"

"Does this mean there's a smidgen of decency left in the world?"

"Yes—there apparently is some decency left. It's good to get a taste of it now and then."

"And how! Anyway, the reason I called: I heard back from my people in Olympia concerning your nephew's shrink, so I thought I'd better get in touch with you right away. Lindsay, are you sure you got his name right?"

"Well, I think so. It's Hadrian Craslowe—Oxford, Cambridge, some mental health institute in Switzerland."

"No middle initial or anything else that might differentiate him?"

"Not that I know of. Is there a problem?"

"Listen to this: The state board of clinical psychologists licensed him to practice about fourteen months ago after he passed the board examination—which he did with flying colors, by the way. They've got copies of his diplomas, peer reviews, certifications, and some papers he wrote for the Royal Academy of Mental Health Consultants in England. Everything looks on the up and up."

"Then I'm authorized to breathe a sigh of relief, right?"

"That might be a little premature, Lindsay. One of the state board's staff guys telephoned Oxford University—let's see, I think it was Trinity College. . . ." Lindsay heard the shuffling of papers on Dr. Cabaza's end. "Yes, here it is: Trinity College, Office of Academic Records, Oxford, England. The people there dug out the records of one Hadrian Craslowe, physician and surgeon—*not* a shrink, because there wasn't any such thing as a shrink back then—who took his degree in medicine in 1754. Needless to say, it can't be the same guy." Esther laughed gustily.

But Lindsay did not. "And that's *it?* No Hadrian Craslowe since then?"

"None on the record. That's not the end of it, I'm afraid. The Royal Academy of Mental Health Consultants has never heard of him, or at least that's what they said on the phone. They have no record of a Hadrian Craslowe or anyone with a similar name who wrote articles or conducted studies for them. The documents he gave to the Washington board must've been extraordinarily well-done forgeries."

"Oh, for the love of . . ."

Lindsay's mind started to race through a maze of absurd but harrowing possibilities, none of them rational, all having to do with the black tale that Hannie Hazelford had spun in Lindsay's living room three nights earlier.

"Esther, there's got to be some other explanation. I can't believe Dr. Craslowe is a fraud."

"It does seem hard to believe, and that's why I wondered whether he had used some other name while attending Oxford and doing work for the Royal Academy. Even so, it wouldn't explain why his present name is on the documents that he gave to the state board. If he'd changed his name for some reason and had updated his credentials, then the folks at Oxford should've known about it. They should have it in their records."

"But how on earth could he have slipped forgeries by the Washington authorities? I thought they were in business to protect us from that kind of thing."

"It wouldn't be that hard to do," answered Dr. Cabaza, "if the forgeries were extremely good ones. The state board relies primarily on the testing process to weed out the incompetents and the charlatans. For what it's worth, your guy is probably qualified to practice, or he wouldn't have passed the exam."

This, coupled with the fact that Craslowe had worked a veritable miracle with Jeremy, might have given Lindsay some reassurance, but for the apprehensions that Hannie Hazelford had planted in her mind. Lindsay had hoped that a check of Craslowe's credentials would give the lie to Hannie's ravings, but the opposite had happened. *Contradiction:* Hadrian Craslowe was a fraud who had worked a very authentic miracle. Lindsay's apprehension sharpened.

"If you want," continued Dr. Cabaza, "I'll ask the board to keep checking, which they'll probably want to do anyway, having found out this much. It you could recall the name of the institution in Switzerland . . ."

Which Lindsay could not, regrettably. All she could remember was that Craslowe had mentioned working in Zurich, meaning that to check further, the state board would have to call every mental health organization in Switzerland's largest city. No telling how long that would take. And what would be proved by discovering that Craslowe had never worked with any of them? Only that he had told yet one more lie to Lindsay Moreland and Carl Trosper.

Lies, apprehensions, contradictions; the sharp little dread of believing the unbelievable, of trusting the untrustworthy— these were the ingredients of the emotional stew boiling inside Lindsay as she thanked Dr. Cabaza, promised once again to bring her mother by for a checkup, and said good-bye. Then she buzzed the front desk and instructed the secretary to cancel her remaining appointments for the day.

Hannie Hazelford's cottage on Torgaard Hill smelled pungently of the potions she had brewed feverishly throughout the night and into the morning, of the herbs and spices and disgusting bits of once-living tissues that she had dug from her vast inventory of magical goods, which she had then chopped or pulverized, shredded or blended, burned or boiled or chanted over, until her rickety old body verged on collapse. And collapse she finally did. But not until she had placed at least one kind of charm—a vial or jar full of some foul suspension, or a skin pouch containing a powerful powder or crumbs of bone from a long-dead animal—at every window and door of the cottage, in the corners of every room, before the fireplace hearth and even over the heating vents. Using unbleached candle wax, she had drawn strange Kabbalistic symbols upon every windowpane, which—like the charms—would prevent intrusion by the forces that Hadrian Craslowe would surely send against Robbie and herself.

The war had started anew, she had told Robbie at the end of their breakneck drive back to Torgaard Hill from Mitch Nistler's house. A war that was as ancient as the human species. The brews, the charms, and the chanted words were their fortress, their armor, their swords.

By sunup Robbie too was exhausted but not sleepy, thanks to the adrenaline rush that came whenever his brain conjured the image of Craslowe's direful face—inches away from his own, glowering through the Jaguar's window with those toxic eyes. Robbie wondered whether he would ever sleep again.

How absurd it all was, thought Robinson Sparhawk, as he stood on his crutches next to Hannie Hazelford's amply feathered bed, having tucked her in for some much-needed sleep. He gazed down at her shapeless lumps under the blankets, at the sparsely haired head that lay as still as a fossil on its pillow. He tried to visualize the child she once had been: a redheaded slip of a Saxon girl, perhaps, with dancing eyes and freckled cheeks and a giggle that could make a father's heart sing.

How absurd that this little girl, having survived in childhood the plagues and pestilences of the Dark Ages, the murderous raids of the Vikings and the bloody upheavals of ancient Britain's native tribes, should evolve to *this:* a senescent witch in twentieth-century America, the owner of a red Jaguar. The managing partner of a team that included an over-the-hill psychic from Texas. A warrior in a supernatural war.

Suddenly he missed El Paso intensely, missed his home and the graying cripple he remembered as Robinson Sparhawk, who really hadn't been such a bad old boy, despite his laziness and a streak of lily-liveredness. A good man inside, committed to decency. Not a complete man, but what the hell? He hadn't *asked* to contract polio, hadn't *asked* for link-sausage legs. You play the hand you're dealt.

Earlier Hannie herself had lamented her dwindling faculties, had blamed herself for failing to take forceful action against Craslowe weeks earlier, when she had mistakenly assumed that the body of Lorna Trosper was to be cremated and put safely out of Craslowe's reach. Months before that, when she had learned that Lorna's unfortunate son was Craslowe's patient, she had recognized the horror that was afoot, having seen the pattern often enough before. But she had found that her spells and hexes were ineffective against Craslowe, that he had evolved a strong countermagic that rendered her own next to useless.

Last night's encounter with Craslowe, followed by nearly nine hours worth of urgent spell-casting, had left Hannie a drained and dry-boned wreck who could barely stand, who actually needed Robbie's help to get to her bed. She would spend the morning gathering new strength, she'd said, and had advised Robbie to do the same. Come afternoon, she would undertake some serious scrying—a psychic reconnaissance of the battlefield. They would then plan their next move.

Robbie felt himself growing pale as he chewed on the question of whether Hannie was strong enough to face Craslowe and his hell-things, whether her tired old body could take the punishment. He himself felt bruised and spent, and the fact that his own psychic powers had strengthened dramatically as the result of his ordeals seemed of small consequence.

Only *magic* could destroy Craslowe, his Giver of Dreams, and its fearful offspring. Only Hannie could wield that magic. And if anything were to happen to her—

Robbie clenched his eyes and shuddered away the awful thought.

26

"Did you know that this car has a name?" Renzy Dawkins asked Jeremy, who rode in the rear seat of the old Roadmaster, his hands pocketed in his acid-washed denims. No answer. Only a silent gaze that Renzy saw reflected in the rearview mirror.

"Well, it *does*," he went on, trading a quick glance with Carl in the front passenger's seat. "It's Leo, like in Leo the Lion. Lions are masters of the jungle, okay? And this is a Buick Roadmaster, so it only seemed right to give it a masterful name."

Renzy had always named his cars, Carl remembered, though not always as elegantly as he had named this one. *Bushmobile* had been a garish Chevy Impala that he had owned in high school. The name had been appropriate.

"Whenever I park this thing in Seattle," said Renzy, still trying to entertain the boy, "I hang a sign in the back window to keep it from being stolen." He pulled a rectangle of neatly lettered cardboard from beneath the driver's seat and flipped it into Jeremy's lap:

DANGER
LIVE SNAKES IN TRANSIT
Acme Herpetarium

"Best antitheft device ever invented, and probably the cheapest. That's assuming the dirtball can read."

Still no reaction from Jeremy, whose eyes seemed hollow and distracted.

"Well," said Renzy, turning into the parking lot of Greely's Cove Marina, then stopping and setting the handbrake, "I've been a regular bundle of laughs, haven't I? What I need is a bag of Whoppers and a beer."

He opened the door and swung out, waiting for Carl to slide over into the driver's seat.

"Why don't you two come by the boat after you've seen Dr. Craslowe? I've got a fridge full of regular food and beverage that I'd be happy to share. We could even call it a late lunch."

"Sounds good," said Carl. "But don't fritter away your day waiting for us. Jeremy and I have some heavy talking to do after the therapy session."

"I understand," said Renzy with a little wave. *"Hasta lumbago."* He turned and trotted toward the docks, his dark hair fanning in the salty breeze.

As Carl drove on toward Whiteleather Place, he tried in vain to engage his son in light talk, eliciting only an occasional nod, an empty glance, or a monosyllable. He stayed away from the subject of the boy's latest nocturnal excursion, wanting first to reestablish some semblance of rapport. But he got nowhere, and the more he talked, the more foolish he sounded, even to himself.

They cleared the forest canopy and rolled onto the grounds of Whiteleather Place, which stood dark against a dazzling afternoon sun. Carl felt a pang of emotion the moment he laid eyes on it. Once this place had been the stage of childhood games, the friendly old theater of boyish fantasies. With Renzy and Stu he'd hunted Russian agents in its maze of rooms and corridors, shot it out with diamond thieves and bank robbers in the musty passages of the basement, stampeded herds of longhorns through the madronas and pines of the sprawling grounds. They had "spied" on Renzy's sister, Diana, pretending that she was a Confederate agent who sold her body for Yankee secrets.

Thoughts of Diana deepened his anxiety. He visualized her alone in a featureless room, sitting on a steel-framed bed and staring uncomprehendingly at the drab walls of a mental institution, her mind a void that had swallowed the horror and grief of her parents' suicide. Renzy, he knew, had loved her intensely and had suffered fearfully over her breakdown.

"Good afternoon, Mr. Trosper," said slim Ianthe Pauling, having opened the creaky oak doors of Whiteleather Place. As ever, she was stiff and formal, but her eyes seemed even sadder than Carl remembered. She wore her customary straight skirt of charcoal and a bone cameo on a flouncy black blouse. Today her raven hair hung down around her shoulders, rather than clinging to the back of her head in the usual tight bun. "And hello, Jeremy," she said. "Dr. Craslowe is ready to see you now."

For the first time that day Jeremy's mood brightened, and he stepped smartly into the front parlor from the foyer, as though eager to get started with his therapy session.

Carl moved to follow. "Mrs. Pauling, I want to talk to Dr. Craslowe. Jeremy and I have had some troubles at home, and I think I need some professional advice."

"Very well," replied the dark woman. "I'll speak with the doctor about it. I'm certain that he'll be happy to set an appointment for later in the week. Also, Dr. Craslowe has asked me to tell you that you needn't wait here during today's session, inasmuch as he anticipates a rather long one. Perhaps you can give me a number where I may reach you when it's ended."

"No, you don't understand," said Carl, feeling a stirring of anger. "I need to see him today—right now, as a matter of fact. And I want to sit in on the session, to see just what this therapy entails."

Jeremy heard this and halted at the mouth of the dusky corridor that led into the innards of the house. He turned to face his father and stared icily at him. But it was Ianthe Pauling who answered: "I fear that's impossible, Mr. Trosper. To be effective, the doctor requires total privacy with his patients. The slightest distraction could prove very damaging when the patient is under hypnosis."

"Well, he'll have to make an exception in this case," answered Carl, squaring his shoulders. "You can assure him that I won't be a distraction. I'll sit in a corner and not move a muscle or make a sound. I'll even hold my breath, if I have to. But I mean to sit in on the session, Mrs. Pauling, and I mean to find out why my son has been behaving the way he has. I *will* talk to Dr. Craslowe, so I suggest you tell him that—right now."

The atmosphere grew heavy with menace, and Carl suddenly felt utterly alone in a place where aloneness seemed ill-advised. He felt a hostility that could only derive from something alive. The feeling shook him, and his gaze wandered around the dim room as though searching for living movement among the antique furniture and woolen tapestries.

"Mr. Trosper, please be reasonable," Ianthe Pauling was saying. "The doctor's techniques are tried and true. You have my assurance that his reasons for wanting privacy are good ones and that what he's doing is best for your son. I must also ask you to reconsider your demand to speak with him today. His schedule is very heavy, and he deems it important to spend the maximum amount of time with Jeremy."

"But the last session was less than four days ago," Carl protested, "and it lasted four hours. I can't believe that he's so pressed for time that he can't take a few minutes to answer my questions."

Questions about the books. Jeremy's malevolence. Something horrible had happened to the boy, was *still* happening.

Jeremy's voice rang out from across the room, slicing Carl to the quick. "Your questions will all be answered in due time, *Dad*." He sounded like a brat from a high-brow British public school, spoiled and hostile and determined to have nothing but his own way. "I'll thank you not to jeopardize my recovery with your insane insistence upon watching my therapy session. Kindly have enough regard for my welfare to abide by my physician's instructions, all right? And have the decency to make an appointment, if you must talk with him, rather than barging in like a backwoods bully!"

Carl's anger sizzled as he stared back at Jeremy, but it was anger in the company of real fear. With a Herculean effort, he reined in his rampaging emotions and forced his mind into a rational mode. He took several deep breaths of the suffocating air and allowed ten leaden seconds to die.

"Very well," he said calmly, "maybe I should make an appointment." He turned back to Mrs. Pauling. "I'll call after I've checked my calendar."

Some deep-seated instinct told him to control his thoughts, to steer them away from his real intentions, and he did so without knowing why.

"I'm sorry if I've embarrassed you, Jeremy." *Yes, that's it, don't think. Just talk.* "And I hope I haven't offended you, Mrs. Pauling. You can call me at home after the session's over. Good-bye." *Now head for the door and get out of range.*

The dual oak doors swung open, and Carl's feet were on the porch, on the flagstone stairs, on the walk, bound for the gleaming old Roadmaster convertible parked in the drive—*Just keep walking, don't think*—his mind a blank. He slid into the driver's seat, cranked up the brawny V-8, and piloted the car in a circumnavigation of the circular drive, then swung onto a course for the crumbling gateposts. Only after he had put those gateposts behind him did he allow himself to start thinking again.

With a final surge of effort, Mitch Nistler twisted the last screw into place. The hasp was installed on the battered old door that led to the stairway of his reeking house, as Jeremy had wanted. He pulled from his pocket the heavy padlock he had bought that morning at the hardware store on Frontage Street, swung the hasp into place, and slipped the lock through the staple. He forced the lock closed, and it clicked satisfyingly. Then he leaned back against the doorjamb and rested.

The lock should do nicely, he told himself. It was a strong one. Not strong enough, maybe, to hold back the thing that lived upstairs, should it ever want out, but certainly adequate to the task of confining a human being, even a very big and heavy one.

This thought gave him a little glimmer of anticipatory joy, and for a moment he forgot the igneous rash that covered his mouth and throat, the lumbering pain in his chest and the ache in his limbs. For the first time in what seemed an eternity, he felt compelled to treat himself to a good stiff drink.

Carl parked the Roadmaster well beyond the precariously leaning gateposts of Whiteleather Place, so that it could not be seen from the mansion. He trotted back along the graveled road to the fringes of the grounds, then left the road to make his way through the holly-choked woodline to a point where he could approach the house with minimum exposure. Though the afternoon sky was clear but for a few patches of cloud, there was a chill in the air that cut through his light jacket and the flannel shirt he wore beneath it. He shivered and wished that he had worn something heavier.

He was now conscious of why he had instinctively blanked his mind the very moment this idea came to him: *Jeremy could read his thoughts*—just as he had been able to read Nora Moreland's mind. The fact that Jeremy had used the voice of

Carl's dead father as an instrument of pain was the proof,
despite Renzy's rational assertions to the contrary. By blanking
his mind, Carl had hidden from Jeremy his intention to
penetrate the secrets of Whiteleather Place.

And to do so covertly, if need be.

Why this new acceptance of Jeremy's mind-reading ability
did not terrify and appall him, Carl didn't know. Maybe he was
simply more afraid of losing his son than he was of some vague
suggestion of supernatural power. He doubted not for a
moment that he had any choice but to march on, to infiltrate the
shadows of Whiteleather Place, regardless of what might wait
there.

It would be a mission to get the lay of the land, to find out
what he was up against. It meant trespassing at the very least,
even breaking and entering, which he was fully ready to do if
the need arose. To be caught and convicted probably meant that
he could forget about practicing law in the great state of
Washington ever again.

As he approached the house, dodging among trees and
islands of shrubs, he saw that the grounds were in even worse
shape than had been apparent from the drive. Vast invasions of
morning glory and thistle had laid waste to the rolling lawn.
The once-graceful madronas had become twisted skeletons,
and the towering native pines were spires of yellow death,
punky with rot. The breeze sighed forlornly through the lifeless
shrubbery and rattled the dead trees as though to mourn their
passing. Even the *weeds* were dead, and not a single bird flitted
overhead.

He crouched against the shadowed foundation of the east
porch, feeling the coarse bite of cinnamon-colored brick
through his thin jacket. He pondered tactics.

Going in through the front door seemed ill-advised, and he
would have bet that it was locked anyway. Even if it was not
locked, the warped old hinges were far too noisy to chance. He
decided to try the rear door, which unfortunately was also
locked. As were the glass-plated and curtained doors that gave
onto the sun parlor in the southeast corner.

Carl crept down the rear again and ducked between the dead
shrubbery and the foundation wall, needing a few moments to
sort through his knowledge of the mansion and its grounds. His
boyhood came back to him in gusts of mental wind—vivid

memories of this house and the games that he had played within and near its walls.

He and Renzy and Stu are U.S. Army Rangers on the beach at Normandy, cowering under the Nazis' withering machine-gun fire from the cliffs above. The order comes from the Headquarters of Operation Overload: Scale the cliffs and take out the machine guns, no matter what the cost. "The success of the whole goddamn Allied invasion depends on you grunts, so move out!"

With the fate of a hundred thousand Allied troops riding on their shoulders, Renzy and Stu and Carl scaled the "cliffs," their toy weapons strapped to their backs, their official U.S. Army canteens banging against their hips. They pulled them-selves ever higher into the branches of the madrona that stood near the porch of Whiteleather Place, up and up toward the balustraded balcony of Mrs. Dawkins's sewing room, where an elite battalion of Hitler's dreaded *Schutzstaffel* was dug in behind sandbags and concrete. Carl reached out from his perch on a creaking branch and gripped the old wooden railing, to hoist himself onto the balcony, selflessly braving a blizzard of hot lead. He and his buddies poured fire onto the German positions until their throats were sore from making shooting noises. But today—

"Good job, men! It's all over now, so you can take it easy for a while. We won!"

Carl was breathing hard, his heartbeats thundering in his neck and temples, his head moist with sweat. Climbing madronas was a job for nine-year-old boys, not for lawyers in their late thirties. His hands were fiery and raw from the rough bark, and his muscles ached from unaccustomed stretching, bending, levering. But the lifeless tree had borne up under his weight, and he was still in one piece.

His spirits sank when he found that the French doors of the sewing room were locked. The thought of descending the way he had come caused him to try the old brass knob again. Locked, true, but there was give in the latching mechanism, a hint that just enough pressure might defeat the aged tumblers. Carl wrapped both fists around the knob and twisted. It gave a little. He upped the pressure, feeling his face turn red, watching his hands turn bloodless white. The lock gave way with a clank that startled him, and he pulled back from the door to press his body against the flanking wall. He listened a full minute for the sound of investigating footsteps within, but heard only the wind wheezing around the terra-cotta inserts on the gables above his head.

He pushed open the doors and slipped inside. The room was dim—thanks to heavy drapes over the windows—and only sparsely furnished. Something in the air spoke to him of Alita Dawkins, the kindly woman who had done charity work in and around Greely's Cove, who had hovered over Lorna during her pregnancy with Jeremy. Alita had brought some much-needed cheer into the Trosper household during those final, difficult weeks before Jeremy came into the world, helping with housework and cooking, giving Lorna charming little figurines that she had fashioned herself in a handicrafts class, and generally being on hand for comfort and good company.

He went deeper into the house, pausing before every door in the corridor to listen for life on the other side. He heard nothing. He came to a rear stairway, which offered an ascent to the third floor or a descent to a main-floor vestibule, which in turn gave onto the kitchen and a corridor leading to the front of the house. He crept lightly down the stairs to the vestibule, straining his ears for the slightest sound.

The huge kitchen, with its islands of countertops and cabinets, its gleaming pots and pans hanging from the ceiling, was empty of life, so he passed it by after quickly poking his head through the door. He went farther down the corridor and checked the dining room, which was a showcase of cherry antiques, but also deserted.

Next was the music room, where Renzy's sister, Diana, had practiced her lessons on the Steinway concert grand that Ted had bought for her. The piano was silent and alone now, an ebony orphan.

Carl turned right into a branch of the corridor hung with placid, overly romantic landscapes—originals, no doubt, set in heavy gilt frames and probably valuable. He halted again and listened hard to the silence, since only a few steps more would bring him to the rear parlor, the room Hadrian Craslowe used as a personal office and the one in which Ted and Alita Dawkins had ended their lives with rat poison. This was likely where Jeremy's therapy session was taking place. After glancing behind him to ensure that Mrs. Pauling was nowhere in sight, he moved forward and pressed his ear against the wooden door.

No sound. No droning, hypnotic voice, which he had expected to hear. No sound of Jeremy talking or answering questions, as would have seemed appropriate to "therapy." Carl pressed his ear still harder to the wood, waited, put his hand to the tarnished brass knob, twisted it, and pushed. The door opened an inch, then wider, and Carl stared into dusky silence. He swept his gaze over the massive desk littered with ancient books, at the empty chairs, the cold fireplace, the tapestries of melancholy brocade, the porphyry busts and the thin rails of stained sunlight from the Dawkinses' "prayer corner."

Where the hell is *everybody?*

A glance at his watch told him that it was almost 1:25— scarcely twenty-five minutes since he had dropped his son here. He mulled the possibility that Dr. Craslowe and Mrs. Pauling might have taken Jeremy away from Whiteleather Place, where and for what reason he could not guess. But they could only have done so during the few minutes since he had entered the house, because Carl would have seen or heard their departure when he was outside. More likely they had taken Jeremy to another room in the house. Daunting a task as it was, he decided to search the entire mansion, from the basement to the third floor, if necessary, until he found his son.

As he turned to withdraw from Dr. Craslowe's personal office, he caught a fleeting impression of movement out of the corner of his eye, down the dusky corridor and to his left, back toward the kitchen. He halted, waiting for the accompanying sound, footfalls, breathing, or the rustle of clothing. The house remained silent as a tomb. He went back the way he had come, walking soundlessly on the dense Persian carpet, and halted at the corner where he thought he had seen something. Gingerly he poked his head around the corner. And saw no one.

He moved around the corner, eyes wide in the spare light that came from the open kitchen and the stairwell beyond the vestibule. As he passed by the kitchen door, he caught another hint of movement in the direction of the butler's pantry, something fluid and rusty in color, airy like crepe paper. Again he halted, but not as long this time. He spun on the heel of his shoe and plunged into the kitchen, intending to get a clear look at whoever had darted into the shadows. But the pantry was deserted. Whoever had been there must have fled down the rear stairs to the basement. His nose picked up a rotting odor that dissipated with the movement of his own body through the still air.

The stairwell to the basement was a cave of esophageal gloom, and Carl waited a moment for his eyes to adjust before taking the first step downward. As he was lowering a foot to begin his descent, a familiar old voice spoke in his mind.

Oh, this is real nice, Old Carl. You've committed the crime of breaking and entering, jeopardizing your lawyer's ticket, your career, and the new life you've wanted so bad—and for what? Because of some half-baked idea about discovering what's wrong with Jeremy, some nutty suspicion that Dr. Craslowe hasn't leveled with you. Do you have to work at screwing up, Old Carl, or does it just come naturally?

He froze again. He needed to get his emotional ducks in a row, to be certain of what he was doing and why, for the repercussions of being caught here could indeed be nasty.

Carl could not turn back now, he knew. He felt, more than knew, that Craslowe was at the root of his and Jeremy's miseries, that nothing substantial could come from merely asking questions. More than this, he felt that deep inside his son lived an ordinary little boy who was not eloquent or prodigious, who did not speak with an aristocratic British accent or read minds, who if given the chance could find simple joy in rock and roll and video games. This was the son whom he loved, whom he meant to save.

He took that first step downward into the dark, and then the next, feeling the air cool as he descended, wishing he had a flashlight. At the bottom of the stairs he became aware of a yellow incandescence from a bare light bulb that hung from the low ceiling, some two dozen steps farther down the passage. He made for it quietly, passing by an iron-grated door that led to the wine cellar. To his right was a wall of grainy foundation stone that gave off the damp smell of earth. To his left were stacks of wooden crates and cardboard boxes, some of which were imprinted with names like *Bekins* and *Florida Oranges* and *Del Monte*.

Like the basements of most old houses, this one had not been meant for living, but rather for storing wine and vegetables and little-used odds and ends. It was dark and damp, a place more suited to rats and spiders than human beings. A network of naked water pipes traveled along the low ceiling, forcing Carl to duck now and again as he drew nearer the light bulb, which was where the passage turned to the left.

He made the turn and walked a path between two mountains of junk that included old bicycles and tricycles, lawn mowers and gardening tools, boxes brimming with moldy toys from someone's childhood. There were kitchenwares and shapeless furniture, statuary and baby cribs, lamp shades and dusted-over pictures in tarnished frames. Carl passed under an arch of heavy masonry into another room, smaller than the first but not as tightly crammed with junk. He remembered that this was the site of the massive old boiler that heated the house. He could just make out its shape, hugging the left wall like a giant squid made of cast iron.

To the right and a few more steps ahead was another brick archway, which—according to his boyhood memory—led into a room that he and his buddies had always thought special. On one wall was a mysterious steel door that would have looked more at home on a bank vault. It boasted the biggest padlock Carl had ever seen.

I want you boys to stay away from that door, Ted Dawkins had more than once told his son and his two pals, Carl and Stu. *There's nothing in there for kids, believe me.*

So, naturally, they had visited the door often. They had pushed their ears against the chilly metal and tried unsuccessfully to scare each other with claims about hearing unspeakable horrors on the other side. They had even tested the lock now and then, hoping against hope to gain access to the mysteries that lay within. But the door had never given up its secrets, never even budged.

Carl's nose wrinkled, tickled by a whiff of the smell he had detected moments earlier near the top of the stairs. He moved through the archway and gasped, for the vault door was standing open, a yawning rectangle of flickering light from a sooty kerosene lantern hanging just inside. Actually *open*, the same door that throughout his boyhood had stayed locked against the prying fingers of curious little boys! The stink densified as he moved toward the opening, but he hardly noticed, and he bowed his head to step inside.

The room was small and empty, walled with rough-hewn stone that gleamed wetly here and there in the muddy lamplight. At the far end was another brick archway, this one barred by a weighty-looking door of dark, very old wood. Something from his boyhood drove Carl toward the door, a rekindled hunger to know secrets that someone had seen fit to lock away. He gripped the cold brass handle that time and dankness had corroded and pulled it open, fully expecting a groan from the rusty hinges. But it yielded smoothly, silently, revealing a circular stone stairway that coiled downward into a well of dim candlelight.

Carl grimaced against the onslaught of odor that wafted up the stairway, for it carried the tang of disease and decomposition. He fought his recoiling senses and went forward, his palms outstretched toward the narrow, curving walls. He moved downward, ever downward, at least a score of steps and then a dozen more, passing candles in wrought-iron holders that were mounded over with gnarly wax. He listened for sound, *any* sound, but heard only his own breathing and the scuff of his boat shoes on stone.

The stairs ended in a long passageway that Carl figured lay at least two stories beneath the basement of Whiteleather Place. At ten-foot intervals were heavy oak timbers that shored up the ceiling and walls, as in a mine shaft. The passageway stretched onward in a straight line for perhaps fifty feet, unlit but for a faint patch of yellow light at the far end. As he moved closer, he saw another wooden door. Light was escaping around the edges of a small shutter that was not quite closed.

So the local rumors about old Captain Whiteleather's treasure chamber were true, he told himself, as he trudged toward the door. This was probably where the skipper stored the ill-gotten booty of his Pacific adventures, the stolen antiquities from the temples of Sumatra or Java or Malaysia, gold and jade and priceless ceremonial masks. What a field day the Greely's Cove Historical Society might have had in this place, if only they had been able to get beyond the steel door.

These thoughts evaporated with the onset of *sound,* a ululating chant from a deep male voice that reverberated low against the surrounding stone walls, oddly rhythmic and yet somber, punctuated now and again by the voice of a boy that overlaid the first voice in a kind of liturgical counterpoint.

The nape of Carl's neck pringled, for he was certain that the second voice belonged to Jeremy.

He pushed himself onward through the thickening stench, which had become nearly unbearable now. The voices grew louder as he neared the door with its small hinged shutter. He raised his hand to the shutter and nudged it open, and the voices seemed very close. He edged close to the rectangle of light and peered in.

His lungs seized up. His heart missed a beat, missed another, then started to pound in his chest like a jackhammer. Beyond the door was a spacious undercroft with walls of stone and a vaulted ceiling hung with torches in mounts of filigreed metal. In the wall directly to his front was a gaping archway that led into a maw of blackness that seemed impervious to the torchlight, and somehow alive. It seemed *hungry*.

Much worse was the spectacle taking place on the threshold of the blackness, the sight of Jeremy floating unsupported in the air, rigid and naked, with his arms splayed wide. Craslowe stood over him, clad in flowing robes of black and crimson, his own feet well off the ground. From the old man's mouth issued a staccato stream of alien words that rose and fell in pitch, that crescendoed and ebbed in rhythmic cycles. At regular intervals Jeremy's voice overlapped Craslowe's, reciting back the exact syllables with a rapidity that seemed impossible for a human tongue.

Carl wanted to believe that this was a dream or a hallucination. But the details were too real, too solid to be made of dream stuff: the fiery glint off Hadrian Craslowe's steel-rimmed spectacles; the silvery array of chalices on the ebony table beneath Jeremy's floating body; the Kabbalistic symbols carved into the stone walls.

Even more real than the solid sights and sounds was the pall of evil that hung in the air, a vaporous presence that flowed from the furrows of Craslowe's long face, from his oily eyes, from his spittle-slick lips. Carl sensed that the evil was flowing from Craslowe into Jeremy, that the boy's lank body was a vessel into which the old man poured power and will and knowledge.

Then Carl's gaze alighted on Jeremy's hands, and he bit his tongue. The index finger on each hand was at least an inch longer than the other fingers.

Carl wanted to vomit: Small wonder that Jeremy nearly always kept his hands in his pockets or out of sight under workman's gloves—to hide this hideous deformity.

Craslowe raised his arms in a gesture required by the hellish ritual, and Carl saw that *his* hands were similarly deformed, but much more radically. Craslowe's index fingers were easily twice the normal length, topped with sharp black nails that hooked inward like talons. He knew now why the good doctor never offered to shake hands.

Carl's intellect switched off, overloaded by contradictions of the sane, rational world in which he had lived until this moment, of all that he had known as truth. Rage took over, tensing his muscles and knotting his fists in preparation to lunge through the door. Battle would ensue—good, old-fashioned physical battle, fueled by a father's righteous rage against a perverted old monster who had corrupted an innocent boy. His fists would smash that loathsome old face, shatter the spectacles and inflict great pain. He meant to crush and rip and shatter that grotesque old body, then snatch his son away and flee the stinking undercroft, back to where the sun shone. He was drawing up to launch himself when—

This could not be.

—human figures began to emerge from the maw of darkness behind Craslowe. Or *almost* human figures. Their flesh hung in ragged tangles from their bones, as though eaten away. Their eyes glowed. Some walked on what was left of their feet, while others floated in the air. One man actually sat in a wheelchair that made an electrical hiss as it rolled along the stone floor. Half a dozen strong, they formed a circle around Craslowe and Jeremy, their faces turned inward, their palms upward in a gesture of obscene worship. Carl's jaw dropped as realization flowed into him. One of the hideous acolytes was old Elvira Cashmore, the woman whose yard he had cared for as a boy. Now she was a barely recognizable scarecrow of exposed bone and rot. Next to her stood the ruinous figure of a young girl with red hair, her Army field jacket ripped and clawed to shreds, her face a third gone, and her arms—

God, her arms! How can she still be alive?

She was Teri Zolten.

Carl shivered and trembled, fought to hang on to his sanity, to keep from screaming at the top of his lungs. These were the missing people of Greely's Cove, or at least some of them—the ones who had not yet been totally consumed by whatever lurked in the dark maw beyond the arch. By some unnatural magic they had survived wounds that should have killed them several times over, possessed powers to float through the air and do God only knew what else.

A hand settled on Carl's shoulder, and this time he *did* scream. He whirled to stare into the wrecked face of Sandy Cunningham Zolten, once his favorite cheerleader at Suquamish High. Her left cheek had been taken by someone else's teeth, leaving her own exposed to the air, along with her fungoid gums. Her rusty hair was ragged and crazy, her jumpsuit shredded to reveal the savaging that her once pretty body had taken.

"Oh, Carl, I can't tell you how good it is to see you," she said with what should have been a smile. "I followed you around upstairs, wondering if I dare talk to you. But since you're here . . ." Her voice was rough and gurgly, which could have been due to the holes in her throat. Her speech was misshapen for lack of half a lip.

"S-S-Sandy?" Carl's own voice had nearly fled, and he pressed his back into the corner of stone wall and wooden door, a pathetic effort to move away. "Sandy, I—I—"

"There's no need to whisper," she said, cocking her head and allowing the stalk of a severed vessel to pop through a gap in her face. "They can't hear us in there. They're in a trance—something to do with Jeremy's final initiation, I guess."

She drew even closer to him.

"I sensed you were coming, Carl. And I was glad. I suppose you know that I've always had a crush on you, even after high school. You must've known."

She insinuated a tattered arm over his shoulder, causing him nearly to retch.

"Sandy, what's happened to you?" he croaked, nodding toward the door. "To *them?* Is it Craslowe? Has *he* done this to you?"

"Oh, let's forget about him, since he won't be awake for hours yet. That means we have some time before you go to the Feast. We should make good use of it."

"What feast? What's going on in there?" He grabbed the

viscous skin of her arm and tried to force it away from his neck.

"It's like a graduation or something. Jeremy is becoming like Hadrian, a steward to the Giver of Dreams. But that doesn't concern you or me—or *us*. Let's make the most of—"

Carl summoned all his strength and wits, dragged his mind back from the brink of blubbering lunacy, and shoved Sandy away. When she came back at him, he kicked her hard in the midriff. She staggered backward and then faced him squarely, breathing with a growling hiss. Her eyes began to show from within, and Carl nearly fainted with fright.

"What's the matter, aren't I good enough for you, Carl? Aren't I high enough on the social ladder to be your girl?"

"Sandy, stay away from me!"

"Do you think I don't know what you and Renzy have been doing with your fucking cameras, taking pictures of me when I'm leading cheers, when I'm kicking? How do you think that makes me feel, Carl? Do you think I like the thought of having my picture in your wallet, so you can show it around the boys' locker room?"

"Sandy, I mean it! Stay away!"

"Or you'll do what, Carl? You're not thinking of leaving, are you? I can prevent that, you know. I have *powers* now, and I can make you do whatever I want. Besides, you don't want to miss the Feast."

Carl made a move along the stone wall, thinking to flee back toward the stairway, but Sandy Zolten laughed out loud with a voice that turned his blood to jelly. Numbness soaked into his arms and legs and torso, staggering him. He fell against the wall and just managed to stay on his feet.

"See what I mean?" said Sandy, coming toward him again. "I have power, Carl, and I'm going to take you to the Feast. There'll be some pain and a few minutes of terror, but you'll surrender to the Giver, and when you've done that, the *dreaming* will start. And oh, you'll dream the most incredible things! You'll move through time and taste the most exquisite miseries, Carl, the most beautiful atrocities that mankind has ever conceived. You'll experience hungers that you never knew you had, and you'll be able to quench them with every imaginable kind of sin. But first—"

Another wave of numbness gripped Carl, and he nearly fell

to the stone floor, heaving and gagging. Sandy was very close now, and he could smell her.

"—there's the little matter of *this*."

She began to wriggle out of her tattered jumpsuit, pushing it down from her horribly mutilated shoulders, down past the only breast she had left, down with the remnants of her ravaged undergarments, exposing great gapes where gouts of flesh had been eaten away.

When naked, she came to him and wrapped her filthy arms around his neck, pushing her encrusted face into his.

"Time to fuck, Carl. Isn't this what you've always wanted, a chance to fuck me? Isn't that why you took all those pictures, so you could see up past my panties? Well, here I am. You want it, you know you do, and so do I."

Carl felt that at any moment his revulsion would kill him, that his heart would simply refuse to go on beating. Sandy was digging into his jacket, tearing away the buttons of his flannel shirt, trying to force a hand into his belt. Carl was smothering, dying, when Sandy's body suddenly stiffened, and her hands flew to her throat. The numbness left Carl instantly.

He saw a tight leather strap around her neck, which she clawed with her hands, her luminous eyes bulging and her tongue thrusting horribly out of her mouth, the wounds in her neck sucking and whistling wetly. Behind her was Ianthe Pauling, who was strangling her with what appeared to be a belt, and doing so expertly. Minutes passed before it was over, before the tragic existence of Sandy Zolten ended and the salacious light left her eyes. The body that had once belonged to a beautiful young woman slapped to the stones in an obscene heap.

Carl cried as Ianthe Pauling led him away from the undercroft, actually shed huge tears that flowed down his face as she pulled him, urged him, *drove* him up the coiling staircase, forcing him to leave Jeremy behind. He cried for his son, for Sandy Zolten. He cried for his sanity, for all the poor souls on whom Hadrian Craslowe's evil had feasted. He scarcely believed his eyes when at last they beheld the light of the winter afternoon, when he discovered that the world still existed.

27

Lindsay Moreland left the library of the University of Washington and headed for the parking lot and her Saab. On any other day she might have enjoyed the memories stirred by the sights and sounds of campus life, having spent nearly six years in this place, pursuing her B.A. and M.B.A. and virtually living in the library for weeks at a time. But today she was oblivious to the bustling students and the familiar landmarks. In her hand she carried a folded slip of paper on which a helpful assistant librarian had jotted the name and address of a small shop in Seattle's International District: *The Man-And-Magic Bookstore*.

The dashboard clock told her it was nearly two hours past lunchtime, but strangely, she was not the slightest bit hungry. She had spent the past four hours wading through volumes about the occult, scouring the indexes and tables of contents for any reference to Hadrian Craslowe, by that or any similar spelling. Though she had not found the name, she had come across numerous references to several books that were purportedly complete encyclopedias of noteworthy characters throughout the history of the occult. But the university library did not stock those particular books. They could be ordered, of course, the librarian had said, but that might take days.

"Try this place," he had advised, scribbling on a notepad. "It's a little store off Jackson Street—wait, I'll look up the address for you. It's supposed to have everything there is on the occult: encyclopedias, histories, how-tos, the whole nine yards. If you don't find them there, you won't find them anywhere."

Lindsay had thanked the guy and left, feeling just a little foolish for having dedicated a precious morning to scratching a mental itch, a little guilty for playing hooky from the brokerage, but no less determined to find out—

335

Find out what? Whether Hannie Hazelford's ravings had contained a grain of truth? The implications of that possibility were too outrageous, so Lindsay suppressed them and concentrated instead on getting across the Washington Ship Canal to Highway 520, and from there to I-5 South, which would take her to the International District.

"Robbie, wake up. We have work to do."

Hannie was shaking him with her bony hand. Reluctantly he opened his eyes, to discover that he had fallen asleep in an armchair in her living room. He sat up straight and saw that Hannie was naked, her pince-nez perched on her nose, meaning that she had been scrying again.

"What time is it?" he rasped, unable to focus on his watch just yet.

"It's early afternoon, and time's a-wasting. Here, I'll help you with your boots." She exuded an English sense of urgency.

"I can't believe I fell asleep," said the Texan. "After last night's little go-around with that Craslowe fella, I doubted that I'd ever sleep again."

"Be thankful that you were able to rest. Now come."

"Aren't you gonna put somethin' on, hon? I s'pect you will freeze if you go out like that."

"Oh, I'll put something on," she answered, as though Robbie had been serious, "but I must first cast a protective spell for you. I doubt that you'll need it in the broad daylight, but it's better to be safe than sorry, wouldn't you say?" Her energy level had apparently returned to near normal, which Robbie was glad to see.

"I'm not so sure I like that idea, Hannie. The last time you hung something around my neck, it blew up and burned the holy you-know-what out of me."

"Really, Robbie, I haven't time to argue with you. There's a young man who needs our help, and he needs it desperately. I saw him just now, while scrying Whiteleather Place. It's Jeremy's father. I told you about him, I think."

Robbie's face grew serious as he pulled himself up and onto his crutches. "Yeah, you did. And I saw him during your scrying last night. He was lookin' for his boy, drivin' around the streets, up and down alleys. He wasn't a happy man."

"He's even less happy now, I fear. He's actually gotten

inside the mansion and gone down to the undercroft where the Giver of Dreams resides. I'm happy to say that he's safe for the moment, but his sanity has worn a trifle thin, and he needs our guidance. We must go to him. Now come along, and roll up your sleeve, if you please, because I'll need some more of your blood."

"Aw, come on, darlin', you can't be fixin' to cut me with that knife again! Shoot, I've got a big scab where Monty Pirtz took a chunk out of my wrist, another one where you cut me last night, a blister on my chest the size of a half-dollar, even a gouge in my hairdo—"

"Will you *please* stop behaving like a child and roll up your sleeve! This won't hurt, I promise you."

But of course it *did* hurt. It hurt like the frigging blue blazes.

"Are you certain you're well enough to drive?" asked Ianthe Pauling, staring at Carl with her huge almond eyes. "It would be no trouble at all to drive you home."

He leaned forward in the passenger seat of Hadrian Craslowe's Lincoln, in which the mysterious Mrs. Pauling had whisked him away from Whiteleather Place to the spot where he had parked the Roadmaster.

"I'm fine now," he lied. "I can drive."

In truth he still felt shaky, as though his equilibrium had evaporated through his ears, as much because of the incredible things Mrs. Pauling had told him as the ordeal he had suffered at the undercroft.

"Very well, then. I shan't keep you any longer." She touched a button that unlocked the doors with an electrical thud, and Carl flinched.

"Mrs. Pauling—" His voice cracked, and he coughed to clear his vocal chords. "Ianthe, are you sure there's no way I can get Jeremy out of there? It just seems so—so *insane* to leave him."

"As I've told you, Mr. Trosper, there's absolutely nothing you can do for your son. He's lost to you forever. Any attempt by you to get him back would only result in your own death, which would be prolonged and excruciating beyond belief. You already have gotten a taste of what I mean. You've seen the victims of the Giver of Dreams, so you know what would lie in store."

Once again Carl felt heat rising from his chest to his throat, the fire of grief and rage. He held back what would have been a most unmanly sob.

"But he's my *son!* He's my own flesh and blood!"

"Not anymore. He's become like Hadrian, the manciple of the offspring. His whole existence is tied to the creature— caring for it, feeding it, keeping it safe and helping it to procreate. This will be Jeremy's life from now on. In return he'll have wealth and longevity, a thousand years or more, and his mind will absorb more knowledge than any human was meant to have. He'll be a great sorcerer, and he'll use his magic to further his ends, to create more of his kind, perhaps. Other mere mortals will serve him, just as many have served Hadrian, lured by the promise of wealth and success, both of which Jeremy will be able to provide through his magic. Or he will simply blackmail them, or hold hostage their loved ones, as Hadrian has done with me. Jeremy will *thrive* on evil, just as Hadrian does. He'll take his sustenance from the agonies that he inflicts, from the fear and grief that will follow him wherever he goes. He has become an agent of Hell, Mr. Trosper, and no longer yours."

Carl swallowed and clinched his eyes for a moment, trying to digest the execrable things he had seen within the past hour, all that Ianthe Pauling had told him. In the space of sixty short minutes, his rational universe had toppled against a barrage of inexplicable events. He had seen them with his own eyes, heard them with his own ears. Who could possibly disbelieve, having survived the past hour?

He opened his eyes and stared straight ahead, seeing nothing beyond the video screen of his thoughts. "This offspring that Jeremy serves," he said miserably. "Where did it come from?"

Mrs. Pauling's silence made him turn his head toward her. When his eyes focused, he saw the turmoil in her face, the glistening tears. He tried again: "Ianthe, I asked you—"

"I heard! There's nothing to be gained by talking about it. Haven't you seen enough, heard enough? For God's sake, Mr. Trosper, go home now! Pack your things and leave this town for good. Forget about everything that has happened and make a life for yourself somewhere else. You're a young man yet, and you still have time."

"But I only wanted to know—"

"Take my advice and get out while you can! Hadrian will consider you a threat for having found out his secrets, and he'll retaliate. He'll send forces against you, the most appalling things imaginable. So get away from here, as far away as you possibly can, like I should have done years ago. That's all I'm going to say." A crystalline tear rolled down her cheek. She jerked her head forward to study the steering wheel. "Now, good afternoon, Mr. Trosper."

Carl opened the door and got out, but he hovered unsteadily a moment, gazing at the woman who had delivered him from something that he had never dreamed could exist.

"Ianthe, I know this will sound inadequate. But thank you. Thank you for getting me out of there. And for telling me the truth about—about Jeremy. I owe you my life. I only wish there was something I could do for you."

"You can repay me by getting yourself to safety, by forgetting all this. Not that I deserve any repayment: I'll always carry the guilt of having had a hand in making your son what he is."

"You didn't have any choice in that. Craslowe has had a hold on you." He didn't mention her brother, who she had said was rotting away in a Welsh mental institution, a victim of Hadrian Craslowe's magic, a hostage to guarantee her continued service. Carl shuddered as he thought of the price she might pay for having saved his skin. "I hope that somehow things go well for you," he managed. "Good-bye."

He closed the door of the Lincoln, heard her start the engine, and watched her turn back toward the mansion. The sun glinted brilliantly off the shiny skin of the car, the breeze stirred the forest that walled the road, and gauzy clouds inched across the blue sky. Carl lingered a moment in the warmth of the sun on his shoulders, trying hard not to think of the poor souls who still languished in the mephitic bowels of Whiteleather Place, and then walked toward the Roadmaster.

"So this is where Jeremy lives," said Robinson Sparhawk, as Hannie's red Jaguar braked to a halt at the curb in front of the squat little bungalow at 116 Second Avenue. "Damn, it looks ordinary."

"Surely you can feel the presence, your being a psychic and

all," said Hannie, switching off the ignition. "Even though Jeremy is not here, the presence lingers. Just look at the lawn and the shrubbery—all dying, even those hardy old trees. It's the effect of the evil that he partook of at Whiteleather Place. It radiates from him, poisoning the air and the elements. Green things are especially susceptible, and so are birds and animals."

"And people, too, apparently," said the psychic, eyeing the ruined yard. "It drove his mother to kill herself."

"Indeed. But there was a purpose behind her dying, as you well know. It was premeditated, part of a plan. The death of the yard is merely incidental."

Robbie buzzed the window down and lit a cheroot. "Are you sure Carl will come back here?" he asked, tucking his lighter away.

"Not positively, but I strongly expect that he will. He's a shattered man, and he'll want the comfort and familiarity of the place he calls home. At the moment this is the only home he's got, so he'll come here to collect himself."

"And we'll be waiting for him. I can't say I envy him, considering what he's going to hear."

"We must be gentle with him," said the old witch, checking her lipstick in the rearview mirror, "but we must hold nothing back from him. If he is to be our ally, he must know the whole truth."

"Even about Lorna?"

"Especially about Lorna."

"What if he doesn't believe us? You've got to admit that this whole thing sounds a little farfetched. To your average old boy in the street, it'd be nothing more than a Halloween story."

"The Giver of Dreams has, in fact, inspired many Halloween stories. Its victims have given rise to the legends of vampires and werewolves and zombies. Carl Trosper will believe, though; of that you can be certain. Don't forget that he has visited the undercroft and seen things that defy reason. I'm certain that he encountered at least one victim of the Giver of Dreams while there. If this is the case, he will believe *anything*. You should know, having yourself encountered one."

Robbie watched as she straightened her blond wig, and he hoped that her aged body was up to the rigors that lay ahead.

For that matter, he hoped that his *own* body was up to the rigors that lay ahead.

They fell silent as a 1954 Buick convertible approached from Frontage Street. It slowed and swung into the driveway of 116, then halted. A lean man with reddish-blond hair and a short matching beard got out, stood beside the car, and eyed Hannie's Jaguar, which was anything but unobtrusive in this modest neighborhood. He waved feebly. Hannie returned the wave, and the witch and the psychic got out to meet Carl Trosper.

KRAZLOV, GADRIAN (ca. 1590–?), early 17th-century magician and physician around whom numerous dark legends emerged throughout eastern and western Europe . . .

Lindsay Moreland read the first line of the entry and developed a sudden case of gooseflesh. She shifted her weight and braced the bulky volume against the bookshelf, popped out her foggy contacts, and groped through the pockets of her coat to find her horn-rims. The light in the Man-And-Magic Bookstore was not conducive to reading, and there were no tables at which to examine the goods—only high-walled canyons of dusty books about magic, witchcraft, vampires and werewolves, and virtually everything else worthy of the term *weird*. The one that she cradled in her arms was *An Encyclopedic History of Western Occultism*, by a scholar named Charles Frederick Stout.

. . . often with varied spellings of the name. Though virtually nothing is known of Krazlov's actual origin, most occult historians agree that he was born in what is now Bulgaria sometime in the 1590s, and that he traveled throughout Europe during his adult life.

Among the outrages ascribed to him was the murderous practice of antinopomancy (reading the future in the entrails of women and children), for which ecclesiastical and secular authorities often sought to put him to death. Krazlov always managed to escape capture and prosecution, however, often with the help of wealthy clients for whom he had effected cures or told the future.

Lindsay closed her eyes a moment and breathed deeply of the stale air, hoping to cure the mild nausea she felt coming over her. The name *Krazlov*, she told herself, probably was *not* a variation of *Craslowe,* notwithstanding that the given names were identical but for the first letters.

In 1657, the witch-hunting "Law-Giver of Saxony," Benedict Carpzov, obtained an ecclesiastical decree from Lutheran authorities in Leipzig, branding Krazlov as the direct descendant of an ancient sorcerer named Hadrianus Craslovius (ca. 1100 A.D.), who according to legend had found the secret of resurrecting the dead. At the time of the decree, Krazlov was under suspicion in connection with the disappearance of more than a dozen Leipzig citizens, whom Carpzov insisted were victims of "lycanthropy and vampirism." Once again Krazlov managed to escape.

Lindsay bit her lower lip so hard it hurt, but she read on. The passage told of other cities and regions visited by the notorious Gadrian Krazlov during his lifetime, where people disappeared but sometimes returned as "vampires" and "werewolves"— Augsburg and Strasbourg and Cologne—where he was vilified and hunted but never caught, never burned at the stake, as so many thousands of others were.

The Krazlov legend revived from time to time in later centuries, notably in England and France. The most recent and best-documented case occurred in Coggeshall, Essex, in 1840, when charges of murder and kidnapping were brought against an itinerant actor and mesmerist who called himself Hadrian Craslowe.

A tremor of disbelief shook Lindsay, nearly causing her to drop the heavy book. There it was. The name. Not under *C* for *Craslowe,* but under *K* for *Krazlov,* which she had checked merely on the off chance that there might be variations in spelling.

No rationalizing it now: There was some connection between the legendary Krazlov and the Dr. Hadrian Craslowe of Greely's Cove, Washington.

. . . no direct evidence implicating Craslowe, he disappeared along with his small retinue of actors and stage helpers before he could be apprehended to face the charges.

Lindsay left the bookstore and drove to her house on Capitol Hill, her mental gears grinding. She quickly shed her business suit and donned a bulky cowl-neck sweater of dark green and jeans that were faded nearly to white. From her study, she telephoned Carl Trosper in Greely's Cove. He answered on the fifth ring, with a voice that sounded weak and distracted.

"Carl, it's Lindsay. I've got to talk to you, and I'd rather do it face-to-face. Are you going to be home this afternoon?"

"Well—yes, I think so. . . ."

What's wrong with him? Lindsay wondered. He sounded unsteady and fearful. She thought she heard another voice in the background, but it did not sound like Jeremy.

"Sorry this has to be on such short notice," she said, "but I've found out some things I think you should know. How about if I catch the next ferry? I can be there in"—she stole a glance at her watch—"about forty-five minutes."

"That'll be fine. I—I have something to tell you, too."

"Okay, I'm leaving right now. Bye."

Later, she sat on the observation deck of the ferry, sipped coffee from the snack bar, and carefully composed the disclosure she planned to make to her former brother-in-law, replete with rebuttals to his inevitable charge that she had gone out of her skull.

Hadrian Craslowe was a phony—a talented one, perhaps, but a phony nonetheless. His credentials were bogus, a circumstance that surely demanded that Carl find another therapist for Jeremy, one properly papered and vetted.

But Craslowe has been the only doctor who's been able to help, Carl would counter. *Why tamper with success?*

This one would be difficult to handle, and Lindsay worried over how much more to tell about Craslowe. She wondered just what she herself believed about the man.

If she were to believe Hannie Hazelford, he was an ancient sorcerer who had lived at least a thousand years, the servant of a monster that ate people. If Hannie was right, then Stout's *Encyclopedic History* was wrong—the numerous stories about Krazlov were all about the *same* man, not about imitators or descendants. But this was lunacy, of course, despite the coincidence of the recent disappearances in Greely's Cove.

Lindsay had read about people who believed themselves to be vampires or werewolves and behaved accordingly—actually killed people and drank their blood or ate their flesh—the sickest of the sick, certainly. The present-day Hadrian Craslowe might have read the legends surrounding the original Gadrian Krazlov and made himself the namesake. He might even be insane enough to think that he *was* the original fiend. Therefore he could be dangerous.

But then Carl might suggest that the good doctor really *was* the innocent descendant of someone named Hadrian Craslowe, maybe even of the same guy who was suspected of kidnapping and murdering people in nineteenth-century Essex. Why would that be so outrageous? You can't hold against someone the fact that he had poor taste in ancestors.

Which would bring her back to the fact that the good doctor had phonied up his sheepskins and misrepresented himself to the state health authorities, which in itself should be a sufficient outrage, certainly enough to justify changing therapists.

Lindsay hoped intensely that Carl would see things her way.

28

". . . And, as I was saying, it was at this time that the Sisterhood came very close to destroying Hadrian Craslowe and his Giver of Dreams," continued Hannie Hazelford as Carl returned from the telephone. He sat down again on the sofa next to Robinson Sparhawk, the crippled Texan who professed to be a psychic.

"The Sisterhood was much stronger then, and I was not so—so *alone*. In the south of England we had seven initiates, all of whom reinforced the magic of the others, protected one another, urged a Sister on when she became weary or frightened. We were very much a family back in those days. And in the English countryside were a simple, robust folk who remembered the old ways, many of whom were willing to help us." She paused for a sigh of sadness. "Ah, but as it turned out, Hadrian was able to evacuate his master—hidden in a large trunk—to a ship in the port of Plymouth, and from there to the island of Sumatra in the Indian Ocean."

"About as far away from England as it's possible to get," put in Robbie, who had heard the tale before, "and still be on the planet. Craslowe'd had enough of this old girl and her friends, so he meant to make himself scarce for a while."

Carl nodded, trying to keep his composure. The story simply got worse and worse, and he longed for the strength to disbelieve it.

"So everything Mrs. Pauling told me was true," he said, just to fill the gap in the conversation. He had never doubted the woman.

"True indeed," said Hannie, her turquoise contact lenses glittering in the afternoon sunshine that streamed through the living-room window. "In Sumatra, Hadrian procured an abandoned Hindu monastery in which to hide the Giver, and he set about in his typical manner to corrupt the local population—

345

one of whom was a young American trader named Tristan Whiteleather, who had just taken a Batak tribeswoman for a wife. That was in 1873, and they were, of course, Ianthe Pauling's great grandparents. They could not have known the price that they and all their line would pay for the wealth and success Hadrian's magic brought them. This is what happens, you see: A man goes in league with Hadrian and the Giver, only to discover that he has cursed his sons and daughters, even his grandchildren and great-grandchildren, with the burden of those obligations. No amount of wealth can be worth the price."

"So it was Whiteleather who brought the Giver of Dreams here to Greely's Cove?" asked Carl.

"Yes. You see, the Giver of Dreams undergoes a period of deep sleep once every three centuries or so, and the sleep lasts roughly a hundred years. We're not sure why this happens. All we know is that shortly after the sleep ends, the Giver of Dreams attempts to procreate. As it happened, Hadrian's Giver was about to lapse into its sleep sometime in the early 1890s, which suited Hadrian, because he detested Sumatra. Too hot, too barbaric, and the local Bataks were becoming increasingly hostile as they deduced that Hadrian had something to do with the rash of disappearances among their people. He was eager to return to Europe, where he meant to pursue his intellectual passion for medicine, of all things.

"After the Giver went to sleep, Hadrian charged Captain Whiteleather with the task of providing a safe resting place for the master, which the captain had no choice but to do. The resting place was the undercroft of Whiteleather Place, which the captain designed for that very purpose. Of course, he had other obligations, the captain did, and he was most competent in seeing them through.

"I doubt that he ever returned to Sumatra, for he took an American wife and lived with her here. Little did he know that one day Hadrian would track down his great-granddaughter from the line of his first wife, murder her husband, and cast a crippling spell on her brother, all to secure her servitude. Hadrian needed a new servant, because the Giver was about to awaken from his sleep."

"Yes, Ianthe told me about that," said Carl. "She'd married an Englishman and gone to England with her husband. They'd sent for her brother—Lionel, I think she said his name was."

"Yes, all very tragic," said Hannie. "Ianthe may pay dearly for having helped you this afternoon."

"But she helped *me*, too," said Robbie, stubbing out his cigar in an ashtray, "last Saturday night. If she hadn't stepped in when she did, old Monty Pirtz would've dragged me down to the undercroft. Why do you think Craslowe let her get away with it?"

"Possibly because he was and still is distracted by the matter at hand," said Hannie, in a tone that suggested some reluctance to go on.

"You mean Jeremy, don't you?" said Carl, massaging a sweaty fist. "Jeremy and the offspring?"

"Yes," said Hannie. She avoided Carl's eyes and glanced down at the heavy silver witch's ring that adorned one of her fingers. "This isn't easy to say, Carl," she went on finally. "You must promise to be strong, to hear me out and not go dashing off . . ."

Carl looked first at her and then at Robbie, silently asking what could be worse than had already happened, what he had already heard. What greater horror could there be than losing a son to the Giver of Dreams?

"Do you remember when you and I first met, the day that followed Lorna's death? I accosted you and Stuart Bromton in the receiving room of the Old Schooner Motel." Of course he remembered, and his eyes told her so. "I made quite a to-do over the matter of an autopsy for Lorna. I had a reason for doing so, Carl." Another pause, more painful this time. "An autopsy, you understand, displaces the organs of a corpse in a way that mere embalming does not. During an autopsy—"

"I know what happens during autopsies," interrupted Carl, showing impatience. "A doctor pulls the organs out of the body, weighs them, cuts them up and examines them or whatever, then sews them back in. What does all this have to do with Lorna? She was cremated, just like I told you she would be."

"I'm afraid not, Carl," said Hannie, her voice heavy with regret. "I've discovered that her body was stolen, that she was forced to—"

Carl's shoulders jerked and heaved as the horror hit him.

"—give birth to—"

He choked and gagged with rage, covering his face with his hands in a pitiful attempt to shut out the egregious truth, to wash it away with his lava-hot tears. But the truth became larger and more sickening with every word from Hannie's mouth. Had it not been for Robbie's strong arm around his shoulders, he could not have faced it.

Lindsay gasped when Carl answered the door. His face was slack with exhaustion and his eyes ringed with red. His voice, his movements, everything about him suggested a man who had lost something precious or would soon. Seeing him like this was a shock, but she held her tongue and followed him into the house.

Having noticed Hannie Hazelford's Jaguar outside, she was not surprised to find the old woman seated in the living room, outlandishly attired as usual, her face as aged and leathery as ever. Lindsay greeted Hannie with as much civility as she could muster. The other man in the room, however, was a surprise: He was fiftyish, square-jawed and tan, dressed like a cowboy but wearing a curious little pouch on a thong around his neck. Carl introduced him as Robinson Sparhawk, a "forensic psychic" from El Paso, Texas.

Robbie struggled gallantly to his feet, sans crutches, and managed to stand long enough to shake Lindsay's hand.

"Right pleased, ma'am," he said with Texan charm. "I've met some pretty women in my time, but I can't say any of 'em had anything on you." The remark would have rankled her had it come from a man who lacked Robinson Sparhawk's combination of age and brown eyes brimming with sincerity. From him it seemed okay. Lindsay liked him immediately, "psychic" or not.

"Carl, where's Jeremy?" she asked, after the Texan had taken his seat again.

"He's—he's not here. He's with Dr. Craslowe." Something about Carl's answer seemed incomplete.

"Oh, that's right. Today's therapy day, isn't it? Just as well, because what I have to tell you concerns him, and I wouldn't want him to overhear. For that matter"—she threw a quick, narrow-eyed glance at Hannie, who had not moved from her armchair—"it might be best if we talked in private."

"I don't have anything to hide from Hannie and Robbie," replied Carl.

"Really, Carl, I don't think—"

"Like I said, I don't have anything to hide from them. Now, what is it you want to tell me?"

Lindsay felt a mild thrill of annoyance. "Very well, it's about Hadrian Craslowe. I've done some checking on him, and I've found out that he's not who he says he is. The credentials he gave to the state licensing board are phony. On top of that—"

Carl's emotion-savaged face suddenly broke into a wide, very disturbing grin. He chuckled, and the chuckles evolved into sharp laughter, but not the laughter of joy.

"Do you mind telling me what the hell is so funny?" she asked.

"Is that all you wanted to lay on me? That Craslowe's a phony? That his *credentials* aren't what they should be?" Another string of chuckles wheezed out of Carl's throat, the kind that could easily become sobs. "That's funny, really funny. You see, we've been talking about him, too—Robbie and Hannie and I—but we're not worried about his fucking credentials. We're worried about something *else*, something a lot more frightening than *credentials!*"

"Wait a minute," interrupted Lindsay, frowning with suspicion and glaring at Hannie Hazelford. "I think I know what's been going on here. You've been hearing a lot about something called the Old Truth, haven't you? Demons and stewards and curses, all kinds of gibberish about corpses giving birth to monsters—am I right?"

She glanced back at Carl in time to see him wince a little. This was incredible: Carl Trosper was a hard-nosed lawyer and professional politician, hardly the kind of man to be rattled by bump-in-the-night tales.

"You're not telling me that you believe all that claptrap, are you, Carl? For God's sake, this is 1986, not 1186. The Dark Ages are gone! Monsters are out and computers are in. If we're going to talk about problems, let's at least talk about real ones."

"If I were you, I wouldn't be so quick to poke fun at something you know nothing about," said Carl with ice in his voice.

"Oh, hey, I've heard the whole bloody story," said Lindsay,

"including the part about how Jeremy drove Lorna to kill herself, how somebody stole her body and worked some sort of magic on it, so that she could give birth to a baby monster. Now, if you're going to try and make me believe that all this is *true*—"

"It's true," said Carl solemnly. "All of it."

"Oh, brother!"

Lindsay thrust her palms into the air and rolled her eyes toward the ceiling. This was bad, much worse than she had feared. Hannie Hazelford's insanity must be infectious, she concluded, and Carl must have caught it. Which meant that things did not look good for Jeremy, who needed care from a sane, competent adult.

"Carl, I'm going to give you one more chance to prove that you're not ready to be hauled off in a net. There's a lot at stake here: your son's future, his recovery, your own—"

"Lindsay, I went to Whiteleather Place this afternoon. I saw Hadrian Craslowe and Jeremy, and they were engaged in some sort of horrible ritual. Jeremy was in a trance, floating in the air with no ropes or wires. I saw Teri Zolten and Sandy Zolten, old Mrs. Cashmore, and several other people who've been missing, and they were all—they were . . ."

Carl seemed at a loss for words to describe the people he had seen, but his eyes conveyed a stark horror that startled Lindsay.

"I—I can't really say it, but it was horrible, detestable. And I saw Jeremy's *hands*, Lindsay!"

These he could describe, as well as Craslowe's, and he did. Lindsay stood as though frozen to the floor as Carl talked on, wondering how anyone could remember a nightmare this elaborate. When Carl had finished, Hannie Hazelford rose from her chair and laid her osteal hands on their shoulders.

"This isn't the time for wrangling amongst ourselves," she said gently. "We have other matters to attend to, such as saving Jeremy and restoring him to a normal human state. If we can agree on nothing else, can we at least agree on that?"

Lindsay spoke first: "Maybe I should ask just what this entails."

"Several things, actually," answered the old witch. "First, we must kill the offspring to which he has become the steward. Then we must destroy Hadrian Craslowe and the Giver of Dreams."

It all sounded so matter-of-fact, like the old English fish recipe that began *First catch a dozen trout.* . . .

"In other words, commit *murder*," said Lindsay. "And I'm sure that it all involves lots and lots of gruesome mumbo jumbo, doesn't it?"

"Lindsay, for once in your life stop acting like you've got a broomstick up your ass!" Carl shouted angrily. He now stood up, straight and tall, his shoulders thrown back. He seemed strong. "Has it ever occurred to you that maybe you don't know everything in the world? That just possibly you could be wrong about something? I hate to be the one to tell you this, but you *don't* know everything, and you *are* wrong about some things! This is one of them.

"I didn't lie to you about what I saw at Whiteleather Place, and I didn't hallucinate it. I don't give a rat's ass whether you believe me or not, but know this: I'm going to save my son from Hadrian Craslowe and his evil, and I'm going to do whatever it takes to get the job done, no matter how sickening or disgusting or vile it might be. I'm going to do exactly what Hannie tells me to do, because that's the only hope I've got. Now, you can believe me or disbelieve me, or you can call me a fucking lunatic, but don't even *think* about trying to stop me. If you want to help, then fine, you're more than welcome, because God knows we need help. But if you won't help, then get the hell out of here!"

Robinson Sparhawk spoke for the first time since the introduction, his face long with concern, his voice heavy. "Don't go high-tailin' it away, darlin', because Carl's right: We do need help. And for what it's worth, I can tell you that he ain't lyin' about what's out at Whiteleather Place, because I've been out there myself. I saw enough to corroborate everything he's said."

He took a moment to lick down a cigar, to fire it up with his butane. Blowing out smoke that swirled dizzily in the rays of the waning sun, he went on.

"Know what else, darlin'? I went through just about the same kind of crisis that he did, the same one you're just now starting to go through—the crisis of belief. It ain't easy to throw away everything you've always known to be true and substitute somethin' that smells like a jug of nitrogenous waste.

But it can be done, and you can live through it, same as he did, same as I did."

"Robbie's right," said Hannie. "The truth always finds a way to be believed, I've always said."

Lindsay's hands suddenly felt very cold, and she struggled with images and thoughts that were most unwelcome. The things her mother had said about Jeremy's powers. The historical account of someone named Gadrian Krazlov, who read the future in the guts of murdered women and children. Carl's description of Jeremy's hands. For a moment, she almost believed she was the victim of some kind of group hypnosis, because the room was swimming and growing dim in the coppery light.

Carl was talking in a low voice, and Lindsay forced herself to listen, to hear.

"Ianthe Pauling begged me to leave town, said that Jeremy was beyond help, lost. But Hannie says that there's hope—"

"Only if we *act*," the old woman put in urgently. "The time is growing short!"

"I can't give up on him, Lindsay. He's my son. I've failed him before, but I'm not going to fail him this time. I don't care what I have to do. I'm going to get him back."

"If everything you've told me is true," said Lindsay, having gotten herself together again, "wouldn't it be best to call the police and let them handle this? It seems to me that they'd be anxious to check out any lead on the missing people, no matter how unbelievable it might sound."

"The police would be powerless against Hadrian Craslowe," answered Hannie. "They'd go blundering into Whiteleather Place with their guns and dogs and bullhorns, but the best they could do would be to force him to flee. He would only start anew somewhere else. More innocent lives would be lost. What's worse, the police could do nothing to help Jeremy—for that we require the assistance of much higher authorities."

"For that, we need *magic*," said Robbie with a gentle smile.

"Let us leave this house now," said Hannie, gathering up her slicker from the chair over which she'd tossed it. "Evening will soon be upon us, and this won't be a safe place after dark. Ianthe Pauling was right, Carl, when she warned of Hadrian's retaliation against you. You will be safe, however, in my cottage, as *you* will be, Lindsay. I've taken certain precautions."

"Your *cottage!*" said Lindsay. "But I didn't come prepared to spend the night—"

"Not to worry," commanded the old Englishwoman. "I've spare rooms and a sofa that converts to a bed. As for toiletries, we can pick up some things at the Seven-Eleven on the way. No food, though, because tonight will be a night of fasting, which is essential to our rituals. Now come."

Incredibly, Lindsay let herself be dragged along, not believing and not disbelieving, but only *hoping*.

29

Vengeance was a cup from which Mitch Nistler had never drunk. Throughout his life he had always been the victim, the target of wrongs, but he had always lacked the means and the will to strike back at the multitude of his tormentors.

As a kid he had suffered taunts, insults and rejection, simply because he was homely and different and, worst of all, poor. He and his family had silently endured the humiliating charity of a local rich man, Ted Dawkins, who had regularly appeared on the doorstep of their shack near the marina, laden with pots of homemade food and weird little hand-carved figurines that were supposed to cheer the Nistlers' bleak lives. The food had always tasted bitter and overly seasoned, the toys had brought no cheer, and the Nistler family had crumbled into desolation.

Mitch had hated Ted Dawkins and his phony show of mercy, but he had never thought of striking back for the humiliation that the man had inflicted. In fact, after getting out of prison, Mitch readily accepted the job that Dawkins had talked old Matt Kronmiller into giving him. Mitch had suffered no pangs when he heard that Dawkins and his wife had eaten rat poison shortly thereafter.

He had craved no revenge against his childhood tormentors, nor, in later life, against Matt Kronmiller, his tyrannical boss and landlord. Not until Corley the Cannibal Strecker had reentered his life did he come to know the thirst.

Tonight he meant to drink deep from that cup, knowing that this could well be the last real joy that he would ever taste. Sickness was burning him up from within, eating away the flesh and leaving hideous red welts and itchy blisters. His lungs were tight with fluid, his joints and muscles stiff with ache. If through some miracle he survived this contagion contracted through sexual union with a dead woman, his future looked

anything but bright, thanks to Jeremy Trosper and the thing
that lived on the second floor of his house.

Even at this moment, the thing was mewling with hunger.

Having made his delivery of crack and money to an alley in
downtown Seattle, he had returned to his own place rather than
drop off the load of unprocessed cocaine at Cannibal's crack
house—a violation of his instructions. He waited now in the
inky darkness of his living room, sprawled in a chair that he
had moved to a front window, gazing out at the nightscape
through the dirty glass. In his fist was an icy bottle of Olympia.

He sipped the beer and relished the sting on his throat. He
gloried in the platinum glow of the full moon and the shadowy
silence of the woods beyond his weed-choked yard. He savored
the fullness of each passing minute. The night was alive with
the black promise that for once in his miserable life, he—Mitch
Nistler—would be the predator and not the prey.

His heart leapt as headlight beams danced among the trees
and swept into the muddy drive of his yard. He heard the
grumble of a large engine and the grinding of gears, the crush
of gravel as someone hit the brakes hard. Without his glasses,
Mitch could not see clearly the dark hulk of the vehicle in front
of his house, but he knew from the sound that it was Cannibal's
Blazer. Cannibal had tired of waiting for him, had grown
anxious about the fifteen thousand dollars worth of cocaine that
had not shown up on schedule, and had come to investigate,
just as Mitch knew he would.

He jumped up from the spot near the window and moved
back toward his bedroom, pausing en route to open the door
that led upstairs.

He heard a voice from the front of the house: "You stay in
the truck, Punkin'. I'll go see if I can find the little puke. I just
hope he's here, so I can get my hands on him."

Another voice, brassy and grating: "He's got to be in there
somewhere, because his fuckin' rust-bucket car is here."

"I know that. I've got eyes, too, y'know. Just stay in the
fuckin' truck, okay?"

Heavy footfalls on the porch. A pause. The booming of a
huge fist against the door. Which swung open, because Mitch
had not latched it.

A gigantesque figure of a man appeared in silhouette against
the Blazer's high beams. Mitch peeked around the doorsill of

his bedroom, staying deep within the shadow and squinting through the glare.

"Mitch, are you in there?"

Mitch's heart started thumping madly. It was happening now, just as he had planned it. The cup was near his lips. The son of a bitch was behaving exactly as Mitch knew he would.

"Mitchie, answer me! I know you're in there, you little shit! What're you trying to pull here, anyway?" Cannibal stepped across the threshold and halted. "God *damn!* It smells like a sewer full of dead rats in here!"

Mitch heard the sound of Cannibal's hand clawing along the wall in search of the light switch, heard the switch snap; but no lights came on. Mitch had removed the bulbs from their sockets.

"What's the deal, Mitchie? Did you forget to pay your power bill?"

Cannibal took another wary step, and Mitch reached into his pocket to finger the heavy padlock that he had bought earlier that day. From the thing upstairs came only silence now, as though it knew what was afoot and was willing to cooperate.

Another step.

"Okay, Mitchie, I'm done fuckin' around with you. Give me the goddamn coke. It doesn't belong to you, man. I don't know what you think you're doing, but whatever it is, it's not worth having Laughing Luis come after you. You're smart enough to know that, aren't you, Mitch? Just give me the coke, and I'll get out of here."

Right. But not until you've pulled my arms and legs off and left me to die like the moths you used to catch in your cell, you sorry mother-fucking piece of vomit.

"I mean it, Mitch. This isn't funny anymore."

Mitch was loving this. His senses seemed sharper than they had been in years. Cannibal Strecker was sweating, worrying, and the first draught of sweet revenge was feeling good going down.

Sweat, you worthless chunk of lard, SWEAT!

Stella DeCurtis's voice sliced through the night: "Is he in there?"

"Yeah, he's in here somewhere!" Cannibal shouted back. "And he's going to be one sorry little mouse-man when I get done with him, you can bet your ass on that! *Unless*, of course, he comes out right now! You hear that, Mitch?"

Cannibal seemed reluctant to take another step, maybe because of the stink. Or maybe because a remnant of childhood dark-fear was stirring in his guts. Time to start phase two, Mitch figured.

He pulled his head back into his bedroom and drew a painful breath. This had better work, or Cannibal would have him, and he would know pain as he had never known it or ever dreamed it.

"I'm up here," he hollered, "at the top of the stairs! If you want your coke, you're going to have to come and get it!"

Mitch heard movement: the sound of a few more steps. Cannibal was taking the bait.

"Is that you, Mitchie? Where'd you say you are?"

"Open your fuckin' ears, you big shit-covered pig! I said I'm upstairs, and I've got your coke. You want it, you come and get it!"

Silence ensued, and Mitch worried that Cannibal could hear his wheezing. If Cannibal were still sweating, he wasn't the only one now. Mitch held his breath, edged his face to the doorjamb, peeked around it, and saw the shadowy silhouette of Cannibal standing a few feet away, staring into the blackness of the open door that led upstairs. Mitch froze. He dared not start breathing again, feeling his face grow hot. He imagined that the big man was quivering with rage.

"Okay, if that's what you want, you little shithead, I'll come and get it. And I'll get *you*, too!"

Cannibal inched forward and placed a foot on the first step, the other on the second, and moved upward to the creaks and snaps of the old staircase. Three steps, four steps, five. Mitch launched himself at the door, grabbed its edge, and slammed it. With cold fingers he slapped the hasp home and slipped the padlock through the staple, clicking it shut.

He heard huge thumps on the stairs—Cannibal coming back down—and fists booming on wood, hands frantically working the knob. The door groaned against Cannibal's weight, but the lock and hasp held fast.

"Mitch, God damn it, you let me out of here! What the hell is going on with you, anyway? Mitch! MITCH!"

For a moment there was silence, perhaps some indefinite

hint of movement overhead, something scuttling across the floor upstairs, and Cannibal had heard it. Mitch leaned his back against the door, worrying that he lacked the intestinal fortitude to endure what would surely come next.

"O GOD, THERE'S SOMETHING IN HERE! GOD, MITCHIE, OPEN THE DOOR!"

But that wasn't possible. The cup was not yet empty. Neither was it as sweet as Mitch had hoped it would be. He heard the scrabbling of claws, the clicking of teeth.

"OH, FUCKING CHRIST ALMIGHTY, IT'S GOT ME! JESUS GOD, MITCH, PLEASE! OPEN THE FUCKING DOOR! IT'S GOT! OH, NO-NO-N-! HELP MEEEEAAAAH-HHHHHHHH!"

Mitch lurched away from the door and staggered-stumbled toward the headlights at the front of the house, unable to bear any more of Cannibal Strecker's screams. He burst out to the porch and fought the glare with an upraised hand, steering himself toward the Blazer, which sat still on its fat tires, its throaty engine idling. Jeremy had done his part, just as he had promised, and stood next to the pickup near the passenger's door, his face a vulpine horror. Inside sat Stella DeCurtis, her comatose eyes fixed straight ahead, her once-cruel mouth hanging slack and open, Jeremy's victim.

Mitch knew she would not move a muscle until Cannibal came for her.

30

The last thing on earth that Stuart Bromton wanted to hear over the intercom was that he had a visitor, and the last person on earth he wanted to see was Dr. Hadrian Craslowe. But he dared not refuse to admit the man, dared not even keep him waiting for long.

"Give me a minute and show him in," he told the dispatcher.

A minute. Sixty seconds. Not much time to hammer his wits back into shape. For the past thirty-six hours or so, ever since his incredible encounter with the doctor in Mitch Nistler's upstairs bedroom, Stu had lived in a kind of limbo. He had gone through the motions of being a police chief, a husband, and father. But in his mind he had seen himself as an actor in a play. It was like watching from the safety of a darkened box seat—removed from the action, interested in the goings-on, but not really involved.

He wondered if this were some sort of an emotional defense mechanism that had been switched on to soften the direful new realities that had entered his life since—

Since Monday night. When he had shaken hands with Hadrian Craslowe. When his soul had taken a little unannounced vacation from his shuddering, drooling body. Had he really been a little boy again? Walking along through a chilly wood? Only to chance upon a hole in the path, a black opening about the diameter of a grapefruit, that sank downward through decades worth of spongy leaves? What had made him get down on his knees and thrust his little hand into that blackness?

Police Chief Stuart Bromton discovered that his body was trembling again, that he was gripping his right hand with his left, as though to confirm that it was where it should be. He forced down a sip of coffee and was struggling to swallow it when the door of his office swung open.

Dr. Hadrian Craslowe walked in, his awful hands tucked

deep into the pockets of a shapeless overcoat, his steel-rimmed glasses impeccably clean and his white hair swept back from his walnut face. He was a kindly patrician today, his head held high.

"Good morning, Chief Bromton," he said with his rich British voice. "I trust you're well."

Stu was not well, but he nodded.

"I wonder if we might have a moment of privacy." To which Stu responded by asking his secretary to take a coffee break and to close the office door behind her.

"Well then," said Craslowe when they were alone, "I've popped in to notify you that your assistance is needed."

"Oh? How so?"

"I've learned that certain people here in Greely's Cove intend to trespass upon the home of Mitchell Nistler. Their motives are most harmful, and you must see to it that they do not succeed."

"Who are these people?" asked Stu.

"The same ones we spoke of the night before last, and two others as well—friends of yours, I think: Carl Trosper and Lindsay Moreland."

Stu felt the wind being sucked from his lungs, as though an invisible fist had slammed into his solar plexus. "Carl is the oldest friend I have," he managed to say. "Are you sure he's involved?"

"Come now, Chief Bromton, you don't really believe that I could be mistaken, now do you?"

No, of course he didn't. "What do you want me to do?"

Hadrian Craslowe told him, and for the tiniest fraction of a second his rage grew monstrously. He nearly launched himself out of his chair and across his cluttered desk, to clamp his hands around Craslowe's neck. But his consciousness altered suddenly, and he was the little boy in the woods again, and he was pushing his hand deep into that freezing hole in the ground. His fingers touched something spongy and viscous. A stinging tentacle wrapped itself around his wrist and pulled, and the pain shot like electricity into his shoulder, his arm, his scrotum, and right down to the core of his soul.

So Stuart Bromton merely nodded, having heard Hadrian Craslowe's orders. To protest would have been useless, and even so, they had shaken hands on an agreement, which was inviolate, which superseded old friendships, long-held values, and all old notions about goodness and decency.

Dr. Craslowe did not have far to travel for his next call of the morning: only upstairs to the mayor's office, where His Honor Chester Klundt received him warmly. The office was small and garnished with framed awards and honors from local civic organizations. Here and there were icons of Klundt's ardent religiosity: a calendar that featured scriptural verses and paintings of biblical scenes, a carving in wood of the ancient Christian fish symbol, a small desk plaque with *"I'm Ready for the Rapture"* printed on it.

Dr. Craslowe bowed deeply, rather than shake the mayor's outstretched hand.

"Gosh, it's nice to get a visit from one of our town's newer citizens," said Klundt, once they were seated. "You know, I usually don't come into the office this early in the morning, so you're lucky to catch me." He beamed his politician's smile.

The doctor, who sat with his overcoat folded over his hands, said, "I'm grateful that you agreed to see me on such short notice, Your Honor."

"Hey, you don't have to call me that," said Klundt. "Just call me Chet. What do I call you? *Hade?* Or maybe *Haddy?* I knew a guy in the Navy named Haddy, but his first name was really Hadford."

"You may call me"—the doctor cleared his throat, smiling to conceal his utter loathing for the fat little man who sat behind the desk—*"Hadrian*, of course."

"Ah, good. What can I do for you, Hadrian?"

"Mayor—or, rather, *Chet*—I come to you this morning not as a citizen of the town or as a voter, but as a fellow Christian"—Klundt's eyes lit up, and he leaned forward slightly in his chair—"knowing that you are a very spiritual man. You are also a powerful one, and you have tremendous responsibilities to the community. I deemed it wise to talk with you before talking with anyone else."

"Well, I'm glad you did, Hadrian, I'm glad you did. I have to say, I never dreamed that you were a Christian. Do you belong to a church here in town?"

Craslowe spun a yarn about having not yet taken time to seek out a church, that back in England he had belonged to a fundamentalist congregation that was "truly spirit-filled." He was on the lookout for a church whose pastor preached "salvation" and not modernist heresy. Until he found one he would content himself with his daily devotions and fellowship with a few close friends. After all, for a born-again Christian, every waking minute is spent in communion with Jesus. Klundt answered with a *praise God!* and naturally suggested the church that he belonged to. Craslowe promised a visit.

"But on to the matter I must discuss with you, Chet," continued Craslowe. "It's a most difficult subject to broach, and I pray you'll bear with me. I'm afraid that the Devil is hard at work here in Greely's Cove."

Which Klundt first took to mean the disappearances, but Craslowe quickly set him straight.

"I'm speaking of sorcery and witchcraft, Chet."

The mayor's face went white.

"I cannot divulge my sources to you, because they are patients of mine, and what they've related to me is privileged. But I can tell you this: There is a woman who lives here in town, named Hannabeth Hazelford, who has been practicing witchcraft with alarming openness. Using power given her by Satan, she has even managed to cast a spell on our city council, I'm told, in order to bring in one of her close allies, a man who calls himself a psychic—"

"Yes, yes, I *know!* His name is Robinson Sparhawk. It pains me to say this, Hadrian, but everything you've heard is right. I naturally opposed bringing this man to our town, but I was outvoted. I can't say I'm surprised that old Hannie's a witch. She even *looks* like one. I've never liked her!"

"She and Mr. Sparhawk are servants of Hell," said Hadrian, putting on his most somber face. "I came to you because these two demon-worshipers are contriving to convert others to their art, one of whom is a patient of mine. They have intimidated him, bullied him, and have even threatened his life. I suppose I can trust you if I were to give you his name, your being born-again."

"Absolutely."

"His name is Mitchell Nistler. Very soon—tonight, as a matter of fact—this Sparhawk fellow and the Hazelford woman intend to hold a sabbat at Mitchell's house, even though he is terrified of the idea. I'm told that they will be in the company

of two other witches—I don't know their names—and that their
ceremony will consecrate Mitchell and his house to the service
of Satan. In other words, Chet, they intend to establish a
working community of witches right here in Greely's Cove."

The mayor's eyelids were fluttering with God-given rage.
His breathing was short and raspy, his lips pale. His eyes saw
but his brain did not register the motion of Hadrian Craslowe's
hand as it tossed a tiny pouch made of skin to the carpet under
the desk, where it began to release its vapors.

The hypnotic voice droned on: "I know that you are aware
of God's commandments concerning witches, Chet. In Exodus
the Lord says, '*Thou shalt not suffer a witch to live.*' And in
Deuteronomy, '*There shall not be found among you any that is
an enchanter or a witch, for all that do these things are an
abomination unto the Lord.*'

"I realize that I can't go to the police, Chet, because I would
only hear from them that this nation's laws protect the beliefs
and religious practices of everyone, even witches. Yet I keep
hearing the Lord's words in my heart. . . ."

Thou shalt not suffer a witch to live.

Craslowe's voice flowed on, and his gaze bore into Chester
Klundt's eyes. The room swirled with a power that Klundt
could neither see nor feel, but he soon drifted into its influence.
He did not notice that his visitor occasionally slipped a foreign
and very guttural word into the conversation, but even if he *had*
noticed, he could not have known the power that the words
unleashed.

31

"Magic depends on many things," said Hannie Hazelford, "but most of all it depends on words."

She stood naked in the center of the pentagram she had carefully drawn in red wax on the floor of her kitchen. At each tip of the five-pointed star she had placed a thick white candle. The combined light fluttered across the surfaces of cupboards and walls, throwing jerky shadows.

Carl forced himself to concentrate on what she was saying and not on the misshapen marvel of her naked body. He stole a quick look at Lindsay, who stood between himself and Robbie: Her eyes were huge and disbelieving, her mouth slightly open. She absently fingered the small pouch that hung on a thong against her sweater.

"The proper combination of words, uttered with reverence and respect for the powers they represent, can set the magic in motion," Hannie went on, moving now to a counter, where she had placed a large collection of vials, jars, and boxes. "It's very much psychological, and emotional, too. Though it's true that the ingredients of potions and charms produce their own kind of energy, more often than not they serve merely to put a person into the right frame of mind for doing magic. By mixing together various herbs and spices, and by executing the required rituals, I simply prepare my mind and body for uttering the words of power."

The Words of Power. Carl had seen that title on the cover of a book in Jeremy's room. The memory of it produced a cramp in his abdomen.

"Lindsay, Carl, Robbie." Hannie peered at all three of them through the thick lenses of her pince-nez. "I must ask you all to disrobe now."

"What?" Lindsay's voice rang out like a rifle shot. "You want us to—you want us *nude?"*

"Yes," answered the old woman. "Nudity is a necessary part of the ritual. The participants must be unencumbered by—"

"Okay, this is where it stops!" shouted Lindsay. "I'm now in my twenty-sixth hour of fasting, and I haven't complained. I've skipped work. I've worn the same grungy clothes since yesterday, slept on a lumpy sofa last night, and sat through an entire day of rituals and lectures and nonsensical hokum. I've let you take blood out of my arm, a fingernail, a snip from my expensive haircut, and I've even given you a jarful of my urine. But I'm *not* going to take off my clothes and get naked with two men and a witch. This is where it stops!"

"Lindsay." Carl turned toward her and tried to say something, but he found himself at a loss. He struggled. "Lindsay, this isn't a game. Something very serious is at stake here. We're talking about—"

"I know what we're talking about! What I don't know is how I let myself get dragged into this! I'm so hungry I'm ready to faint, I'm tired because I didn't sleep last night, and I've had it up to here with hocus-pocus!"

Carl could not say that he blamed her, because he too was near the end of his rope. The cottage seemed like a jail cell, his head buzzed from the oppressive pall of burning spices, and his eyes ached for sunlight. But he had an advantage over Lindsay: He believed in the elaborate, maddeningly arcane exercise that Hannie was putting them through, had been putting them through since the first rays of morning; he believed in it, because he had no choice, because he had visited the undercroft of Whiteleather Place and seen its secrets. Lindsay had not.

"Please don't go, Lindsay," said Robbie, hobbling after her as she darted around the cottage, collecting her jacket, handbag, and the toiletries she had bought last night at the Seven-Eleven. "This stuff all sounds like nonsense, I know, especially to somebody who's never seen—"

"It *is* nonsense!" shouted Lindsay. "I'm getting out of here before I become as crazy as all of you." She made for the door, pulling on her jacket.

"Darlin', it could be dangerous out there. If you don't want to join the ritual, that's okay; you can stay in the back room with Katharine, if you want. But at least wait 'til morning before you—"

"Negatron," said Lindsay. "I'm not staying another minute at this funny farm. Nice meeting you, Robbie."

Carl bounded into the living room from the kitchen as the fire-blackened front door slammed shut. "Christ almighty, you didn't let her go out there, did you?" he asked.

"Didn't have much choice, Bubba."

Hannie appeared at the kitchen door. "If she's kept the charm around her neck, she should be safe from nearly anything Hadrian might send," she assured, "short of a full-fledged demon. If he were to send something like *that,* the whole neighborhood is in dire trouble."

"What if Hadrian himself is out there?" asked Robbie, touching the front of his brightly colored western shirt, under which lurked a painful blister. "I seem to recall that he can make short work of a pouch around the neck."

"Oh, I *do* hope he hasn't come himself," said Hannie weakly. "If Hadrian is close by, then that poor girl—oh, dear."

Lindsay stood in the darkness of Hannie Hazelford's driveway and pawed through her handbag for the keys to her Saab. The wind off the Sound had grown cold since nightfall and had blown a heavy cloud cover over Greely's Cove, dousing the moon and stars. She cursed the chill and the blackness, cursed herself for not cleaning out her handbag weeks ago when she had thought about it. She became more urgent in her search for the keys. Lipstick, eyeliner, pens, coins, Kleenex, candy bars . . .

"Miss Moreland?" The whisper was close. And husky with sickness. Not long ago it had been a young woman's voice. Lindsay's body turned to stone as she stared into the darkness.

Next to the rear fender of her Saab, not four feet away, stood a shadow that looked something like a young woman. But as Lindsay's eyes adjusted to the gloom, they gleaned hints of grievous bodily injury. She nearly swallowed her tongue.

"Miss Moreland, you don't know me, but my name is Elizabeth Zaske," the thing said, moving still closer. "You might've read about me in the papers awhile back."

Lindsay's brain labored, deciding whether she was in danger; and if so, what to do about it. The breeze brought a horrible stink to her nose, and she wanted to step away, but her limbs had become as uncooperative as hardened plaster. Fear gripped her, like a claw, right between her breasts.

"I disappeared, remember?" the shadow-thing said, but it was no longer a mere shadow. It was near enough now to give evidence of its solidarity, of real flesh and bone. "I was the waitress at Bailey's Seafood Emporium."

"What do you want?" demanded Lindsay, with as much authority as she could muster. "I don't have time to talk. I was just leaving."

"Oh, you can't leave, Miss Moreland. I'm supposed to stop you from leaving, no matter what happens."

"And just how do you intend to do that?" A flutter had crept into Lindsay's voice, utterly destroying the authoritative effect.

"It's easy," said Elizabeth Zaske. "I'm doing it right now. I can't finish what I'm supposed to do, though, unless you help me. Please take off that awful thing you're wearing."

Lindsay felt her hand go to the little skin pouch that hung around her neck, the charmed vial that contained ground hair and nail, samples of her body fluids and she hadn't dared to guess what else. Her *protector*, Hannie had called it.

"Wh-why would you want me to take it off?"

"Well, because it's offensive," said the creature, who had lost much of its skin and flesh, who stank like an open grave, who knew what *offensive* was. "If you keep it on, you and I won't be able to have any fun. We won't be able to go to the Feast."

Lindsay had not heard Carl approach from behind. She choked with startlement as he stepped between herself and the one-time Elizabeth Zaske.

Suddenly the creature's eyes glowed bright green. Lindsay nearly lost the contents of her bladder.

Carl seemed confident in the protection of his own charmed vial. He slammed a fist into the creature's face, knocking it backward. Before it could recover, he slammed another into the side of its head. It went down onto the concrete, and Carl delivered a kick to the throat, which dislodged pieces that might have been teeth or bone. They made little snicks as they landed on the concrete.

Incredibly, the thing got back on its feet again. Its breath came with horrible, moist-sounding whistles.

"Hey, you're pretty tough against little girls!" shouted a

voice from the deep shadow, this one male and scratchy with disease.

From behind Robinson Sparhawk's van, which was parked next to Lindsay's car, stepped one of the things Carl had seen in the undercroft.

"Want to try your luck with *me*, Bucko?" It had once been a large and healthy man in his early fifties—probably Wendell Greenfield, the missing service-station operator. He was no longer so large, because he had given up so much of his meaty self to the Giver of Dreams. But there was no telling how much damage he could do, charm or no charm, and Carl backed away, grabbing Lindsay's arm.

"Come on, let's get inside," he said.

"I can't!"

"For God's sake, Lindsay, how can you need any more proof than that?" He motioned toward the Zaske- and Greenfield-things, both of which were approaching now, their eyes aglow with greenish light.

"I don't need any proof, Carl!" Lindsay's voice was cracking now. Tears were flowing. "I can't move! She *did* something to me! *I can't move!*"

Carl waited not another second. He ducked under her arm and looped it around his neck, then swept her up and made for Hannie's front door. At the last possible moment it opened, thanks to vigilance at the window by Robbie. The door slammed shut behind him.

As he laid Lindsay on the sofa, Carl saw that she had fainted dead away.

The ritual finally ended.

The four of them silently gathered up their clothes and pulled them on, for there was work to be done. Midnight work.

None of them looked forward to it, but none shied away from it either—not even Lindsay, who only hours ago had tried to sever herself from the others. Now she was with them, having encountered a sample of the evil that Hannie, Carl, and Robbie had insisted all along was real, an evil that had claimed her nephew and her sister, had worked such horror upon an innocent little town. Hannie had administered an herbal potion that had quickly cured the paralysis inflicted by the Elizabeth Zaske–thing. Along with the others Lindsay had shed her clothes and had participated in the ritual, not yet fully believing that she was living anything but a nightmare.

Carl led the group out of the house to Robbie's van, carrying an immense flashlight and the long rawhide scabbard that Hannie had presented him with during the ritual. As the flashlight beam poked into the shadows of shrubs and the dark places at the corners of the house, it revealed the hunkered shapes of Hadrian Craslowe's victim-dreamers, lurking and hungering to get close. Green fury spewed from their eyes. Hannie's magic kept them back:

> Spell of spice from the good Sister's mouth,
> Raptus of Morrigan, North and South,
> From Heaven and Hell, and from West and East,
> Flow from mine eyes to repel this Beast.

Robbie drove them down Torgaard Hill to Frontage Street, then turned right and followed a route he had come to know too well. Carl sat in the rear of the van with Lindsay, his head bowed and his eyes shut tight. The silence conquered the droning of the engine, the rush of tires over pavement. Another turn, onto Sockeye Drive.

She had worked her magic while the other three sat naked in a triangle, at three tips of the waxen pentagram drawn on the floor of her kitchen. She had bustled to and fro in the candlelight like a twiggy little elf, singing and chanting both in English and the Old Tongue. She had flitted now and again to her hoard of bottles and pouches and boxes and jars, extracted this or that, sometimes interrupted her chants to explain things to her listeners, to reassure or warn. She had mixed and chopped and brewed—

"Of Herb Grace and Sweet Flag, with teeth of a hanged man,
And Sandalwood oil and unripe Cubeb, to flavor the bite,
I murmur this song, I murmur long as I can
To draw Thy tears and dry them with petals of Clove Pink this night,
All here, all here,
Seething with fire,
To fear, to fear. . . ."

—and Carl had felt the power of the words as the fumes of

burning herbs seeped into his head. He had drunk the foul mixture she had poured from an Osterizer into a silver cup and chewed the bitter chunks of something she had chopped in a Cuisinart. And her laughter had fallen like rain. She'd said that blenders and food processors were the best things that had ever happened to witches. . . .

Another turn, this time onto Old Home Road. Not far now to Mitch Nistler's house.

The van halted, and Carl raised his head to look out through the front. A Pontiac sedan blocked the road, and next to it—standing with an arm upraised—was a hulking figure of a man whose broad face was white in the glare of the headlights.

"Well, I'll be dipped," said Robbie under his breath. "It's Stu Bromton, and he looks like he means to rain on our parade."

For the second time this night Mitch Nistler heard the approach of a vehicle on Old Home Road. The first had been less than an hour ago: Stu Bromton's Pontiac, which for some unknown reason had stopped about a hundred yards from the house and switched off its lights.

Mitch had worried frantically that the police chief would storm in and find the fruits of all the hellish doings that had been afoot here: a dead body upstairs; the half-living Cannibal Strecker, whose restless, shuffling footsteps could be heard above the ceiling; the comatose Stella DeCurtis, who sat in a Blazer out back, waiting, waiting; a bag of reasonably pure cocaine that Mitch had brought with him from Seattle last night; and last—oh, this would really be special—the offspring of Lorna Trosper's corpse.

But Jeremy had reassured him, told him not to worry. The situation was well in hand. Best for Mitch to get some rest, the boy had said, and then he had gone upstairs to "commune," or whatever it was that he did with the offspring. So Mitch had sunk onto his old living-room sofa and tried to sleep.

Tried. The darkness of his living room had come alive with the kind of tingling ferment that precedes a violent electrical storm. If it was the product of magic, it certainly was not from Jeremy's kind, which produced only torture and terror and hopelessness. This magic crackled with a curious sense of hope.

He rose from the sofa and pressed his face against the front window. He saw headlights up the road; some kind of van. People were getting out, and Stu Bromton was confronting them, trying to turn them back.

But he shouldn't turn them back! something screamed deep inside Mitch's heart. *These people are hope!* Without really knowing what he was doing, and certainly not knowing why, Mitch got his hurting body into motion, aimed it for the front door, and plunged outside. He needed to hurry, or Jeremy would hear his thoughts and stop him before he could—

What was *this*? The spare-tire compartment of his old El Camino? A crowbar? He took it into his fist, savoring the icy bite of the metal, and strode toward the headlights.

"I'm afraid I can't let you go any farther, Carl," said Stu Bromton, standing his ground like a block of granite. Despite the cold night wind, he was sweating like a butcher inside his padded nylon jacket. The headlights of Robbie's Vanagon were giving him a blinding headache.

"Stu, listen to me," pleaded Carl as he approached. "We've got to get into Nistler's house. I don't have time to explain now, but I'll tell you everything when—"

"That's far enough, Carl!" The threatening tone of his own voice appalled him. This was *Carl* he was talking to, the oldest and best of his friends. He sickened at the thought of ever raising a hand against Carl Trosper, became even sicker with the certainty that he could. And would.

"But you don't understand! Jeremy's in there! And so is *Lorna!*"

Good God, Carl *knew!* Stu's mind reeled with the implications of this. Suppose Carl went to higher authorities with a story about Stu Bromton covering up the theft of a body, and an investigation resulted. Suppose the investigation uncovered the evidence of Stu's involvement with a crack ring, and—*shit!*

"*Please,* Stu! If you don't let us go by, I'll never get my son back! Do you hear what I'm saying?" Carl's face was wretched with desperation. Stu hated seeing him like this, hated more what he himself was doing. But he had no choice in the matter.

"Look, Carl, it's not like I'm doing this for myself."

Lindsay Moreland and Hannabeth Hazelford had gotten out of the van by now, and Robbie was leaning on the open driver's door. Hannie's wig looked as though it were on backward, and she was wearing a pair of those old-fashioned, pinch-nose glasses.

"I'm keeping you out for your own good. Now get back in your van and go back to town. We can all talk about this later."

"So, how do you plan to stop us, Chief Bromton?" asked Lindsay, drawing up beside Carl. "Suppose we decide to go around you. What are you going to do, shoot us?"

The question ignited anger, and Stu reached down to unsnap the holster of his nine-millimeter. Lacing the anger was real fear of exactly how far he *would* go.

"Miss Moreland, I'll do anything I have to in order to keep you from trespassing on this property. Is that absolutely clear?"

There was shadowy movement behind him, which Lindsay and Carl glimpsed for the barest instant: a man crouching behind Stu's Pontiac, coming closer now, staying low. A crowbar connected solidly with the side of Stu's head, knocking him to his knees. With a pitiful little yell, his attacker dropped the weapon and fled into the thicket beside the road.

Stu moaned and cursed bloodily. Holding a hand to his head, he gave chase to Mitch Nistler, staggering crazily and weaving like a man drugged, waving his flashlight and crashing through the foliage like a raging animal.

"Come!" screamed Hannie. "This is our chance!"

The three of them scrambled back into the van. Robbie gunned the engine and steered around Stu Bromton's dirty Pontiac toward Mitch Nistler's house.

Carl had stood in the center of the pentagram while Hannie floated in the air around him—up, down, and around—listening to the songful gibberish of the Old Tongue and somehow understanding the words. He had felt the power, the magic, as though it were flowing over him like warm oil from an invisible cauldron above his head, bathing his naked body.

"Rage of Tempest, singing through the thorny wood,
From the darksome Otherworld, the depths beyond light,
Bearing Vesta's pow'r to me, in tormented plight,
Or by any other Name, She is as good.
I hear Thee, I see Thee, Thou givest Thy Sword
To smite the Offspring of the Misruled Lord. . . ."

And when he had drunk yet again of the silver cup, Hannie produced the old scabbard and placed it in his hands, her eyes tearful in the entrancement. Looking into those aged eyes, he had seen himself.

As he was now, hours later, with the short, heavy sword gripped tight in one fist, the flashlight in the other, pushing through the front door of Mitch Nistler's house. Had he never visited the undercroft at Whiteleather Place, he would not have believed that anything could produce a stink this bad. Hannie was at his left elbow, Lindsay at his right, and Robbie a step behind on crutches. He heard the sound of Lindsay's hand as it searched the wall for a light switch, heard a snap when she found it. No light came.

Scuffling footsteps overhead, the creaking of old floors. A groan? Or was it a growl, low and fulsome with threat?

Carl turned his face toward Hannie, whose huge, rheumy gaze darted upward and then met his.

"Up there," she whispered.

The foursome moved into the innards of the house, their eyes burning with the stench. The flashlight showed incredible squalor. They halted at a door that likely led upstairs.

Stu Bromton toppled over a log and nearly lost his pistol and his flashlight.

"Son of a bitch!" he hissed, struggling to his feet. The wet foliage seemed to have hands and claws, seemed to grab him and hold him back whenever he got close to Nistler. From deep in the woods he could hear the little man crashing onward in terrified flight, occasionally crying out after a collision with a tree.

Stu's head throbbed from the blow Nistler had given him with the crowbar, but adrenaline and exertion had restored most of his senses. He now knew that he had been wrong to give chase, that he should have stayed on the road to prevent Carl and his friends from going into the house. They had already done so by now, probably. Meaning that Stu had muffed the assignment given him by Craslowe. For this there could be hell to pay.

He made his way back toward Old Home Road, cursing with every other step, wishing that he had given in to an urge earlier in the day to pack his car and simply disappear south. Once again he asked himself what the hell was so important about his agreement with Craslowe. So *what* if the good doctor spilled the beans about the crack lab—especially if Stu were in Mexico or Costa Rica? Who would bother with him and his penny-ante haul of bribe money when there were so many big-time crooks in the world, so many cops who took major cash?

As he neared to within a hundred feet of the road, he heard the sound of a passing car, then saw its headlights through the trees. By the time he'd gained the road, the car was halting in Mitch Nistler's drive, next to the battered old El Camino and Robbie Sparhawk's van.

Stu squinted into the dark: Was it Chester Klundt's El Dorado? Something dark and cold tickled his guts, making him break into a run toward the house.

"Well, Bubba, I reckon this is it," said Robbie, squeezing Carl's arm and giving a little smile that was lost in the darkness of Mitch Nistler's house. "From here on out, it's up to you. No matter what you find up there, just remember that you've got the magic. You'll be okay."

Carl tried to smile but could not. Because his face was ice. He turned back to the stairway door and lowered the flashlight beam to the padlock that hung open beside the hasp.

"And remember the *words,*" whispered Hannie Hazelford. "The magic is nothing without the words."

"I'll remember," answered Carl feebly. "Here goes."

His hand closed around the knob, and the old door opened upon a cave of blackness. The beam of his flashlight immediately fell upon the mutilated face of Corley the Cannibal Strecker, who lunged down the stairs with a bellow of murderous fury, his eyes alight with preternatural venom, his ragged hands groping and swiping like a carnivore's claws.

Carl froze with terror, unable to raise the sword or move a muscle, and stood stonelike as Lindsay's shrieks filled his mind, as time slowed and enabled him to follow the movement of Cannibal's hands toward his throat. But the magic was with him—the magic of the potion in the vial. In the pouch. On the thong. Around his neck. The magical protection that Hannie had supplied.

Cannibal's body slammed into an invisible wall, igniting a dazzling shower of sparks that ricocheted off the walls of the stairwell and cascaded down the steps. Cannibal jerked backward, twitching and twisting and screaming, an appalling spectacle of pain.

The grip of Carl's terror shattered. He moved forward, up the steps, as the writhing Cannibal tried to scramble away. Carl caught him and raised the charmed sword, brought it down hard, and saw the blade slice through Cannibal's right arm. A geyser of blood washed over the stairs. Carl raised the weapon and brought it down again, this time through the right shoulder, severing ribs and spinal cord, ripping loose vital organs that wagged and jiggled with Cannibal's every movement. Then yet again, through the neck now. Cannibal's life fled, along with the hideous glow behind his eyes.

Carl stood on the stairs and breathed in great huffs, leaning against the blood-spattered wall of the stairwell. He splayed the light over the carnage he had just wreaked and would have stood there a long time, struck dumb and numb by the magnitude of the deed, if Hannie had not called out to him from below.

"Go, Carl! Go now, and do what you must do! This is no time to weep over what you have become. Remember your son! Remember Jeremy!"

Carl remembered Jeremy and set his feet to moving up the stairs once more, following the beam of the flashlight, trying to be strong. This was *love,* he told himself again and again, a father's love for his son. Nothing can conquer love. *Nothing.* Killing the offspring would free Jeremy, and life would then be good again.

"That's a bunch of sentimental bunk, Old Carl, and you know it!"

The voice nearly shredded Carl's reason, for it belonged to his own dead father. Trembling like a leaf, he swept the flashlight beam across the upper landing and saw nothing. Then he realized that he had not swept it high enough, because Jeremy was lying on the ceiling almost directly overhead, his awful hands laced behind his head and his feet crossed, glaring down at him with laser eyes.

Thou shalt not suffer a witch to live.

Mayor Chester Klundt heard these words in his heart for the thousandth time since Dr. Hadrian Craslowe had visited his office that morning. He slid out from behind the steering wheel of his El Dorado, knowing what he must do, knowing exactly what God wanted from him.

He reached into the rear seat and pulled out the Winchester Model 12 shotgun that he had sneaked out of his house—*sneaked,* because if Millie had known what he was up to, she would've thrown a fit, probably even called the police. His wife had no use for violence or cruelty of any kind.

Chet, on the other hand, knew that in every Christian man's life there came a time for standing up and showing what he was made of, a time for striking a blow for Jesus and maybe being struck back for the effort. That was what Christian courage was all about: a willingness to strike a blow for Jesus, no matter what the consequences.

He heard screams from inside Mitch Nistler's house, high and dreadful *witch*like screams that sent chills up his spine. His courage wavered slightly. These were creatures of Hell he was about to face, and he could not know what horrors they might loose upon him. But then he remembered the words of Hadrian Craslowe's prayer—the prayer that the two men had shared together that morning in his office, right there on the carpet, two Christian men down on their knees.

" '. . . Jesus, we ask Your blessing upon Brother Chester, a blessing of strength and courage to do what You would have him do. Grant him the armor and sword of Your Holy Spirit as he undertakes to follow the command that You gave us in Exodus—*'Thou shalt not suffer a witch to live.'* . . .' "

Chet had felt the power of the Holy Spirit surge through him like electricity as Brother Craslowe gripped his hand in his own. From that very moment he had suffered not the tiniest doubt about what he must do. The earthly consequences were of no importance whatever, be they ridicule or arrest or even prison or execution. All that mattered was striking the blow, ridding the world of Hannie Hazelford's wickedness and reaping the heavenly reward that surely awaited him.

He chambered a round of 00 buckshot and walked toward the front door of Mitch Nistler's house, praying under his breath.

Help me, Jesus, help me. Give me the strength, my Jesus. . . .

The stink of Hell assailed him as he set his foot inside the open door, the shotgun leveled from his shoulder, and he saw a faint glow ahead, the dancing beam of a flashlight. The witches were there—three of them, anyway—clustered around the opening of a staircase. Might as well take these three right now and get the fourth one later.

"Chet, no!" Sounded almost like his son-in-law's voice. Somewhere behind him, running and breathing hard. This was not good, because Stu would try to stop him. Chet tightened his finger on the trigger, wishing that he were a little closer, because the light was so bad, and the *stink!*

"Chet, don't do it! Don't do it! *Nooo!"* First, one shot ripped the night, but a second followed in a heartbeat.

Carl heard the shot but had no idea what it meant and did not care. The green light from Jeremy's eyes bored into his soul and planted cold where once there had been love.

"The *words,* Carl, the *words!"* screamed Hannie from below.

Paralyzing darkness, petrifying cold—not at all what Carl needed to continue up the stairs with his charmed sword, not at all adequate to the task of killing the offspring.

"P-please, Jeremy," he stammered pitifully, feeling molten tears on his cheeks, "can't you understand that I'm trying to help?"

A heartbeat, another shot.

The first, from Stu Bromton's nine-millimeter pistol, was meant for Chester Klundt's legs, because Stu had no wish to kill the man, much as he hated him. All he wanted to do was prevent a massacre, which for some un-fucking-known reason, Chet seemed on the verge of committing. But Stu was running up the porch steps, and the light was bad, and he had never been a good shot with a pistol. The round went high: It entered Chet's back just above the buttocks on the right side, ripped through the old man's bladder, and made a sharp turn, puncturing the stomach before exiting the front.

The second, a reflexive shot from Chet's 12-gauge, lit up the squalid living room of Mitch Nistler's house for a fraction of a second and filled it with a mind-numbing roar. A cluster of hot pellets tore into Hannie Hazelford's shoulder, taking much of it away.

• • •

Carl heard the noise and the screams from below, but he did not care, because his son was coming down from the ceiling now, his horrible hands spread wide as though to embrace his father. Though that embrace would have meant death, Carl was willing to accept it, willing, willing—

"Carl, don't let him touch you!" came Robinson Sparhawk's voice close upon his back. The trance weakened slightly. Carl felt like a small, defenseless animal that a snake had hypnotized.

"The words, Carl! Use the goddamn *words*, Bubba!"

More noise and commotion from below—Lindsay's screams, a man's shout—but Robbie was close by and *with* him, and they pressed on, upward and upward. The trance-fog was beginning to thin, but Jeremy was so close, and the green fire from the boy's eyes would—

—would kill him, Carl suddenly understood.

He raised the stubby Roman sword that Hannie's magic had blessed, and Jeremy drew back, his face a spastic mask of hatred. *This is not my son,* Carl reminded himself aloud, as Hannie had admonished him to do again and again, *but a thing that has stolen my son's body and mind, the thing that Hadrian Craslowe created with a cutting from his own Hell-bound spirit.*

"The *words*, Carl!" Robbie was behind him, coming up the stairs on his crutches, a brave man.

And Carl found the words:

"By Mantis, by Daghda, by the Lord of the Wildwood and His Ten Thousand Names, I turn you back! I turn you back! I turn you back!"

The sword began to glow pinkly, and a ray of color shot from its tip into Jeremy's face. The boy screamed with a demon-voice and flew backward toward the upper landing, where he came to rest and turned around again, facing his father with glowering eyes.

"I'll not let you harm him, *Dad!*" Jeremy thundered, and Carl felt a stab in his heart. But he kept coming up the stairs, closer and closer, with Robbie hobbling along right on his heels. "I'll have you in Hell before I'll let you harm him! I'll call a thousand demons to rip out your eyes! I'll have you on a *spit!*"

"By Mantis, by Daghda, by the Lord of the Wildwood and His Ten Thousand Names, I turn you back! I turn you back! I turn you back!"

"That little speech may work against *me,*" hissed the boy, backing away toward the bedroom door. The door opened of its own accord. "But it will never work against *him!*"

A shattering of wood and glass followed as if on cue from Jeremy's long, pointing finger. Beyond the bedroom door, Carl saw a man-form crash through the window in a blizzard of splinters and shards. It hovered in the blackness above a rickety old bed: Hadrian Craslowe, birdlike or batlike in his lumpy tweed suit and baggy old overcoat, his white hair riotous, his eyes a double dose of hellfire. Jeremy floated up to meet him, and they hung together in the air like a pair of vultures, grinning.

"*Soooo*, Mr. Carl Trosper," boomed Craslowe, as Carl stepped onto the landing, "you come armed with magic, I see. And powerful magic, too. That old sword you have in your hand—it is the one that the Emperor Nero used to kill himself. Fascinating historical tidbit, no?"

He floated toward Carl and Robbie, his arms spread wide, his dark talons gleaming at the tip of each index finger.

"But we're not here to discuss history, except in the sense that it's being *made.* You see, the survival of an offspring of the Giver of Dreams is indeed a very historic occasion, one that I intend to see come off without a hitch. Unfortunately for you, Carl, and for that sorry little specimen of manhood shivering behind you, *survival* is not the operative word."

Carl raised the sword: *"By Mantis, by Daghda, by the Lord of the Wildwood and His Ten Thousand Names, I turn you back! I turn you back! I turn you back!"*

But Craslowe was not turned back, as Jeremy had been. The pink outpouring from the tip of the sword did not faze him, and he moved closer, grinning that bestial grin.

Hannie lay in a lake of her own blood in the hallway below, with Lindsay cradling her head and Stu Bromton hovering with his flashlight.

"Take me up the stairs," she croaked. "Do it now, immediately! Hadrian has come!"

Stu started to protest, to insist that she lay still, because her right arm was hanging by little more than a few threads of skin and she had lost an incredible amount of blood. Stu wanted to call for an ambulance.

But he stood back as an ashen-faced Lindsay Moreland helped the old woman to her feet, and unbelievably they made for the stairway, where light was leaking downward. They went up, step by step.

Craslowe would have been on Carl, would have ripped him to pieces as a small child might rip a paper doll, had Robbie not used his Gift.

The psychic visualized a boulder roughly the size of a baby grand piano, poised it above the old sorcerer's head, and let it drop. The shock was apparent in Craslowe's aged face, in the faltering light from those dreadful eyes. The pink energy from Carl's sword intensified, and the magic seemed to have effect now. Craslowe screeched and staggered backward, roiled and flailed his arms, before recovering from the shock and coming back at Carl.

Robbie screwed his eyes shut and launched another blast of psychic energy, but *damn!* this wasn't easy, and he did not know how many more times he could do it.

Suddenly Hannie and Lindsay were on the stairs behind them, and something was horribly wrong. Hannie was covered with blood, her blond wig was gone, and her *arm*!

She wasted no time but pointed a crooked finger of her good hand squarely at the hovering mass of Craslowe. That most ancient language poured from her lips.

The magic flowed in a torrent from her eyes, assaulted Craslowe and drove him back into the bedroom with Jeremy. The sword in Carl's hand glowed hot now, and the pink flow from the blade enveloped them and drew screeches of pain. Robbie threw chunks of mental energy against the pair as they hovered in the little bedroom, as they turned and writhed and twitched—all within the space of seconds.

Jeremy and Hadrian Craslowe plunged through the window into the cold night, fleeing the magic that Hannie Hazelford had wrought, flying away like two Hell-birds on a storm.

An onerous silence descended.

Carl would have directed the beam of the flashlight to the bed, but he already knew what lay there, and he doubted that either his guts or his soul could endure a clear look. He turned his attention to the breathing sounds in the corner of the bedroom, where something waited.

Something subsumed in near-total darkness.

Carl stepped toward it, keeping the light to one side, worrying that he might actually see its face and that he might lock gazes with it. Hannie was at the door behind him, chanting in the Old Tongue—which was good. The sound of her voice gave him strength. He heard heavy feet coming up the stairs, but this did not concern him. What concerned him was the darkness in the corner, the darkness that seemed alive and hungry.

He raised the sword and waded into the gloom, getting the vague feeling of bulk and slitheriness, of reptilian wings and claws, the definite impression of fangs and teeth and a predatory mouth. He nearly vomited at the babylike cry that came as he brought the first blow down.

But this was not as bad as Lindsay Moreland's scream, or his own quick flight into insanity after throwing a glance over his shoulder to the old bed behind him, after seeing—surrounded by the beam of Stu Bromton's flashlight—his wife, Lorna, the mother of his son.

Sitting up on the bed.

Standing now.

Moving toward him, glowering.

Skin blistered and mottled green and brown, slipping away in places. Hair loose and falling, body distended. Eyes and tongue swollen, her face a chthonic rictus of murderous rage. She tried to speak, to hold out her hands, to keep Carl away from the thing that she had borne. Carl went weak and dizzy.

Pistol shots erupted, pounding deafness into Carl's head. Stu was firing, firing at Lorna. She was jerking and recoiling with every impact, going down, mercifully, going down and dying at last—really *dying*. Carl turned back to his murderous task, sobbing hugely and shoving the charmed blade deep into the slithering matter that hunkered in the corner, *glad* for the deafness. So that he could not hear the screeching as he chopped and slashed. Chopped and slashed. As blue fire consumed the once-living pieces of the offspring.

32

They fled to Hannie Hazelford's cottage, the five of them: the original four soldiers and Stu Bromton, who because of what he had seen and done tonight was now with them. Hadrian Craslowe's hold over the police chief had broken, possibly through the effects of Hannie's magic, or possibly by sheer revulsion against a man who could sponsor such horrors as had taken shape before Stu's very eyes.

Unlike Mayor Chester Klundt, Hannie was still alive and kicking, despite the volume of blood she had lost and the fact that her mangled right arm hung grotesquely backward at her side. She immediately shed her blood-soaked clothing and set about brewing a potion in an earthen jar, employing dozens of spices and herbs and many words of magic. She kept the jar near her and drank of it often as Lindsay bandaged the shotgun wound and bound the crooked old arm in a tight sling. The potion, whatever it was, worked well against both pain and bleeding. But more incredibly, it gave her strength and vigor, even revived her feistiness.

They sat in a circle in the living room, feeling safe behind the barricade of waxen symbols and vials and pouches and jars. They listened silently as Hannie told them what they must do.

Whispered instructions went to Stu. Hannie snipped hair from his head and a nail from his finger, took his blood and urine, performed a ceremony, and gave him back a small skin pouch with a vial in it, marking him a soldier like the others. He left the house on his mission while the sun was still hours away.

Robinson Sparhawk watched Hannie with fascination, listening to her words and feeling a mixture of admiration and dread: admiration for her personal strength and endurance, the potency of her magic, dread over knowing that the magic was devouring both her spirit and body, even as it propped her up

382

in the aftermath of a shotgun blast that should have killed her. How much longer could she last? he worried.

"You've done well this night," she told them, her face a living riddle of creases in the candlelight. "I'm grateful to you. Together we've accomplished a great good, you and I: We've destroyed the offspring of the Giver of Dreams and have thus saved hundreds, perhaps thousands, of our fellow human beings from ineffable suffering. But you know as well as I that we have yet more to do. The death of the offspring did not free Jeremy from the evil's grip, as we'd all hoped."

Carl stiffened at this. He tightened his grip on the bloody sword he still held in his lap.

"But I tell you that there is yet hope for him. The hope lies in killing the Giver of Dreams and its manciple, Hadrian. Unfortunately, this will be no easy task. It will be far harder than destroying the offspring, which was a mere infant—less than an embryo, really, of the mature demon. To succeed against the Giver of Dreams, we must invoke the most powerful magic imaginable. We must carry out a ritual that you may find execrable and utterly revolting. But worse, one of us must make a sacrifice—a totally abhorrent sacrifice—which will be the key to the demon's destruction. Without that sacrifice, we cannot hope to win."

She stared through her silvery pince-nez at Carl, her leathery old head tilted slightly back and her chin thrust out, her eyes magnified to eloquent sharpness. Carl knew that he would be the one to make the sacrifice, and his pair of colleagues knew it, too. Lindsay reached for him and took his hand, held it firmly. Her own hand was cold, but strong.

"This ritual is very old," continued Hannie, "older than any other I know, though it has been amended through the ages with new names and words, added to and embellished. It combines the pure energies of the male and female—the man, who is the defender and warrior, with the woman, who is the giver of life and the provider—in order to loose the fury of the unseen world against mankind's oldest enemy. I say once again, it is not easy magic, my friends. It is demanding and rigorous and dangerous, for we are not dealing with harmless woodland spirits here. We're not speaking of Shakespeare's Mustard Seed or Cobweb or Peaseblossom, but of things with names like Astaroth and Leviathan and Asmodeus the

Destroyer—not their *real* names, of course, but the ones that men have given them. These beings existed tens of thousands of years before any man ever walked on the earth.

"Suffice it to say that we cannot afford to make mistakes. We must be strong in our resolve, for we cannot leave the ritual unfinished once we begin it. We must be prepared to *suffer,* and having suffered, we must even then be ready to accept the consequences of defeat. The magic, you see, only works about half the time, for the Giver of Dreams is so very strong. . . ."

Carl surmised within minutes that the bubbling green potion Hannie had given him was an aphrodisiac, and a powerful intoxicant to boot. He felt warm and giddy as he gazed across the flickering candle flames to where Lindsay stood naked at a tip of the pentagram. His eyes devoured every detail of her lean, blond body, from her delicate toes to the gentle slope of her belly to the mounds of her breasts. She stood golden and still, her blue eyes flashing and her mouth faintly curved in a smile. She too had drunk the potion. Carl would have sworn that she was glorying in his stare, maybe even rejoicing at the spectacle of his engorged penis.

Hannie chanted and brewed, used her microwave and the burners on the gas range—mixing and shaking and stirring, producing occasional flashes of fire and smoke. The air was thick with incense and foggy with the fumes of burning herbs.

Whether morning had come or night returned, Carl did not know, did not care. The windows were shuttered and curtained. He knew only that Stu had come back a moment ago after accomplishing his dark assignment, toting a small bundle wrapped in black plastic. Carl tore his stare away from Lindsay and watched Hannie remove the shiny wrap, feeling his own eyes go wide and his lungs constrict as she pulled out the thing. He heard Stu's deep voice explaining that he had used the computer at the police station to access the county's vital statistics. He had found the record of an infant's recent death, located the cemetery, and—

God, spare us! This can't be!

The corpse of the baby boy was perhaps a week old, bluish and greenish and mottled with fungus, the tragic little remainder of an innocent life that never really got going, thanks to a defective valve in the heart.

In the center of the pentagram Hannie knelt before a heavy cutting block, upon which lay a wide pewter bowl, and went to work with her long knife, singing an old song in a voice that could have curdled blood and maybe had:

> *Comes now yellow Wolfsbane, embrace Aloe Root,*
> *To sharpen the senses when Dark Wind's afoot;*
> *Monkshood and Nightshade, dried up brain of a cat,*
> *Comes now Mandragora, so purple and fat,*
> *Combine with the fat of an unbaptized Child,*
> *An Innocent's Blood, unpolluted and mild.*

Her knife winnowed and flashed with easy speed, separated fat from muscle and muscle from bone, lopped the appropriate bits into the cold pewter bowl where they lay amid the chunks of powders and flecks of spices, the dark globules of—

> *Sweet flesh of a venomous Reptile I bring,*
> *For the Semen of the Wizard needs temp'ring.*

She uncorked an ancient-looking vial and poured a white, almost vaporish fluid into the mixture, then picked up the knife again.

> *Juice of an Innocent Babe's tiny Liver*
> *Is Poison, dread Poison to the Dream Giver!*

The knife entered the infant's body with surgical deftness, found the liver, cut it out, and directed it into the bowl. The act seemed less a defilement than an honor. Next came boiling oil from the range, water from the tap, more chanting, but in the Old Tongue now. And dancing, and mixing, and beating, while Robbie Sparhawk stood nearby with the candle lantern that supplied light. With an amazing display of physical strength, Hannie, who was naked but for her mass of white bandages, held the heavy pewter bowl above her head with the one hand available to her. She danced. Lifted off the floor into the air and danced. She cast her crone's gaze onto Lindsay, who fell immediately into a trance.

The dark came alive with eddies of air, the whining and buzz of unseen powers, the energies of the *words*.

Lindsay ascended, her naked body gyrating slowly and her flaxen hair streaming as though underwater. She floated to the center of the pentagram. The forces in the air focused on the contents of the pewter bowl. The vile mixture formed itself into a thin column that stretched upward to the ceiling, undulating and twisting as though alive, then separated into two streams and snaked downward to flow into the open mouths of Lindsay and Hannie. When they had drunk until nothing was left in the bowl, Hannie lowered it, and Lindsay descended into the center of the pentagram, where she stood next to the pale and shaking Robbie Sparhawk, who looked as though he might throw up at any moment.

Hannie sliced the remains of the dead infant into chunks suitable for the food processor, then processed them into a thick paste, adding more spices and oils and old words. She scraped the mixture into the bowl, which she then handed to Lindsay. Now Carl felt himself being drawn into the center of the star, and he let himself go after casting a worried glance at Stu, who stood as though frozen in the shadow of the kitchen door. Hannie suddenly went rigid as a statue. Carl thought for one wild moment that she had died, but a closer look revealed that she was indeed breathing, but so shallowly, so slowly. It was Lindsay now who was animated, who was alive and vital.

When he was within her arm's length, she scooped a handful of the paste from the bowl—it was more like a salve or a balm—and began to rub it on his chest. Old Hannie must have added something powerful to the mixture, for it felt warm and tingly on his skin. Another handful, more rubbing—onto his shoulders now, his neck, warm, warm. Onto his arms, down his belly—*Jesus!*

He plunged his own hands into the bowl, took gobs of the balm, and rubbed it into Lindsay's skin, marveling at the light in her eyes, only touching on the thought that there was someone *else* besides Lindsay Moreland behind those eyes. His hands found her firm breasts as her hands found his cock, his balls. He was oblivious now to the wide, watching eyes of Robbie and Stu. He knew only that he must touch the rusty mound of hair between Lindsay's legs, that he must press his fingers into that velvety wet fold, that he must knead and knead, which is what he did. Lindsay uttered a cry and began to gyrate her beautiful hips, began to claw at his shoulders with her nails. Suddenly her mouth was on his, and he knew that even if someone else were inside her head, it was still *she*—Lindsay—who was kissing him like this, ramming her tongue against his, pulling him down to the floor, massaging his cock with the greasy, fiery balm.

They went to the floor, she on top of him. She maneuvered his stiff member into herself, sluicing it inward and up to the hilt. Carl pulled her down to him and felt the crush of her hard nipples into his chest, reached behind her and dug his fingers into her satiny buttocks, now slippery and hot with the balm. They began to thrust on the floor. Chanting came out of Lindsay's mouth, old words that she could not possibly have known, but neither she nor Carl cared about this. They fucked with a frenzy and fortitude born of intoxicants and aphrodisiacs, of denial and desperation, of having endured too much terror and too much truth, of needing the elemental physical coupling of male and female to set their spirits straight. Too soon, too late, it was over, an eruption of raw love and bio-fury; Carl jolted and released. Lindsay screamed, fell against him.

The leathered form of Hannie Hazelford jerked back to life, shook and throbbed and distended. From the corner of his eye Carl saw that something was swelling within the old woman and *moving*. Had he not been so exhausted he would have screamed, because the sight was truly terrifying: Hannie bending out of shape, undulating like a snake who was unhinging its jaws to engulf some bulky prey. The mass inside her moved upward through the shapeless sack of her torso, bulged her neck as it passed out through her mouth: a wiggling, squirming *infant*, slick with mucous but lacking umbilical cord or any other accompanying membrane of a normal birth. It dropped from Hannie's mouth into the crook of her waiting arm.

Lindsay and Carl lay in each other's arms, not believing their eyes, though what they had seen in recent days should have made anything believable. The infant appeared to be alive, tiny and very male. It kicked and waved its arms, and, after a few choking breaths, screamed like any other newborn.

Hannie's misshapen head now pulled itself back into normal shape, her jaw reconnected to her cheekbones, and her skin re-formed like flexible latex. She began to chant again in the

Old Tongue as she lay the bawling infant upon the wooden block. She took up the knife.

"*No!*" Carl screamed, because he now knew what had happened: that Hannie had indeed been inside Lindsay. Sharing the repast of the pewter bowl had allowed Hannie's and Lindsay's souls to merge, to fuse. The old sorceress had thus tapped the incredible energy of Carl's and Lindsay's sexual union, and she had used that energy to fuel this atrocious magic, to vomit up a human baby for no other purpose than to—

"*No!*" he shrieked again, because the reality was too fulsome, beyond enduring. But the air grew very cold, and his muscles went numb and heavy like lead. His injured sensibilities seemed laughably irrelevant now, inasmuch as magic makes no value judgments, requires no elegant deductions about what is right and what is wrong. Magic simply *is*. Hannie Hazelford's magic had provided the sacrificial flesh required for the next step. And now that the process was under way, there was absolutely nothing Carl could do about it.

Except cry, which had become so damnably easy for him in recent weeks.

The infant's wailing abruptly ended in a skirling shriek as the knife sank deep, as Hannie's voice sailed high in the dark:

> *Combine with the fat of an unbaptized Child,*
> *An Innocent's Blood, unpolluted and mild.*

The fat came away from the tiny body, flopped into the pewter bowl.

> *Juice of an Innocent Babe's tiny Liver*
> *Is Poison, dread Poison to the Dream Giver!*

Then came more flashes of surgical dexterity and a repeat of the horrible doings that had earlier utilized the corpse of a naturally dead child. But now the bubbling potion was not to be shared by Lindsay and Hannie: It was meant solely for Carl, who was himself to be a sacrifice. Together Hannie and Lindsay held the heavy bowl to his lips, as Robbie and Stu bolstered him into an upright position. That he did not vomit or struggle was because he had accepted the unavoidable fact:

Nothing else could kill the Giver of Dreams, defeat Hadrian Craslowe, or free Jeremy. Nothing but the *magic,* the sacrifice of Carl Trosper—his body and soul poisoned by innocent blood.

So he forced himself to drink the thick stew. To breathe its horrific fumes and chew the bits of offal afloat in it. To swallow it and, with the help of magic, keep it down. The room swirled, the candle flames became shooting stars, the faces of the others were washed-out projections against a tattered screen.

Whiteleather Place, once again, looming black against a stone-silent sky.

Deep night, perhaps midnight—Carl did not know. To look at his watch did not occur to him.

He got out of the van and shivered. The wind drove specks of moisture against his face. Before he could move away, Lindsay touched his arm, and he glanced back at her, saw that her face was pale in the glow of the dome light, her eyes huge with worry. For a few fleeting seconds, Carl saw the past in those eyes, saw the Yesterday of a young lawyer and his pretty artist-wife, their sick little boy, and the field of unknowable Tomorrows stretching before them. He wondered whether he would have chosen to go on living had he faced a choice back then, knowing what lay in the field: that Tomorrow and Tomorrow would bring *this*.

This horror, this sacrifice.

That's what moms and dads and husbands and wives are supposed to do: sacrifice!

Which is what Lorna had told him more than once, usually in response to Carl's insistence that they institutionalize Jeremy. Which certainly would have made their lives easier, would have freed them to live like normal human beings.

Would *this* have made Lorna happy? he wondered absurdly. Did *this* meet her criteria for sacrifice?

Lindsay was talking now, not Lorna: "You're holding up well, Carl. You look strong, and that's good. I can see strength in your face, and I can"—she stammered, searched—"feel your love for Jeremy."

In answer Carl reached out and touched her cheek, feeling close to her in a way that he had never felt with another woman, not even Lorna. Magic had brought Lindsay and him together. But wasn't it magic that brought *all* men and women together? he wondered.

"I just want you to know," Lindsay went on, whispering to keep the others in the van from hearing, "that I'm sorry for all the grief I've caused you over the years. I'm sorry for misjudging you, for judging you at all. I hope you can forgive me. If we come out of this . . ." She lowered her eyes.

"No apology needed," he whispered.

"Best not to waste time," said Hannie with a scolding tone. "The longer we delay, the more likelihood there is of Hadrian discerning our intentions. Go now. But remember, Carl"—her tone changed to sympathy, concern—"we are all with you. We shan't fail you."

Carl shook hands with Stu, who was now the keeper of the stubby Roman sword, and with Robbie, who gave a thumbs-up sign. He then headed for the pair of crumbling gateposts that marked the entrance to Whiteleather Place.

The once–Teri Zolten met him at the front door of the mansion as though she were expecting him and made hideous small talk as she led him down to the undercroft. The sight and sound of her enraged him, but he tried to shut her out of his mind, tried to ignore the treacly stench of half-living flesh that trailed behind her. With every descending step into the curving stairwell, with every new breath of the stinking air, fear tightened its grip: He was about to give himself to the thing that had done *this* to a beautiful young girl.

Lindsay had said a few moments ago that he looked strong, and in truth he felt strong. He felt strong enough to destroy the squad of acolytes who slunk around him in the shadows of the tunnel—physically, with his fists and feet, ripping and stomping and bashing. But he fought down the urge and walked on, like a condemned heretic to Torquemada's dungeon, following the Teri-thing.

His usher pushed through the heavy wooden door to the undercroft, moved aside, and retired into the shadows of the tunnel behind him. Carl stepped into the rubicund light of a hundred candles, then down three steps to the stone floor. Standing before the black maw on the far wall were Hadrian Craslowe and Jeremy, both robed in red and black satin, their eyes agleam and their faces grinning. They had apparently been busy with the array of silver bowls and chalices on the table before them, engaged in some unspeakable ritual that Craslowe had been reading from a massive old book.

"So you've finally come, have you, *Dad?*" said Jeremy by way of greeting, riveting his father with his laserlike eyes and grinning tightly. "So nice to have you, so nice indeed."

The boy's snideness aroused little feeling in Carl. This was not his son talking, not the child he had dreamed of nurturing and guiding to a love of truth and goodness; not the innocent babe he had deserted so long ago. This was an intruder, a thief of bodies and dreams and hopes. What horrified him was the sudden thought that he himself might be infiltrated by that evil, that Carl Trosper would become not merely a sacrifice but a living member of the enemy. The thought shook him to the cellar of his soul.

"Finally given up, is that it?" Jeremy went on, grinning even more tightly. "Finally seen the world for what it really is?"

"I've come to take you home, Jeremy," answered Carl, thinking how laughable the rehearsed words sounded. The candle-lit room started to swim, and tentacles of fear constricted his chest. "Take off that ridiculous robe and get into your real clothes. We're leaving."

Both Jeremy and Craslowe laughed long and loud as Carl had known they would. The peals of their laughter reverberated off the carved stone walls and echoed down the tunnel that led from the undercroft. The arched maw in the wall behind them issued no echo but remained as silent as it was dark, a dead space.

"Really, Mr. Trosper, you can't believe that we don't see through this pathetic charade," said Hadrian Craslowe. "Your Hannie Hazelford isn't the only one in the world who can operate a scrying mirror! We know precisely what's going on, and we know why you're here."

Carl's heart began to beat madly.

"Jeremy," he managed once again, his vocal chords rasping and quivering, "I'm taking you home. Now, come with—"

"Kindly shut your odious mouth!" shouted Jeremy. "You have done me a great wrong, *Dad,* one that I'm not inclined to overlook! You've killed my half-brother, the offspring of the Giver of Dreams, and have thus denied me great power. It will be another three hundred years before that opportunity comes to me again, at the close of the Giver's next long sleep, and only through the brotherliness of Hadrian can I hope to last long enough to seize it. I've eaten of the Giver's flesh, you see, and will continue to do so as long as Hadrian allows it."

"And I intend to allow it indefinitely," added Craslowe. "The Giver's flesh will sustain Jeremy for at least a thousand years—long enough, certainly, for him to become one of history's most potent stewards."

"But as for yourself," said Jeremy, "I've decided that you must pay for the wrong you've done. I've petitioned the Giver to prepare some very special dreams for you." The boy laughed abominably, causing Carl's guts to lurch. "And it has graciously consented."

"Concerning the magic that you believe will save you," added Craslowe, "you may forget it. I've cast strong counter-spells to ensure that your charmed flesh cannot harm my master. I think you'll find that *my* magic is considerably stronger than Hannie Hazelford's. In short, Mr. Trosper, you've delivered yourself into the clutches of the Giver of Dreams, and there's absolutely nothing you can do except endure your fate."

The old man turned his ghastly smile to the lad who stood at his side. "If you please, Jeremy, you may officiate."

Jeremy needed no prodding. His eyes lit greenly, his grin became the slavering yawn of a carnivore. He spewed out a power that seized Carl's heart and rendered him instantly weak. It lifted him off the floor and dragged him toward the maw in the wall.

Carl struggled like a slave in shackles, like a worm on a hook. He was now certain that the beast who waited and hungered in the maw meant to do more than feast on his flesh; it meant to become one with him, to fuse his soul and body with its own and give him its own vile hungers and needs. He floated closer to the blackness, clawing and kicking the air, close enough now to feel its foulness against his skin, to taste the shrieking stink of its evil and hear the groans of its hunger. The dreadful images of Teri and Sandy Zolten flared in his mind. He saw himself becoming like them: willing, panging disciples of the beast, vehicles of its unthinkable cravings, wanting only the dreams it gave.

Blackness closed over him, and he convulsed with the touch of a slithery hand-thing against his cheek, the rough and eager tearing of claws at his clothing.

It had him now, and it was large, many times larger than a man. It was spongy with viscous fat and amorphous underfolds of skin. It had teeth. Carl had never known such fear, such revulsion.

The Giver of Dreams started to feed.

"It's time," said Hannie Hazelford, somehow knowing. The four of them piled out of Robbie's van. Slowly they made their way through the damp night to the front door of the mansion, which was open as though in welcome. There they met Mrs. Ianthe Pauling, a smiling, gliding wraith in the aura of the porchlight, customarily attired in funereal color but lacking much of her face. She had atoned grievously for earlier helping Carl escape the undercroft.

Stu ground his teeth and, forcing his muscles into motion, stepped forward and cut her down with the charmed sword, driving it deep into her rib cage. Something in Ianthe's tortured eyes cried out in gratitude as she died, as she collapsed in a shapeless mound in the shadowed foyer. Lindsay struggled to fight back a shriek. Somehow she steadied herself and followed the others into the screaming silence of the house.

From her scrying, Hannie knew the location of the undercroft, so she took the lead, her ruined right arm wrapped tight to her side, her blond wig pushed down on her head like a clown's hat. She led them to the vault in the basement, pulled open the door that gave onto the twisting stairway, and started down. Stu and Lindsay went next, shoulder to shoulder, Lindsay manning the flashlight and Stu gripping the sword with both sweating hands. Bringing up the rear was Robbie Sparhawk, lowering himself on his crutches, one stony step at a time, sweating profusely and swearing occasionally at his legs.

They were a strong formation, and the pitiful victims of the Giver of Dreams were no match for them: Hannie's magic on the point, Stu's charmed blade on the flanks, Robbie's psychic sledgehammer in the rear. Every half-living acolyte they encountered died a mercifully quick and complete death by the sword: Teri Zolten, Monty Pirtz, Elizabeth Zaske, maybe half a dozen others.

No need to worry about getting them all, Hannie assured. At the moment of the Giver's destruction, the surviving victims would be liberated to the cool void of death, and their very bodies would vaporize.

She halted before the door that led into the undercroft and warned that things could get "nasty" beyond this point. Lindsay was to stay close at Hannie's side, because she lacked Robbie's psychic power and Stu's charmed sword, having only the pouch around her neck for protection. Lindsay felt naked and exposed, like a prey animal entrapped in a predator's lair, able to do little but wait until hunger moved the beast to pounce. Her source of strength was the vision of Carl's strong face and the love it radiated, the selfless commitment to saving a little boy. Lindsay emulated that love, adopted it as her own, directed it to Carl, and hoped that it would somehow find its way to him. She had been wrong about so much, she knew now: about Carl, about herself. About the world.

"Robbie and I will keep Hadrian and Jeremy at bay," whispered Hannie, "and you, Stuart, will proceed immediately through the dark archway in the far wall. By now the Giver will have begun to feast on Carl. The creature will be weak from the poisonous magic that Carl carries in him. You must utter the words I gave you, and you must strike the thing with the sword, again and again, until—"

Suddenly the door of the undercroft blew off its hinges with a roar, showering Hannie and her soldiers with splinters. From the vaulted chamber raged a wind that tore at their clothing and toppled them like bowling pins. The baneful laugh of Hadrian Craslowe assaulted their minds and ears, descended upon them amid the blizzard of forces he had unleashed. Lindsay was flung against the wall of the passage, where her head slammed into stone; she fell unconscious, twitching and gagging. A shard of wood connected with Robbie's forehead and knocked him off his crutches. The wind literally rolled him backward until he too collided with the wall and lay in a motionless heap.

Stu Bromton caught hold of Hannie as the wind lifted her off the floor and, like a human anchor, held her with one hand while clinging fast to the doorjamb with the other. Having lost both her wig and pince-nez, Hannie managed to point her face into the core of the maelstrom, where she could just make out Hadrian and Jeremy hanging in midair, with their deformed hands pointing directly at her. Against the onslaught of demon-force she screamed words in the Old Tongue, summoned influences and energies from the edges of the unseen world where she had poised them, drew in ligatures and called in old debts, directed the flow of power from her eyes and hand toward the sorcerer and his disciple; she screamed the words again and saw Hadrian falter; she saw Jeremy crash rudely to the floor, where he lay still in a heap of garish satin; she saw the green hatred in Hadrian's eyes waver and fail, then grow bright with one final burst of malevolence.

Hannie endured another blast of death-wind but survived it and retaliated with her own finality. Hadrian Craslowe dropped out of the air and landed stiffly against the table, knocking a score of silver plates and bowls and chalices to the stone floor. He came to rest like a figure of bronze that had tumbled from its pedestal in an earthquake, rigid and leaning unmanlike against a wall.

Hannie struggled to her feet, actually helping Stu regain his. Silence beat against their eardrums. Stu found the sword on the floor, clutched it tight, and searched Hannie's face for confirmation of his instincts: *Go to the darkness beyond the arch and—*

The old witch suddenly collapsed again, and Stu just caught her. He edged her through the open door into the undercroft. Her face was an awful shade of gray, her eyes sunken and rolling. Her breath came in very short, shallow huffs. Stu gently laid her against the stone stairs and cradled her head in his arms.

"Hannie, are you all right? Hannie, can you hear me?" Clearly the energy that had passed through her body had taken a tremendous toll, as had the assault she had endured at Craslowe's hands. Combined with the trauma of having recently taken a load of buckshot at close range, having lost much blood . . . *God,* thought Stu, it was a wonder that she was even alive.

"Stuart," she croaked, "the *sword.* Take the sword, and kill the Giver. *D-do* it, Stuart, before Hadrian recovers. I-it's your only chance."

• • •

Carl had expected dreams, but as yet no dreams had come. The thing had planted its horrible mouth onto his left shoulder and started to feast, holding him fast with its stinging claws. This was perhaps the "special treatment" that Jeremy had promised: to endure being devoured without the anesthetic benefits of dreaming, like an insect caught in a spider's web.

The pain was a constant acidic thrill, a continuous jolt that radiated from the wound to every cell in his body. He prayed that his endorphins would soon kick in, the brain's natural painkillers, but still the agony grew. The sounds were as horrible as the pain, the munching of his flesh and the squeaky sucking of his blood, the rip of teeth through his skin. And worst of all were the creature's low moans of ecstasy. He struggled ferociously, clawed at its slimy skin, flailed and gouged with his fists and elbows and knees, only to feel its serpentine limbs close more tightly around him and press him more deeply into its stinking bulk.

He screamed.

Cursed his terror.

Fought to hang on to his reason.

Thrashed against the gristly bone and leathery membrane of engulfing wings—wings like a bat's or an extinct reptile's, wings from the imagination of a medieval painter whose commission was to depict a creature of Hell.

But then, within the interval between jackhammer heartbeats, the pain and fear withdrew to the outer frontier of his consciousness, leaving only a wisp of recollection.

He feels nearly himself again, alive and whole and strong, as he stands with his lieutenants in a sunlit clearing near the border between Poland and East Prussia.

"We are ready now, *Herr Sturmbannführer*," says one of the others, a heavy-browed man with dull, unfeeling eyes. Carl glances to his left and sees that they are indeed ready, that the four machine guns are in place atop their tripods. To his right are the prisoners, kneeling naked in fresh snow before a newly dug trench, their faces slack with horror, their bodies sticklike and white with exhaustion after the long, cold trek from the village.

More than a hundred men, women, and children. Babies

held close to shivering chests. Hands and arms linked, en-twined.

To Carl they are stains on the sparkling winter landscape, infections on the skin of mankind. The latest train to Treblinka is full, jam-packed to the very roofs of the boxcars with Jewish vermin rounded up by the *Einsatzgruppen SS*. So he is forced to deal with the overflow as best he can.

"Very well," replies Carl, "we shall begin in a moment." He is speaking German, naturally. (*When had he learned German?* a tiny inner voice asked. *Could this be?*) "But first, I have some minor business to attend to."

His lieutenants laugh huskily and trade knowing winks with each other. Carl steps smartly over the snowy ground toward the bedraggled prisoners, his mirrorlike jackboots crunching and his swagger stick whipping the seam of his britches. He troops the miserable, huddled line.

"This one will do," he announces shortly, pointing his swagger stick at the bare form of a kneeling girl. She is maybe fourteen, dark-eyed and long-haired—just the kind he likes. A pair of helmeted SS troopers spring forward and seize her, drag her to the edge of the clearing, away from the line of fire.

"Would you care to man one of the guns personally, *Herr Sturmbannführer?*" asks the heavy-browed lieutenant in a tone appropriate to suggesting another piece of strudel.

"Don't I always?"

This too raises snickers among the underlings. Carl takes his place at one of the four tripods, crouches behind it, being careful not to muddy his immaculate gray uniform.

No, I won't do this! screamed that same tiny voice from some remote corner of Carl's soul. *This is abominable, unthinkable! This is evil!*

But it *is* he, Carl Trosper, whose fingers wrap around the wooden firing grips of the weapon, whose steady gaze settles over the gunsights to take in the picture of pathetic families huddled before the rude trench that will be their grave. It *is* he whose penis suddenly stiffens with the thrill of the first barking bursts of fire, whose heart thunders with obscene joy as a storm of heavy slugs rips through torsos and limbs, detonating little explosions of bright blood. It *is* he who—

This isn't me!

—ejaculates and rejoices in this spectacle of suffering and

killing, whose hatred burns hot and beautiful on no other fuel than lies and visceral fear. He sucks in the essence of the evil even as he breathes in the smells of the forest—the vapors of death mixed with the tart smells of birch and fir. His ears glean the choking cries of the dying above the chatter of startled sparrows. He sucks it in, laps it up like good soup. It is delicious, this evil. It is what he was made for.

No!

With an incredible eruption of psychic strength, Carl tore himself out of the dream and fled the horror of actually *being* evil. He almost welcomed the return to the physical agony of the beast's clutches, for here, at least, he knew who he was. His escape from the dream, he prayed, meant that Hannie's poison was at work, that even though the beast could tear him to pieces and devour his body, it lacked the power to eat his soul.

Had it really been a dream, though?

This surely was no dream: the sight of Stu Bromton, framed in the flickering center of the arch, moving forward on unsteady legs, with the charmed sword gripped in his fists. Stepping now into the maw, into the cavern of dark. Causing the creature to pause in its feasting and stir, to groan and growl with apprehension.

Yes! Good old Stu, good old Hippo! Come on, big guy, just a few more steps! The fucking beast is weakening. The grip of claws and wings faltered ever so slightly. *I can feel it! You can kill him! Come ON, Stu! Chop this son of a bitch into a billion stinking pieces!*

The sword was raised high over Stu's head, and Carl would not have cared if Stu had missed his mark and struck *him* rather than the beast, as long as he tried again, *tried again!*

Carl cried out to warn his old friend of the shadow behind him. But too late. Heavy wood whistled through the air: a baseball bat, taken from the riot of discarded goods in the basement above—a child's toy. It cracked down on Stu's skull, caving it in and popping his eyes out of their sockets, ejecting a gout of blood from his mouth. The big man went down like a puppet whose strings had been cut and thudded heavily to the stone floor. Hannie Hazelford's magic sword clattered down harmlessly beside the twitching corpse.

The demon drew a relieved breath and started to feed again, and Carl would have screamed himself to death if he had been able, because the hands around the baseball bat belonged to a familiar and much-loved face.

A face that belonged to Renzy Dawkins.

Without his crutches Robbie could only crawl. He pulled himself with his arms and hands along the floor of the passage, back toward the undercroft. His eyes were awash in blood from the wound on his forehead. He wondered how long he had been unconscious after his collision with the stone wall, if he had broken any bones and whether any of his friends had survived. He wondered too at the god-awful silence, a silence that caused painful knots of dread in his guts.

He found Lindsay lying against one wall of the passage, rummy and bleeding from the scalp, but alive. He left her and made for the door of the undercroft, where Hannie's gauzy head lay just visible against a stone step. Her ancient face lolled toward him as he crawled near. She reached out to grab his collar with a bony hand.

"Robbie," she whispered hoarsely, "we are in great trouble! Stuart has been killed, and the Giver is still alive. It still has Carl!" She coughed painfully, and Robbie could see the life ebbing from her rheumy eyes. His heart weltered.

"We have but one chance, Robbie. It must be you and I together, because I alone am so weak. I haven't much left, Robbie. I need your *Gift!*"

"It's okay, darlin', it's okay," answered the psychic, snaking his arm around her neck and cradling her head. "Whatever I've got is yours, you know that. Now what is it you want me to do?"

Earlier in the day, while the sun still shone, Mitch Nistler had struggled back to his house to die, only to find the house itself dead. Everything in it and near it was dead.

The mayor in the living room, shot in the back, a riddle that did not matter.

Stella DeCurtis out back in the Blazer, cold and glass-eyed, lifeless as alabaster.

Corley the Cannibal in the stairway, chopped into several barely recognizable pieces.

The wormy shell of Lorna Trosper, peppered with bullet holes in an upstairs bedroom, truly dead now.

And nearby, scorch marks on the wall and floor, the sooty silhouette of something.

The *offspring,* surely. Dead and gone, somehow reduced to ether.

There was a peculiar joy in the deadness around him. Mitch felt at peace for the first time in living memory. He lay down on the living-room sofa, utterly spent from a cold night in the forest, and awaited sundown. When the darkness finally came, he welcomed it, resigned himself to letting his sickness consume him. His horrors had ended. He yearned to slip away before new ones sprang to life.

But then the dark air stirred, just as it had stirred the previous night, when some tickling force had enfolded his heart and urged him to attack Stu Bromton with a crowbar. What had he felt in that crackling magic? *Hope?* The magic was back now, and it passed over his face like the breath of an angel.

Robbie's head was a volcano of pain. Each eruption shook the marrow of his bones. His will was linked to Hannie's through some puissant magic that he would never understand. His Gift was turned to feats he had never before contemplated, never dreamed himself capable of.

Like forcing his spirit from his body and flying over the treetops, into the clouds. Searching fields and roads, reaching out and groping, gravitating, gravitating . . .

To Mitch Nistler's house, drawn there like a bee to a fragrant blossom in the golden afternoon.

Communicating, touching, urging the little man to leave his house and come to Whiteleather Place. From somewhere Robbie heard Hannie's voice saying that Mitch Nistler was their only hope, because Mitch Nistler had eaten of the Giver's flesh and had carried its monstrous seed. And whatever his weaknesses, Mitch Nistler was blessed with a certain immunity from the evil magic of the Giver's minions.

"Bushman, you're in there, aren't you?" Renzy stood in the opening of the maw, his head tilted to one side. Carl could just make out his handsome face through a haze of pain and terror. "I can't quite see you, old son, but I can sure as hell feel you.

Can you hear me, Bush? We gotta talk." He rested the bloody baseball bat in the crook of his arm, leaned against the edge of the stone arch, and stared into the blackness.

"R-Renzy, please!"

The beast tore more flesh from Carl's back, causing him to scream with blinding pain. He felt his bladder let go and his stomach heave, but only acid came up, flooding his gullet and mouth with sour heat. Still, through the rage of agony and horror, he could hear Renzy's voice. He wriggled an arm free of the creature's grip and thrust it toward his old friend, clawing the darkness, reaching, begging.

"I didn't want this to happen, Bush, you know that. But there wasn't anything I could do about it. This was all—"

"Renzy, kill it! P-please kill it! The sword, Renzy!"

"Oh, Christ, Bush—I can't do that. I *work* for Hadrian, and I'll go on working for him until I can see my way clear to blow my own brains out, which I hope is soon. I intend to do it the very minute he takes the hex off my sister."

Carl's ragged mind reeled. He caught a vague image of Renzy's once-beautiful sister, Diana, languishing in a mental institution, a prisoner behind blank walls. A prisoner like Ianthe Pauling's brother. Did this mean . . . ? He struggled again, twisting and writhing, but a clawed hand settled over his head and drew him in by the hair.

"Too bad about Hippo, huh?" Renzy went on, glancing down at Stu's corpse, which had by now ceased its twitching and throbbing. "The poor son of a bitch never really got it together, did he? Classic case of wanting more than you're capable of getting. Still, he had his good points, and he deserved better than what he got. I hope he's in a better place, I really do."

Renzy's voice took on an echolike quality. Carl's consciousness began to drift through a field of ripples and blurs, as though he had entered another dream. The creature that held him bit into his flesh again, and against the veil of pain Carl imagined that he could actually *see* Renzy's words.

"I suppose I owe you some kind of explanation," Renzy went on, "considering what we've been to each other. We were like goddamn brothers, weren't we? You, me and Hippo—the Triumvirate."

Carl saw three sub-teenaged boys in a distant playground on

a summer afternoon, chasing a bouncing basketball around a hoop that had no net. Their laughter, their shouts, the smell of their boyish sweat were as real as the razored teeth that were tearing into his shoulder.

"Shit, if anyone had ever told us it would end like this," said Renzy, "we would've laughed them right out of the state! But anyway, Bush, this whole sorry mess was cast in concrete long before you and I were ever born. Know why? Because my mother was the granddaughter of Tristan Whiteleather."

Mitch Nistler left his little house for the last time, carrying the Winchester that had lain next to the corpse of Chester Klundt. He knew vaguely that he must go to Whiteleather Place, but he did not know why. Neither could he have explained why he was taking along the shotgun. He knew only that he was doing the right thing, that the magic in the air was about to resolve the anarchy that had ruled his life for so long. He got into his El Camino, started it, and drove away into the rainy night.

Renzy's words seared Carl's spirit as the Giver's teeth seared his flesh, an exquisite garnishment to the physical torment. The words became clear images, a mental cinema of faces and movement, reality. Carl saw the unfortunate Ted Dawkins, a relentlessly ambitious man who had inherited the curse of the Whiteleathers in taking old Tristan's granddaughter, Alita, to wife.

"It was like a bargain," narrated Renzy, giggling madly now and then. "You marry a Whiteleather, you serve Hadrian Craslowe—know what I mean? Well, Mom and Dad got pretty good at it—doing Hadrian's magic, that is. They got rich—which was part of the bargain—became pillars of the community, respected and loved by everybody in town. My old man was happier than a pig in shit, had everything he'd ever wanted. At least for a while. The problem was that the other part of the bargain wasn't so rosy: They had to find somebody to sire the offspring of the Giver of Dreams, along with a suitable mother for it. As if that wasn't enough, they had to find someone who could become its manciple, its steward."

In the fuming dream fueled by Renzy's words, Carl saw little Mitch Nistler, the homely and unpromising son of a local ne'er-do-well, the sad and retiring child whom other kids mercilessly tormented, a sorry specimen whose destruction would deny the world nothing of value. A perfect candidate to carry the demon's seed.

The scene shifted: Ted Dawkins calling regularly at the Nistlers' shack near the marina, delivering bitter-tasting food laced with magic potions and little "toys" that were really charms. Charity, supposedly—but in actuality, a polluting combination that damned poor Mitch to failure throughout his childhood, that compounded his weaknesses, rendered him malleable.

Ted and Alita Dawkins now, huddling together in the undercroft of Whiteleather Place, brewing potions and casting spells aimed at the local undertaker, Matt Kronmiller. So *that's* how Mitch landed a job after prison, a job that put him in a position to steal a corpse when the time was right.

But this was not a dream, not a nightmare. It was real!

And the steward, of course, was to be Jeremy, selected before the boy was even born. Carl saw Alita hovering and fussing over the pregnant Lorna, all under the guise of friendship, taking every opportunity to pollute Lorna's food with poisonous magical herbs and mixtures, leaving little hand-carved "figurines" around the Trosper house, which were supposed to cheer and amuse, but which were actually powerful charms. Alita's magic proved successful: Jeremy was born an empty vessel, a child who seemed to lack a soul, perfect clay for the hands of Hadrian Craslowe.

And that brings up the matter of *Lorna,* said Renzy.

Carl cried out again in pain and rage—not only because the demon was tearing another strip of muscle from his shoulder, but also because he was seeing Lorna, hearing Lorna, as she announced with dancing eyes that they were going to have a baby.

And later, with tearful and desperate eyes, that she knew something was horribly wrong with their little Jeremy.

And much later, with empty eyes, saying that she would give Carl a divorce, as he wanted.

Carl roared with molten anger, heard his own voice reverberating against stone, felt it batter his eardrums when it bounced back.

Ah, yes, Lorna, who fell into Hadrian's clutches like a ripe berry, said Renzy.

"Bush, I was the one who suggested that she take Jeremy to see Hadrian. And then I helped drive her crazy—even started taking her to bed in order to get the job done. Oh, I can't really take much credit for her killing herself—Jeremy was the one who really pushed her over the edge, which you've probably guessed by now. I just did what Hadrian told me to do. If you've got Whiteleather blood in your veins, you don't say no to Hadrian."

Carl's lungs erupted with another enraged roar. "Why, Renzy? Why did you do it? Why didn't you fight him? You could've fought him!"

"No!" screamed Renzy, stepping deeper into the blackness. "I couldn't fight him, Carl! That's what I'm trying to tell you. I can't let you think that I—"

"You're an obscenity! An animal! Lorna was good, Renzy, the only really good thing in my life!" The Giver's fangs sank again. Its spongy lips closed tight on the wound. Carl felt himself weakening, miring in a lake of pain. In his mind he saw a faded old photograph hanging on the bulkhead of *Kestrel,* Renzy's yacht, the picture of a rumpled seaman, Tristan Whiteleather. At the captain's side stood a somber man with a silvery hair and spectacles that exaggerated his watery eyes. The silver-haired man, Carl knew now, was Hadrian Craslowe, Renzy's lord. The hurt was like a fountain in his chest.

"You've got to understand something, Carl," said Renzy tremulously, sinking to his knees while leaning on the baseball bat. "After my parents died, Hadrian did something to my sister, to Diana—cursed her, made her into what she is now. She hasn't spoken a word since that day—just sits in an empty room and stares at a wall. How's that grab you, Bush? My *sister,* the most beautiful girl in Greely's Cove, the heartbreaker to end all heartbreakers, sitting alone in a room, unable to speak or appreciate music. Remember what an incredible musician she was? Remember the grand piano upstairs?"

Carl's world was swimming, and he could barely hear Renzy's trembling words. He wondered whether he was dying and hoped that he was.

"Hadrian did it to guarantee my cooperation, to make sure

that I would always be around to help him. He promised to lift the curse someday"—Renzy coughed and whimpered—"if I did everything he wanted. Don't you see, Carl? I didn't want to hurt you or Lorna. What happened to Jeremy wasn't my idea. I was only trying to give Diana a chance to live a normal life, to get out of that—that *place*. And when that day comes—"

"*Help* me, Renzy! If you've ever cared about me"—Carl's voice was a tortured croak, and his body had gone limp—"then for God's sake, *kill* it! *Kill it, Renzy!*"

The kneeling man raised his eyes, and his tearful stare bore into the darkness. "I can't, Bush—don't you see? Diana's only hope is Hadrian. I know this sounds a little crazy, but I can't just run out on her. I can't let her live the rest of her life in a fucking cell. Try to understand—"

"*Kill it!*"

"No, I won't, Bush! If I never accomplish anything else, I'm going to free my sister, give her some kind of life. Oh, I'll still end up like my parents, with too much guilt to carry around, and I'll put a fucking bullet in my head. I'll think of you when I do it, all that my family has done to yours, what I've helped do to you and Lorna. And I'll think of all the good times we've had together—*God!*" Renzy choked and sobbed, wiping away tears with the sleeve of his jacket. But when he looked up again his face was hard, his voice controlled. "I'm going to do what I have to do, Bush, and I'll kill anyone who tries to interfere. I just want you to know that I'm sorry."

Lindsay heard a sound that was hard and metallic, and she undertook the monstrous task of raising her head and focusing her eyes. Someone passed by her in the dark, actually stepping over her body and moving toward the ruddy candle glow of the undercroft. A man, apparently, short and painfully thin, a long gun across his arms. The metallic noise had been the chambering of a shell.

She organized herself, got legs and arms under control, willed a halt to the dizzy spin of her vision, and stood up. She inched along the wall on fluttery legs in pursuit of the dark figure who was now stepping into the undercroft, who was carefully making his way around the huddled forms of Robbie and Hannie, heading toward the black archway. Lindsay moved closer.

Carl whistles around the toothpick in his teeth as he drives his clunky Chevy van along the lonely wooded road, and he feels good, very good. The summer afternoon is warm and coppery, he has half a six of cold Rainier on the seat beside him, and there's a pretty whore tied up in the cargo bed.

Her terrified squeals are music, sweet music.

Taking a whore has become ridiculously easy in recent years, especially along Seattle's Second Avenue, where the young runaways have begun to flock like dirty little starlings. Unwary and lacking street smarts, a hungry runaway kid will swallow any line that ends with the promise of twenty bucks and a hit of good dope. And once she's in the van with him, it's Lay Down the Newspapers and Let the Puppy In, Martha, 'Cause It's All Over But the Shoutin'. *And* the Fuckin', of course. *And* the Stabbin' *and* the Slicin' *and* the Dyin'.

Carl giggles, shifts the toothpick to the other corner of his mouth, and turns left onto a forest road marked Lake Morton. He likes this area for its ample cover of trees and brush, for the fact that it's virtually deserted on weekdays and yet so close to Seattle. Having discovered this place, he can now do his thing and get back on the cannery line within two hours.

He halts the van in a shady clearing well off the road, kills the engine, and squeezes between the seats into the sweltering cargo area.

"Time for the main event, sweetie pie," he says around the toothpick, grinning. The spindly, dark-haired girl struggles desperately against the belts that cut into her wrists and ankles, then forces a mewling groan through the wide strip of tape that covers her mouth. Carl thrills to that sound, to the smart scent of her fearful sweat, to the sight of her panicky tears. He gathers her roughly into his arms, kicks open the rear door of the van, and carries her into the brush.

"Wanna know somethin', sweetie pie?" He lays her onto a leafy bed of fern and tawny grass now, withdrawing a long hunting knife from beneath his fishnet shirt. "As of this moment, you've got a new name. Wanna know what it is?" More squeals and sobs from the girl. A shudder of expectant horror. "It ain't Cathy or Jennifer or Amber or anything like that. And it ain't Georgia or Cookie, either. You really wanna know what it is?"

He applies the blade to the front of her flimsy blue blouse, and the fabric rends, exposing her tiny, sweat-slick breasts. Down the blade goes, ripping through the waistband of her acid-washed denim shorts, under which she is bare, trembling.

"It ain't Alice or Judy." His voice becomes hoarse and breathy as he stares at her nakedness. "Or Debbie or Bonnie. You really wanna know what your name is, sweetie pie?" His tattooed hands tear at his own belt and zipper and push his filthy jeans down. His ramrod penis jumps free.

No! This isn't me! I'm Carl Tros—

Oh, but this *is* Carl Trosper, whose calloused hands are spreading wide the poor child's thighs. This *is* Carl Trosper, whose mindless cock is digging deep and almost immediately squirting, squirting. Whose knife is now held high, glinting in a stray ray of sunlight through the forest cover —

No! I won't do this thing! I won't!

—and plunging suddenly downward.

"Seventy-six! *That's* your new name, sweetie pie: Number Seventy-six! Number Seventy-six! Number Seventy-six!"

With every shout the blade plunges, sundering flesh and bone and vessels. Flinging bright webs of blood into the air, onto the mass of ferns and grass. Spattering Carl's face and arms and hands, turning the afternoon red.

"Number Seventy-six! Number Seventy-six!" The sin is exquisite, hideously delicious. The blood and gore, the final tremor of death, the frenzy of bloated hatred unleashed for the seventy-sixth time: He drinks it all in, savors it, relishes the evil.

No! It's not me! It's not me!

Carl drew strength from the remnant of his soul that he still owned and *willed* himself out of the dream, forced his consciousness to flee.

To flee.

Away from the dream and back to—

Back home. To safety. Back to the bungalow on Second Avenue in Greely's Cove, where his mother waits.

Some small sound must have warned Renzy Dawkins, because he rose from his knees, turned away from the friend whom he had forsaken to the Giver of Dreams, and saw Mitch

Nistler, of all people. The little man stood only a few paces away and was holding a shotgun on him.

"O Lord, Mitch, you don't mean this," breathed Renzy, his dark face weary, his eyes bleary. "There's nothing you can accomplish here. Now give me the gun."

But Mitch did indeed mean it, which was clear in the steadiness of his gaze, in the relaxed little smile on his lips. He was about to do something good, and he felt wonderful.

"I said, give me the gun, Mitch. I don't have time for this." Renzy raised the baseball bat and took a threatening step forward. And Mitch pulled the trigger. A white-hot ball leapt from the muzzle and tore most of Renzy's head away, flinging his rag-doll body into the dark maw. Mitch chambered another shell and turned toward the jerking form of Hadrian Craslowe, which leaned against the wall to his right. The sorcerer was sparking back to life now, regaining his faculties, healing quickly from the drubbing Hannie had given him. His oily eyes were bulbous and furiously aglow, his monstrous hands coiling and uncoiling as limberness soaked into them again.

At his feet Jeremy, too, was stirring.

Mitch leveled the shotgun directly into Craslowe's face and fired. The walnut scowl disappeared in another explosion of light and fire, but Craslowe did not go down. The mangled spoilage that had been his face moved and writhed, shaping itself into what could have been a grin. His demon-hands closed about the muzzle of the shotgun and twisted it from Mitch's grip, bending and warping the metal. What seconds ago had been eyes turned toward Hannie and Robbie, and a horrible laugh gurgled out of the indefinite gap that had been a mouth, spraying blood into the air like water from a lawn sprinkler. As Jeremy regained his feet, Craslowe moved stiffly toward Hannie and Robbie, needing no eyes, reaching toward them with his taloned hands.

Lindsay alighted at Robbie's side, helped him shield Hannie Hazelford from the palpable wrath that flowed from Craslowe, and fully expected to die within the following seconds. Robbie traded terrible glances with her, then pulled himself to a kneeling position to face the oncoming monstrosity. He launched a blast of psychic energy, the biggest he could muster—a chunk of granite the size of a cement mixer. The sorcerer reeled under it and staggered backward a step but still did not go down. Though temporarily drained of killing magic, Craslowe still clearly possessed a semblance of his defensive powers. And he meant to destroy these interlopers, not with magic, but with his talons, to slice and shred them into bits of flinching meat. He lurched forward again, laughing out gobbets of flesh and gouts of blood.

Oh, this is better, much better indeed. So good to be *home* again.

His mother stands in the doorway of the little bedroom that she has converted into a watercolor studio, facing him with wide, hopeless eyes. Her jaw hangs loose and her mouth yawns in terror. One hand is thrust deep into the tangles of her blond hair, while the other grips the front of her paint-spattered smock, as though clutching a wound. She seems to be having difficulty breathing.

Carl issues a silken giggle. It won't be long now.

"Surely you understand that there's only one thing left to do, Mother," he says in his child's voice. "There's really no reason for delay, is there?"

His mother staggers against the doorframe, letting her gaze wander over the carnage around her. The furniture is broken and shredded, the walls gouged and holed. Heaps of garbage lie on the floors. This is all Carl's handiwork—weeks and months worth of incapacitating Lorna with his newfound power, smashing her belongings without even touching them, probing deep into her mind and soul to root out her blackest secrets and emotions. God almighty, it's been such fun.

"W-why are you doing this, Jeremy?" she stammers through a wash of fresh tears. "Why do you hate me so much?"

"Quite simply because you're *you*," he answers with British-style matter-of-factness. "Put another way, for the same reason you hate yourself. We both know what you are, don't we? A filthy whore, a slut, a—"

"Just because I've been spending time with Renzy—is that why you hate me?"

"There's much more to it than that, Mother. What about all those times you wished that I was dead, that I'd never been born? Before my recovery, I mean? Don't tell me you've forgotten." He laughs with gusto and thrills to the pain his laughter causes. "I was a helpless child who could do nothing for himself, a pitiful shell of a boy who depended on you for everything. I hadn't asked to be born sick, Mother, hadn't asked to be born at all. And yet, you wished that I would die, that I'd free you to pursue your own frivolous wants and cravings, your ridiculous *art*."

"That's not true! I loved you, Jeremy! I've always loved you!"

"It's senseless to lie to me, Mother. I can see inside you." Which he *can*, of course, thanks to this wonderful power he has gotten at Whiteleather Place. He sees and tells. He tortures his mother yet again with truths uprooted from the darkest depths of her mind.

Yes, there were times when Lorna nearly crumbled under the stress of caring for her impaired son, times when she yearned to shut herself away with her watercolors rather than mop up the fecal messes that appeared daily throughout the house. Times when she craved freedom from her son's mindless screeching and howling, wanting nothing more than to be alone in a world of orderliness and quiet. Occasionally she wished desperately that God would take the boy through some painless accident or disease, liberating her to a normal life.

She shudders and cowers from her son's words, presses her hands over her desiccated cheeks, screams. "But I still loved you, Jeremy! I never would've done anything to hurt—"

I'm not Jeremy! I'm not—

Carl unleashes a surge of energy that chokes off her voice. "Don't try to rationalize, Mother. The fact is, you wanted me dead—*me*, your only child, your own flesh and blood. You wanted me out of the way so you could devote yourself to your stupid little gallery, so you'd have time for your precious painting. You actually wished that I'd be hit by a car, or that I'd stick my finger in an electrical socket so you'd be free to hobnob with your worthless, small-minded friends, the good citizens of Greely's Cove, the same people who laughed at you behind your back for not locking me away in an institution. You loved your community projects, your fund-raising drives and your bloody art shows more than you loved me."

"Jeremy, you've got to understand—sometimes I just got so *tired*! My mind would play horrible tricks—"

"Enough of your fucking lies! You wished me dead, because you were selfish and wanton, because you thought that I was the killer of all your cheap little dreams! You thought of me as your jailor, as the weight around your neck!"

"No, Jeremy!" Her eyes roll hideously, and she wraps her thin arms over her chest, trembling.

He is close now, so very close. Lorna's reason is wearing thin, stretched to the point of breakage. Time for the pièce de résistance, the final hammer stroke that will finish the job. Carl shuts his hazel eyes tight, concentrates, gathers himself to launch a bolt of psychic power. He has been saving this for just the right moment.

God in heaven, I'm not Jeremy! I know what this is!

The walls begin to vibrate and the whole house shudders and squeaks. Sawdust and flecks of plaster seep down from cracks in the ceiling. A riot of wind tears at Lorna's clothing, twists her around to face the interior of her studio, where the walls are hung with a score of her paintings. One by one the wind assaults the mountings, shattering the glass, warping the frames, shredding the paper. Hundreds of hours worth of loving work explode into wreckage before her terrified eyes. When the last painting meets its end, the wind moves on to the other rooms of the house, to other walls where Lorna's art hangs: landscapes, seascapes, still lifes, portraits. Rumbling blows from an invisible sledgehammer. Ripping. Tinkling. Splintering.

"That's what I think of your *art*, Mother," says Carl in the dead-quiet aftermath. Lorna stands before him like a worn-out mannequin, a cold and lifeless woman-image ready for the dumpster. "You'll never paint again, of course. I'll see to that. You have nothing left now, do you? Surely there's no reason to—"

She comes suddenly alive and shakes her head as though to deny the atrocity she has just witnessed. Her hand goes to the light switch on the wall and snaps it off. Darkness floods the room, and Carl catches the desperate words in her mind. She needs darkness. Lorna Trosper needs darkness.

"Come now, Mother." He giggles. "You can't make all this go away by simply dousing the lights." He launches a mental hand and snaps the switch on again.

And his mother turns it off.

And he turns it on.

She wheels out of the studio and into the hallway, then into her bedroom, where a light still burns. She shuts it off and falls against the wall, sobbing. Carl snaps it on without touching it, relishing this little game.

She flees to the living room, turns out the light.

And Carl—

Jeremy, it's you, isn't it? Stop it, you fucking little bastard! Stop it! I won't let you!

Lorna lurches from room to room, shutting off the lights, only to have them snap on again, but still she moves on, wanting only darkness. Only darkness. She pauses a moment to stare at herself in the hall mirror, shrieks and tears at her hair, stumbles into the kitchen. Amid the clutter of garbage and broken dishes she spies a butcher knife, and for a hellish second she considers seizing it and whirling to attack her son. Carl chuckles with amusement, knowing that she cannot possibly harm him.

She moves to a drawer, scrabbles for a pen and pad, scribbles something, and stuffs the torn slip into her smock. She makes for the door to the garage, and Carl knows now that he has succeeded, that victory is his. He sops up the fumy air of terror that radiates from his mother like heat from a stove, inhales it and savors the spicy taste of her pain. He takes strength from the evil, glories in it, giggles obscenely as he hears the engine of the old Subaru station wagon coughing to life. This is what he was made for.

He groped frantically through the depths of his consciousness in search of that glimmering shard of his own identity, that small surviving piece of Carl Trosper that the demon could not devour. Suddenly it flared bright behind his eyes.

". . . Poison, dread Poison to the Dream Giver . . ."

And he clung to it with his mental arms and hands, clung to that floating spar in a rearing sea of evil, clung to that remnant of goodness. In a heartbeat his shoulder was on fire again, his eyes flooded with bloody tears, his body a vessel of pain.

Mitch Nistler stared in horror at the robed figure of Jeremy, who was now coming at him, eyes ablaze and face a gargoyle of killing hatred. The lad's hands would have closed around Mitch's neck, had not some force intervened, some protective power born of the unclean meat Mitch had eaten right here in this undercroft.

Or rather *there,* in the maw beyond the arch.

While in the hypnotic trances inflicted by Craslowe, Mitch had gorged himself repeatedly on that stinking, living meat, burying his face in the putrid breast of the monster. The meals had given him hungers—and the ability to sate them, which he had done with the poor, savaged corpse of Lorna Trosper. But the meals had also made him *of the flesh,* of the same stuff as the Giver of Dreams. Jeremy could not kill him, could not even touch him.

Mitch smiled as the magic stirred within, as he realized that he had *power.* He ducked out of Jeremy's halting grasp, launched himself through the archway into the maw, and immediately toppled over Stu Bromton's dead body. From the blackness he heard a voice, raspy and choked with pain, crying out something about a sword. Mitch did what the voice begged: groped around the blood-soaked body of Stu Bromton until finding a short sword that suddenly glowed with a potent, pink light as his fingers closed over the handle.

He felt more stirrings of magic, heard more pleading screams from the darkness close by. Mitch scrambled to his feet, waded deeper into the stinking night of the maw, swung the sword while laughing insanely, plunged it into the mass that hunkered against the far wall. He heard shrieks that could not have been human, felt the pain *himself.*

Carl once again felt the grip of the demon weaken, a skittering of agony and terror within its bulk. Summoning strength that he thought should have leaked away through the wounds in his back and shoulder, he twisted his right arm free and grabbed the leathery wing that held him. He tore at it wildly, heaved his upper body against it, and finally wrenched himself out of its grasp. He lunged forward and grabbed the sword away from Mitch, who was staggering crazily now, laughing hysterically and careening. Carl whirled and drove the blade deep into the slimy beast and saw its hideous eyes pop open with green rage—not a single set of eyes, but *hundreds,* cruel pinpoints of laser-sharp light from hundreds of tiny human heads that were not quite as big as golf balls.

Male and female heads, old and young.

Each on its separate stalk, every one an individual.

They grew like mushrooms from the mass of the creature's neck and shoulders, comprising a huge reptilian skull. They

screamed and squealed and cursed, arched their necks and
bared their teeth at him. Somehow he knew that each repre-
sented a victim of the Giver, that each contained a piece of
tortured human consciousness that could suffer, grieve, *dream*.

He bit his tongue as he recognized the miniature head of
Sandy Zolten amid the multitude on the brow of the beast,
glaring at him and shrieking curses. And that of her daughter,
Teri, near a nostril. And most enraging of all, his *own* head,
lantern-jawed and bearded in silvering auburn, less discolored
than the others, as though newly sprouted from the riotous mob
that formed a cheekbone. His own head screamed more
piercingly than all the others, writhed and trembled on its stalk,
spat an odious green fluid that burned his skin.

"You don't really believe you can kill me, do you?" it
shrieked in a voice that was an octave above his own, but still
his own. *"I'm one with you! You are one with me! As long as
you live, I live!"*

Carl's legs turned to warm jelly, and his heart nearly
stopped. He forced himself to breathe, to think. "No, you're
not me," he hissed. "Am I'm not *you!* You're going to die!"
The glowing sword grew heavier in his hand, and his wounded
shoulder burned lividly as he drew back to strike another blow.

*"You can't kill me, Carl! My juices have flowed into you,
and our souls are fused! You dreamed with me, and once that
happens, we are one!"*

"No!"

*"Oh yes, Carl. It was easy, because you actually welcomed
it! Deep inside you, deep below the layer of lies you tell
yourself and others, you're like me! You're MY kind, Carl! The
dreams I gave you were from your own heart, from your own
cravings! I didn't invent them for you."*

"You lie! You LIE. You *LIIIEEEE!*"

He plunged the sword again, this time into the scaly throat
of the creature, just below the gaping jaws. The head erupted
in a cacophonous choir of screeching and mewling. A leathery
wing convulsed and slashed the air, connecting with Carl's
cheek. He was flung to the stone floor and nearly crushed by
a thrashing leg. He clambered to his feet again, fought through
scrabbling tentacles and claws to find the handle of the
gleaming sword, and jerked it out again from the sucking
wound.

Screaming his own curses, he drove the blade deep into the toothy gullet that mere moments ago had feasted on his own flesh, that was still bright with his own blood. Out again came the sword. *In* again—this time splitting the horrible little skull that bore his own face, shattering it into a dangling mass of blue and crimson gore. He howled above the din of the screaming heads, demanding that this loathsome beast suffer, that it bleed and weep and die. He struck again and again, until his arms and body were festooned with bits of sundered flesh, drenched in the creature's fetid blood.

Until the thing keened with earsplitting pain and rage, convulsing and choking, trembling and dying.

Until its many eyes were fire spots of green panic that lit the charnel chamber like an alien noon, until its limbs ceased to thrash and its eyes to glow

The room exploded in a blue fire that, in the eternity of a few dazzling seconds, consumed the obscene bulk of the Giver of Dreams, the tattered skulls and discarded bones and all the other rank detritus of its past victims, the bodies of Stu and Renzy and Mitch, even the huge old steamer trunk in which the beast had been transported. Carl lurched away, pressed himself against the wall, and cowered from the blue glory until it ended, until the room was black and still.

He staggered out through the archway and saw Craslowe gathering himself for the killing of the three figures who huddled near the door of the undercroft. Robbie looked exhausted, spent of all his psychic boulders, unable to defend Lindsay and Hannie any longer. Carl charged forward, oblivious to the agony in his shoulder, drew back the sword, which was glowing orange now, swung it in a singing arc, screamed with his last calorie of rage, and chopped off Hadrian Craslowe's head.

The robed body shuddered, erupted gore, thrashed, and fell to the stone floor.

With the onslaught of silence Hadrian Craslowe died, his body crinkling and imploding, glowing green and blue as it dissolved into vapors and fumes, leaving only the satin robes behind.

They got as far as the crumbling gateposts on the edge of the grounds before Hannie collapsed onto the wet grass, but

Lindsay caught her fall and sank to the ground with her. Robbie threw aside his crutches and laid his sheepskin jacket over her thin, misshapen frame, then took her gnarled hand in his.

Hannie had not actually gotten this far under her own power, but on the strong arms of Lindsay and Robbie. They had half-carried her, half-led her, because she was so very weak, and without her pince-nez she was nearly blind. Now she refused to go even one step farther, whether under her own power or anyone else's.

Carl lowered the unconscious body of his son to the ground nearby, then knelt and stared a moment into the faces of the others. Lindsay's and Robbie's were bloodied, both exhausted and gray, the faces of refugees. Hannie's, though, was the more troubling, because it was slack with resignation and drained of life. The skin hung tonelessly off her cheeks and jaw; the ancient eyes lacked their gleam.

Carl himself felt detached and strangely at peace, despite the oozing wounds on his back and shoulder, despite the gore that covered his ragged, shredded clothing. Stoned on my own endorphins? he wondered. He felt no pain.

"Is it dawn yet?" Hannie asked, her voice hoarse and weak. "I did so want to see the daylight one last time." It was dawn, Robbie assured her. The rain had stopped, the eastern sun was casting yellow shafts of morning across the rolling grounds of Whiteleather Place, and birds were beginning to sing.

Yes, *birds*—here at Whiteleather Place!

"Then we have truly won," breathed the old witch. "The birds would not return if the Giver of Dreams were still alive." She closed her eyes a moment, as if uttering a prayer of thanks, then opened them again. "Is everyone all right? Have the rest of us survived?"

Yes, said Robbie. Even Jeremy, who had fallen unconscious at the very instant of Hadrian Craslowe's death. Carl, though horribly wounded, had carried him out of the undercroft with his one good arm. Jeremy was here, lying only a few feet away. The old woman turned her head to confirm the news.

"And what of Mitch Nistler?" she wanted to know.

Carl moved to her side and lowered his face close to hers. "I'm not sure what happened, Hannie," he said. "Mitch started stabbing the Giver, but then he went into hysterics, started laughing and crying at the same time, like he was in pain. I took the sword away from him and finished the job myself. When it was over, Mitch wasn't moving. He was on the floor. Then the blue fire—"

"Yes, the fire. I know what happened now," said Hannie. "Mitchell was *of the flesh* and, being so, was linked to the beast. When the beast died, so did Mitchell, and they were both consumed. I should have known this would happen. Such a tragedy. I'm glad, though, that his last living act was one of courage and goodness."

"Hannie," said Carl, "can you tell me what will happen to Jeremy? Will he be okay? I mean, will he be—"

"He will awaken soon, and he will be nothing like he was as the offspring's manciple," she assured. "The personality that Hadrian gave him is dead and gone, as though it never existed. What remains in Jeremy's mind, I couldn't say, but time will tell. I wish you every happiness with him, Carl, and the very best life can bring to you. The world owes you so much, as do I." She gave him a wrinkly smile. "Do try to be happy, won't you?"

Carl blinked away tears and nodded.

"Robbie, where are you?" demanded Hannie. "I can't see a beastly thing."

"I'm here, sweet pea," said the psychic, squeezing her hand and smiling gamely. "Been here all the time. You need somethin', all you gotta do is ask."

"I don't need anything, except to thank you once more. You're a remarkable man, Robbie, one of the bravest souls I've met in the last thousand years, which I say without the slightest reservation." Robbie's smile faltered; he knew that she meant every word, and this moved him. He tried to swallow the hot lump in his throat. "What I want to tell you, though, is this," she continued. "When a very old Sister of Morrigan dies, great energies are released. At the exact moment of her death, a Sister is usually able to perform one last act of major thaumaturgy, provided she's conscious and not totally bereft of her senses. I fully intend to control my own passing, something I've made provisions for with my magic, and I intend to be in command of my faculties until the very end. So I'm offering you a miracle, Robbie." She coughed and shivered, then fixed him again with her fading eyes. "If you'd like, I'll take care of those legs of yours, give you a set of new ones. I'm certain that it can be done. What do you say, man? Would a pair of strong legs suit you?"

Robbie felt a great rush of heat into his face, the beginnings of tears. He gripped Hannie's hand more tightly and took a deep breath to get his voice under control. "Darlin', I don't know what to say. All my life I've wished for good legs like other men, because I sort of figured you couldn't be a real man without them. Well, I know now that it's not true. If I had some real legs, I'd be somebody I don't even know. I wouldn't know how to act. If you can work a miracle, do it for somebody who really needs it, like a sick little kid somewhere. As for me, I'll be just fine with the legs I got, so long as Katharine's around to fetch my crutches now and then."

Hannie reached up and touched his face, caressing it. "So be it," she answered, smiling. She looked around for Lindsay and located the blurry outline of the young woman's face. "Take good care of yourself, girl. You're a fine soul, someone with principles and good sense. I'm glad to have known you."

Then she shuddered again and gasped, looked startled for a moment. Her gaze darted to each of their faces, then upward to the brightening sky. The eyes that had seen a millennium of sunrises and sunsets closed for the final time.

EPILOGUE

They sat on the rough, wooden dock of Greely's Cove Marina, their legs dangling over the edge, Carl under a pith helmet to protect his fair skin from the blazing August sun, Lindsay in sunglasses and a billowy flowered smock. A gentle morning breeze rattled the halyards of a spanking new Tartan 28 sailing sloop that lay in the nearby slip. A gangling boy with golden hair loaded aboard coolers, sleeping bags, and sacks of groceries for what was to be a long and unhurried cruise.

Six months had passed since the debacle at Whiteleather Place. Summer had come to Greely's Cove, bringing robins and geese and blinding blue skies. With summer had come healing.

Lindsay stole a glance at Jeremy, who seemed oblivious to everything but the task he was doing. She smiled. "My God, that kid's growing like a weed. It won't be long before he's as tall as you."

"I don't doubt it," answered Carl with a proud grin. "As you well know, there's a lot of height on his mother's side. By the way," he added, just above a whisper, "the orthopedist's final report came in the mail yesterday. Jeremy's hands are back to normal—no abnormal growth in the index fingers."

Lindsay slipped an arm around him, pulling him close in celebration.

"Then the miracle is complete," she said. "He's just a regular, healthy boy."

"I never used to believe in miracles," Carl said, gazing out at the glistening waters of the Puget Sound, where sailboats and freighters lazed silently past. "Now I'm afraid *not* to believe in them."

Hannie Hazelford's final miracle had centered on Jeremy—of this Carl and Lindsay were certain. The old witch, in her last moment of life, just before her desiccated body evaporated into

419

fuming ether, had cleansed the boy's soul of every taint of Hadrian Craslowe. She had given him a new start. In a mere six months Jeremy's mind had evolved from that of a newborn babe to the equivalent of an eight-year-old's. The teachers at the school for special children in Seattle reported that his reading and writing skills were coming along nicely and that he seemed to have a special acuity in art, especially painting. The therapists estimated that in three to four years his mind would catch up to his physiological development, and that with special schooling he could look forward to a normal, productive adulthood.

Jeremy finished his chore and strode over to the spot where his father and aunt sat. He was clear-eyed and rosy-cheeked. He wore a red tank top over baggy white trunks with deep pockets.

"Dad, can I have a buck for a Slurpee? I loaded all the stuff, like you wanted." His speech was boyish and very American. He seemed like a regular kid who happened to be big for his age.

Carl dug into his khakis for money, handed over a five, and reminded his son to bring back the change. "And don't fill up on Reese's Pieces, or you won't be hungry at lunch."

"Thanks, Dad!" shouted Jeremy, beaming. "I'll be back in a flash!"

He turned and pounded up the dock toward Halvorson's Grocery, dodging the crab pots and floats stacked here and there at the mouths of slips.

"He's a beautiful kid." Lindsay sighed, watching him go. "He's kind, inquisitive, full of adventure. He's going to make you proud someday, Carl."

"Correction: He's going to make *us* proud. As far as I'm concerned, you've got as big a stake in him as I do." He leaned close and kissed her sun-browned cheek. "If you want to know the truth, I think *you* were the center of Hannie's last miracle. Somehow she made you want to be with me. If that isn't miraculous, nothing is."

Lindsay gave him a peck in return, then leaned back on her hands.

"Maybe it was all part of her miracle," she said, lolling her head to let the sun warm her face, "everything that's happened to us since Whiteleather Place. I mean, think about it: You and

and Robbie were able to pick up the pieces of our lives without ending up in a mental institution, which is nothing short of miraculous. Your wounds healed amazingly fast, and your shoulder's almost as good as new."

"Except for the scars. I'll never be able to take my shirt off in public again, which is a shame for the female population."

She gave him a good-natured punch on the arm. "*And* we were cleared of any wrongdoing by the investigation."

Whether this was indeed a miracle was debatable, Carl-the-lawyer pointed out. Stu Bromton, Hannie Hazelford, Ianthe Pauling, Corley Strecker, and Mitch Nistler had all disappeared and, like all the other victims of Hadrian Craslowe and the Giver of Dreams, had gone the way of their tormentors, leaving only their rags behind. Only the bodies of Mayor Chester Klundt and Stella DeCurtis attested to bloody wrongdoing, but the authorities lacked solid reasons for blaming Carl, Lindsay, or Robbie for it. Though the cases were still officially open, nobody seemed anxious to pursue them aggressively.

"Still, it's hard to believe that things could turn out this well without some kind of magic," Lindsay insisted, resting her cheek on Carl's shoulder.

"You're right, it is. But really, I don't care whether it was magic or not—I'm just glad to be alive and kicking. It's good to be a part of the twentieth century again. I like worrying about ordinary, everyday things like credit-card bills and the ozone layer, watering the yard and getting the car tuned up, instead of—" He cut himself off. For a bleak moment he endured the memory of a shrill voice, his *own* voice:

"*I'm one with you! You are one with me! As long as you live, I live!*"

"I know what you mean," Lindsay said.

Jeremy was walking back toward the boat with a large paper cup full of a purple, snowy substance, sucking it up through a pair of straws. When he reached the boat, he swung smoothly over the lifelines and bounded into the cockpit.

"Let's go, Dad!" he hollered. "The wind's kicking up!"

Carl got to his feet, laughing. "The kid's a born sailor," he said, pulling Lindsay up. "The wind comes up, and you can't keep him in port."

"Buying that boat was a good move. It gives you something the two of you can do together."

"I wish it were the three of us," said Carl. "Sure you won' come along? Jeremy and I'll do all the cooking, cleaning, and sailing. You wouldn't have to think about anything except tanning that gorgeous body of yours. Don't forget, the San Juan Islands are great this time of year."

"I'd love to go, Carl, but I think I'd better stick close to the grindstone for a while. Now that I'm back at work full time, I want to prove that I can carry a full load—which is exactly what I've got."

"I understand. But I'll miss you."

"Miss you, too. It's going to be a long week."

They kissed tenderly and long. They would have kissed longer had not Jeremy urged them to get on with it.

"Time to push off," said Carl, jumping aboard. "San Juan Islands, here we come: a couple of salty swashbucklers with money in their pockets and time on their hands!"

"I'll call ahead and tell them to hide their daughters!" said Lindsay, laughing.

She untied the dock lines and threw them onto the deck, then helped edge the craft out of the slip. She stood and watched as father and son motored toward a gap in the breakwater, beyond which lay the dazzling blue openness of the Sound. Carl glanced back often to wave, or just to look at her, and Lindsay smiled after them. Too soon the boat rounded the breakwater and was gone, and Lindsay stood alone awhile, gazing at the summer water and listening to the cries of gulls.

"Dad," said Jeremy, once the sails were set and the boat was driving nicely northward, "is Lindsay *really* going to call people and tell them to hide their daughters from us?"

Carl smiled and leaned back in the cockpit, steering with his knee.

"No, Son," he answered, shifting his toothpick to the other corner of his mouth. "At least I *hope* not."